WE ALL GO INTO THE DARK

KEVIN LUCIA

Crystal Lake Publishing
Where Stories Come Alive!

www.crystallakepub.com

ALSO BY KEVIN LUCIA

Hiram Grange & The Chosen One

Things Slip Through

Through a Mirror, Darkly

Devourer of Souls

Things You Need

October Nights

Mystery Road

The Night Road

October's End

When the Lights Go Out

Joey Leonard's Last Horror Movie Marathon

The Horror at Pleasant Brook

Billy the Kid and the Lazarus Stone

PRAISE FOR KEVIN LUCIA

"Kevin Lucia is this generation's answer to Charles L. Grant."– Horror Grandmaster, Bram Stoker Award-winning author, **Brian Keene**

"Kevin Lucia's writing is both scary and smart, a lethal cocktail that makes for mesmerizing storytelling." – **Tosca Lee**, *New York Times* best-selling author of *Demon: A Memoir*

"Kevin Lucia writes my favorite kind of horror...the subtle breed, the sort you don't see coming until they're already upon you and you realize it's too late to catch a breath." – **Kealan Patrick Burke**, Bram Stoker Award-winning author of *The Turtle Boy* and *Kin*

"Kevin Lucia is a major new voice in the horror genre." – **Jonathan Janz**, author of *Marla*

"Lucia is a true craftsman of the horror story, with a fine sense of the genre's best traditions." – **Norman Prentiss**, Bram Stoker Award-winning author of *In the Porches of My Ears*

WELCOME
TO ANOTHER

CRYSTAL LAKE PUBLISHING
CREATION

Join today at www.crystallakepub.com & www.patreon.com/CLP

CONTENTS

PROLOGUE

Law Offices of Spellman & O'Hara
Main Street
Monday, 9 AM

When I entered Barry Spellman's office at Spellman & O'Hara's law firm, it was clear from his cheerful smile and relieved expression he was happy I'd come. Almost as if he'd expected me not to and was pleasantly surprised. That was all well and good, but it only made me even more confused as to why he'd called me to his office at 9 a.m. on a Monday. To discuss a "matter of utmost importance regarding the final affairs of Mr. Archibald K. Leopold." Apparently, I'd been named in Mr. Leopold's will.

The problem?

I had no idea who he was.

It didn't even sound like a real name, honestly. Or, at the very least, it didn't sound like a Clifton Heights kind of name. Also: What in the world had he left me in his will? Even better: Why?

I tabled these questions as Barry reached across the desk for a handshake. "Mr. Patchett. Thank you so much for coming. I know how valuable your time is. With the writing, of course, and teaching."

I accepted his handshake, again marveling at his always firm grip, so atypical of a lawyer. Of course, his father, Kurt Spelling, worked as a foreman at the lumber mill for over twenty years. Barry worked there during his high school years and college breaks. He wasn't a stranger to hard work.

"Thanks. Although I must admit, I'm confused and a bit intrigued—as to why I'm here."

Barry gestured to the leather chair facing the desk. I sat, saying, "I'm afraid I don't know any Archibald K. Leopold. I can't imagine why he'd mention me in his will."

Barry's smile grew as he sat in his own chair, as if enjoying a delightful secret. I discovered what it was when he said, "That's only because you've never heard his full name. Archibald Kretzmer Leopold is better known around town as 'Old Man Kretzmer.'"

I grunted and crossed my foot over my knee. That indeed solved some of the mystery. Old Man Kretzmer had always been one of Clifton Heights' more mysterious citizens. Reclusive and solitary, he'd owned more businesses and property in Clifton Heights than most realized. I only knew of The Motor Lodge, the Mobilmart on Haverton Road, The Golden Kitty, and the Great American Grocery.

Rumor had it he'd also footed the bill for much-needed renovations to our Halloween exhibit THE FELDPAUSCH HOUSE OF HORRORS on Clinton Avenue. His name was often connected to the Science & Discovery Education Center on Samara Hill Road, as well as the Briar Nature Conservatory. He'd also made a big splash over the past year in announcing (through the newspaper, of course), his intention to upgrade and renovate the Raedeker Park amphitheater.

Of course, though I now knew who Archibald K. Leopold was, it still left the questions as to why he'd mentioned me in his will. I'd never met the man. Didn't even know what he looked like. Not sure anyone my age did. He'd withdrawn from the public eye nearly thirty years before.

"To be honest, I'm still at a loss," I admitted. "I've never met Old Man...Mr. Leopold. I can't imagine what he'd leave me. I doubt he even knows who I am."

Barry smiled as he opened a desk drawer and pulled out a very large manila envelope. He set it in the middle of his mahogany desk and said with an air of satisfaction, "On the contrary, Mr. Patchett. Of course, Mr. Leopold knew of you. Being our very own Stephen King, as it were."

I nodded, having the good grace to accept the compliment on its own merits while trying to remain modest, but without too much self-deprecation. "I'm flattered, but that might be overstating things a bit."

Barry folded his hands over the manila envelope—which looked suspiciously like it contained a manuscript—and said, "Regardless, he's a completist when it comes to his favorite authors, and you indeed are—were—one of his favorites. He owns first printings of all your books, including your science fiction novels. He left his entire collection to the Webb County Library System, on a reservation-only status."

"Wow. I'm touched." And I was, quite frankly. I also didn't know what else to say, so I opted for, "I'm still not sure why I'm here."

"For this, actually." He patted the fat manila envelope—which made a manuscript-sounding thump—and then pushed it across his desk to me. Feeling even more intrigued and yet, oddly reluctant, I made no move to accept the envelope.

"What is it?"

Barry settled back into his plush leather chair and folded his hands in his lap. "Not only was Mr. Leopold an avid reader, he loved writing as well. Not for publication, mind you. Purely for himself. He understood the limitations of his abilities. He loved writing, however. Wrote every day from his teenage years up until he passed."

This was getting more intriguing, I had to admit. "What did he write?"

"Mr. Leopold considered himself something of an archivist. He wrote about everything he saw and heard in this town since his teenage years. And over the years he saw many, many things. Ordinary and mundane things, and...some not so ordinary, at all.

"One might think that Mr. Leopold's reclusiveness impaired his ability to keep in touch with Clifton Heights. On the contrary, the more he withdrew from the machinations and mechanisms of society, the clearer his vision became. Unlike most who live here, he was able to see Clifton Heights as it truly was...

"Much like you."

There it was.

Since returning to Clifton Heights over ten years ago, my writing has become... a portal? A conduit? A lens into a dark, shadowy world that exists next to ours. For whatever reason, these past few years, I'd gained an insight into what may or may not occur behind Clifton Heights' closed doors and in its darkest corners.

May or may not occur.

An important distinction, for sure. I couldn't say with any degree of certainty the things I'd written had actually happened. There are odd parallels and an unnerving synchronicity at work in my fiction; anything past that was beyond me.

Maybe I was a good guesser.

Maybe I had a skill for taking local rumors and strange news items and turning them into convincing fiction. Maybe the tumblers in my mind unconsciously worked on the many "locked box" mysteries our town had. Or maybe I was...plugged into something. Like a radio station only partly in tune.

Quite often, it made me uneasy. Occasionally, it unnerved me. Sometimes, downright scared me. But in the end, writers write. We had no other choice.

I nodded at the fat manila envelope, (which most certainly contained a manuscript, I felt quite sure now), and said, "Is that what this is? Something Mr. Leopold wrote about this town?"

Barry nodded. "Mr. Leopold's will stated this manuscript be turned over to you, because—and I quote—'Gavin Patchett will know what to do with it.' He said there are many others, should you wish to read those after this one."

I took a deep breath and stared at the envelope. Surely, I could pass. Say, "Thanks, but no thanks." Or accept the manuscript and toss it in the trash later, or even better, burn it in the fire pit at the cabin. I was a creature of free will.

Wasn't I?

Writers write.

Of course, more practical concerns loomed. It had been nearly two years since *October Nights*. The only thing I'd published since had been a novella, *The Night Road*. The novel I'd labored over for years, *In the House of the Dream Witch*, had fallen dead in the water. Much as I dreaded accepting this manuscript, I also, paradoxically, couldn't resist.

The moment of truth reached, I gave in. Took the manila envelope and slid the manuscript out. The cover page read in plain typeface: THE MOTOR LODGE: CABIN 14.

I grunted. The Motor Lodge, on Chester Road, rented out fourteen self-sufficient cabins. It was our sole lodging for out-of-town visitors. Having never stayed there myself, I'd heard the cabins were nice enough.

I glanced up at Barry. "I'm assuming he's written stories which are about The Motor Lodge in some way?"

Barry offered a spare nod. "The will states this in broad terms, yes."

"Have you read this? Why 'Cabin 14'?"

Barry offered me an apologetic smile. "I haven't any idea. I've not read it, because Mr. Leopold's will made it very clear. Only you are to read these stories. No one else."

I placed my hand on the manuscript gently. Compelled to show the same reverence I always felt when Clifton Heights shared its strange stories with me. Staring at the cover page, not looking at Barry, I said, "What am I supposed to do with this?"

"The will doesn't make any stipulations other than it be given to you, and that other manuscripts have been stored away, should you wish to read them. As Mr. Leopold stated, he felt you'd know the best course of action."

Silence fell as I continued to stare at the plain typeface reading THE MOTOR LODGE. I thought again of declining. Mr. Leopold—Old Man Kretzmer—was a stranger. Didn't matter if he was my biggest fan and had owned everything I'd ever written. I didn't owe him a damn thing. I had free will. I could say no.

Couldn't I?

I stared at the manuscript for a heartbeat longer.

Writers write.

I stood. Gently slid the manuscript back into its manila envelope. Nodded at Barry Spellman without speaking. Turned and left, thinking it was a good thing—and maybe a bad thing—it was summer break, and I had nothing else to do.

Zoo Town

Come away, O human child!
To the waters and the wild
With a faery, hand in hand,
For the world's more full of weeping
than you can understand.
– W. B. Yeats

1.
Sunday, October 6
6:00 PM

When Jim O'Connell turned away from Raedeker Park's old amphitheater, he saw something he'd initially missed. Several trailheads and an access road, winding into the woods. Wooden signs marked the trails with names and distances. The access road, however, was barred by an old, sagging wooden gate.

He stared at the gate; interest piqued. An avid explorer of abandoned places, Jim loved finding new and unusual sites to poke around. He enjoyed reconstructing their histories in his mind. Thinking of what they used to be. Who'd lived there or spent time there. Jim felt a pleasurable melancholy witnessing Time's signature on edifices once revered.

Raedeker Park's old amphitheater had proven disappointing, however. The concessions had been torn down long ago; the stands were completely overgrown. The only thing visible—the stage itself—sat crooked in a quagmire of mud, impossible to reach. Hard for Jim to envision a crowded theater enjoying Shakespeare, for sure.

Which made the access road behind the old gate intriguing. Jim took a few steps toward the tottering wooden gate, eyeing the road beyond. From where he stood, he couldn't see a trailhead sign, but he also didn't see a sign prohibiting access. He'd already decided to sneak around the gate when he heard it and stopped dead in his tracks.

A woman, singing.

He felt sure of it. He couldn't make out the words. Nor did he recognize the melody, but he could hear it. A woman singing a rich, melancholic tune. It came from the access road.

However, even as Jim strained to hear more, the haunting voice faded. For several more minutes, Jim listened. All he heard was a slight autumn breeze through the trees. A bird calling, and its wings flapping as it took flight.

Jim rubbed his mouth. The singing had produced an interesting effect. Though he hadn't recognized the tune, the melody's sentiment rang clear. Longing. Wistful, and a touch sad. Everything he felt when exploring abandoned places.

More than ever, he wanted to walk up the access road.

He glanced at the sky. The sun was burning a hazy orange-red, but decent light still remained. Of course, it would be darker under tree cover, but he'd walked and camped in the night woods before. He always carried a pocket flashlight. The Adirondack forests had nothing on the woods near home in Franklin, Massachusetts.

Jim decided. He'd explore the access road. If he didn't immediately encounter anything interesting, he'd return to his cabin at The Motor Lodge and save a more extensive exploration for daylight. His vacation lasted all week. He'd have plenty of time to explore. He approached the gate, certainly feeling more enthusiastic than when he'd seen the amphitheater's unimpressive remains.

At sixty-four years old, Jim O'Connell still possessed an active lifestyle. He loved the outdoors. He especially enjoyed camping overnight in an abandoned area, if possible.

For nearly thirty years, Jim worked as a technical associate at Carion Filters and Mirrors in Franklin, Massachusetts. He'd been in charge of a vacuum chamber that made and refined optical filters for the medical industry. As jobs went, he hadn't loved it but hadn't hated it, either. He'd occasionally found it tedious, but sometimes he'd also found it interesting. At the least, it had kept him busy for thirty years, making time pass.

He'd felt relatively fulfilled working at Carion. Had earned a good living. Enjoyed an amiable relationship with his co-workers. He would've been happy to work there for ten more years.

Instead, he'd been forced into early retirement, due to a declining economy. Better to pay someone with less experience to do the same job, he supposed, than pay someone with over thirty years of experience.

Whatever the reason, Jim O'Connell only had two months left at Carion.

Jim told himself he didn't mind. It was time for something new. He'd make out okay with his retirement, and he'd built his savings up over the years. He hadn't lost his purpose or direction. He'd simply gained more time for rural exploration. He told himself this, and most days, he believed it.

Most days.

He'd dated several women over the years, but no one had ever compelled him toward permanence. They'd all been nice enough. Decently attractive in varying degrees. All reasonably intelligent and certainly "marriage material." However, he always parted amicably with them, eventually.

He still dated occasionally, but for the most part, he saved his free time for exploring. It had occurred to him, occasionally, that he'd yet to meet any women who shared his interest. How important this was, Jim didn't know. He also didn't care to ponder.

Every year, he took a week-long vacation to rural areas. Usually, destinations with ample abandoned places to explore. Always within driving distance, usually within a day. He'd spend the week hiking, and, of course, exploring. Usually, if circumstances provided, he would camp for a night at one of his destinations.

Most vacationers prepare by searching Google for restaurants and local attractions. Jim searched Google for abandoned warehouses, churches, schools, and factories.

He took his vacation whenever it was most convenient. This year, it had been the first week of October. Ironically, he'd scheduled his vacation a week before he learned of his "retirement" in December. There was some irony there, though Jim preferred not to think about it.

The last few weeks leading up to this year's vacation passed, but it had been twice as hard as usual to concentrate. He supposed it just had to do with his impending "retirement." This was also something he chose not to examine. Regardless, for the last three weeks, all he could think about was this vacation and the places he'd explore.

The access road proved surprisingly easy to walk. Especially considering that old gate, which looked as if it hadn't been opened in over twenty years. It certainly didn't serve as an effective barrier. Its posts were rotten through. Jim thought one good push would knock it over.

The road itself, however, looked oddly worn and was clear to navigate. Almost as if driven regularly. No grass or brush had grown up over it. The ruts in the road were worn smooth and straight. The road was even fully free of debris.

Interestingly enough, he saw no evidence of teenagers. Normally, he saw remnants of their presence in most of the abandoned places he explored. Soda and beer cans and bottles. Whiskey bottles, crumpled cigarette packs, candy wrappers, and even occasional panties or used condoms. He saw no debris here, however, which he found intriguing. Teens were drawn to abandoned places. Of course, for different reasons. To escape the prying eyes of adults, find shelter with gossiping friends, or sanctuary from bullies.

As he walked, Jim noticed something else. An unusual sense of peace settled over him the farther he walked. He'd always enjoyed nature. It calmed him in a way few things could. This felt different, however. Perhaps peace wasn't the right word. Thinking about it, he thought "unburdened" fit better, as if he'd been cut free of something. Of his obligations? His duties? He wouldn't have them much longer, so he didn't need to be cut free from them. Perhaps...cut free from the haunting specter of his empty house, and a directionless future? He shied away from these thoughts.

Ahead, the access road curved left and inclined sharply. Jim slowed his pace, adjusting to the steeper terrain. As he continued to walk, the air changed around him. He couldn't have said how. It felt cooler, which made sense. The temperature would change more the deeper he went into the woods.

Even so, the air felt still. Heavier. Pregnant. Quietly expectant, with a hushed reverence similar to what he'd felt in his holiday visits to St. Mary's Church in Franklin. A sense of reverence permeated the air.

The access road leveled out and continued straight. Jim stopped and took in the sight before him. He felt slightly out of breath, though from the walk or what he saw, he wasn't sure.

On both sides of the access road, Jim saw dozens of meticulously arranged rock piles. Stones of all shapes and sizes had been fit together with the utmost care to form eerily symmetrical cones. Laid out in a grid, as if marked off with a square and compass. From his years of exploring, Jim knew what they were.

Cairns. Often used as landmarks or trail guides. Folk horror movies increased their pop culture allure over the past fourteen years. It had become faddish for hikers to leave random piles of rocks in the woods. For amusement's sake, for manufactured photos, or the novelty of it. What lay before him, however, wasn't the work of a hiker who'd enjoyed a faddish novelty. There were far too many, and far too much care had been taken.

In his mind, they could only be grave markers.

He didn't count every single pile, but at a cursory glance, he estimated nearly five dozen cairns stood on either side of the access road. More than he'd ever seen in one place. The symmetrical arrangement of each cairn was unmistakable. He stood at the mouth of a cemetery, filled with perhaps more than fifty souls that had long gone to rest.

The strange feeling in the air made sense, now. He'd felt similar sensations in abandoned churches and their graveyards. Though he wasn't much of a believer in the supernatural, he thought the air always felt heavier in those places. A more imaginative person might say it was the pressure of the lingering dead or the resonating psychic vibrations left by decades of mourning visitors.

A woman's voice interrupted Jim's thoughts. Faint, singing the same haunting melody that had drawn him here to begin with. He looked up, bizarrely expecting to see a woman dressed in flowing robes, wild hair flying free, a garland crowning her head, hands outstretched, singing an ancient ballad of grief and longing as the song faded into silence...

He didn't see a woman, but what he did see proved astonishing. Even more so, because he hadn't seen it when he'd first crested the hill.

A town.

A small town, in the middle of the woods. As he walked forward, his gaze traveled more carefully than when he'd examined the cairns. At the far edge of the cemetery, the access road forked and split into two parallel roads. Whether they merged at the end, Jim couldn't see.

Mindful of the approaching dark, Jim didn't walk far past the first few buildings. A long structure on his left, maybe an old storage building, and a shotgun shack on his right. Both buildings appeared remarkably well preserved. He stood, hands in his pockets, gazing down the neatly paved dirt road. Questions buzzed in his mind. Where had the singing come from? Who it had been? Where it had gone? Also, what purpose had this town served? How old was it? How long had it been abandoned? Even more intriguing, why hadn't he found mention of it on Abando nedWebbCounty.com when he'd researched his vacation?

He teetered on the edge of risking a quick exploration before dark, but a sound checked him. An easily recognizable fluttering. To his right, he saw, on the nearest shack's sagging porch railing, a large raven. Larger than he'd ever seen. Unlikely as it seemed...it was staring at him.

Impossible, of course. It was a bird. An animal. Animals didn't stare at people. Jim could accept an animal might examine a person's threat potential. Size them up, so to speak. But they didn't stare disdainfully at people, as this raven was doing now.

As if to prove his own point, it croaked once. Dug its beak under its wing in a mundane, bird-like gesture, then took flight. It flapped away, out of sight. Any imagined dread he'd felt left with it.

Jim chuckled, amused at his reaction. "Too easily spooked, old man," he muttered. However, as he glanced around, he realized the raven's appearance had served a purpose. So caught up in his discovery, that he hadn't noticed how dark it had gotten. If he'd given in to his urge to explore, he would've had to return to his car in the dark. In this instance, instead of being a harbinger of doom, the raven had warned him away from a foolhardy venture.

As Jim turned and walked through the cairn cemetery, back down the access road toward his car in the parking lot, he resisted the urge to think the raven had been warning him away. Such a thought wasn't rational, and Jim considered himself a rational man. The only thing dangerous about exploring those ruins in the dark was possibly hurting himself falling over debris.

That was all.

2.

The Skylark Diner
8:00 PM

Jim had left Franklin, Massachusetts at eight in the morning. After a six-hour drive, he'd arrived in Clifton Heights around two. He hadn't stopped for lunch and didn't eat anything until he'd gotten settled in his cabin at The Motor Lodge around three. Because of the late lunch (a pre-made ham and cheese sandwich), he was ready for dinner after leaving Raedeker Park. His cabin featured a fully equipped kitchen, but he hadn't bought groceries yet. He'd do so tomorrow. Also, refresh his camping supplies.

Google Maps produced several eateries. Dooley's Ice Cream and Subs, Chin's Pizza, Pizza Joe's, The Skylark Diner, and Henry's Drive-In. Jim chose The Skylark Diner. He found it easily enough. Within fifteen minutes he was seated, waiting on an open-faced hot turkey sandwich, with a side of fries.

While waiting, Jim consulted the list of sites he'd made on his smartphone. Raedeker Park Zoo had been nice enough, though it had appeared to exist in an enduring state of disrepair. Renovations to walls and sidewalks looked half-finished. Many exhibits had been "under construction," and looked like they hadn't seen fresh paint in at least twenty years.

A highlight had been The Lion House. It hadn't been used since a lion killed a zoo employee in the early seventies. According to Abandoned WebbCounty.com, rumors said if you walked through The Lion House near dark, you could hear distant screams of the ill-fated zoo employee. He hadn't heard any screams of course, but he'd enjoyed the ambiance of walking through the abandoned lion cages more than he'd thought he would.

It had made up for the letdown of the amphitheater. Only abandoned for twenty years, the pictures of it online had clearly been taken years ago. They still showed concession stands, a full stadium of wooden benches, and adjoining platforms surrounding the main stage. To find nothing but a crooked platform sinking into mud had been disheartening, to say the least.

His waitress—a young woman with short black hair named Cassie—brought his dinner. Jim settled in and ate, thinking about his discovery of the abandoned hamlet in the woods behind Raedeker Park. He worked it over in his mind. The cairn cemetery, and the abandoned buildings. What had it been? Any connection to the zoo? Why wasn't it listed on Abandoned Webb County?

Who was the mysterious singer? A fellow explorer? His imagination?

Jim had never considered himself much of a talker. He didn't mind the company of others, or listening to them. He, however, had always been soft-spoken. Reluctant to draw attention to himself. He harbored no fear of talking. He just preferred to stay in the background.

Even so, as Cassie cleaned his table and asked, "How was everything?" he worked up more than a standard response. "Very good. Also...I wonder if I could ask something. I'm vacationing here this week, and have questions about the sights."

Cassie's eyes lit up. She offered a friendly smile. "Sure! Where are you from? Staying at The Motor Lodge?"

He nodded. "Yes. Cabin 14. Nice place. And I'm from Franklin, Massachusetts."

Cassie collected his plates and silverware onto a bus tray, balancing the tray against her hip. "Nice. Always wanted to visit Massachusetts. Especially Salem. Hear it's wonderful this time of year." She deftly plucked his receipt from her waist apron and handed it to him. "What brings you here?"

Jim smiled, feeling remarkably relaxed around Cassie. She was easy to talk to. "I suppose you could say I'm an amateur explorer. Love poking around old schools, churches, houses. Maybe even camping overnight in a spot, if possible. Every year I take a vacation somewhere with lots of abandoned places. Over the summer I found a website called Abandoned Webb County, and decided to vacation in Clifton Heights this year."

Cassie nodded enthusiastically. "Nice. We've got lots of cool abandoned spots here, for sure. Been anywhere, yet?"

"I just came from the first spot on my list. Raedeker Park."

"Ooh. Did you walk through Lion House? It's silly, but it gives me the creeps. Especially right before dark."

Jim tipped his head. "Yes, Lion House has an interesting vibe, for sure. The amphitheater, however,..."

Cassie's nose wrinkled. "Yeah. Not so great, right? It used to be cooler when the stands and concessions were still there. Isn't much to look at, now." She nodded at his phone, on which he'd brought up his list. "Where else?"

"Two abandoned houses. Bassler House, on Bassler Road, and La Pierre House, off Allen Road, along the railroad tracks."

Cassie nodded. "Go to La Pierre House. Skip Bassler House. Lots of kids have gotten hurt there over the years. A few of them have even died. Don't think it's safe. Anywhere else?"

Jim consulted his phone. "An abandoned koi pond and flower garden, also on Bassler Road, but not far past the Commons Trailer Park. An old farm on King Road, and an old titanium mine along the railroad tracks, not far from the farm."

Cassie shook her head. "No to the mine. County finally boarded it up last year. Too many kids partying in there, I guess." She smiled. "You got a full schedule. Sounds like a blast. I dig abandoned places myself. Too bad the old elementary school on Route 79 wasn't still standing. Heard it was a great place to explore, back in the day."

Jim nodded. "The website did mention it." He took a breath. It occurred to him that, even though he'd been talking far more than he usually preferred, he hadn't minded at all. Cassie had a way about her. "I actually found another abandoned place tonight, by accident. Past the old amphitheater, there's a few trailheads. Boden Hill Trail, Owen Pond Trail, Ford Hollow Trail, and a gated access road. I walked up the access road and found..."

Cassie's shift in stance was subtle, but detectable all the same. A slight shadow flickered across her face. Her smile dimmed slightly. Jim could hear a flat note in her voice. "Oh. Zoo Town. You found ...Zoo Town."

Intrigued by Cassie's reaction, Jim leaned forward. "Zoo Town? Know anything about it? Been there?"

Cassie coughed. It was clear the topic bothered her. "I haven't. No one goes there. Not sure why. And I don't know much about it. I guess back when the Zoo was bigger, lots of their employees lived up there. Why it's called Zoo Town."

She shrugged limply, in a manner that seemed out of character. Though of course, Jim had only just met her. "No one talks about it much."

Jim nodded slowly. He didn't think Cassie was lying. But she certainly wasn't comfortable talking about Zoo Town. Whether because she knew something she didn't want to share, or because of an ingrained taboo, he didn't know.

Her reaction heightened his intrigue. As an avid explorer, he'd encountered varied reactions when scouting abandoned locations. They ranged from vague airs of discomfort to cliched warnings. Without fail, these places had proven to be harmless.

Jim held up his receipt. "Thanks. Dinner was great. Pay at the counter?"

Cassie smiled. "Yep. Have a great night! Hope you enjoy your stay."

Even though she'd recovered her easy-going manner, Jim couldn't help thinking she was fleeing him, and the topic of Zoo Town.

3.

9:30 PM

When Jim returned to his cabin—which had a modestly sized bedroom and den, and a small but efficient kitchen—he grabbed a Heineken from the fridge (he may not have brought groceries, but he'd certainly brought beer), sat down on the futon and woke up his laptop, which he'd set up on the coffee table shortly after he'd unpacked. He connected to the cabin's Wi-Fi, opened Google, and searched "Zoo Town, Raedeker Park Zoo, Clifton Heights, NY." It was getting late, but he'd worked the second shift at Carion for almost thirty years. He had several hours left in him.

His initial search turned up nothing, which made Jim think "Zoo Town" was a local nickname, not official. He spent another twenty minutes searching variations of "ghost town in Webb County," "abandoned town, Raedeker Park," and "abandoned village, Clifton Heights."

He finally found a result through searching "abandoned hamlet in Webb County and Clifton Heights." Even then, it turned out to be nothing but a scanned article of a local history retrospective column from a defunct periodical called *The Web County Gazette*. It was dated 1985. Not much more than a footnote, it read:

> A little talked-about aspect of
> the Adirondacks is its Irish
> immigrant heritage. From the
> 1920s–1940s, Irish immigrants
> settled in varying numbers
> throughout Adirondack Park

and worked largely as manual laborers. Mining, logging, and construction being the common trades. They worked wherever they could find it, but they often preferred to keep to themselves, so they could observe their own customs and way of life. Even their own burial customs. Because of this, it wasn't uncommon for larger groups of Irish to settle and build small hamlets outside the towns in which they worked. These hamlets varied in quality. Some were respectable settlements. Others, little more than shanty towns.

One such hamlet existed here in Webb County, in Clifton Heights. What made it unique is that, while some men worked at the lumber mill or on Clifton Heights' farms, most worked at Raedeker Park Zoo & Carnival, in various capacities. Cleaning animal cages, cleaning the zoo and carnival grounds, running rides and attractions, working concessions, and performing maintenance. Thus, the hamlet became known as 'Zoo Town.'

Unfortunately, it wasn't necessarily an affectionate name. Anti-immigrant sentiment did exist in Clifton Heights, and the town's name was used as a slur by some to indicate the Irish living there were little more than animals. Even so, history shows that, for the most part, the residents of Zoo Town steered clear of trouble.

1974 saw the beginning of Zoo Town's end. Several rides malfunctioned in the Spring of 1974, causing numerous accidents and injuries, including two fatalities. Raedeker Park, facing a huge increase in their insurance and a drastic drop in business, as well as legal threats, discontinued its carnival. They tore down the rides and laid off nearly all the Irish who worked there.

The lumber mill and area farms followed suit. With no work and rising anti-Irish feelings, the younger families and young men and women of Zoo Town quickly left to live and work elsewhere. The last Zoo Town resident—ninety -year-old Liam Bodher—was discovered passed away in his sleep by Clifton Heights Sheriff Cliff Danford on August 5, 1980. The remains of Zoo Town still stand in the woods behind Raedeker Park.

Jim sat back after reading the article twice, thinking. Originally published on August 5, 1985, the article was remarkably informative yet tight-lipped at the same time. On the one hand, it provided a concisely written background for Zoo Town. On the other, it offered no speculation at all on the ruins themselves.

Jim also continued to be surprised by the rather conspicuous lack of information about Zoo Town elsewhere. He revisited AbandonedWebbCounty.com, but after forty-five minutes of searching, found not one mention of Zoo Town on the site. Likewise, when he modified his web search to "Irish laborer hamlets in Webb County," he found nothing.

What did that mean?

Considering Cassie the waitress's reaction, it seemed likely a local taboo existed regarding Zoo Town. Though she'd tried to cover her discomfiture at the subject, Jim had picked up on it clearly. What had she said?

No one goes there.

He remembered, as he thought of those words, how there'd been no litter on the access road to Zoo Town, which still struck him as odd. Litter – the marks of younger, less respectful explorers – was a typical hallmark of most abandoned places.

Jim kept returning to Zoo Town's omission from AbandonedWebbCounty.com. Usually, the more taboo connected to a place, the more notorious it was. "No one talks about it" usually meant everyone talked about it, in hushed whispers and grapevine rumors. But if the scarcity of information about Zoo Town served as an example, literally no one talked about Zoo Town, at all. This intrigued Jim even more.

Jim knew, even as he shut down his laptop and prepared for bed, that Zoo Town was the place he wanted to camp overnight. Though the access road hadn't been marked with a trailhead sign, it hadn't been marked with "no trespass" or "no camping" signs, either. Likely enough, if he took a cab there right before the zoo's closing time tomorrow evening, he could slip up the access road unnoticed. No one would ever know he was up there.

Feeling pleased at this decision, Jim fell into a deep sleep almost as soon as he slipped beneath his bed sheets.

4.

Jim lay in bed, drowsing. Partially awake. Drifting on a hazy borderland, listening. To what? Something moving around his room. Something fluttering. Skipping and hopping. Scuttling across the bare wooden floor...

Another fluttering, louder. Something taking flight. And then, a deep, throaty croaking. A sound that invoked nightmarish visions of black-winged things flooding the sky, blocking out the sun and all hope, black death, winging toward him...

Another croaking screech brought Jim fully awake. He sat up in bed, heart hammering in his chest, breath roaring in his ears. Pressing his back flat against the headboard, cowering (without knowing why), he fumbled for the bedside lamp.

He gasped as yellow light spilled over the bed, revealing the source of the screech. Sitting on the end of the bed, yellow talons clutching the footboard, wings outstretched, was an enormous raven. Its eyes—a bright, almost hellish yellow—gleamed. It fluttered its wings. Leaned forward and hissed at him. He'd never heard a bird make such a sound before. The feathers on its powerful neck were standing on end. Jim swore he could see its muscles rippling.

He pressed himself back against the headboard even more. Mind whirling, trying to tell himself he was only dreaming. This must be a nightmare. It had to be. But the fear pulsing through him had none of a dream's surreal haze. Rather, an adrenaline-fueled reaction held him in its grip. His thudding heart told him this was real.

The raven screeched again, shattering his thoughts. It exploded forward into a storm of black flapping fury, leaping off the footboard for him. Talons extended, beak snapping. A small part of him felt silly (it was a bird, for God's sake!) but he cried out as instinct flung him away and to the side. He rolled off the bed as the enraged bird slammed into the headboard, talons and even beak clicking against the wood. He flopped onto his belly and covered his head with his hands while peering awkwardly upward to see if the raven would resume its attack.

Nothing happened.

Silence settled over the bedroom.

Jim waited a heartbeat longer. When he heard nothing—no wings, no croaking screeches, not even a fluttering—he risked raising his arms off his head and dared a glance around the bedroom.

He saw nothing. No raven. No threatening shadows winging around the ceiling. He didn't see anything out of order. More importantly, he didn't feel anything out of order.

He was alone.

Of course, the bedside lamp didn't provide the best light. It was conceivable the raven sat lurking in one of the room's darkened corners. Maybe it had even ducked into the bathroom, which he'd left open.

Taking a deep breath (feeling ridiculous because it was, after all, only a bird) Jim stood on shamefully weak legs, bracing his back against the wall. He stood there for several tense seconds; certain the raven waited for him in the dark. It was foolish, but even so, the feeling persisted.

No Gothic screech split the night. Jim's breathing eased. His heart slowed. He cracked his neck, flexed his shoulders, and pushed off the wall. In a brisk, stiff gait, he walked to the light switch by the bedroom door and flicked it on. Again, feeling foolish, he turned and flattened against the door, facing a now fully lit bedroom, muscles tensing.

Nothing.

So far as Jim could tell, the bedroom was empty. There wasn't anywhere a bird could hide. No room under the bed, and he'd thankfully closed the closet before going to sleep.

Which left the bathroom. Emboldened but still wary, Jim approached it slowly. Once there, he carefully pushed the door all the way open, ears straining for the flutter of a wing, or a croak in the darkness. When he heard nothing, he reached a tentative hand into the darkness and spent several seconds groping for the light switch. He found it and bathed the small bathroom with light.

Silence.

Taking a deep breath, Jim peeked around the corner. It was a small bathroom. Shower stall to his right, toilet to the left, linen shelf above the toilet, sink and mirror straight ahead. It didn't take long for Jim to make sure the raven wasn't hiding in there.

Jim turned slowly and surveyed the bedroom again, half-expecting to see the raven perched on the headboard, wings spread, ready to strike. He didn't see it, but he did see how it had gotten in. The window next to the bed was open, the curtain ruffling in the breeze. The screen had been knocked off its track, allowing enough space for the raven to have gotten through.

Jim crossed the bedroom quickly. With fumbling fingers and slightly shaking hands, he hastily tried to fit the screen back into its track, but it wouldn't fit. It was warped. Almost as if the raven had slammed into it. No matter how hard he tried, he couldn't fit the screen back where it was supposed to go. Cursing, he tugged the screen loose, dropped it on the floor, and closed the window. He locked it for good measure.

Jim picked up the screen to examine it more closely. It certainly had been bent out of shape, lending more credence to the theory the bird had rammed into the screen so it could get inside. Which was a ridiculous thought, of course. He didn't know much about birds, but so far as he did know, they didn't ram through screens to get into buildings. Even a raven accidentally flying into the screen at night didn't make sense.

Jim shook his head and set down the dented screen. Because something was unlikely didn't make it impossible. If animals caught rabies, they acted strangely and out of character. Maybe the raven was sick? Could ravens catch rabies?

As Jim returned to bed, he tried to shake the even more ridiculous notion it was the same raven he'd seen in Zoo Town. Almost as ridiculous as thinking the raven had been staring at him, or warning him away. Ridiculous. A flight of fancy.

Even so, it took him at least an hour to descend into a thin, uneasy sleep.

5.

Monday
10:00 AM

Tired from his interrupted night, and the uneasy sleep he'd gotten after, Jim didn't wake until mid-morning. His foggy head pulsed with a mild headache. He felt faintly sick. An hour later, however, a shower and a cup of coffee put him to rights. He'd never been much of a breakfast person, so he figured a sausage and egg sandwich from the local gas station would do.

Before leaving for groceries and camping supplies, Jim logged onto his laptop and double-checked the camping guidelines of Adirondack Park. Every area had slightly different rules when it came to primitive camping instead of camping on regulated campgrounds. On a few occasions he'd stretched those rules, but for the most part, he tended to obey them. Especially if fines were involved.

A quick perusal revealed the standard rules. While campers were advised to stay on regulated campgrounds or near marked trailheads, they could primitive camp elsewhere, as long as it wasn't marked private property, or marked camping prohibited.

Jim put his laptop to sleep. If he remembered correctly, he hadn't seen any camping prohibited signs on the access road at Raedeker Park. Nor had there been any on the three trailheads next to the access road.

Jim stood. He didn't know what kind of police force Clifton Heights had. Based on the town's modest size, he guessed it wasn't large. Also, he thought the nearest state police barracks was in Woodgate, nearly two hours away. He supposed there was also Webb County Police to account for, but he hadn't seen any patrol cars since entering Webb County.

Collecting his jacket and heading for the door, Jim figured camping one night in Zoo Town would be an acceptable risk. He knew how to keep his campfires small. He'd wait until late so its smoke wouldn't be as visible. He'd pack a dry breakfast, so no campfire smoke in the morning. Also, because the park was open later than the zoo, it would be easy to slip up the trail. The chances of anyone seeing him would be relatively small.

Something bothered him, however, as he got into his car, started it up, and pulled out of The Motor Lodge. He couldn't put his finger on what. Of course, it had nothing to do with last night's freak incident. Or the strange similarity between the raven in his room, and the one he'd seen at Zoo Town.

Nothing at all.

As a seasoned primitive camper, Jim had all the main necessities. A small pup tent which, once unrolled, immediately snapped into form. Much better than the old tents, which had been frustrating to assemble, because their aluminum poles never fit quite right. The tent folded into a tight rectangle which he latched to his backpack. The backpack, of course, had a lightweight aluminum frame and was exceptionally durable, as well as flexible. He had a tarp to pitch the tent on, and he'd learned over the years how to roll it tight. A thin sleeping bag, because despite his age, Jim had no difficulty sleeping on the ground. He never suffered much in the way of soreness the following day.

Of course, he had all the necessary tools and accessories. A hammer, a small ax, a flashlight, and a compact but powerful LED lantern with long-lasting batteries. He had extra batteries, of course.

For a one-night stay such as this, he wouldn't worry about his small propane stove, though he'd packed it. He'd simply roast some hot dogs over his fire. Jim wasn't a big eater under normal circumstances, so that and pre-made sandwiches would work fine. He had a small first aid kit and insect repellent. Usually, five bottles of water sufficed.

With these essentials packed, Jim's trip to the quaintly named "General Store" on Main Street proved brief. All he needed were extra matches, some silverware (forks and tongs, which he'd forgotten at home), hand sanitizer (also forgotten), and a jackknife, because he'd lost his only knife on his last camping trip.

A kindly man with longish white hair and a bushy white beard checked him out at the sales counter. Novak was stenciled on the breast pocket of his red polo shirt. As he scanned Jim's items, he nodded with a friendly grin. "Going campin'?"

"Yes. For one night, off a trail. I've got a cabin at The Motor Lodge for the rest of the week."

"Uh-huh. Folks do that often enough." Novak scanned the batteries. "Which trail you campin' off? One in town, or outside?"

Mindful of his answer—remembering Cassie's odd reaction last night—Jim said carefully, "One of the three trails up at Raedeker Park. Not sure which, yet."

The old man's bristly eyebrows rose. "Oh? Raedeker Park, you say? Hiked all three myself. Owen Pond Trail is tricky. Hilly, twists and turns on itself. Worth it, though, especially if you're a fishin' man. Owen Pond is a beautiful sight. Got some nice bullhead and smallmouth bass in it, too. Father Ward—he's our local clergy—and Sheriff Baker both have pulled some big 'uns outta there."

"Now, Ford Hollow Trail is more straightforward. Easy walkin', and it leads to a nice hollow which would be a fine place to camp overnight. The last, Boden Hill, is short but vigorous. Gets you up high, quick. Not a mountain trail, but it offers a nice overlook of Owen Pond," he continued.

Because Novak was acting talkative and free with information, Jim decided to risk a little. "What about the other one? The access road behind the old gate near the amphitheater? Didn't see any signs. Know where it goes?"

Novak's expression shifted slightly, as Cassie's had last night. He glanced down and quickly scanned and bagged the rest of Jim's items as if the clerk suddenly didn't want to meet his gaze. "Naw, you don't wanna go up there. It's an old county access road. Ain't been used in nearly thirty years. Twists and turns all over the place, and don't go nowhere. Lots of branches off it, too. Apt to get yourself lost up there. 'Specially if you're from out of town."

Jim nodded, assuming a properly thoughtful expression, as if carefully considering the man's words. "I see. What's up there?"

Novak hit 'total' on his register. "Nuthin' much sides deadfall and debris, I expect. Not nearly as nice as them other trails. I'd avoid it, I was you."

He finally met Jim's gaze. In the clerk's eyes, Jim recognized the same furtiveness he'd seen in Cassie's. "Thirty-seventy-five, sir."

Jim paid in cash. The man handed over his bag with only a nod. Jim accepted with one of his own. He turned and left the store, mind buzzing.

As Jim pushed his cart down the bread aisle of Great American Grocery, he continued to puzzle over the odd reactions he'd received regarding Zoo Town and its access road. Both Cassie and Novak had acted strange and skittish. Almost afraid. Cassie had brushed the topic off, saying she'd never been there, that no one went there. Novak hadn't even mentioned the town. Only said there was nothing but "deadfall and debris."

This only made Jim even more eager to explore and spend the night there. From his cursory examination last night, the buildings had appeared remarkably well preserved, which directly contradicted the old clerk's claim of "debris." Clifton Heights folks obviously entertained a powerful taboo about the place. The sparse details he'd found online hadn't given a clue as to why, past the possibility of anti-Irish sentiment. He wanted to believe such sentiments couldn't still exist in these more progressive times, but he knew better. It seemed unlikely he'd find anyone in town willing to talk.

"There's gotta be someone," he muttered as he paused before the hot dog rolls. "Someone who can tell me more..."

His thoughts stopped when he heard it, coming from the next aisle. More clearly than last night. Now he could hear the words. Even if he couldn't, he would've still recognized the melody, its tone, and the voice. It was the same woman he'd heard singing at Zoo Town last night. His heart sped up slightly (why, he wasn't sure), as he listened closely to words he could now discern...

Where dips the rocky highland
Of Sleuth Wood in the lake,
There lies a leafy island
Where flapping herons wake
The drowsy water-rats;
There we've hid our faery vats,
Full of berries
And of reddest stolen cherries...

As the last line faded into an indistinct humming, a cart turned into the aisle ahead. Pushing the cart—which was filled with several cartons of eggs, frozen vegetables, and two cartons of milk—was a tall woman with lustrous, shining black hair pulled into a ponytail. She wore black running tights, and a black windbreaker, her feet shod in bright yellow running shoes, completing the image of an athlete dressed for a run.

Her face, however—which held a faraway expression as she hummed—was anything but "standard." In perhaps her mid-thirties, perhaps even mid to late forties, her face was proud. Almost regal. Her jawline was firm yet somehow graceful, with high cheekbones and an aquiline nose. Her eyes burned a startling hazel, almost gold. She seemed confident and at ease. The kind of woman most men (Jim included) found attractive and intimidating.

However, when she noticed him, she smiled pleasantly and said in a genuinely friendly voice, "Oh. Hello. I about ran into you. Sorry! Daydreaming, I guess."

He'd fully expected her to push past with nothing but a spare nod. Instead, she'd spoken to him and stopped her cart before his. He realized she was actually waiting for him to say something, so he managed, "No worries. I do it all the time. What's grocery shopping for, if not to let your mind wander?"

The woman smiled wider, eyes sparkling with warmth. "That, and to buy food."

It could've been a sarcastic remark, but it wasn't. Offered in levity, and completely benign. "Well, yes. That too."

She gave him an appraising eye. "Are you new in town? Visiting? I don't know everyone in town, but I'm good with faces. Don't recognize yours."

"Ah. Yes. Vacationing. Staying at The Motor Lodge. Hey..." he paused, hardly able to believe his forwardness, and before he lost his nerve, plunged ahead, "Did I hear you...singing last night?"

The woman smiled wider, showing immaculate, white teeth. In a surprisingly intimate gesture, she sidled her shopping cart next to his, leaned in, and said, almost coyly, "Well. Depends on where you heard me."

Jim laughed, his face suddenly feeling warm. Women had certainly hit on him before. It hadn't happened in quite some time, however. Also, he'd never been hit on by such a striking woman. If, of course, that's what she was doing.

"Uh. Well." He coughed, cleared his throat, managed an abashed smile, and said, "It's going to sound crazy...but in the woods behind Raedeker Park? In an...abandoned little village called Zoo Town?"

"Hah!" The woman clapped her hands once and beamed. Whatever trace of seductiveness Jim thought he'd sensed vanished in her delighted surprise. "Yes! That was me. Around dusk?" He nodded, and she laughed again. "It indeed was. I run every day," she gestured at her attire, "as you probably guessed. The access road which runs through Zoo Town also runs through the old cemetery on Shelby Road. I live out on Shelby Road, and I run out to Zoo Town and back at least once a day. Sometimes twice, if I really need to clear my head. I sometimes sing while I run, so it most definitely was me."

She extended a hand. "My name is Morgan."

Jim accepted her handshake and found her grip firmer than he'd expected, but not overbearingly so. "Jim," he replied. "Pleasure."

"All mine." She withdrew her hand. "So. You discovered Zoo Town all by yourself. Alone. You're definitely not a local. Folks around these parts pretend that place doesn't exist."

"So I've learned. I...Well, I enjoy exploring abandoned places. A lot. So I'm used to folks acting spooked about a fallen-down church or burnt-out house, but usually, it's all bluster. The more spooked people are about a place, the more people go there and whisper about it. But not..."

"...not here. Not about Zoo Town," Morgan finished with a slow smile. "Absolutely not. Don't think anyone besides me has ever been up there. Not recently, anyway."

Jim crossed his arms, skeptical despite Morgan's seeming sincerity. "Not at all? Not a single soul in over twenty or thirty years besides you?"

Morgan shrugged, appearing thoughtful. "An exaggeration, maybe. I'm sure hikers and hunters have stumbled over it, not thinking about where they were. And I have occasionally seen a jogger running the access road on the other side of Zoo Town, out to the old cemetery on Shelby Road. But no one talks about it, sure enough. And I don't think folks ever intentionally go there."

"Why, do you think?"

Morgan shrugged again. "Honestly? I don't think anyone in Clifton Heights knows. Not today, anyhow. Everyone's been conditioned by their parents, grandparents, adults, and other authority figures never to go there. For the usual reasons, I'm sure. 'It's dangerous, falling down buildings, you could get hurt.' Etcetera."

Jim sensed an addendum. "But?"

She pursed her lips. "I imagine it's a holdover from the anti-Irish sentiment many felt towards the folks who lived there, back when Zoo Town was alive and well. Are you familiar with its history?"

Jim nodded. "A bit," and proceeded to recount what he'd learned from the scanned article last night.

"Indeed. What the article didn't mention, and what isn't included in the pitiful local history unit in area high schools is the Irish who lived there were considered godless pagans who worshiped tree spirits, nature, and maybe even Satan himself. The irony? Most of the Irish who lived there were either Catholic or Protestant. Although...a small few did preserve their old ways."

She raised a speculative eyebrow. "You saw the cairns, of course."

"Yes. I'm assuming their cemetery."

"Indeed. They preferred to conduct their burial services among themselves instead of at Clifton Heights churches and preferred to bury their dead near them. Which, of course, ignited whispers that Zoo Town sat on a fairy path."

"Fairy path. Sounds familiar, but I can't quite place it."

Morgan waved. "They're the supposed supernatural highways of the Fey. Routes to and from their Otherworld, their Nether Realm, or any of the other names it was called. Sometimes they're called ley lines. Routes of elemental power crisscrossing the Earth. Another term was the 'night road.' It was supposedly guarded by The Phantom Queen. Any mortal daring the night road unbidden risked death, or...worse. Although what the 'worse' was, legends never made clear..."

"Anyhow, I'm sure the original admonition to avoid Zoo Town had to do with townspeople's superstitions about such things. 'Don't go to Zoo Town, or the godless pagans will corrupt you.' 'Don't go to Zoo Town, or The Phantom Queen will take you.' Over the years, the message got diluted to: 'Don't go to Zoo Town.'"

Jim scratched his chin, even more intrigued than he'd been before. "Fascinating. How do you know so much about it?"

"I'm Irish. One of the few left around here. It's become my 'thing,' I guess you could say. My hobby. To know the stories." Before Jim could question her further on this point, she added, "Is exploring abandoned places your hobby?"

"It is." He briefly sketched his annual vacation excursions, the places he'd visited before, and some of the places he'd thought about visiting in Clifton Heights. "But honestly, all those pale in comparison to Zoo Town. I'm surprised the local website omitted it."

She tipped her head. "You'd be amazed how far the hands of rumor and prejudice reach."

Jim agreed with the idea in principle, but again, in his experience, rumor usually made abandoned places more notorious, not less. Before he could offer his thoughts, however, Morgan continued, "And you actually camp for the night in some of these abandoned places? Are you going to," a mischievous smile spread, "spend the night in Zoo Town?"

He was about to say 'yes' but something held him back. He didn't know what, and he didn't understand why. This woman acted more open and unafraid, and she certainly wasn't inhibited by the same taboo as Novak the clerk and Cassie the waitress. And, if she jogged up there regularly...wouldn't she likely encounter him later tonight?

Still, something held his tongue, which felt odd, and out of character. While he certainly wasn't a big talker, he'd also never been secretive. So why the reluctance to share his plans?

Even so, all he did was smile and say, "I'm weighing my options."

She nodded. "Fair enough. Well, in any case," she pushed her cart past him, heading down the aisle, somehow smiling coyly and demurely at the same time, "Maybe I'll see you later, on my run? Depending on how you weigh your options, of course."

Again, Jim felt a flash of warmth creep past his collar, sure this time she was flirting. "That would be great. Depending on how I weigh my options. If so, you'd be welcome to join me for dinner." He waved with great flourish at the package of hot dogs in his cart. "Such as it may be."

Her smile widened, becoming less coy and more genuine. "Sounds delightful. I'm not picky, at all."

She continued on her way. Jim was about to let her go when a thought struck him. "Oh," he said, turning, "out of curiosity. That song. What is it about?"

She turned her cart around the corner, paused before disappearing with it, and said casually, "It's actually from a poem by W. B. Yeats, called 'The Stolen Child.' It's about changelings." She offered another mischievous smile. "Maybe, if I see you tonight, I'll tell you more about it."

She turned the corner.

Jim stood there for several minutes, stunned. A woman hadn't flirted with him so openly in a long time (if ever), and a younger woman, too. Jim had never been overly concerned with attracting women, but he couldn't deny his encounter with Morgan had him feeling ten years younger. Happy about this, he continued shopping, whistling quietly to himself. If Morgan were there and said his whistling sounded similar to her song, he wouldn't have been surprised, at all.

Something happened to dim his excitement over meeting Morgan as he pulled out of the grocery store's parking lot. It jarred him badly, for some reason, though hours later the experience receded into his memory as a brief startle, nothing more.

He hadn't noticed the man standing on the corner of Main and Canon Street as he approached, so caught up was he in thinking about Morgan. He couldn't make up his mind about her. Had she been coming on to him? Was her proposal to meet later an invitation to something more than conversation? Why hadn't he told her outright he'd be camping at Zoo Town?

His mind consumed by these thoughts, he only got a brief glance at the figure standing alongside the road, and only because it turned to watch Jim pass. The man was wearing the exact same outfit he was. Jeans, and an unzipped blue fleece jacket over a white T-shirt.

When he risked a quick glance in the rear-view mirror, however, his heart skipped. The man dressed exactly like him...

Had no face.

No eyes, nose, or mouth. Only smooth, uninterrupted skin.

He glanced forward again in time to see the stop sign at a four-way intersection. He managed to brake without screeching to a tire-shuddering halt. Thankful he was alone at the intersection; Jim turned all the way around.

The man was gone, making him wonder if Jim had ever seen him in the first place.

6.

He spent the afternoon going through his camping supplies, checking the tent for tears, and reviewing his camping checklist. He prepared several sandwiches—four more than he'd normally make—and packed those with the hot dogs, rolls, and small packages of ketchup. If Morgan did run through Zoo Town, he had enough for them to eat. Not a gourmet meal, of course, but something. In addition to the sandwiches and hot dogs, he packed the protein bars and individual packets of trail mix.

While he packed, try as he might, he couldn't keep his thoughts from returning to the man standing at the corner of Main and Canon. The one dressed like him. The one without a face. He must have had a face, of course. Jim had driven by too quickly to see it. He'd only a brief glance in the rearview mirror. And so what if the man had been wearing similar clothes? It was the Adirondacks, in early fall weather. A fleece and jeans were perfectly appropriate.

On another level, Jim wasn't sure what bothered him more. The eeriness of the optical illusion, or the fact it even bothered him. He didn't spook easily. If he did, he certainly wouldn't enjoy exploring abandoned places.

Finished packing, Jim glanced over his shoulder at the dented window screen, still leaning against the wall. He'd meant to take it to The Motor Lodge's office today to find out how much of his room security deposit he'd lose. He hadn't, though. Wasn't sure why.

He didn't remember leaving the window open last night. It made sense he might've. The cabin had been a bit stuffy, and he preferred an outside breeze to air conditioning. Even so. He hadn't left the window open. Birds didn't barge their way through window screens in the dead of night.

As Jim stared at the screen a strange, chilly sensation settled onto his shoulders. He'd never been a big believer in omens, or foreboding signs. He didn't believe the universe warned people of impending doom. The stereotype of the scared local who warned out-of-town strangers not to "trespass" on a "forbidden" place belonged in horror movies, not real life. Over the past twenty years, he'd visited countless abandoned sites he'd been "warned away from." They'd turned out to be nothing more than abandoned, forgotten, sad places buffeted by Time and the elements.

Even so.

He couldn't shake an odd feeling. Maybe, all things considered, he should opt out of camping at Zoo Town. Maybe he could visit some of the other abandoned places in Clifton Heights. The La Pierre House. The koi pond. The French Farm. He could poke around one of those sites, enjoy another dinner at The Skylark, and call it an evening.

The strangest part of all? He wasn't dwelling on Cassie or Novak's reactions. No, he kept coming back to his conversation with the attractive, pleasant, and slightly enigmatic Morgan, and her theory that a taboo had developed decades ago about Zoo Town because it sat on a fairy road. That mortals daring trespass risked a "fate worse than death." It was a figure of speech with no real expectations attached. But the way Morgan said it...

Jim sighed noisily and rubbed his face, his irritation winning out over his odd uneasiness. This wasn't like him. At all. He wanted to spend the night at Zoo Town, and he was going to. Maybe if he was lucky, he'd get to spend time with Morgan. Maybe he'd misread her signals, and they'd share a nice evening together, nothing more. But if he hadn't misread her signals...well, the pup tent was a tight fit for two, but he was sure they'd manage.

Focusing his thoughts on Morgan herself and where the evening might lead, Jim finished his preparations for the night's excursion. It was about noon. He'd take a nap, make himself a late lunch, go over his supplies once more, and then make his trek up the access road to Zoo Town.

7.

4:00 PM

"You from out of town?"

Jim nodded absently, staring out the window as the Yellow Cab he'd called turned off Chester Road onto Main Street. He had to admit, Clifton Heights was a picturesque slice of small-town Americana. Franklin, Massachusetts, was mostly suburbs, and nice enough. Clifton Heights, however, belonged in a Norman Rockwell painting. Neatly maintained houses and lawns. Businesses and storefronts that obviously saw regular upkeep. The abandoned zoo had been a bit neglected, true.

But from what he'd seen so far, that neglect hadn't extended to the rest of the town.

Even so, as the houses and storefronts passed in a bucolic smear, Jim felt a slippery unease he couldn't quite identify. A presentiment which clashed with Clifton Height's pleasant exterior. A whiff of decay lurking beneath the surface. A decay he was used to finding in dilapidated, run-down, derelict buildings. Places left behind by the world. Sensing this aura here, in a town with such a charming exterior, felt more and more disconcerting with each passing moment.

"See you've got hiking gear. You heading up one of those trails at the park?"

"Yes," Jim said, glancing into the taxi's rearview mirror and quickly glancing away because he couldn't see much of the cab driver's face. It was too easy to let himself think the cab driver had no face. "Not sure which one, though."

"Don't go up the old access road. There's bad mojo up there."

"Oh?" Jim risked a glance into the rearview mirror, relieved this time to catch a glimpse of the man's lips and nose, and also annoyed at himself for feeling so out of sorts. "How do you mean?"

The cab driver waved casually, but a certain flat quality to his voice belied the gesture. "Lots of stories floatin' around about what they used to do up there in the thirties. Pagan rituals, Satan worshiping, and such. I dunno. An out-of-towner wanted to hike it a few years ago. Called a cab and got me. I dropped him off. He ducked by the gate and started right up the access road. Not twenty minutes later, Dispatch called me back. Guy is waitin' there, white as a sheet, and shakin'. Asked to be taken back to The Motor Lodge. Heard tell he checked out and left town later that day."

"No plans on going up that one," Jim lied, avoiding the rearview mirror for fear the cab driver would meet his gaze, and sense his lie. "No worries."

"Good," the cab driver said in his flat, emotionless voice. "You never know what's in the woods. Me, I stick to town. Safer."

Jim had no response to this, so he said nothing. Discomfited by the cab driver's manner (and annoyed, because he wasn't usually so easily knocked off balance), he simply stared out the window and watched the town pass by.

Both he and the cab driver remained silent the rest of the way. When the cab stopped before the three trailheads at Raedeker Park, Jim grabbed his backpack with one hand and passed a ten to the cab driver without looking, mumbling, "Keep the change."

The driver thanked him. Jim quickly exited the cab. It bothered him, on some deep, primal level, that he'd never gotten a good look at the cab driver's face...

if he even had one

...but still, he couldn't bring himself to glance over his shoulder, until the cab was already pulling out of the parking lot.

Though the three trailheads were hidden from the zoo's admission gate, Jim made a good show of reading each of their signs, as if he were undecided. After about fifteen minutes had passed, however, and no cars had driven by, Jim ducked past the old wooden gate and headed up the access road to Zoo Town.

The instant his foot touched the access road, all his anxieties (which still felt so strange) faded. A sense of peace filled him. Whatever burdened him about Zoo Town and the strange reactions to its mentions faded. For the briefest of instants, a small voice in his mind whispered perhaps he should feel concerned about the road's almost-narcotic effect on him, but he dismissed the voice instantly. He always felt this way when walking in the woods and exploring abandoned places.

Twenty minutes later, however, he still hadn't reached the cairns and Zoo Town. The walk seemed much quicker yesterday. Of course, he hadn't been carrying a backpack full of supplies with a pup tent fastened to it. Even considering the pack's lightweight aluminum frame, and how conservatively he'd packed, it had to have added at least ten to fifteen pounds. Maybe even twenty. He didn't feel tired, but the backpack was starting to weigh on his shoulders. Obviously, it was slowing him down.

Still, as he walked, not much about the scenery changed. Admittedly, in his excitement yesterday, he hadn't paid much attention to the woods on either side of the path. He'd simply been too focused on where the path would lead. Today, however, he examined the trees and undergrowth. Nothing appeared distinctive. Everything looked the same. Adirondack pine crowding together and thick brush which he couldn't see through. Not see far, anyway.

He didn't remember the woods being so dense, yesterday. He remembered in his quick glances seeing small hills, rocks, and deadfall at least ten to fifteen feet away. Now, when he glanced left or right, all he saw was a virtual wall of trees. He couldn't see more than a few feet into the forest. If that.

With each step, he was beset by a dawning apprehension. Not only was something watching him from deep cover, but something was following him. Tracking him.

Hunting him.

"Okay," he muttered, "this is stupid." He stopped, closed his eyes, and took a deep breath. He tried to recapture the sense of peace he'd felt when he first set foot on the access road. It had slowly leaked out of him, gradually replaced by a mounting sense of dislocation. He felt as if he'd been walking forever, yet nothing changed in his surroundings. It had not taken this long to reach Zoo Town yesterday.

He stood still. He'd been hiking and camping in deep woods for over twenty years. Danger abounded in the woods, of course, depending on the region. Snakes, bears, wolves, coyotes, even mountain lions, if you believed the rumors. Still, these were natural threats, and in all his years of camping and hiking, he'd seen only one rattlesnake, and once thought he'd caught a brief glimpse of a black bear crashing through the woods away from him.

As he stood there, however, eyes closed, breathing steadily, his strange apprehension grew. He felt it. A cold prickling down his spine. An itching along his shoulders. Mounting claustrophobia, as if the trees pressed in on both sides...

Something cracked, loudly.

To his right.

Jim opened his eyes. Resisting the urge to run (what was there to run from?), he slowly turned and peered into the dense trees to his right. He could see little. Trees, brush, some deadfall. It didn't seem possible the trees could be growing so close together, and now he felt positive the woods hadn't been this way last night...

Another crack.

Closer. More cracks, successive ones, as if something large was breaking through the branches as it approached. He heard nothing else. No growling, snarling, or grunting. No heavy breathing.

No footsteps. Only those branches breaking. Coming closer, and the growing sense something wrong and unnatural was out there. Crashing its way through branches toward him.

Jim began walking stiffly forward, ignoring the backpack's weight on his shoulders. He wanted to reach the end of the access road. This desire swelled into a blinding urge driving him forward. Retreating to the parking lot wasn't an option. Going forward to Zoo Town became his all-consuming goal. Though it was irrational and made no sense, he knew his only escape from the thing crashing through the woods was making it to Zoo Town.

He increased his pace. Heart pounding, breath roaring in his ears. Despite the crisp fall air, sweat peppered his brow and glued his T-shirt to his skin. The backpack weighed heavier with each faltering step, as his feet grew clumsier with fatigue. Panting, suddenly in the grip of a near-blinding hysteria he didn't understand, he stumbled forward. His surroundings didn't change. The crashing sounds came closer...

Hot pain slashed across his forehead, and he cried out. He stopped, breathless, and touched his brow, fingers coming away with the faintest dabs of red. A low-hanging branch must've reached over the road and scratched his forehead. Pressing his hand to the line throbbing across his temples, Jim cursed. Turned to continue forward...and stumbled to a confused halt.

Ahead, as far as he could see, the trees crowded so close to the edges of the road, their branches stretched into his path. The higher branches touched, making a ceiling almost low enough to brush his head. He would have to duck under them. Or in some cases, push through them, risking more scratches. Even cuts.

"What...what the fuck?" His voice sounded raspy and small. Yesterday the road had been extremely well-maintained and used, certainly clear of branches stretching across it. Had he accidentally taken a fork he'd missed yesterday? He must have. This wasn't the same road.

When he turned and looked behind him, a tight fist squeezed his heart, making it hard to breathe. He'd expected to see the road as it had been, wider and easily navigated, the trees gradually growing closer to the road. Instead, as far as he could see, trees crowded so close to the road, that their upper branches formed a full canopy. He couldn't see any traces of the wide-open road he'd started up on.

Something crashed through the woods, this time on his left, moving closer. He faced forward, took a deep breath, lowered his head, and continued. Hands up, warding off branches as best he could. Panting, he quickened his pace as the crashing grew nearer. He paid no heed to the increasing weight of the pack on his shoulders, and the increasingly rocky and rutted road, which was intent on catching his feet and throwing him to the ground. He stumbled forward, knocking branches aside. Wheezing and coughing, as things in the woods crashed closer on both sides, the sharp wooden cracking sounds filling the air and he saw nothing through dense stands of trees but flickering shadows and gnarled tree trunks which snarled at him as the crashing sounds grew closer...

His right foot caught on something. A rock, root, or something else. Already overbalanced because of the pack's increasing weight and his stumbling lurch, Jim pitched forward. Fortunately, his hands had already been up to ward off branches, so he caught himself before slamming his head against the ground. However, the pack's weight drove him downward, and he landed hard enough to knock the wind out of him. Hard enough for him to lay there for several seconds, hands covering his face, heart pounding in his chest as the crashing came even closer...

And stopped.

The air fell still. Jim lay there, panting. Straining to hear the crashing as it descended upon him. Instead, he heard, clear as he'd heard it in the grocery store earlier in the day:

> *Come away, O human child!*
> *To the waters and the wild*
> *With a faery, hand in hand,*
> *For the world's more full of weeping*
> *than you can understand.*

He could hear every word, though it sounded distant and far away.

"Morgan?"

He breathed in, collected himself, and with a heave, pushed himself to his knees. His pack suddenly felt half as heavy as it had moments before. He wiped his face, mopping sweat off his cut brow as he caught his breath.

The singing faded into silence.

Another breath and Jim lurched to his feet. Before him lay the cairn cemetery, at the end of the access road. Past the cairns, the silent ruins of Zoo Town stood.

Jim glanced over his shoulder, oddly not surprised to see the wide open and clear access road he remembered from yesterday. Panting, his chest heaving, he tried to understand how that could be. Maybe there'd only been a handful of branches blocking his path, and he'd imagined the rest? That didn't make sense. He wasn't prone to flights of imagination. He wasn't.

He tried to come up with an explanation for the crashing and cracking sounds and failed. The forest made sounds. He'd spent enough time in them to know. He'd only ever seen the one bear, but he felt certain he'd heard them on more than one occasion.

Loggers, maybe? On one of his walks back home, he'd strayed near men logging in the woods, and the sounds had been somewhat similar. Regardless, Clifton Heights did have a lumber mill, though it was on the other side of town.

Jim closed his eyes and rubbed his face. Unbidden, the cab driver's warning about the access road flickered through his thoughts. He debated turning back. Sleeping at The Motor Lodge tonight and camping somewhere else tomorrow night.

After a few minutes, he rejected the idea. He'd come all this way to camp in one of the most unique abandoned sites he'd ever discovered. It would be stupid to turn tail because he'd gotten spooked by sounds in the woods and the unexpected narrowing of the access road (which he must've not noticed yesterday; it was the only explanation). He'd made it here. He might as well stay.

As he slowly walked down the path through the cairn cemetery, another reason for staying lingered in his subconscious, half ignored. Tonight's trip to Zoo Town had gone much slower than last night's. It would be dark, soon. He didn't want to make a return trip in the dark, because if he heard those crashing sounds again, in the cover of night...

Jim brushed those thoughts aside.

8.

Much as Jim wanted to explore Zoo Town right away, he knew making camp was priority. After a quick but thorough examination of the immediate area, he decided on a relatively flat patch of ground in an empty lot between two shacks, across from the long building, which he thought maybe had been a general store once.

It didn't take long for Jim to set up. In about twenty minutes, he'd erected the tent, stored his gear inside, and built a small fire ring with rocks. Once finished, he checked his watch and saw it was nearly eight. Most likely he'd missed Morgan's evening run (assuming the singing he'd heard earlier was his imagination, and not her). Even though that bothered him more than he'd thought it would, the prospect of exploring the old town before night brightened his spirits.

LED lantern in hand, Jim approached the closest shotgun shack, to the right of his tent. On this branch of the access road, there appeared to be ten shacks in total. Tomorrow, when it was light, he'd check the other branch, and see how many were there. Had only families lived in the shacks? Or single men and women, also?

Nearing the shack, he marveled once again at how well-preserved it was, even up close. Time had certainly left its marks. The shack had aged to a dark greenish-gray color. The railing around the narrow deck appeared rickety. A good yank might pull it apart. The deck itself was slightly tilted, many of its boards warped and curled upward at the ends. The wood also looked soft enough Jim didn't want to risk stepping on it, for fear his foot would go right through. The shack's front door was missing, also.

When Jim got as near as possible to the front porch without mounting it, he raised his lantern and saw, with little surprise, the walls inside the shack still stood. The ceiling was intact. He could also discern shadowy shapes of tables, chairs, maybe even an old iron stove. He wondered, if he were to go inside, would he find remains of hand-made toys scattered on the floor? Old books? Maybe even shoes or tattered remnants of clothing?

As he rounded the shack, lantern held high; he wondered how the people had lived. He didn't imagine they'd enjoyed the comforts of indoor plumbing, running water, and electricity back in the thirties and forties. Light probably came from oil lanterns and candles, while heat and cooking came from cast iron stoves. How had they bathed? Wash their clothes? Did a water source exist nearby?

Rounding the back, even in the gathering darkness, Jim found answers to some of his questions. An old washboard, remarkably intact, lying in a rusted-out metal basin. The tattered remnants of a clothesline hanging between two trees. And, at the tree line, the leaning remains of what had most likely been an outhouse. Holding his lantern higher, Jim saw similar, intact outhouses behind the other cabins.

He approached the cabin's back doorway, which was bereft of a door, also. Because it had no back porch, only a small step, Jim could walk right up to it, stick his head and lantern through the doorway.

His lantern's light flickered across the floor and walls. The skeletons of several cots floated in the gloom. Depending on how many people had lived here, this back room had been at least one sleeping area, Jim supposed.

He was about to risk entering—the floor appeared more stable than the front porch—when he heard a distant but familiar melody sung by a familiar voice, out on the access road. Jim left off a closer inspection and walked around the cabin to the road out front. To his great surprise and delight, he was met by Morgan walking down the road toward him, holding her own lantern, and singing softly.

She saw him step onto the road. "Well," she said, smiling, "fancy meeting you here."

Jim marveled over Morgan's ease as she sat cross-legged on the other side of the small campfire he'd made, eating a slightly singed hot dog as if she hadn't a care in the world. Again, he was struck by the contrast between her almost regal beauty and her down-to-earth nature. He supposed at his age he should know better than to judge a person on first impressions, but this morning in the grocery store, Morgan hadn't seemed the type to sit on the ground and eat a cheap hot dog roasted over an open fire.

Yet here she was. Not acting self-conscious in the slightest as she finished her hot dog. "You know, the funny thing about eating outdoors," she remarked as she wiped the corners of her mouth with the napkin Jim had provided, "is that you're hungry for food you'd never eat, normally. Take hot dogs, for instance." She gestured at Jim's half-finished one. "When's the last time you wanted a hot dog?"

Jim thought about it, shrugged, and smiled. "Last time I went camping. About a year ago, I guess."

She snapped her fingers. "Exactly. You may have eaten a hot dog or two over the past year because it was convenient, or it was all you had in the fridge that night. But you didn't want it. I don't have anything against hot dogs myself, but I don't remember the last time I had one. But can a girl turn down an invitation for roasting hot dogs over an open fire?" She shrugged, smiling. "No way."

He chuckled, feeling more relaxed. "I'll remember that. Hot dogs roasted over an open fire. It's a can't-miss proposition. I've got a can of baked beans I could cook up too if you'd like...?"

She snorted and waved. "Oh, no. That would be bad. Mostly for you, trust me."

They shared a laugh at this. He took another bite of his hot dog, and after swallowing, asked, "The poem you sing. By Yeats? You said it was about changelings?"

"Oh, yes." She folded her hands in her lap and settled herself into a story-telling pose. "Changeling myths span the globe. Go back centuries. Every culture has them, though most folks think of Irish, Celts, Scots, or the English first.

"The generic story is that fey folk—faerie, wee people, fairies—stole children and replaced them with inhuman look-a-likes. After a day or so, the baby would transform into a wooden doll, or some ungodly beast which would flee and return to the Otherworld, leaving the human parents in despair."

Finished with his hot dog, Jim sat forward, interested. "Did they always take children? And why?"

"To answer the first question, no. It wasn't always children. Betrothed virgin women and pregnant women, also. And, often enough, older men who lived solitary lives. As to why, well... Children were considered magic, and open to magic. Easily malleable. Some myths said faeries stole children with strong magic to consume them, in order to absorb their magic." Morgan's eyes widened theatrically, the firelight making her eyes sparkle. Jim could tell she was enjoying her role as an ominous storyteller, playing it to the hilt. "Other myths claimed when numbers in faerie troops dwindled, they stole children strong in magic to raise as faeries, to revitalize the troop."

"And the betrothed virgin women, pregnant women, and men?"

"Betrothed women, same as the children. Either consumed or absorbed into the troop, to bear new faeries. Pregnant women were never consumed, however. Either they were assimilated into the troop, or after their child's birth, returned to the world of man, woefully empty-handed."

"The men?"

"Different case altogether. Immortal life may seem a paradise, but for some faeries, it becomes burdensome and wearying. Myth says that when that happens, the faerie would find, entice, and steal away solitary mortal men disconnected from the world, and replace them with a faerie who wished to end their days as a mortal."

Jim grunted, trying not to find too much resonance with her description of 'solitary mortal men disconnected from the world.' He was only partly successful. "What happened to these men?"

A half-shrug. "It depends on the story, as always. If the men accepted their fate willingly, they were offered a sort of half-life in the Otherworld. They could also choose a painless death and oblivion. Those men who didn't choose willingly, and tried to flee their fate?" She shrugged again. "The 'fate worse than death' I mentioned in the grocery store earlier."

"I noticed they're enticed first. Not stolen outright. Why?"

Morgan tipped her head thoughtfully. "Most likely because the faerie was asking for the privilege of finishing their existence in the mortal's form. They could act without the mortal's consent, of course. However, they wanted to make it appear as if, at some point, the mortal could've chosen to walk away." She offered him an almost sly smile. "Even if the deck was stacked to begin with."

Jim leaned forward with a smile of his own. "Here's the real question: You believe any of it? You certainly speak with some conviction."

She shook her head, smile turning wistful. "I'm a broken record, I know...but it all depends on one's perspective. Myths were so often used to explain what we feared or didn't understand. Better to believe our loved ones have been snatched from us and replaced with supernatural copies than believe they've changed in unpleasant or even terrible ways. Easier to claim—especially in medieval times—'That's not my child!' or 'That's not my wife!' than admit the truth."

Jim lifted an eyebrow. "But?"

Morgan smiled slyly. "There are so many things in this world we don't understand. Things we can try to explain rationally...and things we simply can't. But who is to say the things which can't be explained, need to be?"

Jim was about to remark on Morgan's cryptic response but didn't get the chance. She abruptly stood, brushed off her thighs, and held out a hand. "C'mon. Let's do a night-time tour of Zoo Town."

Jim smiled, stood, and took her hand.

Hand-in-hand (feeling a little ridiculous, and wonderful), Jim followed Morgan down the access road deeper into Zoo Town. Their respective lanterns threw ghostly flickers ahead of them. Morgan talked, and Jim felt content to listen to her free, easy, almost musical chatter.

"...believe it or not, right up until it was finally abandoned in the early seventies, most of the cabins and buildings up here didn't have running water or electricity. They kept right on using outhouses and lighting houses with candles and oil lanterns, heating their homes with wood stoves. The two exceptions were the infirmary and the general store."

She released his hand and gestured at the two long buildings in between the forks of the access road. "By 1955, the infirmary did get a basic plumbing system connected to the zoo's water main, allowing them running water. The same year, electricity was wired to the infirmary and the general store." She pointed upward, then took his hand again. "Can't see it in the dark, but if you look close enough during the day, you can see the old hook-ups on a few electrical poles. The wires themselves are long gone."

She steered them toward the second large building. He followed her lead without hesitation, delighted beyond measure. He'd never before found anyone who shared his love of abandoned places. In its own way, the night was unfolding as his version of a "dream date."

"This was the general store, which allowed the people of Zoo Town to buy necessities, so they didn't have to travel into Clifton Heights as much." She ascended a short flight of rickety wooden steps and pushed through an old door hanging crooked on its hinges. Jim followed.

Their lanterns illuminated the immediate surroundings with a hazy light. Jim saw a front counter. To his right, rows of wooden shelves. Some of them tipped over, most fallen into disrepair.

"I can't get over how well-preserved everything is," he said, his voice hushed. "In fact...I don't think I've ever seen anything this well preserved."

Morgan tipped her head, smiling slyly again. "Of course, everything's well preserved. Zoo Town sits on a faerie path, doesn't it?"

Jim laughed again, marveling over the woman's capacity for enigmatic statements. He held his lantern up and peered into the murk at the other end of the building. He could barely make out what appeared to be an old, cast-iron stove. "Where did they get goods to sell?"

Morgan shrugged. "Various places. They worked out consignment agreements with the stores in town, as well as with local farmers, hunters, and fishermen. And many Zoo Town residents hunted, fished, and planted small gardens behind their shacks."

"Where did they worship? Did they collectively worship? You mentioned a mix of Catholic and Protestant beliefs, but was there any truth to the rumors of pagan practices?"

She gave him a small, strange smile. Almost a sad expression, different from her free and easy manner. "Follow me," she whispered and led him out of the old store.

Instead of walking down the access road back to where it forked, Morgan led Jim between the store and the infirmary to the other road. Few weeds had grown between the two buildings. Jim once again felt surprised at how Time's hand had been slowed in Zoo Town.

They stepped into the middle of the road on the opposite side. Morgan raised her lantern. Jim followed suit. She said nothing for several minutes, a noticeable departure from her previous easy-going chatter. As Jim beheld the sight across the road, he readily understood why.

The building stood taller than the shotgun shacks and was three times as wide. Also, it was circular, and so far as Jim could tell in the dim light, made entirely of stone. The roof consisted of logs, lashed together into a point. He didn't see a door, only a gaping doorway twice as large as normal, filled with a darkness that appeared dense and liquid.

Morgan had lapsed into an uncharacteristic silence. Jim whispered, "Was this their church?"

"Yes," Morgan said quietly. "Many Irish American immigrants came from either Catholic or Protestant backgrounds. Zoo Town's residents were no different. On Saturdays, Catholic mass was often performed here by the priest serving in Clifton Heights at the time, if he was able and willing. On Sundays, the Protestants gathered and worshiped, laymen taking turns at the pulpit. Once a month, however, some gathered here to practice...much older beliefs."

Gazing at the massive stone building, Jim needed clarification as to what Morgan meant by "older beliefs." The building spoke for itself. It looked impossibly ancient in comparison to the shacks and long buildings as if it had been plucked from medieval Europe whole and dropped into the middle of the Adirondacks. Jim couldn't imagine how the people of Zoo Town had built the thing so perfectly from the stones found in these woods.

"It's...amazing," he said softly. He usually felt a pleasing sort of melancholy when exploring ruins, but this felt different. A deep, primal sense of longing. A longing so strong, he'd taken a step toward the building without realizing it, only stopping when Morgan restrained him with a strong hand squeeze. "Not yet," she whispered.

He looked at her. Her lantern's soft glow made her black hair glisten, casting her features in an almost ethereal light. "Okay. Where to next?"

She stared at the building. The church. For a heartbeat, maybe more. Then she faced Jim, eyes wide and shining, her red lips parted slightly. "Your tent," she said, voice husky as she squeezed his hand again. "Let's go back to your tent."

The leisurely and quiet walk back to his tent flowed in a warm, liquid dream. Jim had little memory of it. It passed in a floating haze. As if gasping awake from a deep sleep, he came to awareness lying on his back in his tent. Naked, with a likewise naked Morgan astride him. Bent over so the top of her head cleared the tent. She pumped her hips in a slow, languid rhythm. She mewled and moaned softly in the back of her throat. He gripped her buttocks and squeezed, but despite the building urgency of his pleasure, he didn't force her pace. She was in control. Though each thrust of her hips sent him closer to release, he intuitively understood she wasn't ready. When she was, he would know.

As if sensing she was bringing him to the brink, Morgan slowed. She leaned over and kissed him deeply on the mouth, pressing her breasts against his chest. Her long black hair fell over his face in waves. He released her buttocks and clasped her face gently as they kissed. He still throbbed inside her, aching, but slower, now. Backing away from the precipice.

She broke off the kiss and gazed into his eyes. Untold depths swam there. Her eyes were no longer hazel. They burned a golden yellow, and he never wanted to look away.

"Be mine," she whispered in a deep, throaty voice. "Be mine. Roth bo'thar na haiche liem, go deu."

He had no idea what the last part meant, but the command in her voice was unmistakable, her imperious desire irresistible. He nodded breathlessly. Her wide and hungry grin nearly drove him mad with lust, but also chilled him to his core.

She straightened. The tent expanded with her, as if they weren't in a pup tent at all, but in a voluminous, lavish tent for royalty. Staring at him from a wonderful and terrible height, she slammed her hips down onto him, pumping him over and over with unrestrained fury. Crying out, he grabbed for her hips, but before he could touch her, she snatched his hands, bending over him, and pinned them to the ground as her pelvis hammered him, full breasts swaying hypnotically in his face.

He expanded inside her. Swelling, on fire. She thrust even faster, unmercifully, and something else stared out of her eyes. Something which not only wanted to devour him sexually but also wanted to devour his essence. Her face no longer belonged to the Morgan he'd met in the grocery store. It had transformed into a terrifying but beautiful visage. Eyes flashing madly, nostrils flaring, lips pulling back from her clenched teeth as she snarled, "B'othar na haiche! B'othar na haiche! B'othar na.. .haiche!"

The last word she screamed. She released his hands, and to his confused, lust-addled horror, clamped both her hands onto his neck and squeezed, instantly cutting off his air. He clawed at her fingers, to no avail. He couldn't pry loose her iron grip. And amazingly, he'd grown even harder inside her, as she pumped furiously on.

It happened as the edges of his vision started to blacken. He felt her sex clutch and spasm around him. He exploded, melting inside her. She screamed again and squeezed harder. The pain and fear and orgasmic oblivion blurred together as he fell into darkness, but before he did, Jim screamed because she had no face, nothing but smooth, empty flesh...

9.

The voices woke him. Rough, gravelly, with an accent he knew but couldn't place. He couldn't quite make out their words, but their tone sounded congenial as they bantered amicably back and forth. Every now and then someone would laugh or curse with glee. Then they'd all laugh, stomping the ground, slapping their backs or thighs in their mirth.

He heard other things, too. Distant singing. Maybe even a guitar playing. But the singing. That voice...

Come away, human child!

To the waters, and the wild

with a faery, hand in hand

for the world's more full of weeping...

Jim sat up, slowly. A pleasant fog clouded his thoughts. He rubbed his face and tried to piece together his thoughts, which were shot through with scattered images and sensations. He felt bone weary from working on McCallister's farm all day...but the thought snagged in his mind. It didn't seem right. He hadn't worked on a farm all day. Had he? He'd hiked to Zoo Town was all. It had taken longer than expected, but it hadn't actually been work.

Had it?

He opened his eyes and rubbed the back of his neck as a fresh round of laughter and swearing broke out near his tent. He wondered who could be out there. He also wondered why he didn't feel surprised. Of course, the Dolan and Murphy boys always stayed up late carousing, especially Friday night, after a hard week's work. He'd expect nothing less. Except...

Who the hell were the Dolan and Murphy boys?

Still struggling to knit his jumbled thoughts into coherence, Jim reached to his side, expecting to feel a warm, soft body there. Instead, he felt nothing but slightly damp, twisted wool blankets...

not a sleeping bag?

...indicative of someone who had been sleeping there, but who had left. Only a short time ago, as the sweat-damp blankets still retained some warmth. The only question was, where had...Morganna gone?

He drew his knees up to his chest and was puzzling this out when he heard a rumbling voice call, "Jimmy! Jimmy McConnell! Getchyer skinny ass out here!"

Wondering what the hell Daniel was going on about (also wondering, idly, who the hell Daniel was), Jimmy grunted and rummaged around for his trousers and chambray work shirt. As he dressed, he felt a momentary spat of confusion, not remembering packing such clothes, but also not feeling worried about it, either. He buckled his belt, shrugged into his shirt, and crawled out of his tent to drunken hoots and lewd whistling.

He stood and approached the revelers taking great entertainment at his expense. Rough-looking but amiable men, warming themselves at a barrel fire. Something about their clothing struck him as out of place. That, of course, didn't make sense. They weren't wearing anything he wouldn't. Especially after a long day working down at the zoo. They probably hadn't even stopped to change when they got home. In fact, knowing the Murphys and Dolans, they probably hadn't even stopped to eat dinner or kiss their wives and kids, or girlfriends, but came straight here to drink and raise hell around the fire. It was Friday night, after all. Pay day.

Wait. Was it Friday? He thought Monday. But it had to be Friday night. Especially if the boys were drinking around the fire.

One of the Murphy boys—Connor, he thought—clapped Jimmy on the shoulder and handed him a brown jug as he joined them. "How're you doin', Jimmy? Didja give the fair Morganna an entertainin' ride? Or did she give you a ride? She don't play around, that one!"

The men broke out in good-natured guffaws and Jim—Jimmy—chuckled with them. "Hard to tell. When you're with her, you don' know what's up or down." He shrugged, sipped from the jug, and swallowed. "Don' matter, do it? So long as both parties come away satisfied."

"Yeah," Daniel leered across the barrel at him, flames casting his craggy face in an eerie orange light, "so long as both parties come. Eh? Maybe she didn', and she gone down to Liam's shack to get her sat'sfaction!"

They all roared, even Jimmy. Liam was a dour-faced, stern, and unlikable fellow who cared more about the Bible than he did women. One of the men who took turns preaching to the Protestants in Zoo Town, he was more apt to lop off his own willy than take up with the likes of Morganna. Cast out the eye which offendeth, and all that.

Jimmy took a deeper drink of the poteen. Swallowed, and sighed as a pleasant, boozy warmth seeped into his belly. "Naw, she's probably at the church. Prayin' to her moon goddess and her phantom queen, or some such. It's near full moon, y'know. Holy time for her and her people."

He grinned, and said before taking another sip, "She says a good sweaty jag puts her inna holy state o'mind."

The boys chuckled at this, but carefully, lacking their previous raucous glee. Jimmy knew why. Much as any of them would trade their right arm to take up with the beautiful and ferocious Morganna Defay (regardless of their wives or girlfriends), they were leery of her and her people's beliefs. They weren't Catholic or Protestant. They kept to the old, ancient ways, which set them apart, for sure.

They were all Irish. Shared the same blood, and stood together. They had to. Especially because townsfolk in Clifton Heights were sometimes suspicious of them, often downright dismissive. Even so, the folk in Zoo Town gave Morganna and her people a decent berth. Jimmy often wondered if the fellows were envious he'd taken up with her...or fearful for him, instead.

In a blatant attempt to change the subject, Patrick Dolan—a tall, gangling fellow with shaggy red hair and equally red face—cleared his throat and gestured at Jimmy's tent with his poteen jug. "So, Jimmy. Been livin' in that tent almost two months, now. Lucky it ain't been a rainy summer, but fall's comin'. Gonna get cold. Buildin' yourself a place soon? Ain't no one else got a claim on that lot, yet. Better take it while ya can."

Danny nodded and piped up. "You let me know. I can get lumber from the mill at a fair price. Might even be able to convince old man Dickie to give it to you on credit."

Jimmy glanced back at his beaten but tried and true canvas tent he'd bought at Handy's Thrift when he'd first moved here (the tent should be blue and vinyl, bought at Gander Mountain three years ago, but what the hell was Gander Mountain?) and shook his head. "Dunno," he said, glancing back to the men, "still ain't landed a job at the zoo, and there won't be much work at the farm soon, with winter comin'. Not sure if I can afford it."

Danny nodded at him. "I'll talk to old man Dickie. Betcha he has somethin' at the mill fer ya. We'll get you set up, Jimmy. Don't you bother."

As if to punctuate his point, Danny leered at the men. "After all, ridin' with Morganna may be hot enuff, but not so much as to keep that tent warm through the winter!"

The men broke out in deep belly laughs at this. Drinking, stomping, and hooting. Connor threw an arm around Jimmy's shoulder and shook him with great mirth. Jimmy laughed himself because it was all in good fun. As he tipped the jug back and took a healthy swallow of poteen, he almost choked on the homemade hooch at the sight before him.

The men were all dead.

Dead and rotting. Greenish-black skin peeled off their faces and hands in liquid strips of sagging flesh, but they were still laughing. Snorting, calling each other names, and drinking...but dead.

Danny regarded him across the fire with his only putrid eye, which rolled sickly in its exposed socket. The other socket spilled wriggling maggots down his bare cheekbone. They stuck in the crevices with the little bits of flesh that clung there. "What's the matter, Jimmy?" Danny's loose jaw clicked and snapped, broken and jagged teeth gnashing. "Still a wee bit fuck-struck, are ya?"

Sean O'Mare Dolan, a short fat man standing next to the dead and rotting Danny, giggled wetly. Most of his flesh still hung on his face, but it gleamed a sickly pale yellow in the barrel fire's flames, hanging loosely around his eyes and teeth, exposing black and slimy gums. "His willy may've got free from her snatch, but his mind's still stuck there, I reckon."

Everyone laughed again, but their voices had taken on a sinister quality. Jimmy had to fight not to shrink back in revulsion. The cottage cheese flesh of Sean's sagging cheeks wriggled with his laughter. Things squirmed beneath their pock-marked surface.

Connor's arm squeezed Jimmy's shoulders again. This time, it felt all sharp angles. Jimmy glanced sideways and saw nothing but a bare skeleton dressed in rotting and dissolving rags. Darkness roiled in its eye sockets. When its jaw clicked open, he couldn't stifle a gag at its rotten, charnel-house stench. "Don't fret, Jimmy boy. We're pickin' fun at ya."

Jimmy gazed in mute horror at them—the rotting corpses—clustered around the fire. Their laughs had turned to rusty croaks and screeches, not unlike the calls of thousands of ravens. The sounds grated against his nerves. Felt like bony fingers digging into his brain...

All of Jimmy's whirling thoughts screeched to a halt. Out on the access road, walking past the men at a leisurely, relaxed pace, was a figure dressed rather strangely. He wore denim pants which looked different, somehow, and a white T-shirt, with a blue jacket over the shirt. Also, this person was healthy and whole, with all of its flesh, except...

It had no face.

No eyes, mouth, or nose. Though its head turned as it passed and stared at him, it had no face.

The faceless figure turned away and walked past. It melted into the crowd of mingling, laughing, and talking corpses meandering in the road. Somehow managing to wrench himself from Connor's bony grip, Jimmy walked away from the dead carousing men, in pursuit of the faceless one. He averted his gaze from the ragged and rotting corpses walking around him.

"Hey! Where you goin', Jimmy?" This from Colin McDoughal. Bellowed, somehow, without a lower jaw. His rotting tongue flapping and wriggling in the air. Jimmy muttered something about finding Morganna, and walked stiffly away, in the direction the faceless man had gone.

As he tried to make his way down the road, he found himself walking through what could only be a necromantic nightmare made flesh. Everyone he saw was dead. Flesh melting from their bones in varying degrees. Clothes torn and rotted. Oily and slick innards—intestines, kidneys, pulsing stomachs, and quivering lungs—shining wetly through ragged bellies. Walking in the road, sitting on front porches, in rocking chairs, or leaning on porch railings. Dead children grinning with lipless teeth, gums slick and blackened, running through the street.

Dead.

All, dead. But they waved to him. Said hello. Those who still had flesh smiled madly in greeting. He stumbled past, the faceless man's back receding into the crowd. Jimmy tried to focus on the blue jacket (which looked so strangely familiar) and not on the dead milling around him.

Once, in his mounting delirium, he bumped into a man who turned his eternally grinning skull at him, saying, "So sorry, fella!" while clutching a roiling mess of innards in his guts with gleaming white, skeletal hands.

Jimmy stumbled blindly on. The blue jacket ahead bobbed and weaved through the crowd. Everyone was dead and rotting, but didn't notice, nor care. They walked, chatted, and drank.

The blue jacket turned and abruptly left the road and people behind. It slipped into the alley between the infirmary and the general store, fading into the darkness. Eager to escape the rotting crowd, wondering if his poteen had gone bad somehow and was making him hallucinate, Jimmy followed the faceless man in the blue jacket, ducking down the same alley. The darkness between the two buildings brought relief from the horrid sight of the dead walking, but halfway through the alley, grunts and moans of pleasure froze him in his tracks. His stomach surging, he pressed back against the general store, fighting to keep the gorge from rising in his throat.

Behind a high stack of crates against the infirmary, a couple enthusiastically fucked. A man taking a woman roughly from behind. Based on her enthusiastic whines of pleasure, it was a welcome roughness. Such clandestine and frantic couplings in such a barely secluded spot on Friday and Saturday nights weren't unheard of in Zoo Town. There weren't many other places for secret lovers to meet.

But what he saw before him wasn't young lovers stealing a too-brief moment of passion. He saw a flesh-crawling abomination. The man was a bloody, rotting caricature of a human being. Chunks of flesh had fallen away from his torso, hips, and legs. Revealing bone, tendons, and blackened, rotting muscle. What flesh remained was cracked and oozing. Riddled with small holes, out of which squirmed worms. The man's bone fingers literally dug into the pallid and sagging flesh of the woman's buttocks, as he repeatedly slammed home—in soggy wet slaps of flesh—whatever might be left of his member into whatever might be left of her sex. Both mercifully hidden from view.

With each thrust, viscera squirted through ragged tears in his abdomen onto the woman's back, which was spotted with slick green mold. Something resembling hair lay on the man's head, and while both eyes gleamed in sunken eye sockets, the man's facial flesh hung in ragged strips ending mid-cheek, exposing the bottom half of a skull that grinned forever in mad, orgasmic glee.

He saw little of the woman, which was a blessing. Flesh covered her entire face, though it hung loose and jiggled every time the man slammed into her from behind. It made her pleasure grimaces appear even more grotesque. Her matted and tangled hair was falling out in clumps. While one full breast almost swayed seductively, any lust dissolved at the sight of the mangled flesh where the other breast should be. Through the green-black dripping mess, her white rib cage glinted.

Jimmy finally tore his eyes away from the sickening tableau and inched along, back pressed against the general store, desperately praying he could steal away unnoticed. If they heard him and acted embarrassed or angry, as would any normal couple caught jagging behind a building, Jimmy didn't think he could handle it.

Still, even as he stared forward, the animalistic sounds of grunting pleasure recreated the image of them in his mind. Images of two corpses fucking with great energy. With every tentative step, he feared he might lose the battle and vomit into the weeds.

Until he saw him, standing at the end of the alley. Facing him, staring at him with no face. Mercifully, the sight of the faceless man dressed in the strange but familiar clothes banished images of the amorous corpses from his mind. He carefully increased his pace towards him, leaving behind the sounds of rotting flesh smacking together.

The faceless man turned and continued walking away from him.

Jimmy continued until he finally left the alley and stepped onto the other road on the opposite side of town. He nearly sagged in relief, basking in the sudden night silence. The homes on this side of town were dark and quiet. No one walked the road. No rotting corpse children played and screeched. No dead men stood around barrel fires, their croaking laughter sounding like the calls of sickly birds.

He couldn't even hear the revelries on the other side of town. This side of town always remained reverent at night, even on the weekends. With good reason. It played home to the old stone church. The first building erected in Zoo Town.

Ahead, the faceless man walked through the doorway of the old stone church and disappeared into its swirling darkness.

Jimmy slowed as he approached the imposing edifice, which loomed over him as he drew near. Closer now, he could see the tiny flickering glow of a candle inside. He knew who it was, in his heart. As he'd told the boys.

Morganna.

Praying to the Ancients.

He took a hesitant step toward the stone church, then stopped. What would he find inside? Morganna, kneeling before a candle, uttering prayers in some strange, ancient Celtic tongue long since lost to man? Would the sound of her prayers send cold shivers up his spine?

Or perhaps she'd be engaged in something...profane. Unholy, even by his secular values. Sacrificing an animal? He'd never once intruded on her worship or prayer, or whatever she did in here, and they'd never talked about it. He didn't know what he'd find, or if his intrusion would be welcome.

Would she be whole? Alive? Or a tattered, rotting corpse? Maggots and worms spilling from her mouth as she prayed? Nightmarish images of everything he'd seen rushed back into his mind, making his stomach churn once more. Had it been...real? Couldn't have been. Maybe he'd gone mad with fatigue. Or had Connor slipped some root or herb in his poteen? Something powerful enough to make him see things. It could be done, he knew. He was the fresh face around town, after all. Prime for breaking in.

Jimmy shook his head, mentally pushing aside images of the dead walking and talking, laughing, drinking, and fucking. Morganna could explain. He felt certain, though he didn't understand why.

He took a deep breath. Came nearer to the stone church. The small light still glimmered faintly within. He stepped into the doorway and saw the hazy silhouette of a woman sitting. Facing him or back to him, he couldn't be sure. But it was Morganna. Alive? Or dripping phantasm of the dead?

"You'll never know unless you come in," he heard a soft, firm, and familiar voice say.

Jimmy placed a hand on the stone church's cool rock. Before he could move, a cavalcade of thoughts, memories, emotions, and images flooded his mind. A torrent of sensations powerful enough to make him gasp, and stagger. He leaned against the stone church's doorway, remembering.

He wasn't Jimmy McConnell. He was Jim O'Connell. He didn't live in Zoo Town, Clifton Heights. He lived in Franklin, Massachusetts. He wasn't an itinerant Irish laborer of the thirties, he was a—soon to be unemployed—lab technician at Carion Filters and Mirrors. He enjoyed visiting abandoned places, and he'd come here to camp in the ruins of Zoo Town. The woman he'd met at the grocery store—Morgan, not Morganna—joined him here to roast hot dogs over a campfire. They'd toured Zoo Town by electric lantern light, and then they'd...

Jim's stomach lurched. He felt sick and disoriented. The ground felt unstable beneath his feet, his legs weak and rubbery. Had any of what he'd seen...felt...experienced...been real?

"It's all quite real," the soft voice said in a compassionate yet oddly commanding tone, "depending, of course, on how you define 'real.' However, I suppose that's irrelevant at this point."

Jim braced himself against the cool stone doorway and forced himself to straighten. "Who...who are you? What are you? What's happening to me?"

The voice continued as if it hadn't heard him, or hadn't cared. "I've watched you for a long time, Jim O'Connell. From afar. Visiting your beloved abandoned places. The empty spaces where the world has moved on. I've measured and weighed you. Watching as your isolation and loneliness grew, increasingly drawing you to all these places, and inevitably...to me."

Despite his fear and confusion, something inside Jim bristled at the voice's accusations. "I'm not...not lonely, not..."

"...isolated? That's what you tell yourself, of course." The woman's head tilted, but Jim still didn't know if she faced him, or if her back was to him. All he saw was indistinguishable darkness, which made him think of the faceless man. "When you return home from work every day and collapse into a cold and empty bed, you tell yourself you're not lonely, or isolated. You say the same thing when you eat take-out or microwaved meals alone. Or when you spend your free time exploring the broken-down, forgotten places of the world. When you see others progressing in life. Getting married. Having children. Ascending the corporate ladder. While you stand still on a treadmill of your own making."

"That's why I ultimately chose you, of course. Because of your isolation, and growing stagnation. If an Elder takes your place to live out their life as you...no one will notice."

Deep within the gloom, a torch in a wall sconce flared to life. It revealed the faceless man, standing with his back against the wall. Staring at him. Except now, the man had a face. One Jim knew well. It was his, after all.

Jim's mind spun. "But...those were stories. Stories."

The woman—Morgan—chuckled. "As I said to you. Stories are simply ways to explain what we cannot and will never understand."

"Step closer. Come inside. Please."

Jim marshaled what little remained of his resolve. "What if I don't? What if I leave? Hide out until morning?"

Another chuckle. One which sounded sinister, and callous. "Morning will never come, and you'll wander forever among the rotting dead."

The thought of seeing nothing but shambling, decayed, maggot-riddled abominations for an eternity sapped the last of Jim's will. He weakly pushed off the cool stone doorway and entered the church.

10.

The instant Jim entered the church, light flared in points around the interior. Other torches, hanging from more wall sconces, lighting on their own. Half-expecting the church to be filled with a congregation of rotting dead, Jim saw only Morgan, sitting cross-legged in its center, and from the corner of his eye, the blue fleece worn by the faceless man who now looked like him. He forced himself to focus on Morgan, however, and nothing else.

She sat facing him. Wearing a black, full-body stretch outfit similar to the running tights she'd worn this morning in the grocery store. He couldn't tell for sure, but he thought she wore the same yellow running shoes, also.

She didn't speak immediately. Only stared at him with hazel eyes that glowed molten gold. Her gaze penetrated deep inside him. It was neither welcoming nor malicious. It was. Cold, analytical, and measuring. He grew uneasy under its weight, so he glanced around the church to escape its power.

Straight ahead stood a simple pulpit. Next to it, a simple table, which Jim supposed—in a flight of dread fancy—doubled as a profane altar for ancient rituals. There were no pews or chairs. Perhaps worshipers and penitents sat cross-legged on the ground, as Morgan was.

As his eyes traveled the room, he mentally skipped over the faceless man who now had his face. There were no windows. In regular intervals, symbols had been painted on the walls in black paint. The Christian cross, and other symbols Jim didn't recognize, alternating with the cross. He didn't know why, but the symbols made him faintly sick, for some reason.

"As I told you earlier, Catholics, Protestants, and those who followed the old ways took turns worshiping here. They shared this church faithfully. Made it a place of great power. That's the real reason why Zoo Town is so well preserved. Why it shows so little decay." She gestured in a broad circle. "Because of the power which still resides in these walls."

Morgan's gaze settled on him once more. This time, Jim forced himself to return it. Mustering what little reserves remained, he managed, "What are you?"

Morgan smiled. It wasn't necessarily a kind expression, or cruel, either, or without a kind of sympathy. The kind a stern adult shows a willfully ignorant child. "I'd think that would be obvious, by now."

Morgan stood in a motion more graceful than anything he'd ever seen. She walked toward him, supple muscles flexing in her arms, shoulders, and thighs. A vision of terrible power and beauty, all at once. As she drew near, Jim gasped in shock and awe.

She wasn't wearing a black body suit at all. Black, downy feathers covered her body, neck to ankles. And she wasn't wearing yellow running sneakers. They were yellow feet, but not human feet. Claws. Hard. Pebbly. With three talons each.

He gazed into her golden eyes, remembering. "The Phantom Queen," he whispered.

Morgan smiled, showing human, white teeth. "The Morrigan. Goddess of war, fertility...guardian of the night road, and the Otherworld."

Jim swallowed down a dry, tight throat. "And this...this is the Otherworld?"

Morgan—Morrigan—tipped her head. "One of many. Actually, it would be more appropriate to say there are many, and one. They exist in countless places, and the same place, simultaneously. The night road connects them all."

She gave him an arched eyebrow, lips pursed in a mischievous smirk. "You've visited several of them over the years, in the lonely, abandoned places you love to haunt. I watched you in all those places. Every step you took, I was near. Waiting."

Jim looked at her anew, a strange wonder replacing his fear. "Why didn't you show yourself? Those other times? Why now?"

She stepped closer, her expression softening, almost becoming sad. She placed a feathered hand on his face. He flinched slightly, expecting her touch to feel revolting. It didn't. Rather, it felt soothingly warm and soft. "You weren't ready. Now you are. Ready to be offered a choice."

Jim thought of his job, which was ending in December, despite decades of faithful service. Thought of the vacations he'd no longer be able to afford, how it was unlikely he'd find meaningful employment elsewhere at his age. Thought of his solitary, empty home filled with little to mark his time on this Earth.

"Choice. What choice?"

She removed her hand from his face, and clasped both hands before her, assuming an aristocratic, even regal air. "I have selected you. Regardless of what you desire. One of my kind wishes to live out his last days as a mortal. He will have your face. Your life."

The faceless man who now wore his face stepped into view. Jim glanced at him briefly, felt himself slip close to madness at seeing his own face, and looked back to Morgan before he lost his mind completely. "I have no say. Do I?"

"No."

"What happens to me, then?"

"Therein lies your choice. If you had rejected me and fled, you would've been trapped forever in a nightmare world of the dead, and you would've been treated to sights far worse than the dead making love, for all eternity. Sights which would drive you mad."

An awful chill rippled across his shoulders. "What else?"

"You could live here in the Otherworld as Jimmy, with those others you met upon awakening, and Morganna. They'll be whole, however. Uncorrupted, and without decay. You'll stay young forever, and would enjoy an approximation of a good, simple life."

The word approximation stood out. "It wouldn't be real, though. Would it?"

"As real as you wanted it to be."

"Would I know? That it wasn't real?"

She shrugged. "Occasionally you'd glimpse the truth. Feel as if something was out of place. Maybe you'd accidentally sneak tiny peeks behind the Veil. But you'd dismiss those incidents as your imagination. After an eternity," she conceded, "you would eventually grow insane, I'm afraid. But you'd enjoy a long, benign, peaceful existence until then."

"Until I went crazy trying to figure it out, you mean."

"Yes."

"Would I be with you? This Morganna...would that be...you?"

She hesitated. "Morganna is a shade of me. So to speak."

"But not you."

She sighed, almost regretfully, Jim thought. "No. I am The Phantom Queen. I take no consort. I walk alone."

Jim covered his face with his hands, rubbed his temples with his fingertips, and took a deep breath. After several minutes of silence, he uncovered his face and ran a shaking hand through his hair. He whispered, "Is there another choice?"

"Yes. You'd wake up in your tent in the morning. All of this will be a dream. Zoo Town would be as you found it. However, your existence, as you know it, would end. You wouldn't be allowed to reclaim your former life.

"What is your choice?"

11.

Gauzy blue light fell on Jim's face, teasing his eyelids open. Several different birds called far away. One of them screeching like a raven. A slight breeze rippled the tent. Another bird, closer—this one definitely a raven—croaked, bringing Jim fully awake.

He lay there for several minutes, trying to pull his scattered thoughts together. His mind felt sluggish and hazy as if he were suffering from a mild hangover. Which, of course, didn't make sense. He hadn't brought anything alcoholic, and neither had Morgan. Of course, they'd gotten drunk on something else entirely, and...

Vivid memories of their wild lovemaking (no, fucking was the better word) sent a jolt of energy through him. Faint arousal, also. He rolled over onto his side, but instead of Morgan, all he saw was a human impression of where she'd been lying in his rumpled sleeping bag.

She'd left. Had slipped out before he woke, apparently.

His arousal faded, replaced by a casual resignation. Of course, Morgan had left. Whatever last night had been, she was most certainly out of his league. There'd be no repeat of their escapades, and he didn't expect to see her again the rest of the week. If they did happen upon each other, he fully expected her to dismiss him casually, or ignore him completely.

Thinking about the rest of the week reminded him that several days remained in his vacation here in Clifton Heights, with several more abandoned sites to visit. Energy and a new purpose filled him. Oddly, as he rummaged around for his clothes, he didn't think about his impending "retirement" at all. It didn't feel important, anymore.

As he broke camp, a mild headache persisted, insisting he had been drinking last night. Of course, he only remembered vague snatches of how long he and Morgan had gone at it, or if it had happened once or multiple times, or when they'd finally fallen asleep.

Also, he didn't think he'd slept soundly. Garish, nightmarish images of walking dead people kept flashing through his thoughts. Remnants of bad dreams run wild. He couldn't remember much past the images, or recall any context. Only revolting flashes of degradation and decay. Nothing more.

He was probably tired. That's why he had a headache. Fatigue. However, by the time he'd cleared the camp, kicked dirt over the campfire's coals, and watered them down, his headache had mostly cleared. He felt rested and ready for something new. Again, thoughts of impending retirement didn't bother him. He'd cross that bridge when he came to it. Right now, he wanted to hike down to Raedeker Park and call a cab to The Skylark so he could eat breakfast. Maybe Cassie the waitress would be working. He wanted to see her reaction when he told her he'd spent the night in Zoo Town and survived, unscathed.

However, after he passed the cairn cemetery, all his good feelings died. He stumbled to a halt. An icy dread filled him. Tight bands constricted his lungs, and his breathing became short and labored as he tried to make sense of what he saw.

A wall of closely packed trees and dense undergrowth where the road back to Raedeker Park should be. Indeed, he saw no signs of a road, or that one had ever existed. All he saw was a dense forest.

He opened his mouth. Closed it. Opened it again, but his mind couldn't form any coherent thoughts, much less form words for him to speak. He scanned the tightly packed trees and bushes, hunting for a gap or a space of any kind. Some clear ground he could step into. He reached a shaking hand out, to brush a branch aside...

Something cracked in the woods. A footstep. A large body, snapping off a branch as it shouldered its way through the woods. More cracking sounds followed as if something incredibly huge was lumbering towards him. He didn't hear any grunting, growling, or breathing. Only crashing sounds, getting closer and closer...

He dropped his hand.

Stepped back from the tree line.

The cracking stopped. Silence fell. A voice from a half-forgotten dream or nightmare whispered in his heart...

you wouldn't be allowed to reclaim your former life

Jim turned and looked down the road running through Zoo Town. He had no doubt on the other end of the abandoned town he'd find another impenetrable wall of trees and brush. Should he try to breach it, he knew, also, something large and horrible would crash through the woods toward him.

Jim stood still for several more minutes. Staring at Zoo Town, until he numbly started walking past the cairns, back to re-pitch his tent. He had some more snacks and hot dogs, as well as water. Though he didn't feel hungry or thirsty, and idly wondered if he'd ever need to eat or drink again, at all. He supposed he would if he needed, and left it at that.

He would make camp. Undertake a more thorough exploration of Zoo Town. The thought filled him with a strange peace. Maybe later, Morgan would return. He didn't think it likely, but he contented himself with hoping she would. As he hoped maybe one morning, the path away from Zoo Town would reappear.

Maybe.

The Man Who Sits in His Chair

There is a man who sits in his chair in front of his small yellow house on Chester Road. He is as much a town fixture as Raedeker Park Zoo, The Orpheum Movie Hall, or Handy's Pawn and Thrift. No one knows what he does besides sitting in his chair. He's old—somewhere between his sixties and eighties—but he's always been old. Of that, everyone is sure.

His backstory changes with every generation. Some say he served in Vietnam, and because of what he saw there, he now lives alone. Twenty years ago, he fought in Korea. In the nineties, World War II. And so on.

No one ever bothers to learn more. The man who sits in his chair is simply part of the landscape. An interesting aspect of a larger tapestry. Of course, the children whisper epic tales about him. But by adulthood, the man's allure fades. If you remain in Clifton Heights, he simply becomes part of your existence. If you leave, he becomes a curious footnote to your childhood. Nothing more.

The man sits in his chair in front of his little yellow house during the warmer months. During the colder months, he can be seen sitting inside, through his small living room window. Townspeople unconsciously mark the seasons by him. Clifton Heights knows Spring is near when he moves outside. Winter is just around the corner when he moves indoors.

Chester Road climbs uphill above Clifton Heights. From his vantage point, the man enjoys a panoramic view of everything. Even if folks only give him a passing thought, it's reasonable to assume they subconsciously know he watches them year-round. And it is also reasonable to assume many wonder...

How much does he see?

How much does he know?

The answer their subconscious whispers back?

Everything.

1.

Sunday Night
July 14

"How long will you be staying with us, Mr. Roth?"

David Roth jerked slightly; his attention having drifted. He blinked, gripped by a crawling sense of dislocation, for a moment unsure where he was. He stood at a counter in a somewhat charming and rustic lobby. Behind the counter sat a blond, nondescript middle-aged man with watery-gray eyes, and thin lips pressed together in the slightest expression of impatience. "Mr. Roth?"

It came to him. The Motor Lodge. A small resort of self-sufficient cabins just outside Clifton Heights, a small Adirondack town west of Old Forge. He'd planned on driving straight through, hoping to reach Syracuse by evening. His flight home to Alabama left tomorrow afternoon from Hancock International.

Just outside Clifton Heights, however, his rental car—a 2015 Nissan Ultima—had slowly started losing acceleration. He'd crawled along at twenty miles per hour, despite pushing the pedal to the floor, before the Nissan shuddered once and died. He'd coasted to a stop along the shoulder of Bassler Road.

After waiting an additional two hours in a sticky humid warmth he wouldn't have thought possible so far north, the tow truck called by the rental company's insurance arrived. It took his car to a shop in town. Rich's Auto Care. After another hour sitting in their small (but air-conditioned, thank God) waiting area, a distantly sympathetic mechanic named Jesse informed him the Nissan's transmission had stripped several gears. It had to be replaced.

Fortunately, David opted for extra insurance with his rental package, guaranteeing him a replacement car. However, after spending forty-five minutes being shuffled from one phone representative to another, David learned that due to an odd shortage, no cars were available at the nearest rental company in Utica for at least another week. Because of the insurance he'd purchased, however, the rental company would cover all the repair costs...but the policy stipulated new or reconditioned replacement parts. Not used. According to Jesse, the quickest Rich's Auto could procure even a reconditioned transmission was four days.

So here he was at The Motor Lodge, the only place to stay in Clifton Heights. Fourteen cabins on the eastern rim of Clifton Lake. Boasting one bedroom with a queen mattress, a small den, a fully equipped kitchen, and a small bath. Free Wi-Fi and basic cable on a flat-screen television. His rental insurance also paid for a loaner from Rich's Auto. A 2005 Kia Optima, which proved a tight fit for his six-foot-three, slightly paunchy frame. He managed, however, and had driven to The Motor Lodge on Jesse's recommendation.

"Mr. Roth?"

David swallowed and forced his strangely drifting attention back to the man behind the counter. "Sorry. Four days, at the moment. Maybe longer. My rental car is at Rich's Auto, waiting for a new transmission."

The clerk nodded dully, showing little emotion, his expression blank. He slid a generic form across the counter. "The only cabin I have left is nonsmoking. We don't allow pets."

David numbly accepted the paperwork and started filling it out. "That's fine. I don't smoke, and don't have any pets."

"Just you?"

He nodded, feeling slightly guilty at the relief Kathleen wasn't with him. Irritated as he was by this situation, his wife would've been even more so. Though he loved her dearly, Kathleen's added irritation would only have made an unpleasant situation worse. At least alone, he could let himself decompress. His only immediate worry was how to entertain himself over the next four days.

"There's a $150 security deposit. It'll be returned upon check-out, which is Thursday, 11 a.m."

David pushed the finished paperwork back across the counter, along with his American Express card and driver's license. "What if the repairs are delayed? Can I stay longer?"

"Let me check." The apathetic clerk tapped a few keys on a nearly obsolete DELL desktop. "You should be fine," he said after a few minutes, "I've got no one else booked for that cabin."

The clerk examined David's completed paperwork and then ran his American Express card. Waiting for its approval, he looked up and offered David a small but genuine smile. "I wouldn't worry. Rich's Auto will fix you up fine."

He handed the receipt to David for his signature. Though David wanted to take comfort from these assurances, he couldn't help but sense a hollowness in the clerk's words.

David had been practicing business law at the same firm in Birmingham, Alabama for twenty-five years. A licensed member of the Alabama Bar Association, he was required to attend at least one annual "continuing education" convention. His firm had resources to cover his costs, within reason. Because David had conservative tastes, he always chose conventions his firm could fully cover, hotel included, with a modest meal budget.

After the kids left home for college—his son to pursue a degree in Education, his daughter in Veterinary Science—the annual convention became an enjoyable getaway for him and Kathleen. She shopped and took in the sights during the days. They dined out and took in more sights in the evening. All at the low price of sitting through seminars on "best practices" and "business law ethics" while surreptitiously completing the Times crossword puzzle in the back row, under the guise of taking notes.

This year, however, fate rolled snake-eyes for Kathleen. She'd been put on weekend-call at the pediatrician's office where she practiced. This was the first time in fifteen years she hadn't been able to accompany him. Despite his guilty relief, that she wasn't here in the midst of these troubles, he'd missed her considerably the last few days.

However, as David keyed open cabin number 14, he had to admit an even deeper guilt. Relief Kathleen hadn't come at all. He'd felt out of sorts the past two months. Short-tempered, irritable, and he hadn't slept well, plagued by a recurring nightmare from which he always woke bathed in cold sweat.

Usually, he and Kathleen talked about everything. They shared an intimate relationship built on mutual communication. Still, he'd been oddly reluctant to discuss his recent troubles with her, simply because he didn't know why he felt so ill at ease. He'd played off his discomfiture as stress from work, a cold, or general fatigue.

He didn't know what was bothering him, or why. So when circumstances required Kathleen to stay home, he thought a weekend alone might be good. That was also why he'd decided to drive from Montreal to Syracuse. Extra time alone to sort out what the hell was wrong with him. Maybe this layover would be helpful because even after the weekend alone in Montreal, he'd gotten nowhere in diagnosing his troubles.

David stepped into the cabin, and flicked the wall switch on, bathing the interior with welcoming soft light. He shut the door behind him, set down his suitcase, and turned to survey the room.

He saw a modestly sized den. Against the wall to his immediate left sat a rustic-looking futon, its frame made to imitate felled tree limbs. Against the wall to the far left sat a cushioned Adirondack chair, next to a lampstand in a similar aesthetic to the futon. Before the futon was an unadorned wooden coffee table which, in its simplicity, looked more genuine than either the futon or its accompanying lampstand. Against the far wall hung a flat-screen television.

To his right was a small kitchen, featuring a refrigerator, combination oven and range, sink, and a microwave and coffee maker. Not a Keurig, but a standard instant coffee maker. In the center of the kitchen sat a small square wooden table, with two chairs.

His inspection of the bedroom revealed the advertised queen-sized bed and nightstand similar in style to the futon and lampstand in the den. A stained oak clothes dresser, and an empty closet in the far corner. To the left of the bed, a doorway led to the small bathroom and its narrow shower stall, toilet, and sink. The tiny bathroom actually made him smile, reminding him of his first cracker-box apartment (before Kathleen), which had a bathroom so small, that he claimed he could do all his business at once.

His survey complete, David hoisted his suitcase onto the dresser. Perhaps these circumstances weren't so bad. The cabin was nice enough, and if "Jesse" from Rich's Auto proved a fair representative of Clifton Heights, his stay could actually be pleasant.

Something nagged David in the back of his mind, however, as he unpacked clean clothes from his suitcase into the dresser. He couldn't help feeling the action—even though it was consistent with his love of organization—was resignation to staying here longer than four days. That bothered him, though he couldn't say why.

2.

After he'd settled into his cabin and called Kathleen with an update so she wouldn't worry, David's stomach finally made its hunger known. He sat on the futon, opened his laptop, connected to the cabin's Wi-Fi, and searched Google for restaurants and diners. He didn't care where or what he ate. He wasn't picky. He just needed a place still open at 8:00 p.m.

The first several hits turned up establishments that had closed at seven. Dooley's Ice Cream and Subs, and Chin's Pizza and Wings. That left Henry's Drive-In Diner, The Skylark Diner, and another pizza joint called Pizza Joe's. The diners were on the other side of town, while Pizza Joe's, according to Google, was up the road from The Motor Lodge, on Chester Road. David decided he'd try there first.

When David got into his loaner from Rich's Auto, however, and tried to get directions from Google Maps, nothing came up at first. His phone only flashed: LOST GPS SIGNAL. Google Maps didn't provide directions until the fourth try, saying it was six minutes away. Pushing down irritation and the same odd unease he'd felt checking into The Motor Lodge, he pulled onto Chester Road and drove off in search of Pizza Joe's.

His sense of unease only increased, however, as his phone's GPS continued to glitch. Three times in a row, a slightly robotic and oddly feminine voice intoned "*Recalculating,*" before adding time to its projected route.

After the third recalculation, David was nearly out of patience. In all this time, he could've already been eating at one of the diners. He was about to turn around at a tall, crooked elm on his right, when he heard the soft robotic voice say, "Your destination is on the left."

With a curse on his lips, assuming Google Maps had failed once again, David looked up. Indeed, he saw a rectangular building with a huge red and white-striped awning. Its windows and doors glowed with a welcoming yellow warmth against the night.

"What the hell?" David frowned. He gently braked and executed a slow U-turn into the other lane. He coasted to a stop on the road's shoulder. He hadn't seen anything before Google Maps announced his arrival. Not even the tiniest flicker of light. It was almost as if Google's soft robotic voice had summoned the building into being.

Almost on cue, Google cheerily informed him, "You've arrived at your destination."

David put the car in park. Above the red and white-striped awning, Pizza Joe's blazed in tall neon letters. At least twenty cars sat in the front parking lot. On either side of the building stood motorcycles and other cars and trucks. Only one parking spot in the front lot was vacant.

Music played from speakers hidden underneath the awning. He couldn't place its tune, but the music sounded old. Maybe something his grandparents had listened to as teenagers. Abruptly, the music came to a stop with a flourish of drums and a twanging guitar, followed by a DJ. The thing was, David couldn't quite make out what the DJ was saying. He followed the cadence well enough. The DJ spoke in a rapid, jive-talking tone he remembered from movies of a much earlier era. But no matter how hard he listened; he couldn't make out what the DJ said.

An odd realization crept over him. He hadn't made a move to get out. Hadn't shut off the engine, or even taken his hand off the shift. Also, the longer he listened to the fast jive-talking DJ machine-gunning nonsense words, the more frustrated he became. He couldn't understand what the DJ was saying. He should understand, and that made him almost angry, except...

He didn't want to understand what the DJ was saying.

Did he?

Deep inside?

The cadence and the rhythm of the fast-talking DJ sounded human, but he couldn't make any sense of the words. Underneath the jive, David thought he detected a low hum. A buzzing. As if thousands of voices were speaking at once, all in a hissing rush.

His unease increased when he looked closer at Pizza Joe's. Despite the almost full parking lot (except for one space, saved for him?), he didn't see anyone inside. He saw booths, tables, and chairs. A front counter and a register. Rows of narrow rectangular doors behind the counter, which he assumed were pizza ovens.

But no people.

Despite all the cars, trucks, and motorcycles, he didn't see a single soul inside.

Something curdled in his belly. He tasted something sour in the back of his throat. His hand tightened instinctively on the shift, preparing to put the car into gear and drive away...

When he heard it.

The rusty screech and wooden slam of an old screen door opening and closing. Followed by the sound of boots scraping asphalt...

Coming toward him.

He turned away from the sound. Put the car into gear and drove off, barely restraining his impulse to floor it. He also resisted the urge to look out the rear view mirror and didn't take the time to look up The Skylark Diner on Google Maps until he was well away from Pizza Joe's, and near the bottom of the hill.

After David put more distance between him and the strangely disquieting Pizza Joe's, his unease faded. He didn't know what to make of it. A packed parking lot with only one space open, but an empty building. The strange DJ that he hadn't been able to understand and wasn't sure he wanted to. The cold feeling in his belly from that screeching screen door, and the boots scraping asphalt toward him. He didn't understand any of it, but the further away he got from Pizza Joe's, the less inclined he felt to try. He was hungry and tired. He wanted to eat and go back to his cabin and sleep.

He opted for The Skylark Diner because it was the closest. When he pulled into the parking lot, the diner looked moderately busy, but with several spaces open (not just one, reserved for him). He heard muted music coming from inside the diner, but it sounded current. Something his kids would've listened to. Even more comforting, he saw plenty of people inside. Sitting at booths and at the front counter, waiters and waitresses busily serving them. Still, his uneasy feelings about Pizza Joe's lingered. Several minutes passed before he could force himself to turn his car off and get out.

However, once a waiter had seated him at a booth near the back, his unease faded. It settled into a dull pressure in the back of his mind, eclipsed by hunger. He vaguely toyed with the idea of exploring Chester Road in the daylight, but at the moment, he only wanted to eat.

"Hey there!" A waitress with short black hair and bright green eyes sidled up to his table, notebook in hand. "My name's Cassie and I'll be your server tonight. Start you off with a drink? Coffee, water, tea, or soda?"

The young woman's cheer proved contagious. David felt the last dregs of his unease fade away. Though his daughter had light brown hair and blue eyes, Cassie's energy and goodwill reminded David of her. "Water, with a slice of lemon? Been a long drive. At my age, caffeine and sugar make it hard to fall asleep."

"Sorry to hear. From out of town?"

David nodded. "Been on the road since ten this morning. Wanted to reach Syracuse by night. I was making good time until my transmission died. Spent the rest of the time getting my car towed to Rich's Auto and booking a cabin at The Motor Lodge."

"What rotten luck!" Cassie offered a sympathetic smile. "But Rich's Auto does good work, and The Motor Lodge is a nice place. This is also the best time of year to visit, next to Fall. Hopefully, your stay will be a good one."

His spirits considerably lifted, his memories of Pizza Joe's almost completely erased, David returned her smile. "I'm beginning to think it will. Thank you."

"Not to pry, but where are you traveling to?"

"Home is in Birmingham, Alabama. Was going to catch a flight out of Syracuse tomorrow, although now I'll have to call and cancel."

Cassie beamed, looking even more like his daughter. "The South! I've always wanted to go there. What brings you up this way?"

"A law conference in Montreal, Quebec. I flew up, but decided to drive to Syracuse, because..."

He paused, thinking of the nightmares and ill feelings that had plagued him for the past few months. He managed a smile and continued. "I thought some open road might do me good. A pause before jetting back to work."

Cassie nodded. "I get that. I love driving. Always clears my head." She gestured with her notebook. "Ready to order?"

David chose the Burger Deluxe. Well-done, with a side of steak fries. Cassie jotted down her approval and nodded her approval, claiming it was a favorite. About twenty minutes later, after finishing the burger, which had been topped with onion rings, lettuce, and tomatoes, he understood why.

Cassie had cleared his dishes. The thought occurred to ask her about Pizza Joe's. The moment passed, however. Cassie handed him the check, told him he could pay at the register, and wished him a good night. He let the chance slide by, telling himself he could easily ask around about Pizza Joe's tomorrow, though a deep part of him knew he wouldn't.

3.

Before retiring for the night, David sat down at his laptop and searched for places to eat again. Oddly enough, Pizza Joe's didn't come up this time, no matter how many times he refreshed the page. When he tried to find it on Google Maps, all he got was a GPS ERROR message. He thought about Googling for Pizza Joe's by name, but a combination of fatigue and a return of his unease stopped him. He switched off his phone, closed down his laptop, and prepared for bed.

However, despite his physical and mental fatigue, he didn't fall asleep right away. He tossed and turned throughout the night. What little sleep he did get was shot through with dreams.

David's breath roars in his ears and his heart pounds in his chest. He walks briskly down a gray, subterranean hallway. Fluorescent lights buzz overhead in a low, maddening hum. Speakers are spaced intermittently in the ceiling. From them, a voice gibbers madly. Though David thinks he recognizes a syllable here and there, the voice mutters inhuman vocalizations impossible to understand.

He breaks into a run. This unending hallway is lined with doors on both sides and even though he's not sure why...

something's coming

...he needs to get to the next door before it opens, because if he doesn't...

The door ahead and to the left starts shaking in its frame. The knob jiggles wildly. Something is on the other side, and it wants to get in.

Something horrible, dark, and full of hungry teeth. David doesn't know how he knows this. He just does. If he doesn't get to that door it will mean pain, death, destruction, and chaos.

With a burst of frantic speed, David reaches the door. He grabs desperately for the knob. His hand slips and he scrambles for a grip on its cool, slick metal. He loses hold and cries out when the knob turns, clicks, and the door jerks open about a foot. He yells, grabs the knob. This time he gets it. Something on the other side pulls with immense strength, jerking the door open another inch. Fear pulses through David. His hand slips again, and he almost loses his grip. Acidic terror curdles his guts. He has to close this door or all is lost, all is...

He hears it.

The DJ mutters unintelligible and strange words in an excited, high-pitched jive-talking voice. He looks up. Through the partially open door, he sees, far away in a black sea of nothingness...

Pizza Joe's.

Its neon sign and yellow lights blaze insanely against the dark. A wooden screen door screeches open and snaps shut. David can barely make out a silhouette against the darkness, walking toward him.

David screams, his sanity near breaking. With every ounce of strength left, he jerks on the doorknob. Whatever is pulling on the other side lets go. The door slams shut. David stumbles backward and almost loses his grip. Before he can, he brandishes a massive keyring full of keys and fumbles through them until instinct identifies the right one. He inserts the key into the doorknob and locks it...

The door falls still.

David steps back, panting. Clutching the keys so tightly their edges dig into his skin. He swallows and stares at the door for several nerve-jangling seconds, expecting the knob to start turning again, the door to start rocking in its frame.

Nothing.

He's closed the door in time.

His relief is short-lived, however. He can't stay here. The hallway is full of countless doors with things trying to get through from the other side. He has to keep moving. Has to stay alert because it won't be long before…

On cue, David hears the clicking of a doorknob down the hallway. He turns and moves toward the sound. Sees it, about ten feet away. A door on the right, shaking. Cold terror pulses through him. He races forward, keys at the ready, because he knows even if he manages to close this door too, there are endless more, and how can he ever close them all…

4.

Monday, July 15

Freshly showered and mostly dressed (still barefoot, navy blue polo shirt untucked), David stood in the cabin's tiny bathroom, shaving. Also, thinking about his nightmare—the same one he'd been having the last two months—and its new aspects.

The doors.

The doors had never opened before.

In his recurring dream the past two months, he rushed through a subterranean network of hallways in the basement of some corporate building. The walls were painted a bland gray, the floor white tile, the fluorescent lights buzzing madly above. There were no windows, and the hallway split into branches at intersections or turned at sharp angles, without end. In some versions, he rushed past stairwells which only led down into darkness. He never took them in his dreams, filled with a mild hysteria over what might be hiding at the bottom in the dark.

However, the doors had never opened before. In his past dreams, they'd bang against their frames while their knobs jiggled. He'd rush down the hallway faster, increasingly terrified at the sounds coming from behind the doors, fear consuming him with the certainty they would open, releasing nightmarish creatures from beyond.

Also, he'd never carried a huge keyring full of keys in the dream before. And, in last night's dream, when the door did open...Why had he seen Pizza Joe's?

David drew his razor over one last patch of stubble. Rinsed it under the faucet. Turned the water off, set the razor on the sink's edge, grabbed a towel, and wiped his face, cleaning the excess shaving cream. He returned the towel to its rack, folding it neatly. He looked back into the mirror and ran a hand through his still-robust brown hair, shot through with traces of gray at the temples. He wouldn't win any beauty contests any time soon, and he was more pear-shaped than he'd been in his youth, but he supposed he'd held together well, all things considered.

David felt happy enough. He enjoyed his job. Sometimes, he even loved it. Especially when knee-deep in red-lining legal documents, getting down to brass tacks. However, he couldn't say he felt passionate about the law, or climbing the corporate ladder. To him, the law was an intricate system of rules and regulations, of which he'd learned the inner workings. Most of the time, he could use his knowledge to accomplish whatever he needed to. That was enough for him.

He and Kathleen lived comfortably, but not extravagantly. Between their salaries, they'd sent their children to private high schools, and helped cover the college tuition leftover after their respective academic scholarships. They owned a vacation home in North Carolina. Had money in the bank. Invested some in the stock market. They owed nothing past the mortgage for both homes and their American Express card. Neither he nor Kathleen were retiring any time soon.

Things were good. They'd suffered ups and downs, but they loved each other and had remained close despite the years and miles between them. Someday soon (in his son's case, who was engaged), he might even become a grandfather. The idea appealed to him.

Life was good.

So why the hell was he having these nightmares? What had gotten under his skin the past two months?

He scratched the back of his neck. Grabbed his comb off the sink and started combing his hair. He also still didn't understand why he'd never told Kathleen about the dreams. They talked about everything. Why not this? Did he fear her reaction? That she'd think he wasn't happy? He didn't know. Whenever he felt the urge to tell her, a panicky feeling blossomed in his gut, silencing him.

He'd briefly debated seeing a shrink but had dismissed the idea almost instantly. Again, for some reason, he wanted to keep the dreams to himself. He didn't fully understand this compulsion. He wasn't normally a secretive man. Maybe it was a strange form of denial. His life, while certainly not perfect, had always run on course. Admitting a reoccurring nightmare to his wife, or anyone else, was a deviation from that course. Maybe that scared him more than anything else.

The most he'd done was break down and Google "trapped in hallway nightmares." The results—"Sensing great life change, desiring great life change, fearing great life change"—had left him feeling ill at ease. He'd closed the browser without reading more. What change could he possibly be sensing, or fearing? What change was coming? And he didn't want change...

Did he?

Finished with his hair, David tucked in his polo shirt and buttoned it. He adjusted his belt and smoothed the wrinkles in his shirt. He was about to walk out when something in his reflection caught his eye. He stopped to peer closer.

He frowned. It had to be his imagination, but the grayish white in his temples had spread recently. Ridiculous thought, obviously. He just hadn't looked closely in the mirror lately. That's all. His father had gone all-white at about the same age yet kept a full head of hair right to his death at the ripe old age of eighty-two. David figured it'd probably be the same for him.

Even so, David couldn't help spending a few more minutes examining the spreading grayish white in his hair, frowning, before he walked out.

5.

David's plans for the day were flexible. He'd called Kathleen and enjoyed a pleasant talk with her over a cup of coffee, relating in greater detail his weekend in Quebec and his arrival in Clifton Heights, omitting, for some reason, his strange experience at Pizza Joe's. He also left out his strange paranoia about the increasing white in his hair (a stupid notion he couldn't quite banish).

After laying out his plans and wishing her an affectionate goodbye, he called the office. He spoke with them briefly, getting a quick update on the week's business. He wasn't due back until Wednesday, but even so, he thought it prudent to keep abreast of things. If need be, he could attend to matters remotely.

After that, David's stomach reminded him he'd neglected to make provisions for breakfast. Considering the cabin's small but fully equipped kitchen, he added the grocery store to his itinerary, which only included checking in at Rich's Auto for an update and visiting the only bookstore in town, which he'd found on Google. Arcane Delights, a new and used bookstore on Main Street.

David's one enduring hobby was collecting books of all kinds. His towering bookshelves at home contained genres ranging from non-fiction to science fiction and fantasy. He owned hard-to-find limited editions, shelved next to battered hardcovers and yellowed, dog-eared paperbacks bought at thrift stores and library sales. The thought of finding something special at Arcane Delights to remember this little side trip pleased him.

However, when David pulled out of The Motor Lodge, he didn't turn right and proceed directly into town. Instead, he turned left onto Chester Road, heeding his half-formed thought from last night: Find Pizza Joe's in the daylight. He didn't bother searching for it on Google Maps. He'd already tried in-between calls to Kathleen and the office and had gotten the same GPS ERROR message. Based on his memory of last night, it had ended up being six to seven miles up the road. Also, he remembered the crooked old elm he turned around at. He'd keep an eye out for it, on the right.

Pulling out of The Motor Lodge's parking lot, he saw something interesting on the other side of the road. A small yellow house—so small it could've been a garage—with a tiny square front lawn. On the lawn, an older man (perhaps seventy, or seventy-five years old) sat in an Adirondack chair. He had a flowing white beard and long white hair. He wore sunglasses, tan cargo shorts that exposed knobby knees, and a plain white T-shirt. The man didn't move, but because of the sunglasses, David couldn't shake the feeling the man was watching him as he drove past.

It took only about five minutes for David to find the crooked old elm tree. David put his left blinker on and executed a tight U-turn across the road. He parked on the shoulder opposite the crooked old elm. He shut the car off, got out, and walked to the edge of the road. The early morning sun bore down on him with a surprising edge, causing sweat to pepper his brow almost immediately. Insects buzzed a high-pitched song. The air felt still and flat.

There was no Pizza Joe's.

On an initial sweep, David saw only waist-high grass and weeds. However, a few steps off the shoulder and into the weeds revealed the clearing to be a large patch of cracked asphalt overgrown by grass and weeds. A parking lot, maybe? One which had been abandoned for years, it seemed.

Parking lot to what?

He took a few more steps. Where he thought Pizza Joe's might've stood, he saw mounds of overgrown rubble in what could easily be a crumbling foundation. An urge to explore further was instantly quashed by the ghostly memory of the rapid jive-talking DJ he couldn't under-stand, and the sound of boots scraping asphalt toward him.

David turned and walked stiffly back to his car. He got in and started it up, welcoming the icy blast of AC washing over him. He sat there for several minutes, turning things over in his head. He needed to make sense of things, but he was struggling to fit all the puzzle pieces together.

He must've been mistaken about the elm. Had to be. The one from last night must be further up Chester Road, along with Pizza Joe's. He definitely remembered driving much further last night. Also, it would be hard to remember during the daytime an elm he'd seen at night. Pizza Joe's obviously must be further up the road. All he had to do was keep driving.

But David didn't do that.

He continued down Chester Road. This time, when he passed the old man sitting in his chair, David felt eyes on the back of his neck all the way into town.

6.

David's visit to Rich's Auto—which was near the center of town, on Harding Avenue—proved uneventful. Jesse must've had the day off, or had been out back working, because the only person at the desk was a lanky man with a goatee whose name tag read "Skip." He informed David in a rather bored tone they'd be pulling the bad transmission from his rental car later in the day, but the new transmission still wasn't due until Wednesday.

David had assumed so. He'd merely stopped by to keep his name fresh in the auto shop's mind. He'd learned from experience it was a bad idea to leave auto places to their own devices.

Instead of going straight to Arcane Delights, David first stopped at Great American Grocery, which turned out to be on Main Street, not far from the bookstore. He bought enough food to fix his own breakfasts (something his stomach was already harshly criticizing him for skipping), lunches, and the occasional dinner.

At around ten in the morning, he pulled into the side parking lot of Arcane Delights, which proved to be perfect timing. According to Google, the bookstore opened at ten. To give the store's employees a few more minutes, he called Kathleen.

Her phone rang once, then went to voicemail, which made sense. She was probably already seeing patients. "Hey there. Just me. Wanted to see how your morning's been so far. Checked in at the auto place. They're going to pull the transmission today, but they're still not expecting the new transmission until Wednesday. What's the chance it'll come early? Zero, knowing my luck.

"I've stocked up on food, because I just didn't think about it last night, and my gut is yelling at me because of it. Also? There's a used bookstore in town. You know I'm a sucker for those. Will try not to empty our retirement savings in one trip."

He paused, about to say something else. About his dreams, Pizza Joe's, or even the odd-looking old man sitting in front of his house. Instead, he opted for, "Have a good day. Call me if anything pops up. Will probably call back after lunch. Love you."

He hung up, feeling better. He always did after leaving Kathleen a message. Even so, he felt dogged by the vague suspicion he'd left something unsaid, though he wasn't sure what it was.

He shook off the feeling. Got out and entered Arcane Delights.

Upon first glance, Arcane Delights appeared to be exactly the kind of used bookstore that hid the treasures he loved collecting. David had visited many used bookstores over the years. Some were "used" in name only, featuring mostly remainders from big box stores. Others had been cluttered, chaotic disasters with overflowing bookshelves and haphazard stacks of books on the floor which reached waist-high, showing all the order of a psychotic whirlwind. Still others were stuffy establishments that didn't allow patrons to peruse on their own and were open by appointment only.

Arcane Delights was none of these. Great care had been taken with both display windows on either side of the front door, displaying seasonal fare for the summer months. Beach thrillers, Adirondack Hiking and Fishing guides, mystery and romance novels, and summery children's books. The display didn't feel pretentious or showy, however. Simple, neat, and organized.

An aisle ran down the middle of the store. Three steps led to a back room. On each side of the front aisle stood three tall bookshelves running the length of the store. The books were shelved in an orderly fashion. At either end of the store sat older but comfortable-looking recliners, with a small rectangular table next to each. Paperbacks lay strewn in pleasing jumbles on each table.

From his vantage point, the aisle continued after the three steps down the back of the store, with shelves on either side, also. At the very back. several chairs stood in rows. For public readings, David guessed.

To the right of the steps was a small L-shaped counter with a computer, cash register, and telephone at the end. In front of the counter was a big wire basket filled with yellowed, beaten paperbacks. The sign hanging on the basket read: FREE.

"Hey there! I didn't expect to see you again so soon!"

David glanced toward the counter, startled by the jaunty, cheerful tone. One he recognized. To his delighted surprise, a familiar impish grin and bright green eyes greeted him.

He smiled. "Hey. Carol. Casey?"

"Close. Cassie. No worries. People call me those other two all the time."

He approached the counter, shaking his head in mild wonder. "You work here too? You don't...run this place, do you?"

Cassie waved and snorted. "Well, my boss might say yes, but not really. I work here part-time. Usually, I don't open Monday mornings, but the owner, Kevin Ellison, was out of town over the weekend with his family. He'll be here tomorrow."

"And...you work here all day, then at The Skylark in the evenings?"

She tipped her head and smiled. "Tonight I'm off at The Skylark, but I do work the overnight shift at the Webb County Assisted Living Center. Then I have tomorrow off, and work the evening at The Skylark."

David smile-frowned, both confused and impressed by the young woman's diverse resume. "Wouldn't it be easier to simply work one job?"

Cassie shook her head, lip curled in good-natured disgust. "Ugh. No thanks. I'm easily bored. Terminal ADHD. Three jobs keep me busy with three different things. I never zone out, because I'm always getting ready for something different. Believe it or not, it's easier for me to focus."

David shrugged. "All right then. You certainly don't lack energy or initiative."

Cassie beamed, reminding David once again of his daughter. "Aw. Thanks! So." A subtle shift occurred in her demeanor and expression. She effortlessly assumed a more business-like posture. "Was there anything you were looking for today?"

David thought for a moment before answering. He had an extensive book collection – two whole rooms of wall-to-wall, floor-to-ceiling bookcases – and though he'd always meant to, he'd never ended up cataloging what books he had. Far easier to keep a running list of books he didn't have. Even then, he'd occasionally bought books he already owned.

After a moment, he said, "How about some horror and Gothic fiction? You have a section for those genres?"

Cassie smiled again. "We do." She gestured behind her to the back room. "Last bookcase on the left. Both sides." She looked at him again, smiling wider. "I'm sure you'll find something. We've got an extensive collection. Mr. Ellison is a fan of horror in particular."

David ascended the steps. "Thank you. Don't let me keep you from your duties. I'll shout if I need anything."

"Not a problem. Good luck! I hope you find what you need."

David nodded, wondering at her wish of "Good luck!" and also wondering why his stomach had twisted slightly when she'd said: "Hope you find what you need."

Fifteen minutes into browsing, however, David had largely forgotten his reaction to Cassie's odd phrasing, so impressed was he with Arcane Delights' horror and Gothic collection. Meticulously and alphabetically organized by the author's last name, the section contained everything from commercial horror fiction, from the seventies, eighties, nineties, and the last twenty years, to pulp novels from the twenties and thirties, to Gothic novels from the eighteenth century.

David found novels by Ramsey Campbell, Charles Grant, T. M. Wright, Richard Laymon, Ray Garton, Brian Keene, Jonathon Janz, and Ronald Malfi. Also, collections of work by Robert Aikman and Arthur Machen, *Frankenstein,* and *Dr. Jekyll and Mr. Hyde,* to the earliest Gothic novels of Matthew Lewis and Anne Radcliffe. He even found a battered, cloth-bound edition of *Melmoth the Wanderer,* by Charles Maturin, priced at an unbelievable $10. This turned out to be his first selection because it was one of the few early Gothic novels he didn't own.

His second find proved even more astounding. *Who Fears the Devil,* a collection of Manley Wade Wellman's Silver John short stories. He owned several Silver John books and collections, but not this one. The last time he'd seen it on Amazon or eBay, it had been priced at roughly $90. Arcane Delights had, unbelievably enough, priced their copy at only $20. Another purchase he couldn't pass up.

David had eclectic tastes, so he left the horror and Gothic section and drifted from bookcase to bookcase until he found literary classics, on the right shelf closest to the front of the store. He wasn't looking for anything in particular. Was only planning on browsing, until he reached the Shakespeare section near the end, toward the bottom. Out of idle curiosity, (he owned collections of all Shakespeare's plays, including the bard's posthumously published sonnets), he ran his fingers along the spines. Maybe he'd find a commentary he didn't have or an illustrated edition. He'd been thinking about getting one of those for a while, now.

His breath caught, finger stopping on a slim, red cloth-bound volume. He read the title. Read it again, sure his eyes were playing tricks on him. After reading the title a third time, confirming he hadn't misread it, and also wasn't hallucinating, David withdrew the book reverently, fearing it would simply disappear if he handled it too roughly. He held it tightly in shaking hands. He wasn't sure if he could believe what he read on the cover, but there it was, regardless.

The Tragical Historie of Cardenio.

By William Shakespeare.

One of his famous lost plays. Rumored to have been performed, but never preserved in print.

"This is impossible," David muttered, gazing at the gold-embossed title in disbelief. "Impossible. Or a joke? A stunt. Has to be."

Self-publishing was easily affordable these days, after all. David had a friend who dabbled in poetry. She'd self-published several hardcover volumes of her work through Lulu.com. Someone with knowledge not only of Shakespeare's famous work but also of self-publishing could easily make a convincing facsimile and print up a copy for roughly $20, plus shipping and handling.

To what end? A prank for the few Shakespearean scholars and aficionados familiar with the bard's lost play? Or maybe a keepsake or novelty item as a gift for said scholar?

The problem was, this edition looked old. The red cloth-bound cover had faded to a dull pink. The corners looked frayed and worn. The spine was well-used, though not broken. He flipped through the slim book quickly. Not only had the pages yellowed with age, but he also detected the quaint and wonderful smell of a musty old book.

Near the end of the book, he discovered the crown jewel. In the upper right-hand corner, David noticed a neat hole drilled through the remaining pages. He knew what it was. The tell-tale trace of an actual bookworm, which, of course, was just the larvae of any insect. Usually, the sign of a book that had lain for years in damp, musty storage. He owned several books with the same holes, from his own purchases over the years. Who would fake a bookworm hole? Then again, vanity publishing had existed for thirty years or more. Even so, in its earliest days, it had been an expensive venture because it required bulk printing, which wasn't logical at all for a prank or a novelty gift.

He turned to the copyright page. Few details were there. Only a supposed publication date of 1864 in London, England. Hard to believe, because despite how old the book appeared...it just wasn't possible. On the cover page, the price, written in pen, was $20.

David closed the book and stared at the title again, thinking. According to his studies of Shakespeare, *The Tragical Historie of Cardenio* was a rumored lost play Shakespeare had written about Cardenio, a lovelorn and insane character in *Don Quixote*. Though several texts referenced it as having been performed by Shakespeare's troupe, no physical copy existed.

David grinned, slowly. Even though this had to be an insanely clever forgery (what else could it be?), it would prove an interesting addition to his collection. An intriguing conversation piece, to be sure. Certainly worth $20. And...what if, somehow...the book was...real?

David shied away from the thought. It made him uneasy, for some reason.

He stood and took his selections up to the front counter. Cassie was busy looking over paperwork. When he descended the steps to the front of the store, she looked up with a smile. "Find everything okay?"

David smiled in return. "Yes, indeed." He handed her the books. "Some remarkable finds, really. I don't suppose you have a website I could order from later?"

With impressive dexterity, Cassie totaled the books on the cash register with one hand. With the other, she produced a bookmark from beneath the counter and handed it to David. "We do! We have listings on eBay, Amazon, and Abebooks, too. All the info is right here."

David accepted the bookmark and pocketed it. "Excellent. I'll check this out when I get home."

Cassie rang him up and gave him his total. He handed over his American Express and asked, "Any idea where you obtained Cardenio? It's a...unique find."

Cassie ran his card through the reader, handed him the receipt to sign, and then grabbed Cardenio. "I'll look it up. We get books from everywhere. Estate Sales, garage sale leftovers, review copies from publishers, library discards, donations, and book auctions. We do keep a running list, but" she glanced at him apologetically, "if it was a trade-in or a private donation, I won't be able to share. Sorry."

David nodded. "Understandable."

Cassie looked at the title and frowned slightly. "I'm not a Shakespeare buff, but I read enough of him in high school and college. Don't recognize this one."

David chose a glib half-lie over the truth. "One of his more obscure works, I believe."

"Interesting." Cassie typed the title into the computer, and after several seconds, shrugged at the results. "It came in an anonymous donation back when we re-opened about four years ago."

She bagged his books and handed them over. "Sorry, I can't tell you more."

David smiled. "No worries. Curious is all. Maybe I'll stop back in later this week when Mr. Ellison returns?"

"Sure. He might know more about it. I'd not started working here yet then."

"Thank you. Have a good day."

"You also!"

'David turned and left Arcane Delights, once again feeling the same uneasiness he'd felt when he'd found a cracked and heaving patch of asphalt instead of Pizza Joe's.

7.

When David pulled out of Arcane Delight's parking lot, he briefly considered getting a sub at Dooley's or trying Henry's Drive-In. He decided against both, however. He'd bought groceries and could easily make a sandwich. Also, he wanted to sit down and read Cardenio as soon as possible.

When he turned into The Motor Lodge, he glanced across Chester Road. The old man was still sitting in his chair. He'd taken off his shirt (understandable, considering the weather), and appeared to be reading either a book or a magazine, though David couldn't tell which. For some reason, David felt better the old man wasn't watching him. He didn't know why, exactly.

David tried to call Kathleen after he'd stored the groceries, but for some reason, his call wouldn't go through. It just kept ringing until it finally ended in dead air, and not her voicemail. He tried two more times with the same result. On the third try, it rang twice before David heard a tinny robotic voice say, "All lines are busy." He then tried to text her, but the message was returned with the error code: UNDELV. Checking his phone, he saw only one bar of service. That made sense. Clifton Heights was remote and secluded, which he supposed would also account for Google Maps' difficulty in finding Pizza Joe's the night before (odd in today's world of 5G coverage).

When he tried to connect both his phone and then his laptop to Wi-Fi so he could email Kathleen, he got mixed results. He had a strong connection on both devices, but while he could access the internet and Google easily enough, the browser on his laptop couldn't open his email. His phone's email application wouldn't open, either. Thinking he should talk to someone in the lobby office about their Wi-Fi connection, David gave up, deciding to make a sandwich and begin Cardenio.

After making himself a ham, cheese, lettuce, and tomato sandwich on rye, David filled a glass with water (he'd bought a six-pack of Stella Artois at Great American Grocery, but it was still lukewarm), and settled into the cushioned Adirondack chair. His food and water on the coffee table, he opened *The Tragical Historie of Cardenio* and began to read.

Two hours later, David closed *Cardenio,* set the book on the arm of the chair, and stared at nothing. He felt a strange mixture of excitement and the odd unease which had nipped at his heels since arriving in Clifton Heights.

The play he'd just read corresponded neatly with the plot of Shakespeare's rumored lost play. Don Quixote and his sidekick Sancho, in a turn of events, encounter a madman named Cardenio who has fallen into despair over his lost love, a wealthy and beautiful woman named Luscinda. The play told the story of Cardenio's attempts to woo her through his noble friend Don Fernando, how Fernando conspired to steal Luscinda from Cardenio, and her eventual flight from her new husband, while Cardenio retreated into mountain exile, where Don Quixote and Sancho discover him.

David didn't consider himself a Shakespearean scholar by any means. He'd studied business law in college, not literature, though he'd taken Shakespeare electives when he could fit them into his schedule. Most of his Shakespearean insight came from those electives and his study over the years, including reading and re-reading the bard's plays and sonnets. However, in his layman's estimation?

The Tragical Historie of Cardenio wasn't a forgery.

It hadn't merely been written by someone imitating Shakespeare. It sounded Shakespearean. The cadence, the rhythm, the open verse, and the use of iambic pentameter at crucial moments in the play. The sense of balance and structure. The spirit of it. At the least, if Cardenio was an imitation, it sounded so close to Shakespeare that it would be a matter for linguistic experts and Shakespearean scholars to discern, regardless of how well-read David considered himself.

The thought occurred to contact someone who could verify the play's authenticity. He dismissed the notion almost immediately. Oddly enough, he wasn't worried about discovering the play to be an imitation. That would almost be a relief. However, discovering the play was real? Which he'd discovered here, of all places? This only intensified the crawling unease he'd felt off and on since last night.

David yawned abruptly, suddenly tired. He checked his phone and saw it was two in the afternoon. Maybe he should take a nap. After, he could try and call Kathleen again, call the office for updates, and wrangle something in the kitchen for dinner. Maybe afterward, if it had cooled outside, he'd take a walk. Either down into town or up Chester Road...and maybe past the man sitting in his chair.

David retired to the bedroom for his nap.

8.

David napped peacefully until about four o'clock. A little later than he preferred, which meant he'd be up later in the evening, but he didn't mind so much. He wanted to read *Cardenio* again, anyway, and he did so until he started feeling hungry around five-thirty.

Even though he hadn't finished his second read, David closed the play and started working on dinner with vague relief. Despite a closer analysis, he hadn't encountered anything suggesting it wasn't genuine. He didn't know why that bothered him so much. It just did.

David broiled a steak, made instant garlic mashed potatoes, and steamed carrots. Everything tasted passably well, but he decided tomorrow night he'd try dinner at either The Skylark again, or Henry's Drive-In. Oddly enough, the thought of trying Pizza Joe's again never crossed his mind.

After cleaning up, David left. When he stepped outside, he noticed the evening had cooled considerably. It already felt pleasant. Any cooler, and he might've needed a long-sleeve shirt.

His first intention was to walk into town, curious about the bars in Clifton Heights. Instead, on instinct he started up Chester Road. His shoes scuffing the road's sandy shoulder, he looked out over Clifton Lake. The sun had lit the water a brilliant blue. From his vantage point, he saw boats dotting the water. Far across the lake was a beach. Private docks and picturesque cabins abounded. David had never considered living on a lake before. Now, he understood the allure.

"Evening. Enjoying the view?"

The voice sounded gravelly, with a slight accent. It sounded familiar, though David couldn't place it. It sounded cultured, but also warm and cordial.

He turned and with little surprise saw the man sitting in his chair, in front of his house. His shirt was back on, but he still wore the same tan cargo shorts, his feet shod in leather moccasins. His thick and white hair flowed from his head. His voluminous white beard touched his chest. Those tinted glasses hid his eyes, but his smile looked free and easy.

David responded with, "Yes, I am. I live near the coast, so I see the beach often. But I never realized a lakefront could be so beautiful."

The man nodded, smiling wider. "Yes. I think until someone has actually seen a fine lake from this view, just before sunset, they don't. And Clifton Lake is a fine lake, indeed."

The man tipped his head, expression inquisitive. "You're not from around here." It was a statement, not a question.

David stuck his hands into his pockets, checked the road both ways, and crossed over. "No," he said, approaching the man, "I was just passing through when the transmission in my rental died. It's at Rich's Auto, waiting on a new one."

"Rich's Auto is good people. They should get you fixed up quick enough."

David came to stand next to the man's chair. "So I've heard. Young woman who works at The Skylark—Cassie—raved about them."

The man nodded. "Ah, yes. Cassie Tillman. Fine girl, she is. Capable of extraordinary things, I believe. Once she finds her place in this world."

David nodded, thinking the man's assessment was accurate, even though he had only encountered Cassie twice. "Sounds about right. She's got some energy, for sure. Works three different part-time jobs because she prefers to. Says she'd get bored working just one full time."

"Yes indeed. Young people with her kind of energy usually struggle with boredom. She just needs to find herself. She will, eventually."

He turned, and even though David couldn't see the man's eyes behind those dark-tinted glasses, he could feel the power of their gaze. "We all do."

Not sure how to reply, David asked, "Do you know Cassie well?"

The man shrugged. "I know most everyone around here. It's not a large town, after all."

David persisted, surprised by his tenacity. "Still. You talk like Cassie's a friend or a relative."

"She's a kind girl. Has time for everyone in town. Even the local crazy who sits out in front of his house all day." The man looked at him from behind those glasses—he could still feel those eyes on him—but his smile was gentle. "She runs past here every Saturday morning. Always stops and chats. Been doing it for about seven years, now. So, yes. I guess you could call us friends."

This made sense. "So. The town thinks you're crazy?"

The man chuckled heartily. "Oh, they do indeed. Why does he sit there all day? Just sitting, sitting. Staring at nothing, looking down on all of us. He must be crazy."

David chuckled himself. He finally realized who the man's voice reminded him of. The late actor Angus Scrimm, who played the ominous *Tall Man* in the Phantasm horror movies.

"How long have you lived here? Does it bother you? People thinking you're crazy?"

The man waved. "Lived here just about forever, so I don't care much what others think. One thing I've learned is people will believe what they want about you, no matter what you do or say. Best to accept it, ignore it, and be grateful for the good ones."

David nodded. "Wise. Something we should all remember, I think."

"Indeed. Enough of me, more about you. How long will you be staying in Clifton Heights? What do you do for a living?"

David shrugged in response to the first question. "Hopefully only until Wednesday, Thursday at the latest, depending on when the new transmission comes in. And I'm a lawyer. Been working at the same firm for twenty-five years."

"A lawyer." The man's bushy eyebrows lifted. "Trial lawyer? Defense attorney?"

It was David's turn to chuckle. "Nothing quite so exciting. I'm certainly no Clarence Darrow. More a Bob Cratchit. I spend most my days going over contracts and legal documents, checking them against existing laws and precedents, redlining the legalese."

The man tipped his head. Once again, even though David couldn't see the man's eyes, he felt them. "And this work...satisfies you? Fulfills you?"

David paused, taken aback by the man's choice of words, and his directness. "Well. My life isn't a flashy John Grisham novel, by any means." He shrugged again, feeling oddly insecure. "I do enjoy the actual letter of the law. Analyzing certain solutions for different cases, editing the wording and phrasing of legal documents."

He smiled. "I suppose, in another life, I could've been an English teacher or an editor. I do love my red pen."

"But you believe you're making a difference? Impacting people's lives?"

David opened his mouth. Closed it and looked down at the ground. In any other situation, he might've found such questions intrusive, especially coming from a complete stranger. The man had a way about him, however. A presence. A manner of speaking that made David feel more thoughtful than annoyed. And of course...

Hadn't he been grappling with these same thoughts himself, lately?

After a few minutes, David looked up, but away, over his shoulder and at Clifton Lake, which looked even more striking under the now-setting sun. Choosing his words carefully, he said, "I make a difference. It's just hard to see. In the courtroom, working with a client on a case, there's more tangible results. What I do, the kind of law I practice...not so much."

He sighed and looked at the man. "I know, deep down, I've made a difference. I've impacted people. I know I've helped businesses—small and large—by examining their contracts and legal documents, making sure everything is squared away. When a co-worker or a client comes to me with a legal problem or a question, and I can provide an answer, it's satisfying. I enjoy my job."

"But?"

Again, David found it amazing he wasn't annoyed at the man's prying. What he felt instead was a strange, unfamiliar melancholy. "I sometimes wonder if there's something more I could be doing. Something bigger. I just don't know what."

The man smiled gently, his serious demeanor evaporating. "The age-old question all men struggle with at some point. 'Isn't there something more I can do?' I wouldn't worry, David. Cassie Tillman will someday find her place, and you will, too. Perhaps sooner, rather than later."

David nodded, feeling like something important had just happened. As if a crucial moment had passed between him and the man, though he didn't know what it was. Or, if he even wanted to know.

He glanced around, for the first time noticing dusk had fallen while they'd been talking. "Well. I'd planned on going for a walk, but I got an illuminating conversation instead." He nodded at The Motor Lodge. "Guess I'll head back."

The man nodded. "Indeed. Delightful to talk with you. I wouldn't worry, David. You'll figure things out. I'm sure of it."

David nodded again, feeling slightly uneasy for the first time since talking to the man. He waved, turned, crossed the road, and walked back to The Motor Lodge. When he unlocked his cabin door, he realized the man had called him "David" twice, even though he didn't remember giving his name.

9.

Before bed, David tried once more to call Kathleen, but all he got was the same "All lines are busy" message. Upon opening his laptop and browser, the Wi-Fi connection appeared stable, and this time he was able to open his work email. He had several messages, most of them being the usual legal spam. One, however, was from work, assuring him everything was fine, though asking several questions about documents colleagues were handling in his absence.

He was also able to open his personal email. Kathleen had responded to his earlier message, relaying the day's events at work in a lighthearted manner, also expressing her hope the transmission might be fixed earlier than expected so he could get home sooner. She also mentioned she'd tried to call his phone several times and had received an "out of area" message.

David typed a rather lengthy reply relating the day's events (again, omitting his unease over discovering *Cardenio*) and his conversation with the old man, although he condensed his recounting of it, making it sound like an interesting encounter with an interesting person, nothing more. When he clicked 'send,' this time, his message went through, unlike the text earlier.

Despite his intentions of finishing his re-read of *Cardenio*, David got ready for bed. For some reason, the last thing he wanted was more confirmation that the play might be genuine. Better to believe it was a clever forgery. Better, and safer. Also, he felt oddly worn out from his conversation with the man in his chair.

Getting into bed, he caught his reflection in the mirror over the dresser. Though he told himself it was only a trick of light, the grayish-white streaks in his hair looked even more pronounced. Almost completely white. Of course, it was only a trick of light.

Had to be.

10.

Something crashed. Something glass, smashing against a wall or floor, in the near distance. Followed by a grunt, and then a curse.

You bitch!

David blinked his eyes, slowly coming awake. For a moment he wondered where he was. His thoughts felt heavy and fuzzy with sleep. It finally came to him in bits. The rental car's transmission. Clifton Heights. The Motor Lodge. It was Monday night—Tuesday morning? —His second night here, and...

More crashing.

Maybe a chair thudding into a wall. A table being overturned. More inarticulate cries...a woman, David thought, and then...

"Shut the hell up, you fuckin whore!"

The sound of flesh hitting flesh, and a body thumping to the floor. Adrenaline and a surge of fear brought David awake. A domestic dispute, in one of the cabins next door. David had never dealt directly with domestic abuse cases, he'd only assisted by examining documents, arrest records, and restraining orders. What he heard, happening right now...he usually only dealt with second or third hand, and on paper.

More crashing sounds. Then, a door slammed open. "Get the hell out!" He heard thumping steps, a cry, and the sound of a body hitting the ground.

do something more

something bigger

Moving on instinct, David scrambled out of bed. He grabbed his phone on the nightstand. Moving toward the den, he snagged his bathrobe from the hook on the open bathroom door and clumsily shrugged it on. He crept into the cabin's den. Pressed on the phone's screen, waking it up, and dialed 911 on the emergency call screen.

He brought the phone to his ear. It rang once, and then came the same hated message: "*All lines are busy.*"

David cursed. How the hell could lines be busy at this hour? Why couldn't he call 911?

Another slap and a woman's wail sent shivers through him. Keeping his phone handy, thumb hovering above redial, David crouched low at the door. With a trembling hand, he slowly turned the doorknob. Pushed the door open a crack, and peered outside.

He saw a scene from a hellish fever dream. A woman on her knees at the cabin next to his, sobbing. He couldn't see much in the poor light thrown by the halogen lamp over the cabin's door, but she was dressed simply. A dark T-shirt and jeans with ragged cuffs. He couldn't see her face, but she had cropped blond hair.

A man wobbled drunkenly before her. He looked unshaven, with lank, greasy hair falling to his shoulders. He also wore ragged jeans, and a faded, garish rock T-shirt for a band called Dokken, a name which only sounded vaguely familiar to David. He hadn't listened to much heavy metal as a kid.

In one hand, the man held a bottle of what David assumed was liquor, which would explain his unsteady stance. In the other hand, he held a sawed-off shotgun, pointed into the woman's face.

The blood in David's veins ran cold. An uncontrollable shaking spread through him. He couldn't move, speak, or think. Couldn't raise his phone. All he could do was stare helplessly through his cracked open door.

The sobbing woman raised her hands in a pitiful, placating gesture. She had the posture and air of a doomed penitent praying to a remorseless god from whom she expected no mercy. "Deke…Deke, please. I didn't mean any disrespect. I'm sorry. I'm sorry!"

The man—Deke—scowled. "Fuck you, bitch. I'm done listenin' to your whore mouth. No one tells Deke Sommers what to do. No one."

"Deke, no, please..!"

Deke said nothing. Simply raised the shotgun, pulled the trigger, and emptied both barrels into the woman's face with a thunderous banging.

The woman's head jerked.

The shotgun blast shredded her face.

Her body twisted and flipped onto its side. David's stomach roiled as he caught a glimpse of the mangled flesh of the woman's face, and the white of bone gleaming through wet red tissue.

David fell forward and stumbled out his front door and down its steps, numb with shock. For a moment, forgetting completely about the drunken Deke and his shotgun. David stumbled toward the woman's body, which mercifully had landed face-down. Distantly, he heard the clack of a shotgun's breech being snapped open. This didn't register. He stared in horror at what used to be a living human being. Now laying shredded face down in the dirt, bleeding into the ground.

David's bladder twitched. He'd always thought the literary convention of characters almost wetting themselves in fear to be an exaggeration. No longer.

He looked up at Deke, who was calmly and drunkenly inserting shells into his shotgun. His mind, dazed by the horror of what he'd seen, struggled to understand what he was watching Deke do. He mumbled, "Why...why did you...Oh Jesus, why did you..? Why did you kill her?!?"

His voice rose into a high-pitched screech. He instantly felt ashamed. It wasn't the commanding voice of outrage and moral disgust. Rather, a terrified cry of despair.

The man named Deke snapped the gun shut. "Because I fuckin' could," he slurred. He aimed at David. "Just like I'm gonna do you, gramps."

Before David could plead for his life, or even raise his hands in pitiful defense, Deke pulled the trigger. The shotgun roared. David cried out. He flew backwards with the force of a horse kicking him in the gut and slammed into the ground. Blazing hot and cold pain exploded in his guts and spread across his chest and shoulders and down his arms. His hands flailed weakly against his torn guts. Wet and sticky things slid and oozed against his fingers.

Writhing in eternal pain and choking on blood, David heard footsteps scuffing toward him. Also, the sound of the gun's breech snapping open again. A distant part of him knew what was coming next. All he could do was lay there, gagging on his own blood while his hands twitched uselessly in the mess of his intestines.

Deke loomed over him. He snapped the shotgun shut. Two black and bottomless holes filled David's world. "Teach you to fuckin' mind your own business. Old fuck."

David tried to scream. All he could manage was to gurgle and spit up thick blood all over his chin.

The man called Deke pulled the trigger.

The world crashed and roared. David felt blazing heat and then fell into darkness.

David cried out and rolled over onto his belly. He lay face down in the dew-damp grass, his mind spinning, trying to make sense of everything he'd just seen, heard, and felt. His mind struggled to process it and failed, miserably.

Was he dead?

Guts shredded, and his face blown away by a sawed-off shotgun?

He quickly felt his face. Ran his fingertips over his cheeks, nose, chin, and forehead. If he could trust their report, his facial features were intact.

What about his guts? If he put his hands to his midsection, would squirming and wet intestines slide through his fingertips? He sucked in a hitching breath first and felt no pain. Nor did he gag on blood. Breathing in once again, he rolled over onto his back. Feeling nothing amiss in his abdomen, he sat up. Looked down and inspected his belly. All he saw was his white T-shirt, peppered with bits of grass and dirt. With a tentative and slightly shaking hand, he pulled it up to reveal a pudgy but unmarred waistline, of which he'd never complain, ever again.

A sigh shuddered through him. David closed his eyes and covered his face with his hands. What the hell had just happened? A nightmare that turned into an episode of sleepwalking? Had he been sleeping the whole time?

David uncovered his face and rejected the idea instantly. What he'd just experienced had nothing of the surreal horror of his "hallway" nightmare. It had felt real. His fear had been the product of a genuine, adrenaline-fueled reaction. The blazing hot and cold pain of shotgun pellets ripping through his flesh, the oozing sensation of blood—and organs—squirting between his fingers, the sensation of choking on his own blood. It had felt real.

Something was wrong, though. Even now, trying to recreate the events in his mind, something felt out of place...

When David looked up, he understood immediately. Where he'd seen Deke's cabin was nothing but waist-high grass. The Motor Lodge only had fourteen cabins. David was staying in Cabin 14. There was no cabin after his, and yet...

He'd seen Deke stumbling out of a cabin after his. A Cabin 15. Now, he saw nothing.

David slowly stood. A familiar unease oozed through him. The same unease he'd felt finding Shakespeare's "lost" play. The same discomfort he felt whenever he thought about Pizza Joe's, an overgrown patch of cracked asphalt, and boots approaching him.

Briefly, he thought about going back inside. Downing a few beers and going back to bed. The last few days had proved incredibly stressful. His frazzled mind was seemingly playing tricks on him.

However, David thought of what he'd told the man sitting in his chair, about doing things differently. About aspiring to something bigger. He resolutely pushed aside his desire to forget. He wrapped his bathrobe around himself and walked carefully over to the waist-high grass, already suspecting what he might find.

He didn't savor the idea of walking through the grass barefoot, so he stood at the edge. It didn't take long. Hiding in the grass right about where a cabin's bathroom should be, he saw what appeared to be rusty, jagged-end pipes sticking out of the ground. Probably for the sink, toilet, and shower.

It was hard to tell in the dark, but if he looked just right, David could almost pick out the foundation's outline. Also, here and there, David thought he saw chunks of concrete and other bits of rubble scattered among the weeds.

He needed to check one last thing. In front of each cabin, at the head of the driveway, was a log with the cabin's number burned into it, marking the parking space for each cabin. His loaner from Rich's Auto sat, of course, before a log marked 14. He poked around next to his parking space. Sure enough, in the weeds which had been allowed to grow over gravel, he found a log. He brushed the weeds aside. A 15 was burned into it.

David shook his head, emotional and physical fatigue slamming into him. His mind had officially absorbed more than it could process. He turned, perhaps for the first time in his life finally feeling old, and he walked back to his cabin. He went inside, locked his door, checked all the windows to ensure they were locked, and proceeded to drink three beers. Methodically, one right after the other, sitting on the futon, staring into nothing. He'd pay for it tomorrow, but all he wanted to do was dull his senses enough so he could get something approximating sleep.

After he finished, he left the beer bottles sitting on the coffee table and stumbled to bed. He slowly drifted off into an uneasy sleep filled with visions of hallways, doors, and a man with a sawed-off shotgun who kept trying to force his way through every door. No matter how many times David frantically slammed the doors shut and locked them, another door further down would shake in its frame. He knew it was only a matter of time before something slipped through.

11.

Tuesday, July 16

David woke slowly Tuesday morning. He lay in bed for a long time, trying to piece together what happened the night before. He'd half-expected (hoped?) the incident to fade with sleep, so his fuzzy head would convince him everything had been a nightmare.

He remembered, however. Deke with his sawed-off shotgun, shooting the pleading woman in the face, then shooting David in the guts. The feel of blood and slick intestines against his fingertips. Dreams felt hazy. He remembered last night with hard-edged clarity.

It had happened.

Somehow, it had happened...and yet, it hadn't.

After lying still for about an hour, maybe longer, David rubbed his face and sat up with a grunt. He winced. A slight headache throbbed in his temples. He drank on the weekends, but usually only a beer or two, well-spaced out. He rarely overindulged. Hopefully, he'd feel better after a shower, some coffee, and breakfast.

David took a deep breath. Swung his feet to the floor and stood. He closed his mind and headed to the shower. Once clean, dressed, fed, and caffeinated, he'd let himself seriously think about what the hell was going on.

It wasn't until about ten in the morning that David finally allowed himself to start analyzing the things he'd experienced since arriving in Clifton Heights, and it wasn't at his cabin. He finally opened the mental floodgates on the other side of town, at Bassler Memorial Library.

A long, hot shower, a solid breakfast of eggs, toast, and bacon, and a strong cup of coffee refreshed him. However, when he tried to call Kathleen again, he got the same busy message, which was strange. His calls to the office had gone through fine.

He'd briefly debated asking his administrative assistant to relay a message to her, but he decided against it. They'd be busy enough at the office without him adding to their work with his personal requests.

When he logged onto his personal email account, he was happy to find Kathleen's reply to last night's email. He typed a quick response, but this time when he clicked send, an error message flashed in his browser, saying "poor connection/cannot send." He got similar results on his phone, both using data and connected to the Wi-Fi. He thought about calling The Lodge's office to ask if anything was wrong with their internet but decided he didn't want to be a bother. Instead, he searched Google Maps to see if Clifton Heights had a library. He found the listing for Bassler Memorial Library immediately. He called, confirmed they had free public Wi-Fi, then packed his satchel and headed there.

On the way, he stopped by Rich's Auto to check on his rental car's status once again. Unfortunately, the auto shop was unusually busy, with one lone mechanic working the front desk. Nearly a dozen customers crowded the small waiting area. The mechanic—a bald man with glasses, whose nametag read "Brian"—treated him professionally and courteously but admitted he wasn't familiar with David's car. He politely asked him to call or stop by later. He again didn't see Jesse. Though David left with no comment, it bothered him that he also didn't see his rental car anywhere.

It took David ten minutes to reach the library. As he parked out front, he noticed a sign across the street, on the corner of Main and Acer. It read: Handy's Pawn and Thrift. We Have Things You Need. David took note of it, perhaps for after he visited the library. As a boy, he'd been an inveterate packrat, collecting any trinket he found even remotely interesting. Maybe he'd find something of interest at Handy's.

After being directed to an area for Wi-Fi, David settled at a table farthest from the front desk. He pulled his laptop out of his satchel and had no problems signing onto the library's network. The first thing he did was type a slightly longer message to Kathleen. When he sent it, he encountered no connection issues or error messages.

He then searched Google for "Pizza Joe's/Clifton Heights, NY." Several results turned up. Links to scanned newspaper articles and retrospective essays on Adirondack landmarks. They told a disturbing story. Pizza Joe's had, at one time, been a mainstay at Clifton Heights, all through the fifties and sixties. One article described it as "the heartbeat of the town's youth." A main hangout, where all the teens went. Especially on the weekends.

In the late seventies, however, ownership changed hands. The clientele also changed. It slowly morphed from the main teen hangout to a central location for gangs, petty criminals, and even low-level drug dealers. Its nefarious end came on July 14, 1979. In what the local and county police called "a drug deal gone wrong," a conflict broke out at Pizza Joe's. Witnesses reported hearing gunshots. At some point, an unidentified person tossed a Molotov cocktail through one of the windows. By the time Webb County Fire arrived (this was before Clifton Heights had its own fire department), flames had consumed Pizza Joe's, killing fifteen customers, three waitresses, and three cooks.

The new owners never rebuilt. They took their insurance payout and left town. For years townspeople spread rumors about "arson" and "insurance fraud."

After he finished reading, David sat back, his mind working out the details. The facts were before him in digitized black and white. Pizza Joe's, on Chester Road, had burned down on July 14, 1979. He'd seen it, however. He knew he had. He'd seen it, heard the strange DJ mumbling inhuman words, and boots scraping asphalt toward him. On July 14. But when he'd gone back the next day, July 15, he'd found nothing but a cracked asphalt lot overgrown with weeds and grass.

Instead of puzzling it out further, he leaned forward and typed into Google: "Murder at The Motor Lodge in Clifton Heights, NY." His search produced more archived newspaper articles. He clicked a link leading to scans of *The Webb County Gazette* and found something almost immediately. In 1982, a couple from nearby Tahawus—Deke and Candy Sommers—had checked into Cabin 15 at The Motor Lodge. Details emerged later about the pair's considerable background of petty crime.

According to sources in Tahawus, their relationship had always been contentious, Deke always claiming Candy slept around. The second night at The Motor Lodge—July 15, 1982—the tensions simmering between them exploded. After several hours of drinking and arguing, around 1 a.m. in the morning, crashing and screaming were heard from Cabin 15. Followed by several gunshots. Four gunshots, witnesses reported.

The police arrived at a grisly scene. Three dead. Candy Sommers, her face blown away. A man who had been staying in Cabin 14—a traveling vacuum salesman from Pennsylvania, named Robert Ford—was shot in the abdomen and face. It was surmised he'd heard the first shot and had stumbled from his cabin onto the scene. Inside Cabin 15, police found Deke Simmons had turned his shotgun onto himself, sticking both barrels into his mouth and pulling the trigger.

David sat back, closed his eyes, covered his face with his hands, and rubbed his temples with his fingertips. A faint ache—maybe a leftover from the beers last night, maybe from him reading—reappeared there. He thought of the innocent salesman (him), thought of the salesman getting gut-shot, and felt the ghostly hot and cold pain in his belly. Remembered the feeling of innards oozing against his fingers. Behind his closed eyes, he saw Deke Sommers standing over him, shotgun barrels filling up his world, before the final blast came...

What the hell

No.

What the hell is going on?

David uncovered his face, opened his eyes, and forced himself to finish the article. Shortly after the incident, ownership of The Motor Lodge changed hands (David was beginning to think such a practice was commonplace in Clifton Heights). The new owner tore down Cabin 15, never rebuilt it, and let the lot go to seed. Business continued on without missing a beat.

David stared at the laptop's screen, his mind still trying to assemble disparate pieces into an understandable picture. He enjoyed a good ghost story but as entertaining distractions only. Pleasing diversions from the mundane. He'd never once believed ghosts existed and had always maintained that "strange events" could most often be explained rationally.

However, he couldn't explain any of this rationally. The only explanations were supernatural. Which he didn't like, at all. Even worse, discovering Shakespeare's "lost" play at Arcane Delights served as an eerie addendum.

I have to get out of here, he thought suddenly and passionately. *I have to get out of this town before it's too late.*

The last part stopped him. Too late? Too late for what?

When he checked his email, his unease only intensified when he saw his latest email to Kathleen had been returned, with the error code: "UNDELIVERABLE." Forcing down stirrings of panic, he fished his phone out of his pocket and tried once more to call Kathleen.

It rang once. Twice. Three times. After the fourth ring, he heard a click, then dead air.

He hung up his phone. Placed it gently on the table. Took a deep breath and forced his mind to try and make sense of things. *Email glitches happen all the time. How many times have emails bounced back at work, or from clients? Usually a server problem. Even Internet super-companies must experience occasional server outages.*

Also, he'd already established how poor the service was in Clifton Heights. To test his theory, he grabbed his phone and called the office. He felt no surprise when he heard four rings, a click, and then dead air.

He hung up. On a whim, he reached into his satchel's side pocket and pulled out the promotional bookmark Cassie had given him at Arcane Delights. He found the store number and dialed it. After three rings, a pleasant male voice answered. "Arcane Delights, Kevin Ellison speaking. How can I help you?"

"Uh, hello," David stammered, because he'd half-expected the same dead air, "I...uh...visited your store Monday and bought a few books, and had a question about one of them. Your assistant—Cassie—tried to help, but didn't come up with much. She suggested I call back later and ask you."

"Well, I'll certainly do my best." A brief pause, and then, *"What book do you want to know more about?"*

For the briefest of moments, David considered backing out of the whole thing. He could tell Ellison he'd made a mistake and didn't need any help. Why confront what he already suspected?

"Sir?"

David cleared his throat and plunged ahead. "I bought an old, cloth-bound edition of a Shakespeare play. I'm curious to know—if you can tell me—where you obtained it. I'm...somewhat of a bibliophile. These things interest me."

"Sure. I'm the same. I keep a database of where all our books come from. Obviously, if the book came from a private individual, I couldn't share their contact info without their permission. Best I could do is pass your info on to them and let them contact you if they want."

"I completely understand."

"Okay. What's the title?"

David swallowed, and then managed, *"The Tragical Historie of Cardenio."*

A weighty pause on the other end, until *"Shakespeare's lost play."*

David wasn't sure if Ellison's apparent knowledge of Shakespearean lore comforted him or not. "You know your Shakespeare, I'm guessing."

"*Yes,*" Ellison said, his tone carrying just the slightest hint of suspicion. "*Before I retired to take over Arcane Delights, I taught English at All Saints High.*" Another pause, until "*Are you sure of the title?*"

David licked suddenly dry, chapped lips. "Yes. Monday morning. I have the receipt. Your assistant Cassie rang me out."

"*Okay,*" Ellison said, still sounding doubtful. "*Let me check our database.*" Another pause, filled with the distant clicking of a computer keyboard, until "*What did you say your name was?*"

"David Roth."

"*I'm sorry Mr. Roth, but I'm not showing it in our inventory at all. It's not in the 'sold items' column, either. You bought it Monday morning?*"

"Yes," David replied stiffly, suddenly angered—and alarmed—though he couldn't explain why. "I also bought *Melmoth the Wanderer*, and *Who Fears the Devil,* by Manley Wade Wellman."

Some more typing, and then in a confused tone, Ellison said, "*Sir, I still have both those books in my inventory database. They aren't listed in the Monday morning sales. In fact, I don't have any sales recorded for Monday morning.*"

David rummaged around in his satchel for the books he knew he'd bought Monday morning. All he could find was Cardenio. Obviously, he'd been in a hurry and left the other two books back at the cabin. Obviously.

"I'm sure I have the receipt," he said again. He dug his wallet out of his back pocket with his free hand. Holding his phone between his ear and shoulder, he opened his wallet, looking for said receipt.

It wasn't there.

"I...I must've left the receipt where I'm staying, along with the other books. But I bought them there, Monday morning. I can assure you."

"I'm not sure what to say," Ellison said, sounding apologetic, now. *"I'm certainly not calling you a liar. But while you were looking for your receipt, I walked back to the horror and gothic section. Both books are there. And the other book doesn't show in our inventory. But you've got to admit...it would be strange if it did. I mean,"* David heard the shrug in Ellison's voice, *"it's not supposed to exist."*

Bands of anxiety tightened around his chest. A slight chill rippled through him. He fought to slow his breathing and speak calmly. "Could there...possibly be something wrong with your computer program?"

"Sure," Ellison admitted. *"It's an old system, and it has glitched before. Plus, I've only been at this for about five years. Certainly not perfect. Listen, I'll talk to Cassie when her shift starts. She can probably help straighten this out. Honestly, sometimes I think she should be running this place instead of me."*

Ellison's relaxed tone calmed David considerably, even though a small voice inside insisted something was dreadfully wrong. Even so, he ignored it and said, "Thank you, Mr. Ellison. Much appreciated."

"No problem. Okay if I call you at this number?"

"Absolutely fine."

"Okay. I'll talk to Cassie, and get back to you. Have a good day."

"You too."

David hung up and gathered his things. He was still unsure what to do next. The discoveries concerning Pizza Joe's and Cabin 15 still swam through his mind. His conversation with Ellison from Arcane Delights had only served to muddy the waters further. The only thing he knew clearly was his side trip had morphed into a discomforting experience he wanted to quit of, soon. The quicker Rich's Auto fixed his rental car and the quicker he was on the way out of Clifton Heights, the better.

David descended the library's front steps, realizing he was far too keyed up to return to his cabin. He remembered the sign for Handy's Pawn and Thrift. A detour might provide a welcome diversion. After stowing his things in the Kia, he walked across Main Street, thinking he could kill some time looking for knickknacks to decorate his home office. Even while thinking this, however, something inside wondered if he'd ever get to see his home office again. A ridiculous notion, to be sure.

Even so.

12.

From the moment David stepped into Handy's Pawn & Thrift, a delighted sense of nostalgia settled over him. The cluttered and haphazardly arranged thrift store reminded him of the various such stores he'd frequented in his youth.

Initially, there was no discernible order in the store's wares. On gray metal shelves, piles of old tools sat next to piles of thirty-year-old board games. Old shoes and ice skates, spools of wire, linked chains, and old hats lay in piles that seemed to blend into each other. Old tin posters hung on the walls. Everything from beer advertisements to Coke and Pepsi signs. David even walked past a dusty wicker basket full of old cellphones and their charging cables.

However, closer to the sales counter, a more definable—though still loose—order emerged. One whole section of shelving held children's picture books. Some of them looked over forty years old. In sections of their own, David saw collections of Dr. Seuss, The Berenstain Bears, and Little Golden Classics. On the shelf opposite, David saw paperback and hardcover novels. Paperbacks on lower shelves, hardcovers on upper shelves.

In the other rows, David caught glimpses of folded clothes (why they weren't nearer the shoes or hats puzzled him), a rack of costumes, and a section devoted entirely to Christmas decorations. On the wall closest to the sales counter, to David's right, hung fishing poles. Next to those were organizers full of hooks, lures, sinkers, bobbers, and other fishing accessories.

A tall man with white, closely trimmed hair stood over a tray containing lures. "Don't mind me," he said in a deep, pleasant-sounding voice. "I came upon some new fly-fishing lures, and I'm sure it won't be long before Father Ward or Sheriff Baker come looking for them. It's Sheriff Baker's weekend off. That's usually when they go fishing."

The man—the shopkeeper, David assumed—looked over his shoulder and offered a wide, friendly smile. His blue eyes sparkled with mirth. He had a trim white beard. "Take your time. Search to your heart's content. We're never in a rush, here."

David smiled in return, though he felt...at odds about the shopkeeper. Something in his air and his smile instilled a feeling of peace and simplicity. He seemed nothing more than a gentle shopkeeper enamored with his wares, content to putter around his shop and chat up whoever happened to visit. This reminded David even more of the thrift stores of his youth.

Even so, something glimmered in the shopkeeper's blue eyes. A kind of knowing which David recognized. This put him on guard, somewhat. Whatever this congenial shopkeeper appeared to be, David somehow sensed he was also...more.

Ridiculous. It's been a weird few days, and you're jumping at shadows. Assigning meaning where there is none.

He smiled and said aloud, "Thanks. Not looking for anything in particular. Just killing time."

The shopkeeper chuckled and resumed his sorting. "Oh, we're all looking for something. Most of us just don't know it."

David realized where he'd seen that perceptive gaze. Or, at least, where he'd sensed it coming from. The man who sat in his chair. Watching the world from behind his tinted glasses.

"Yes, we're all looking for something," the shopkeeper continued, "whether we realize it or not. Our time here is short. Truth is, we're not killing time. Time, in its slow and creeping way, is killing us. Every single day."

Feeling even more uneasy, but scoffing at himself for it, David knelt to inspect the shelves of paperbacks below the hardcovers. "I suppose so," he managed in a neutral tone. "Although that sounds a bit...morbid."

The shopkeeper chuckled again. "I suppose it depends on your point of view. If you focus solely on the concept that time is killing you, it does sound needlessly depressing. However, if the realization of time's fleeting nature prompts you into discovering your purpose...it becomes rather life-affirming."

Thinking the shopkeeper's words bore an odd similarity to those spoken by the man who sat in his chair, David only said, "I suppose so." He ran his finger down the spines of the paperbacks, which were proving to be mostly commercial romance and thrillers, the kind you'd find in an airport gift shop or grocery store.

"Don't mind me. I'm just an old codger who spends most of his time alone, and who'll talk the ear off most anyone who wanders in. Sometimes I'm sure I love the sound of my own voice."

David pulled out a Leisure Horror novel, *Coffin County*, by Gary Braunbeck. It was in decent condition, and it was also the only book he lacked in Braunbeck's *Cedar Hill* series. "You been in Clifton Heights long?"

The shopkeeper snorted. "Longer than I care to remember. Several Sheriffs ago, certainly."

David turned Coffin County over in his hands, noting the spine was only slightly cracked. He opened it and saw .50 written on the inside cover.

"I'm assuming you're from out of town?"

"Yes. Staying at The Motor Lodge. And I was wondering about..."

"The man who sits in his chair? Outside his little yellow house?"

David glanced up. Apparently finished with organizing the lures, the shopkeeper faced him, brushed his hands off, then stuck them into the pockets of his black slacks. "He's a town staple. Everyone knows him. Everyone who visits asks about him. Sometimes, I'm not sure there'd be a Clifton Heights without him sitting in his chair."

The shopkeeper smiled. Again, the odd knowing in his deep blue eyes belied his friendly expression. "Maybe a little hyperbolic, but even so."

David tucked *Coffin County* under his arm and searched the paperbacks some more, feeling conflicted over the genuine warmth he felt in the shopkeeper's expression and the almost cold analysis he saw in the man's eyes. "How long has he been around?"

Another snort, one which didn't sound so friendly, this time. "No one knows. The story is mostly the same. He grew up here, went to war, and came back to live in solitude. What's up for debate is what war he served in. It changes with every generation."

Ironically—or perhaps, maybe not—David pulled out an edition of *Don Quixote* he'd never seen before. The book's cover was all red, with a simple illustration of Don Quixote attacking a windmill. On the inside cover, he saw it was priced at only $2, so he added it to *Coffin County*. He continued to look through the books, reluctant to meet the shopkeeper's gaze, though he didn't fully understand why. "I suppose it's none of anyone's business...but has anyone tried asking him?"

David heard the shopkeeper's shrug in his voice. "It wouldn't matter if anyone did. There's no getting a straight answer from him. Speaks in nothing but riddles and cryptic platitudes which have no context. Quotes from movies and books without meaning. No one can make any sense of what he means."

This shocked David into glancing up at the shopkeeper, but if the shopkeeper noticed David's reaction, he didn't let on. "What do you mean?"

The shopkeeper pulled his hands from his pockets and crossed his arms, not looking at David, but vaguely out the store's front window. "Fellow's a locked box. Common belief is it's an after-effect of whatever traumatized him in whatever war he fought in. Fact is, he doesn't actually speak to anyone in any real way. I mean, he uses English words strung together in complete sentences which can be understood in isolation, but nothing he says results in any kind of real communication. And, like I said, much of what he says comes from memorized movies, stories, and songs."

David wanted to stand, but his thighs felt weak, for some reason. "No one...no one understands him?"

A sad smile flickered on the shopkeeper's face. His eyes softened slightly. "It's a little heart-wrenching, really. If you listen closely, what he's saying almost makes sense. But in the end...it never does."

The same unease David had felt the last few days wound its cold fingers up his spine. His stomach twisted; his shoulder muscles tightened. "Has...anyone ever understood him?"

The shopkeeper tipped his head, lips pursed. "Cassie Tillman—she's a waitress at The Skylark, and also works at Arcane Delights—claims she catches snippets. She stops and speaks with him on her Saturday morning run, every Saturday, without fail, so I suppose you could say she understands him best. But even then, she'll admit to only occasionally getting a vague sense of his meaning. Not a real understanding of what he's saying."

David swallowed and cleared his throat. "What if someone could understand him?"

The shopkeeper raised his eyebrows. "Well. They would be a special person, indeed. I'm of the private—if, perhaps, a bit fantastic—opinion no one understands him because we're not supposed to. So, someone who could understand him? A special person indeed."

something more

something bigger

"Anyhow," the shopkeeper said, turning back to the sales counter, "feel free to take your time. Find what you need. I'll be out back, sorting through some new inventory. Let me know when you're ready to check out."

David nodded. The shopkeeper left. He remained there, kneeling before rows of paperbacks. He closed his eyes. Breathed once, and tried to sort out everything in his head. He simply couldn't. The shopkeeper was obviously mistaken. Maybe the man who sat in his chair did speak gibberish most of the time, but David had understood him fine. David didn't know much about disabilities or PTSD, but maybe he'd caught the man in a good moment.

Part of David wanted to leave right then and there. For some reason, he couldn't make himself. Though it was silly, the shopkeeper's words resonated inside. Find what you need.

David continued scanning the shelves of paperbacks, and discovered one shelf labeled: "Local Authors." Some of the books were the usual kinds David would expect. Low-budget, self-published nonfiction books about the Adirondacks. Legends, hauntings, trail and fishing guides, Native American histories and legends. One shelf in the local author section, however, was dedicated to an author by the name of Gavin Patchett.

David pulled out and examined several of Patchett's books. Though they'd clearly been published through a small press, upon a cursory examination, they appeared to be professionally printed and formatted. The covers were striking and artistic. He counted five titles. *Things Slip Through, Devourer of Souls, Through a Mirror Darkly, The Night Road,* and *In the House of the Dream Witch.*

At the end of the shelf was a slim, leather-bound volume with no cover art or plot synopsis on the back. When David pulled the book out for closer examination, the only thing printed on the cover was:

David frowned, wondering what the symbols meant. They'd been engraved in the leather cover, inked in black. There wasn't an author's name on the cover, either. He opened the book and was surprised to find the pages rough and textured instead of print-on-demand commercial paper.

He found no copyright information on the inside cover, where it should be. On the title page was the symbol again. Above it, in hand-written script, a title read:

The Man Who Sits in His Chair.

Underneath, written in the same, careful script:

Gavin Patchett.

David read the title again, his anxiety spiking. What was he holding? Some ultra-rare special edition? Where was the publisher's information? The price?

David flipped back to the inside cover. He felt a shiver of surprise to see a carefully inked $35 in the upper right-hand corner. Confused and afraid without knowing why, David ran his thumb over the price. It didn't smear or disappear. He could've sworn it hadn't been there before. Obviously, he must've turned the pages too fast and missed it.

He opened to the first page of writing and began to read.

There is a man who sits in his chair, out in front of his small yellow house on Chester Road. He is as much a town

fixture as Raedeker Park Zoo, The Orpheum Movie Hall,
or Handy's Pawn and Thrift.

As David continued to read, something greasy flipped over in his stomach. Cold hands played along his shoulders. The old man. Sitting in his chair. On Chester Road. In front of his little yellow house. What the hell was this?

When he reached the last three lines of the first section, his stomach dropped out.

How much does he see?
How much does he know?
Everything.

David stared at *"Everything"*. Obviously, this was a work of fiction inspired by reality. Ironically enough, this Gavin Patchett had written a book inspired by the man who sat in his chair, on Chester Road.

Not so odd, of course. Stephen King's fictional town of Castle Rock had been inspired largely by his experiences growing up in rural Maine. Also, Ray Bradbury's fictional "Greentown, Illinois" was essentially his childhood town Waukegan, Illinois.

Patchett had done the same thing, though perhaps a little more on the nose. It was just an odd coincidence David had actually met the man sitting in his chair. Obviously.

David stood there, staring at the word *"Everything"*, wondering why it bothered him so much, debating whether or not he should read further. Even the thought bothered him. Why *shouldn't* he read further?

"Screw it," he muttered, turning to the next page, titled simply: 1. He began reading, but only made it through the first two paragraphs before he muttered under his breath, "What the fuck?"

The first line had been unnerving enough. "How long will you be staying with us, Mr. Greene?" The rest had set his hands to shaking, and he didn't know if he could make them stop.

The next two paragraphs, however...

David Greene jerked slightly; his attention having drifted. He blinked, gripped by a crawling sense of unease and dislocation, for a moment unsure where he was. He stood at a counter in a somewhat charming and rustic lobby. Behind the counter sat a blond, nondescript middle-aged man with watery-gray eyes, and thin lips pressed together in the slightest expression of impatience. "Mr. Greene?"

It came to him. The Motor Lodge. A small resort of self-sufficient cabins just outside Clifton Heights, a small Adirondack town west of Old Forge. He'd planned on driving straight through, hoping to reach Syracuse by evening, for his flight home to Alabama tomorrow, from Hancock International. Just outside Clifton Heights, however, his rental car—a 2010 Toyota Corolla—had slowly started losing acceleration. He'd crawled along at twenty miles per hour, despite pushing the pedal to the floor. The Toyota

shuddered once and died completely. He coasted to a stop
along the shoulder of Bassler Road...

David snapped the book shut, his heart racing. He broke out in a cold sweat and found it hard to breathe. He wouldn't read any further—couldn't bear to—because those first two paragraphs were about him. Some details were different. The last name, the year, and the make of his rental car. But it was about him.

How?

"Find what you need?"

David barely suppressed a frightened yelp. He quickly turned to see the shopkeeper standing behind the sales counter. Almost as if he'd been summoned, somehow. Part of David wanted to drop the books and walk out of the store. Instead, he felt himself walking on unsteady legs toward the sales counter. Drawing near, he once again marveled at the disparity between the shopkeeper's warm smile and his calculating gaze.

David stepped to the sales counter, cleared his throat, and laid down the Braunbeck and Cervantes paperbacks. "I'll take these. And..." he forced his hands not to tremble as he laid the leather-bound book next to them. "Do you know what this symbol means? And...could you tell me a little about the author? Gavin Patchett?"

The shopkeeper smiled widely, but it didn't quite touch his ever-cold eyes. "Ah, yes. Our humble Ray Bradbury and Stephen King, you might say. He got his start writing science fiction tie-in novels. His most recent works in the last few years, however, come from a more personal place of inspiration. This town, and the things he sees in it. He used to teach high school English at Clifton Heights High. Currently, he teaches at our small community college just outside town, Webb Community College."

The shopkeeper's smile faded slightly. He picked up the leather-bound book and turned it over in his hands. "Strange. I don't remember shelving this one. In fact, I hadn't realized it was already out." The shopkeeper flashed David his wide smile again. "Happens often enough at my age. You'd be amazed at the things stocked here, which I've forgotten about."

"It's about the fellow we were discussing. The man in his chair, on Chester Road?"

The shopkeeper flipped through the pages, nodding slowly. "Yes. I remember Gavin talking to me about this not long ago. This was his next project. However..."

The shopkeeper closed the book and scanned the cover, then opened it, looking for the copyright information. "I could swear Gavin spoke to me about this only a few months ago. Hard to believe it's already in print." He shrugged and grinned at David again. "Perhaps it's a special edition of some kind."

"What about the symbols?"

"Indeed. Apologies. I tend to wander in my old age." The shopkeeper closed the book and looked closely at the cover. "Hmm. This appears to be derivative of Cree." He looked up at David, smiling, and he could see the shopkeeper was excited in a bookish way which almost made David forget about his detached gaze. "The Cree were one of the largest Native American populations in the North, mostly situated in Canada, though some migrated down into the Adirondacks over the years. Certainly not unheard of."

"What does it mean?"

The shopkeeper handed the book back to him. "Monetoo. Or, more commonly known today as the mythical manitou. Native American theology believed it to be a fundamental life force which existed everywhere, in everything, in all of time. To them, it was the literal force which held existence together and stood in the way of the 'otsee monetoo, which was its antithesis. It strove to tear apart life, while the monetoo—or Manitou—strove to bind life together."

David looked down at the book. He traced the symbols with a fingertip, thinking...

sees everything

knows everything

Still looking down, he said softly. "You know a lot about these things."

"I run a thrift store, filled with bits and pieces of countless lives. I suppose I've become a treasure trove of bits and pieces myself."

David looked up.

The shopkeeper offered him a warm smile which clashed with his eyes of chipped blue ice. "Have you found what you needed today, David?"

He nodded. The shopkeeper rang him out, put his books into a generic plastic bag, and bid him good day, encouraging him to stop by again before he left town.

It wasn't until David returned to The Motor Lodge that he realized he'd never given the shopkeeper his name, either.

13.

He returned to The Motor Lodge by noon, but his stomach was churning too badly for him to eat. He tried to call both Kathleen and the office, but both times, he received the same four rings, a click, then dead air. When he tried his laptop, it connected to the Wi-Fi without incident, but his emails to both Kathleen and the office wouldn't send. They simply kept coming back "undelivered."

By the time he was able to get through to Rich's Auto—whose number had been busy for nearly fifteen minutes—his nerves hummed with anxiety. He felt poised on a razor's edge. "Hello, this is David Roth. My rental is there, waiting for a new transmission. I had it towed there Sunday night."

"Hold on, sir. I'll check." Keys clicked, and papers shuffled, until a confused voice said, *"I'm sorry, sir. I don't have a car here for a David Roth. It was towed here Sunday night? Waiting for a new transmission?"*

"Yes," David said tightly, holding tenuously to the shreds of his patience. "I have one of your loaner cars. A Kia. License plate 642-4UH."

"One moment, sir." More clicking. *"I'm sorry, but not only does our system not show any pending transmission deliveries, but our inventory also shows the loaner car is still in our lot."*

David cracked his neck, forcing himself not to grind his teeth, which he always did when angry. "I dealt with a mechanic named Jesse, on Sunday. He's the one who arranged the loaner and ordered the transmission."

There was a longer pause. When the voice spoke again, it vibrated with disgust and barely restrained anger. *"Listen, I don't know who the hell you are, but this is a rotten prank. You better get the hell off this phone, asshole."*

David's irritation and anger morphed into confusion. He'd offended this man, but he didn't know how. "I'm sorry. I don't understand, but if you could just talk to Jesse and confirm…"

"Jesse Southard died in a fucking car crash on Bassler Road, a year ago this past Sunday, you sick fuck. Don't call here again, or I'm calling the sheriff."

The line slammed into dead air.

David stood there, staring at his phone, for a long time.

After trying in vain to call Kathleen, the office, and this time both of his kids, David accessed the browser on his phone and Googled "Gavin Patchett, Webb Community College." Oddly enough, despite how bad the service in the area was, several hits came up at once. Of course, his attempts to email Kathleen and the kids from his phone had failed.

He found his way to WCC's English Department Faculty Page and to Patchett's office phone number. His summer office hours were ending in fifteen minutes. David took a deep breath and clicked on the number. His phone autodialed.

After three rings, he heard, *"Gavin Patchett."*

David opened his mouth, but nothing came out. He swallowed, cleared his throat, and tried again. "Mr…Gavin Patchett?"

"Speaking. How can I help you?"

"Gavin Patchett…the writer?"

"Uhm. Yes. Who is this?" The voice sounded confused, and suddenly wary.

"I…uh. This is going to sound strange, but I wanted to ask a question about one of your books."

Patchett sighed. David thought he detected the slightest air of resignation. *"Listen, I don't mean to sound ungrateful, but this number is for my students and fellow faculty only. If you visit GavinPatchett.com, you can send me an email from there, and I'll be happy to answer any questions you have."*

"No, I can't...I mean," David collected himself, forced his breathing to slow, and tried again. "It's important. I need to know about a book you wrote called *The Man Who Sits in His Chair*. It's about the man on Chester Road? The one with the symbol on the cover."

Silence.

A silence that stretched out so long, David was convinced Patchett had hung up. As he was about to hang up himself, David heard, *"Who is this? Is this some kind of joke? Is this Fitzy?"*

"No. No. I just wanted to ask some questions about this book..."

"I haven't written it yet. Just started outlining it two weeks ago."

David stood still, phone pressed to his ear, mouth opening and closing, but he wasn't able to find any words.

"Who is this?"

David ended the call. He shut off his cell. Stuffed it into his pocket. Turned and walked out of his cabin, toward Chester Road.

14.

David walked slowly up Chester Road until he reached the little yellow house. Out in front sat the man in his chair. Without looking for traffic (he supposed it didn't matter at this point) David walked across Chester Road, right up to the man sitting in his chair.

The man looked up from whatever book he'd been reading, and David once again felt the weight of the gaze behind those tinted glasses.

"David. So good to see you again," the man said in his gravelly Angus Scrimm voice. "How's your stay been so far? Any progress on your car?"

"I can understand you," David said. "The shopkeeper at Handy's says no one understands you. That you only speak in riddles. Is this true?"

"Well. Straight to it, then."

The man closed his book, laid it in his lap, and folded his hands over it. "I hate to give that blowhard points for being right—the old stiff loves to hear himself talk—but he's correct. No one in this town can understand me. Certain facets of my...existence precludes clear communication with anyone. It's for the best."

"Why can I understand you?"

The man smiled gently. He almost looked sad. "Because you're meant to."

David suddenly felt feverish and weak. He wiped his sweaty brow with a trembling hand. "I don't understand. This is...impossible."

The man chuckled. "Humanity is surrounded by impossibilities. Your average human encounters the impossible countless times throughout life. And yet, most simply walk right by. They shrug their shoulders, scratch their heads, concoct rational explanations to ease their troubled minds, and they go on their merry ways."

The man arched an eyebrow. "Seen any impossible things lately?"

David couldn't find the words.

The man leaned forward. David felt his gaze even more powerfully. "Having nightmares lately? For maybe the last month or so?"

Against his will, David found himself speaking haltingly. "Y...yes. About two months now."

"Of what?"

"I'm lost in some basement hallway. There's all these doors, and I'm...running down the hall, turning at intersections, running faster and faster...but I don't ever get anywhere."

"Interesting." The man sat back and regarded David thoughtfully. "Has it changed, recently?"

David wanted to say 'no.' He wanted to tell the man they were dreams and nothing more, and that his dreams were no one's business but his. Instead, he swallowed down a tight throat and said, "Yes. Now the doors are...opening. Things are trying to get through..."

"Yes," the man whispered, "things are always trying to get through."

"...and I'm running from door to door, locking them. I've got this big set of keys, but when I lock a door, another one starts opening. I keep running and closing them in time, but I'm always afraid..."

"...something will slip through." The man looked up at him. "Things always slip through, eventually. You can't close them all, I'm afraid."

The man sat up straighter and regarded David closely. "My nightmare was similar. I was running through my house—the one I lived in before—trying to shut and lock all the windows and doors. But it didn't matter how many times I locked them. Another would always pop open again. Over and over."

The man stopped. Looked at the closed book in his lap, appearing to be deep in thought. After several minutes, he looked up at David with a somber smile. "You're the one, then."

David stared at the man blankly, his mind a riot of fear and confusion. "The one...for what?"

"To sit in this chair. I've done all I can. Closed as many doors as possible. I'm tired. Too many things have slipped through, lately. I'm just about all in. Time for someone new."

David waved a weak hand, shaking his head. "No. No, this can't be happening." He looked away, down Chester Road and into Clifton Heights, which was spread out before him in finite detail. A tiny, scale town on a model railroad set. "This is impossible."

The man chuckled. "There it is again. Impossible. And yet...you have seen some impossible things this week. Haven't you?"

David nodded. He opened his mouth, but the man in his chair held up a finger and spoke first. "No, don't tell me. Everyone sees different things. What you need to know is you saw those things because you've been chosen. You've been opened to all the things which—every moment of every day—try to slip through the cracks into our world. Ghosts. Vibrations. Psychic echoes. Quantum fluctuations. Inhuman entities. Other realities. And so much more."

"Chosen. By what?"

The man shrugged. "I have no idea. Maybe a cosmic clockmaker who needs to replace a worn gear now and then. Maybe it's Fate. Or a weird sort of natural selection. If it hadn't been you, it would've been someone else before long. But it's you and here we are."

David swallowed down a tight throat. "What...what are you? Why do I have to...sit in that chair?"

The man tipped his head, looking aggravated for a moment. Then, his features smoothed, and he looked sad. "I'm sorry. This must be terribly confusing. I've been at this so long, and have absorbed so many memories, that it's easy to forget how jarring it all is at first. Simply put: You are the last line of defense between this small town and the Great

Unknown, which tries to get into this world every single hour of every single day. It's going to be your job to close as many doors as you can for as long as you can."

The man shifted in his seat and looked down over the town. "Of course, you'll never be able to close all the doors, all the time. Things slip through. It's the nature of existence. Some of those things are harmless, mostly. Like the *Tragical Historie of Cardenio*. If anyone else had found it besides you, they would've considered it an oddity, a fake, nothing more. They might not have even recognized its importance. Happens more often than you'd think."

He looked at David, his features firm. "Other things. The thing walking toward you at Pizza Joe's? Far worse."

David couldn't accept what the man was saying. He couldn't. It was delusional madness. He must be delusional, just standing here and listening. He shouldn't keep talking to him. He should turn and walk away before it was too late, because as the man kept talking, more of a creeping awareness slid over and into David. Invading him. Changing him.

"What's wrong with this town?"

The man smiled and waved. "It's not just this town, David. It's everywhere. We're needed in all sorts of places. You've seen us. Everyone has. They just don't remember us, because we're the outliers. The homeless person who lives in an alley. The drunk who lives in a cardboard box under an overpass. The crazy man who dresses up like an old west sheriff and stalks up and down Main Street. The nice old lady who stands on the street corner and waves all day long. The man who sits in the back of the same subway car every single day and never gets off, who sits there and rocks and mutters to himself. Surely you've read the Bible at some point? 'Be kind to strangers: for thereby some have entertained angels unawares.' Hebrews 13:2."

The man breathed in deeply. "We are the bulwarks, David, between this world and the howling cosmic madness which rages in the Beyond."

The man sighed and ran an alarmingly shaky hand through his flowing white hair. "And I'm tired, David. I need a replacement. Soon."

Something in the man's urgency lit a rebellious fire in David's belly. The man was nuts. Crazy. The shopkeeper had been putting him on, saying no one understood the man in his chair. There weren't any "doors" to keep closed. No "things" trying to get through. Forget the odd experiences, the nightmares. David lived in the real world. He believed in the real world. Kathleen, the kids, his job. Not fantastical tales of doors holding back chaos, and crazy people holding back madness.

David stoked the flames of his anger so he wouldn't give in. He pointed to the town below. "You're all nuts. Aren't you? This whole fucking town. You're all crazy, and in on it. The thrift store and its nutty shopkeeper. The folks at the auto place, and your local hack, this Patchett guy. This is all just one sick game, isn't it?"

The pitying look on the man's face angered David even more. "I'm so sorry, David."

David jabbed a finger at The Motor Lodge. "I'm gonna pack my bags. Jump in that loaner car and get the hell out of town."

The man nodded slowly. "Of course. Free will still exists, even in the middle of all this. People have refused the call before."

He gave David a long, piercing look. David could almost feel the man's eyes burning into his soul from beyond those tinted glasses. "You must know, however...every choice carries a price. A consequence. You certainly can pack up and leave for home. In time, the memory of this place, and me, will fade. Become nothing more than the hazy fragments of a bad dream. But your choice will come at a cost. One you will bear forever. Be assured."

David pointed in the man's face. "Fuck you. Fuck this crazy-ass town. I'll pay any price to get the hell out of here."

Before the man could respond or he could say more, his phone rang. Confused, still flushed with anger, David pulled his phone out and nearly yelped when he saw Kathleen's face flashing on the screen.

He turned and walked away from the man, intent on heading back to The Motor Lodge to pack. He answered the phone, nearly gasping in relief and joy. "Kathleen! Oh, God! Finally. You have no idea what kind of madness I've been dealing with..."

"David! I've been trying to get you for hours!"

David's stomach clenched. His throat closed tightly at the fear he heard in his wife's voice. He slowed to a halt. "Kathleen...what's wrong? The service here is awful. I've been trying to call and email since Monday afternoon, but..."

"It's Jamie! I...I guess she was coming home for a surprise visit, and a drunk driver...if she hadn't been wearing a seatbelt, she would've died instantly...but her spine's been fractured, the arteries to her kidneys are lacerated...and she won't wake up! David, she won't wake up! The doctors don't think...they don't think..."

David closed his eyes.

Swallowed.

a price

one you will bear forever

He opened his eyes. Turned and looked at the man sitting in his chair, out in front of his little yellow house on Chester Road. He wanted to be angry. Furious. He wanted to scream at the injustice of it all. Instead, all he did was whisper, "It'll be okay, honey. I promise. It'll be okay."

He didn't wait for her answer. He hung up, stuffed the phone into his pocket, and walked back to the man sitting in his chair.

15.

The man looked up; his facial features etched in sorrow. "I can't tell you how sorry I am, David. Truly."

David opened his mouth to ask if Jamie would be all right, but again, the man held up his hand. "I don't know the circumstances. My knowledge isn't quite omniscient. But I do know once you sit in this chair, no price need be paid."

"Are you...a Manitou?"

The man shrugged. "Perhaps. Perhaps what I am is the origin of the manitou myth. Who knows?"

"What...what about Kathleen, and the kids...and..."

The man sighed. "No longer your concern. Suffice it to say: driving is dangerous. More dangerous than flying, actually. Accidents do happen, and people move on afterward."

"But all my things...in the cabin..."

The man shook his head. "This won't be the first time someone has visited Clifton Heights and left without their possessions. As I'm sure you can imagine."

David gestured at the chair. "What do I...how..."

"When you sit, you'll know. You'll need this, however."

The man held out a leather-bound book. David accepted it, seeing with little surprise the same symbol on the cover as the one written by Gavin Patchett. Or, not written yet. This edition looked much thicker, however. Nearly twice the size.

"Not Gavin's version," the man said. "He won't finish for another two years or so, now. You spooked him with your call." He pointed at the book. "That's the...definitive edition."

David opened the book to where the man's bookmark—ironically, from Arcane Delights—had been left. He read one line, and one line only:

That's the...definitive edition.

David closed it and looked at the man. "Who writes it?"

The man shrugged. "Who knows? But in it, you can read about all who have sat in this chair, and you'll read everything which happens in this town every single hour of every single day until your time comes."

"What about you?"

The man, for the first time since David had encountered him, wobbily stood. The motion made him look impossibly old and frail. "I'm tired, David," he whispered in his gravelly voice. "Like all the others who came before me, I'm now going inside to take a nap. I won't be there when you turn in for the night. Where I'll be, I don't know. Nor did any of my predecessors."

He reached a shaky hand up to his face. Removed his sunglasses and handed them to David. For some reason, David avoided meeting his gaze, afraid to see the man's eyes. "You'll need these, son. Trust me. It gets powerful bright out here, some days. Powerful bright."

The man turned away and stiffly limped to his little yellow house. He opened the door, went inside, and closed it behind him.

Without a second thought, David sat in the chair. Put the tinted glasses on, which, oddly enough, fit perfectly. And the lens didn't seem tinted at all. He could see through them, clearer than he'd ever seen before. He opened the book to the first page and began to read...

There is a man who sits in his chair, out in front of his small yellow house on Chester Road. He's sat in that chair for as long as anyone can remember. He is as much a town fixture as Raedeker Park Zoo. The Orpheum Movie Hall, Handy's Pawn and Thrift, or old abandoned Bassler House...

In the Court of the Spider King

"The dark form ran toward him with incredible swiftness. When it came near he saw that there was a kind of face on the squat ebon body, low down amid the several-jointed legs. The face peered up with a weird expression of doubt and inquiry; and terror crawled through the veins of the bold huntsman as he met the small, crafty eyes that were circled about with hair."

– Clark Ashton Smith, "The Seven Geases"

1.

The Motor Lodge
Clifton Heights, New York
Wednesday, September 10
5:00 PM

Ras Seager took a tentative step closer to the wooden fence behind his cabin at The Motor Lodge. Nikon steady in his hands, attention on the camera's viewfinder. He tapped the zoom button with his thumb, then eased closer to the fence.

There it was.

An *Argiope Aurantia*. Better known as a yellow garden spider. An orb weaver, known for its distinctive webbing and its striking bright yellow markings against its black body. Common in the countryside, most often found around gardens. Hence its common name the yellow garden spider. Certainly, a favorite of his to photograph, though he always had to repress an involuntary shiver every time he saw one, because of an unfortunate childhood encounter with...

No, he thought, shutting the door on that memory with practiced ease, *we don't need to think about that.*

Especially considering he'd photographed at least four dozen yellow garden spiders over the past few years. He'd posted better than two dozen pictures of them to his website. He never got tired of shooting them, uneasy childhood memory be damned. Something in their beauty spoke of a special kind of majesty. He'd referred to them as "spider royalty" more than once.

He inched closer. Tapped the zoom once more, adjusting the focus. He preferred shooting in early morning light, but he'd decided to poke around the back of his cabin after settling in. He wasn't about to waste this opportunity. Besides, the light wasn't bad at all. If unsatisfied with the results, he could easily adjust the lighting digitally later.

He gently depressed the speed shutter, as if such slight movement alone would send the magnificent specimen scuttling away. It didn't. The Nikon clicked several shots in a row.

He straightened slowly. Held up his camera, paging through the shots. He grunted in approval. Several of them looked excellent. He smiled and moved along the fence.

Ras' flight from his home state of Kentucky had arrived in Utica around two in the afternoon. After a two-hour drive in his rental, he'd arrived in Clifton Heights, where he'd booked a cabin at The Motor Lodge in advance. It was the first leg of an Adirondack photo tour he'd been planning for a year. Over the next week, he planned on shooting in nearby Old Forge, White Lake, Eagle Bay, and Inlet. He'd then book a place in Indian Lake and do the same, before moving to his final stop, Lake George.

A light buzzing caught his attention. He froze instantly. Turning slightly, he saw a green-black blur hovering over a clutch of flowers against the fence. He brought his Nikon to bear.

The Nikon clicked. Unlike the garden spider, the green-black blur buzzed away. Hoping for the best, Ras checked the Nikon's screen. He smiled in delight. Several shots had framed his buzzing subject perfectly, in mid-flight.

A *Hermaris thyshe*. A magnificent little creature many mistakenly referred to as a "humming bee" because it hovered over flowers. It was actually a moth. A hummingbird clearwing, to be exact. Notoriously hard to photograph because of their lightning-quick movements, Ras had managed to capture several wonderfully clear shots of the elusive moth. Though he'd found himself focusing solely on spiders for the past few years, these shots would look wonderful on his website.

He'd never planned on a retirement career touring the country photographing nature. What began as a hobby had somehow blossomed into a full-time job. Slowly, more people found their way to his website. Eventually, he opened several social media accounts, thinking only of sharing his pictures with the internet. Unexpectedly, he developed an extensive following on all his accounts.

However, when website visitors and his social media followers started requesting prints of his photos, he'd thought it'd be too much hassle. Though he had his own dark room, the last thing he wanted to do was fulfill orders from his website.

Having to pay for shipping and packaging? Buying and fitting frames? Dealing with the inevitable shipping mishaps, and issuing refunds? Potentially dealing with unsatisfied and maybe even surly customers? No thanks. Trying to make a profit from his photography didn't seem worth the effort. He didn't want to turn a passion into a tedious job. In his retirement years, no less.

Things changed when a frequent website visitor posted a link to Fr ameYourworld.com. A professional and user-friendly online art gallery that specialized in printing, framing, and shipping user photos to buyers around the world. The overhead costs were minimal and automatically deducted from each month's earnings.

After creating an account and uploading some of his photos, Ras experimented by ordering framed prints for himself. When he found the product highly satisfactory, he then shared his profile discreetly with a few old Navy friends, promising to reimburse them if they weren't satisfied. When their response proved quite the opposite—they wanted to purchase more—Ras decided it wouldn't be much of a hassle at all. Especially because the website handled complaints and refunds, not him.

Over the following months, he slowly moved select photos from his collection to Frame Your World. When he finally felt confident with his gallery, he posted about it on his website. He also shared the link on social media. The response proved overwhelmingly enthusiastic. Orders flowed in immediately. Satisfied to ecstatic responses to his photography filled his email inbox. Three months later, he was earning a full-time salary without feeling even an ounce of tedium. He'd entered a new chapter of his life.

Ras spent the next six years traveling the country, photographing nature, and getting paid to do it. The revenue he earned from his prints covered his travel and lodging expenses. He wasn't rich, and he never would be. However, affording a week-long trip to California for a photo tour on a moment's notice felt rich enough for him.

He also didn't mind keeping busy. He'd never envisioned retirement as one long vacation. Quite frankly, he had little use for one. To him, sitting on a beach was no better than sitting on a mound of fire ants. Traveling the country photographing nature—for money, no less—not only kept him busy, but he also got to travel to unique locales, which was a natural extension of the traveling he'd done in the Navy.

He'd put some limits on his newfound venture, however. A few nature websites and magazines had approached him, offering commissions for specific kinds of photos. He'd politely turned them down. He didn't need the money and didn't want anyone dictating what kinds of pictures he took. He was done working for other people. He chose his destinations. He chose his subjects. Over time, his focus had drifted from scenery to bodies of water to birds, animals, reptiles, and different kinds of insects. Whatever he wanted.

The last few years it had been spiders of all sizes, shapes, and kinds. He'd always entertained an odd dread/fascination with spiders, ever since that one childhood experience he wasn't going to think about. Recently he'd felt drawn to focusing on them in particular. He loved being able to do so without worrying about having to shoot certain pictures or in certain locations for "this website" or "that magazine."

Ras smiled as he paged through the rapid shots of the humming-bird clearwing. They all looked equally good, capturing the moth in different angles of flight, revealing different perspectives of the moth's unique thorax markings. This, perhaps, was what he enjoyed most about his photography. Capturing something so wonderful completely by happenstance.

Ras grunted and switched the Nikon back to 'camera view.' He walked a few more paces. He was about ready to call it a night and go back inside when he saw something rather large scuttling from the nearest fence post to the tree line. Something whitish-gray, with eight legs. An odd-looking spider, he thought.

Instinctively he raised the Nikon and eased closer to the fence. Whatever it was (could a spider so big live here in the Adirondacks?), it had crawled to the base of an Adirondack pine. As he crept closer, he saw indeed it was a spider. He'd also been right about its size. Its thorax was a hair smaller than a pinecone, though its leg span made it appear bigger.

"Son of a bitch," he muttered as his thumb descended on the shutter, "what the hell are you doing here?"

Almost as if the spider had heard him (ridiculous, of course) the abnormally large and oddly-colored arachnid darted away into the undergrowth as he depressed the shutter. The Nikon clicked, but even without looking, Ras knew he hadn't managed to get a clean shot of the weird-looking spider.

He confirmed this a few minutes later, paging through his pictures. For the most part, he'd caught nothing but a white-brown blur. One picture had captured enough to produce a smeared, passable image, but it certainly wasn't high enough quality to post on the site.

"Damn," he whispered. He looked at the spot where the weird spider had disappeared into the undergrowth. It would've been special to capture a shot of such an odd-looking spider, especially for his frequent website visitors. He was no expert, but he'd gotten good at recognizing different kinds of spiders over the years. This one he hadn't recognized at all. That intrigued him. It had looked abnormally large for this area, too. As far as he knew, spiders this big didn't live in the North.

Also, something bothered him, deep down, about how the spider had moved. They were fast creatures, to be sure. This wasn't the first time he'd failed to get a shot of one because it had quickly darted away. Even so—and he felt sure this was his imagination—the spider had acted as if it had known he was trying to take a picture of it. Though it was silly, Ras almost felt as if the spider had been teasing him. Offering him only a brief glance before darting away.

Ridiculous.

Even so, Ras stood there for several more seconds, staring into the undergrowth where the spider had disappeared, gripped by the certainty the spider wasn't gone. It crouched under cover, hidden, watching him. Also ridiculous, but still. Ras stood there for several more minutes before finally deciding he'd taken enough pictures for now, and it was time for dinner.

2.

Hyland's Place
Main Street
7:00 PM

"So. You were in the Navy. What did you do? Or was it all secret and classified?"

Ras chuckled and sipped his beer. The woman sitting next to him—Sandy Loughlin—had struck up a casual conversation with him as he'd been finishing his burger and fries at the bar. Over something utterly mundane, about the beer he'd been drinking, a Founder's KBS Stout. The banter had developed into a relatively banal discussion about trivial things until they reached the standard "you're not from around here" part of the conversation. A line he'd grown increasingly familiar with on his travels the past few years. This inevitably led to talking about his post-Navy hobby, which of course had led to the question at hand.

He smiled and tipped his head. "I can give you broad strokes. I started out in Photographic Surveillance, but I didn't take pictures. I analyzed those taken by our pilots. Eventually started working for Intelligence. And no," his smile turned into a grin, "I can't tell you anything I worked on. It is classified. Still is, to this day."

Sandy—who appeared anywhere from late twenties to late thirties—smirked and sipped from her mixed drink. "Wow. Real-life spy action. 'I could tell you but then I'd have to kill you'."

He shrugged. "Yes...but believe it or not, it was mundane classified stuff. Critical information and data about military tactics and weaponry...but nothing sexy. I didn't help insurgents retake their country from dictators, or run point on any assassinations or anything."

"Ah. So it was secret stuff, but not fun secret stuff."

He nodded. "Kinda. I mean, I did spend some time in Mexico on drug surveillance, but again. It was surveillance of low-level pushers and dealers making corner drops and deals in back alleys. I wasn't tracking the Mexican Drug Cartel bosses, for sure." He shrugged again. "Half the time, I had no context for the pictures I was analyzing. Nor did I ever know what results—if any—came about because of those pictures."

"Huh. And now you travel all over the country taking pictures of bugs, spiders, snakes, and all sorts of animals."

He grinned and gave a mock shiver. "Yes to everything except snakes. Those I'm not so fond of."

She laughed and he continued. "I loved photography before the NAVY, though. And I've always loved nature. Studying it and collecting it." He winked. "I was that kid. The one with an extensive bug collection."

Sandy wrinkled her nose. "Ew. Really?"

He laughed, not offended by her reaction, as it was common. Bug collecting, apparently, had gone out of vogue long ago. If it had ever been in vogue. "Yep. Although, I didn't stab them through the guts with a pin. I gassed them to death in a little jar, then went to elaborate efforts to mount them on little placards with their genus name and other info. I'd spend hours arranging their wings and legs, trying to make them appear alive. Must've done a good job, because some of my friends were always convinced a few of them were alive."

Sandy gave him an odd look. "You don't...still collect bugs and spiders. Do you?"

He chuckled, though for a moment he thought she would've been offended if he'd said yes. "Heavens, no. After a while, the idea soured for some reason. I realized how awful it would be if some huge, alien, and incomprehensible being gassed me and then pinned me to a card. So I stopped collecting bugs and spiders when I was fifteen or so. Photographing nature felt kinder to the insect and arachnid population."

The subtle relief spreading across her features confirmed his suspicions. Sandy, in some way, would've been mortally offended if he still gassed bugs and spiders and mounted them. He supposed he could understand. That's why he'd quit himself, after all. But something fierce had flashed in her eyes when he'd been describing his childhood hobby. Something powerful and vibrant had made him feel oddly uneasy, for a moment.

That moment had passed, however. Now Sandy was all smiles again, appearing a bit abashed, to boot. "Sorry if I came on too strong, there. It's not the insects I care much about, honestly. It's the spiders. I've always loved those. I was one of those weird kids who wanted a tarantula as a pet. I was always throwing bugs into spider webs, to see how fast the spider could wrap them up."

Ras laughed. "Yes! We used to do the same thing with the garden spiders around our gardens as kids. Especially Japanese beetles. I hated those things. I actually took some pictures of a wonderful garden spider earlier this evening, behind my cabin at The Motor Lodge."

"Nice. You'll have to show them to me. I mean...if you want to."

A pause blossomed, filled with the sudden but pleasant weight of unspoken things. The implication of her returning to his cabin to look at the pictures he'd taken carried something else. As a two-time divorcee who had no desire for long-term commitment, he enjoyed the prospect.

She sipped from her drink, swallowed, and said, "So. Spiders. Are you a fellow devotee? I mean, now that you're not killing them and pasting them to cardboard."

She was smiling when she said this, but once again, Ras thought he heard a slight, biting undertone. Dismissing it as his imagination, he said, "Well, it's complicated. I'm not sure if I love spiders, exactly. Drawn to them, certainly. The construction of their webs, or in the case of trap-door spiders, their lairs, are fascinatingly intricate. And they're such efficient predators. Thank GOD I'm not small enough for a spider to eat."

She chuckled, tucked several strands of her blond hair behind her ear in an engagingly demure gesture, and said, "But."

He nodded. "But. Okay, this involves a rather embarrassing childhood story. Try not to laugh at an old man. Much."

She made a show of settling herself to listen. "I make no promises." She paused and offered him a penetrating gaze with a slight smile. "And you're hardly an old man."

Ignoring the flush of heat in his cheeks, Ras cleared his throat and continued. "This happened when I was ten years old. My friends and I were playing a game by another friend's cornfield. Tag or Capture the Flag, I can't quite remember. Anyway, to avoid capture or tag or whatever, I dodged into the cornfield, plunging through a wall of cornstalks. I took two steps, and felt something soft and kind of itchy on my forearms."

Sandy's eyes lit up in anticipation. She covered her mouth with her hand and whispered in dread delight. "Oh. Oh, no."

"Oh yes. Plastered from my upper chest to waist in spider silk. I'd run through ten to fifteen spider webs strung between the corn stalks."

Sandy was shaking her head, quietly laughing and clapping. "Oh, shit. I'm sorry...but shit."

"Shit is right. Hanging on those webs, tangled up in them, and pressing against my skin or T-shirt were a dozen garden spiders. Each of them the size of a half-dollar. You know that scene in *Stand By Me*, with the leeches? When the boys are ripping their clothes off and screaming?" She nodded, hands clamped over her mouth, "Well, that was me. I left my shorts and shirt behind in the cornfield, and streaked out of there in my tighty-whities." He picked up his beer, cringing slightly at the memory. "I stayed away from cornfields for a while, believe me."

Sandy slapped the bar, trying—with mediocre success—to stifle her laughter. "Oh, shit. I'm sorry, you must've been scared out of your mind...but that's hilarious."

He sipped from his beer, swallowed, and smiled in return. "Oh, it is. Believe me. Now, anyway. Back then, not so much."

Somewhat calmer, Sandy ran a hand through her hair. As she did, Ras noticed something colored on the inside of her wrist. A tattoo, of sorts, he thought. He didn't think about it further as she asked, "So after your childhood experience...are you afraid of spiders? You said you're drawn to them. Why?"

He thought for a moment before answering, then said, "I think spiders inspire an instinctive reaction. Especially if we come across them unexpectedly. Maybe a fragment of race memory from thousands of years ago? When spiders were more plentiful and more dangerous? I dunno. Anyway, the reaction intrigues me, and I'm drawn to photographing spiders because of it. In spite of the childhood memory of my unfortunate encounter with them, which makes me uneasy to this day."

She smirked at him, a playful look in her eyes, which once again implied pleasant, unspoken things. "It's spider webs, isn't it? They gross you out."

"They do. Running into a spider web unexpectedly is worse than running into a spider itself. Gets on my nerves." He shivered again—completely for real, this time—and swigged from his beer.

Sandy gave him another odd look and said, "Y'know, this is definitely the best time to photograph spiders. This is The Time of the Spider, after all."

Ras shifted on his bar stool to face her directly, intrigued. "The Time of the Spider. Never heard of it."

"Cultures which revere spiders see this as something of a holy month. They view it as a time to honor spiders and their various deities. Which makes sense, of course. This is when spiders are out and about, trying to mate and get inside homes to escape the coming cold."

"Huh. Y'know, I read about that somewhere. Didn't realize there were spider deities, though."

"There are many myths about spiders, in many cultures." She gave him a different kind of look, this time, one he did understand. "Maybe we should go back to your cabin where it's quieter, and I could tell you some."

Ras smiled slowly, this time feeling heat somewhere else beside his cheeks. "Maybe we should."

3.

The Motor Lodge
Cabin #14
10:00 PM

Whatever heat Ras had felt blooming between him and Sandy at Hyland's Place cooled slightly when they arrived at his cabin. Not completely. He could still feel it there, simmering beneath the surface. But as he handed Sandy a Sam Adams lager from the kitchen's small fridge, she appeared content to settle herself on the futon in the den. She made no movement toward the bedroom. Which was fine by Ras. At his age, he enjoyed a platonic evening with a woman as much as an amorous evening, so long as it wasn't boring. Sandy seemed anything but.

She looked around the den with an appraising eye. Took a sip from her beer and said, "I've never been in any of these cabins before. It's quite nice."

Ras sipped from his beer and sat in the armchair instead of joining her on the futon. It was odd. He still felt tension simmering between them, but he suddenly felt slightly on guard. He instinctively knew if he came on too strong at this moment, she'd react badly. And having only met her, he had no idea what "badly" meant.

"It is nice," Ras said as he settled into the chair. "No offense to your town, but I was actually surprised *how* nice. On the outside, the cabins appear plain. The interior, however, far exceeded my expectations."

Sandy nodded vaguely and sipped from her beer again, her gaze wandering around the cabin's small den, not focusing on any one thing.

"So," he said, for some reason feeling awkward and fidgety, "you were going to tell me some spider myths?"

Sandy's eyes lit up as if he'd flipped a switch inside her. She straightened, face suddenly animated. "I have many stories," she said with a wide—almost hungry—grin, "but I don't want to tell them at the moment."

"Oh? What do you want?"

She folded her hands in her lap and looked at him, her green eyes (which he hadn't noticed before), saying exactly what she wanted, without using any words whatsoever.

4.

3:00 AM

In the bedroom, they undressed in a leisurely silence. Sandy said nothing as she pulled her sweatshirt over her head to reveal two pleasantly round and firm breasts sheathed in a flimsy bra. As she pulled her pants down, Ras noticed he'd been right. She did have a tattoo on her wrist, of a multi-colored spider. He meant to comment on it, but then Sandy straightened, unhooked her bra, and set her breasts free. His mind was immediately occupied with other matters.

Their lovemaking—the first time, anyway—proved to be fierce and passionate, coming from a place of great hunger. It wasn't especially erotic by any means, but more basic. Instinctual. Primal. Two beings seeking to satisfy their desires. In many ways, though it proved extremely satisfying, it didn't differ from any of his other sexual encounters in the past few years. They were two relative strangers fulfilling their needs, nothing more.

Their second run-through, however, proved more startling, and—dare Ras even think it—breathtaking. Startling, because at his age (though he managed his romantic interludes fine) repeat performances in one night weren't usually the norm anymore. The few times a partner had shown interest in a Round Two, Ras simply hadn't felt the urge.

However, when Sandy—after lying in a sweaty heap with him for twenty minutes—lithely climbed on top and started pressing her sex against his member while she playfully bit his neck, Ras felt himself harden in response almost immediately. It wasn't long until she mounted him, and this time, rode him with a gentle yet commanding rhythm.

Everything about their second encounter was tinged with a humming, low-level intensity. Each languid thrust of her hips sent ripples of pleasure throughout him. A pleasure that slowly built into a towering crescendo. Near the end, it felt as if every nerve ending in his body was on fire, as their skin-on-skin contact sent continual waves of shuddering chills through him, down his spine, and radiating out through his body.

He'd suffered one bad moment, however. Right before Sandy had started riding him faster. Her hair had fallen over him, the strands brushing against his forehead and cheeks. Suddenly he was transported back to when he was ten, realizing with horror his arms were plastered with clinging webs filled with spiders. Her hair brushing his face felt like spider webs, and a strange, panicky sensation rose in his chest. She'd started pumping him harder, however, and brought him to a shouting climax.

Now, Ras twitched awake. Lying on his side, spooning with Sandy. Staring into the dark. Something had woken him, but he didn't know what. He lay there, seeing Sandy's rough outline under the blankets, nothing more.

He lifted his head slightly. As he did, several strands of Sandy's hair brushed his face. Even though Ras instantly chided himself for the knee-jerk reaction, a wave of revulsion pulsed through him. It didn't feel like hair. It felt like the gossamer strands of webs he'd run through all those years ago. Uncomfortable (and also annoyed with his juvenile discomfort) Ras swept an agitated hand over his face, brushing away the delicate strands of Sandy's hair, which clung to him...

Something scuttled, lightning quick, over the back of his hand. Ras jerked back with a hiss, knowing what it was. He'd of course encountered the sensation many times before in his sometimes-reckless pursuit of nature photography.

A spider had darted across the back of his hand. It hadn't been the feather-light touch of a Daddy-Long Legs or a Huntsman. It had been hairy, and he'd felt its thorax brushing against his skin. A wolf spider, perhaps, or...

He felt more hairy legs and another body scuttle across his flesh. And another.

Ras jerked back and scrambled out of the bed. The blankets twisted up in his legs and he almost fell. As it was, he pulled the blankets partially off Sandy, who remained eerily silent. He'd expected her to mutter or at least grunt her displeasure, but he'd heard nothing. Her sleeping form remained still in the bedroom's dim murk.

With a shaking and reluctant hand, Ras fumbled with the lamp on the bedside table and clicked it on. Sickly yellow light spilled across the bed. For a heartbeat, Ras couldn't comprehend what he saw. A black fuzzy blanket—an afghan, though he didn't remember the bed having one? —draped across Sandy's shoulders. Except, it wasn't an afghan, at all.

It moved.

Twitched and jittered. It scuttled along Sandy's neck, shoulders, and exposed back. It took a few seconds for his brain to make sense of what he saw, and when he did—as several bits of the "blanket" dropped off Sandy's shoulders and scuttled across the bedsheets toward him—his throat constricted and hot bands of pressure tightened across his chest, making it hard to breathe.

Spiders.

Thousands of them. Tiny, fuzzy black spiders of indeterminable genus, swarming over Sandy's shoulders and back. Clambering over each other, dropping to the bed, skittering under the covers.

Sandy didn't move. Not a twitch. She lay there, as spiders swarmed over her. Ras tried to move, but his thighs quivered weakly. His stomach roiled with fearful nausea. He'd once taken a picture of a wolf spider with thousands of tiny baby spiders clinging to its back. That hadn't bothered him. It had been a natural photo. This, however. Baby spiders swarming over Sandy's back. Ras felt the food he'd eaten earlier lurch in his stomach.

A ripple passed down Sandy's back, pressing her flesh through the teeming spiders, which now dropped in fuzzy, many-legged clumps onto the bed, where they rolled and clambered over each other. The ripple passed down Sandy's back again. Something inside of her was pressing out against her flesh.

Something wet and fleshy ripped.

The gassy smell of rot filled the room.

A ragged tear opened down the middle of Sandy's back. Out of the tear scrambled even more spiders, covered in a clear, viscous fluid. They dropped to the bed in heavy, wet patters. Then...

Something fuzzy, the size of his wrist, poked out of the tear in Sandy's back. A foreleg. Something pressed against the skin of her back and shoulders again, making more wet flesh-ripping sounds.

The tear in her back widened. More forelegs poked out and probed the air, dripping the same clear, viscous fluid. Ras fell back and screamed as he saw uncountable eyes glittering in the dark cavity of Sandy's ruined body...

5.

Thursday, September 11
6:00 AM

Ras jerked awake and sat upright in bed, a hoarse shout dying in his throat. Instinctively he slapped his chest and arms, for a moment driven mad by the ghostly sensation of thousands of fuzzy legs skittering over his soft flesh.

When he glanced frantically down at his arms and legs, however, he saw bare skin. No black spiders swarming over him, or the sheets. No strands of webs clinging to him. Only his bedsheets, twisted up in his legs, damp with night sweats.

Ras pressed back against the headboard and closed his eyes. He rubbed his chest as if he could slow his pounding heart by massaging it. He fought to steady his breathing. He felt oddly chilled and flushed at the same time. For a moment, he wondered if he was coming down with something. He certainly felt as if he'd wakened from a fever dream.

As the minutes passed, however, the flushed sensation faded. His heartbeat and breathing slowed. For a moment, his stomach twitched uneasily, but those rumblings subsided, also. He rubbed his face, sighed, and opened his eyes.

Morning sunlight filtered through the small window's blinds, casting a dim haze throughout the bedroom, which caught dust particles in its glare, suspending them. It was light enough, however, for him to see his bed was clear. No spiders scuttling in one fuzzy blanket across him.

He looked to his side. For a moment, he expected—his heart stuttering—to see Sandy's body engorged with spiders, and something huge and unnatural tearing out of her body. He saw nothing, however, but rumpled blankets and a folded square of paper. A note, probably. He picked it up, already suspecting its contents. He'd left a few in his time and had received a few, also.

He opened it and found the expected. "Had a wonderful time last night." Followed by a rather unexpected: "I want more. Meet me at Hyland's again for dinner if you want."

He read the note, thinking. He should toss it and go about his business. Clifton Heights wasn't big, but it wasn't exactly tiny, either. If he spent the next few days focused on shooting, he felt reasonably confident he wouldn't see Sandy again. Especially if he ate somewhere else. Last night had been great (amazing, actually), but as much as he'd enjoyed it, he didn't want to get sidetracked. He knew nothing about this woman. Best not get tangled up in something unpredictable, and possibly messy.

Ras had never been averse to running risks. His time in the military certainly hadn't made him timid, and he'd carried his sometimes foolhardy bravado into photographic pursuits. Even so, the last thing he needed was to get caught in some sort of *Fatal Attraction* scenario. As far as he actually knew, Sandy was married to a good old boy who loved shotguns. He wasn't worried about the ethical ramifications, so much. Mostly, he was worried about the shotgun risk.

That settled things. He crumpled the note and tossed it into the wastebasket next to the bed, got out of bed, and headed for the shower.

6.

Something unsettling happened while Ras showered. A normally mundane occurrence which set him on edge slightly. As he washed his hair, he felt something brush his big toe with a feathery tickle. He pulled his foot back, glanced down, and saw a spider. An ordinary, everyday wolf spider. Struggling to skitter across the scrim of water flowing toward the bathtub's open drain. A drain that had lost its grate long ago and was now an open, black hole.

Ras stopped washing his hair and stared at the struggling wolf spider, which was starting to lose its battle against the tide sweeping it closer to the drain. He'd encountered numerous spiders in similar circumstances countless times in his life, especially during his military service. And it was September, after all. When spiders were migrating inside to escape the cold. The "Time of the Spider," as Sandy had said.

The unconscious use of the phrase sent a nasty jolt through him. Looking at the vainly struggling spider, all he could see were the teeming hatchling spiders swarming over Sandy's back in his nightmare. It was silly because nightmares meant nothing. Even so, all he could see in this one struggling wolf spider were thousands of newborn spiders clambering over each other.

Revulsion pulsed through Ras. He swept water with his foot at the struggling spider. The wave upended it and sent it spinning to the drain. It hit the drain, and overcome by the water, toppled over the edge, into the darkness.

Before the water engulfed it entirely, two forelegs caught the drain's rim. For a moment, he thought it would clamber out. In seconds, however, those fuzzy legs disappeared, and the spider vanished.

Despite feeling a sting of guilt for dooming an innocent creature to a watery death, the briefly flailing legs reminded Ras so powerfully of the legs tearing through Sandy's back, that he shivered in disgust. He finished washing and exited the shower as quickly as possible.

7.

Thaddeus Briar Nature Conservatory
Pellingston Street
10:00 AM

"This may be an odd question, but where are the best places around here to photograph spiders?"

The docent—a skinny young man with lank black hair, a scraggly goatee, and John Lennon glasses—straightened, an excited gleam in his eyes. "You photograph spiders?"

Ras grinned. The guy's excitement was infectious. He was acting like the lonely kid on the school playground discovering an obscure common interest with another kid. "Well, I take pictures of all sorts of things. Birds, deer, landscapes, sunsets, dragonflies, and other kinds of insects. But the last two years, yeah. I've kinda focused on spiders." He proceeded to loosely sketch his reasons for visiting Clifton Heights, his hobby-turned-career, the website, and the pictures he sold from it. He handed over a business card with his website on it—rasman.net—and the young man accepted it almost reverently. He gazed at it as if committing its information to memory. "Wow. Awesome. I'll have to check this out later."

He stowed the card into his pocket and beamed at Ras with a wide smile. "You're in luck. I'm the only practicing arachnologist on staff here at the conservatory."

Ras raised an eyebrow. The young man's smile flickered slightly as he admitted, "Well. I mean. I'm studying entomology at Webb Community College. I'm a sophomore. My focus is arachnology, but they don't offer that degree at Webb. Anyway."

The kid took a deep breath in an apparent attempt to shore up his confidence and said in a firmer voice. "I interned here all through high school, and now I work here. If I'm being honest, I don't have a degree or any credentials yet. But, I'm the one here who knows the most about spiders. So."

Ras offered what he hoped was a reassuring grin. "You're the guy I need to speak to, then." The kid visibly relaxed. Ras knew he'd taken the right approach. When he asked again about the best places to photograph spiders, he could see he'd made the kid's day.

Which was probably no small thing, because it was apparent the Thaddeus Briar Nature Conservatory didn't appear to attract many visitors. Perhaps it was an off day, but the empty parking lot out front (save his car, and a Hyundai he assumed was the kid's) looked like it didn't get much use. It was cracked and slightly heaved; the cracks filled with weeds determined to make their presence known.

The inside of the conservatory appeared as if it hadn't changed its decor since the mid-eighties. Though the floor appeared swept and the ceilings free of cobwebs, a lingering sense of benign neglect hung in the air. In the small foyer stood a rack of dusty, yellowed nature brochures. Upon inspection, Ras saw they hadn't been updated in more than twenty years.

The young clerk—named Aloysuis Baston—was quite frankly starving for attention. Ras didn't begrudge him. Nor did he find the town's casual dismissal of the conservatory strange, however. He'd visited many such places on his travels over the past few years. For every robust, large, and well-funded conservatory, there existed three or four underfunded and forgotten ones languishing on the borderlands of small towns across the country.

Aloysuis spread a map on the small, cramped counter. Ras noted with amusement how sharp the map's creases were. This was probably the first time it had ever been opened.

"According to the most recent spider population survey, the densest cluster would be here, in Freivald Hollow." Aloysuis tapped a spot on the map. "Freivald Road is a dead-end road off Bassler Road, a mile past The Commons Trailer Park. It's about two or three miles long. The hollow is at the end of the road, on the right."

Ras smiled again, but he did his best to make it a friendly expression, not a mocking one. "I'm guessing you conducted this survey?"

Aloysuis nodded eagerly, his expression so somber and serious Ras wanted to laugh, though he didn't. "Yessir, but not as a lark or anything.

It was a long-term project for my Entomology Seminar at school. I had to use all the methods an official entomologist would've used, had to gather all the same data, even had to use the same equipment, which they had at the college. The numbers are legit, I promise you."

He tapped the map again. "Trust me. You want an abundance of different species; this is the best place in Clifton Heights to go."

"Sounds great. Will Freivald Hollow show up on GPS?"

"It should, yeah. Even if it doesn't, the old Freivald Spa is right at the end of that road anyway. Signs for it are still on Bassler Road. Shouldn't miss them."

"Great." On instinct, seeing as how he had access to someone knowledgeable about the local spider population, Ras pulled his Nikon out, turned it on, and started paging through the pictures he'd taken. "By the way. I got a partial shot of an odd-looking spider last night. Didn't recognize it. Mind taking a look?"

Aloysuis' eyes lit up. "Sure! I'd love to."

Ras found the picture in question—of the blurred white-brown spider—and handed it over. "Here it is."

Aloysuis accepted the camera eagerly, a smile on his face. A smile that gradually faded and was replaced by a blank expression Ras couldn't read. "Huh," the intern said carefully, "doesn't look familiar."

For some reason, the young man's sudden and odd ambivalence didn't surprise Ras. In fact, he realized with a start he'd been expecting it. "Seriously? Budding arachnologist doesn't recognize a spider?"

As soon as the words left his mouth, Ras knew he'd made a mistake. The young man's face stiffened and something hardened in his demeanor. He handed the Nikon back to Ras without looking at it further. "No sir," he said in an oddly robotic, emotionless voice. "Don't recognize it."

Ras accepted the camera, puzzling over the young man's sudden shift in attitude. As he took his camera from Aloysuis, he caught the briefest flash of something multi-colored with several legs inked on the young man's wrist, under the sleeve of his long-sleeve polo shirt. Though he hadn't gotten a good look, it had appeared startlingly similar to Sandy's tattoo of a multi-colored spider. In the same place as Sandy's tattoo, also.

Ras knew he should walk out. It would be the polite thing to do, especially after his snarky question. It would be the smart thing to do, also. However, with a recklessness that bordered on maliciousness, Ras smiled and leaned over the counter. "Aloysuis, you know a woman named Sandy? Hangs out at Hyland's Place?"

If the kid did know Sandy, he performed a masterful acting job hiding it. He turned his blank expression on Ras, and his gaze was eerily empty. "No, sir. Don't know a Sandy. Anything else I can help with?"

Ras stood there for a moment, returning the kid's distant gaze, debating the wisdom of prodding further. In short order, however, practical sense won the day. Either he'd needlessly pissed the kid off with his jab, or he had gotten too close to something the kid didn't want to talk about, for some reason. Either way, Aloysuis wasn't having any of it. Any attempt to get more information out of him would be futile.

Ras shook his head, taking care to smile amicably. "I'm good. Thanks for the advice. If I get some good shots...want me to stop by and show you?"

This cracked Aloysuis' plastic expression the tiniest bit. He smiled faintly, a little of his former excitement glimmering in his eyes. "That'd be great."

Ras nodded; happy he'd mollified the kid before he left. Aloysuis' quick shift in mood still bothered him, however. But he'd keep it under wraps for now. "Okay. Have a good one."

The kid nodded, smiling slightly, but he said nothing more. Ras turned and left, suddenly eager to be away from Aloysuis Baston and the small, dusty, forgotten conservatory center, though he didn't know why. Regardless, he had no intention of coming back and showing any pictures to the kid.

8.

Freivald Hollow
11:00 AM

His phone's GPS found Freivald Road easily. Even if it hadn't, Aloysius had been correct. Signs for the Freivald Health and Wellness Spa popped up soon after Ras turned onto Bassler Road. A giant billboard (faded and covered with decades' worth of graffiti) marked the turn-off onto Freivald Road clearly enough. It pronounced the spa—and, presumably, the hollow—only four miles away.

The old spa piqued Ras' interest. Abandoned structures often teemed with spiders. Depending on the state of the old spa, he might do a little rural exploring after he searched Freivald Hollow.

When he pulled up to a drive marked by a sagging sign that read "Freivald Health and Wellness Spa," he found the way barred by a chain-link fence. It blocked the drive and extended several hundred yards on both sides of the drive, then back into the woods. Ras couldn't see the spa itself. The long and partially overgrown drive wound back into the woods. Even so, he assumed the chain-link fence surrounded the property.

On the gate hung a white metal sign which read in stark black letters: WARNING. GROUNDS CLOSED DUE TO POSSIBLE CONTAMINATION. WEBB COUNTY HEALTH. As he stepped closer and read the sign again, Ras found its warning curious. The sign bore no official symbols associated with pollution, chemical spills, runoff, or contamination from hazardous materials or chemicals. A quick walk up and down both sides of the drive revealed no security cameras of any kind or any additional warnings about local police patrolling the area.

Ras returned to the sign and stood there, thinking. The fencing and sign didn't appear old. Its padlocked chain appeared even newer. He wondered if maybe the contamination warning was merely a bluff. Maybe the fence had only been erected recently to discourage adventurous teens.

Ras smiled. He'd almost certainly decided he'd somehow find his way into the old spa. The fence wasn't high. He'd kept himself in decent shape over the years. He could probably scale it with only moderate difficulty.

He decided to share this with his social media followers. He took his phone out and raised it to take a selfie in front of the gated drive for his various social media platforms. He positioned the phone's camera so the drive wound away into the woods behind him. Though he wasn't paranoid by nature, he took care to exclude the warning sign. Also, when he posted it to Hootsuite, he didn't tag his location. Just wrote: *"Thinking of Exploring Later. Should I?"*

He returned his phone to his pocket and unzipped his camera bag to check the Nikon's battery. As he rummaged through the bag, he found himself glancing repeatedly at the winding drive beyond the chain-link fence. Something about it called to him. He didn't know why. He supposed it was because he'd been toying with the idea of adding an "Abandoned Spaces" category to his website. Here was an abandoned building. Almost too convenient to pass up.

Then again, just as he didn't want to get involved with any messy romantic intrigue, he also didn't want to get busted for trespassing. He turned to cross the road and headed to Freivald Hollow, which, according to Aloysuis Baston of the Thaddeus Briar Nature Conservatory, possessed the highest density and most diverse spider population in Clifton Heights. He pushed thoughts of the old spa aside, but despite his best efforts, his mind kept drifting back to the chain-link fence all the way to the hollow.

9.

Ras knelt carefully, one steady hand holding a rock on its side, the other hand tenuously gripping his Nikon, aiming it at the magnificent wolf spider that had been hiding under the rock he'd slowly tilted up. He gently tapped the zoom with his thumb and framed the wolf spider—*Lycosidae*—perfectly. He then thumbed the rapid shutter. The Nikon whirred and clicked as it shuttered away. The wolf spider darted away almost immediately, but Ras felt certain he'd captured several clear shots. He slowly lowered the rock. Paged through the most recent images and saw with great satisfaction he'd indeed gotten several.

As he looked at them, however, he was uncomfortably reminded of the eerie incident in the shower this morning, when—for some unfathomable reason—he'd brushed a wolf spider to its watery death down the shower drain. He still didn't understand his visceral reaction. Sure, his weird nightmare had probably spooked him. Especially because he rarely, if ever, had nightmares. Still, he usually didn't react with such disgust.

Feeling oddly discomfited, Ras brushed the thought aside and straightened. He glanced around, wondering if he wanted to keep shooting or head to lunch. Aloysuis' data had been correct. Freivald's Hollow boasted a wide variety of spider life. He'd already gotten several shots of some interesting orb weavers he hadn't recognized (though they hadn't appeared strange or out of place) and had even discovered a funnel weaver far enough out of his hidey hole to get a good picture. He'd seen another yellow and black orb weaver—slightly different size and shape from the one he'd shot last night—and, of course, several different kinds of wolf spiders. He'd even caught a quick snapshot of what he'd believed was a huntsman spider, but he'd have to check it against Google references later.

Ras turned and was deciding to make his way back to the car when he stopped cold in his tracks. Clinging to the trunk of an Adirondack pine about five feet away—roughly at stomach level—was a gray and black spider which was easily larger than his hand. Larger than the strange spider he'd seen last night. Its thick thorax was gray. Its eight legs were banded in alternating strips of black, gray, white, and tan. Its legs were terribly long. Long enough, almost, to wrap around the young pine's trunk. He felt sure the spider was big enough to engulf his entire hand.

Ras stared at the spider, trying to remain as still as possible. As he had last night (though this had to be his imagination working overdrive), he felt as if it was tracking his movements. Observing him. He felt certain if he tried to raise his camera, he'd never get a shot off in time.

Sure enough, this spider proved even faster than the one last night. Ras hadn't even positioned his finger over the rapid shutter, and the spider darted up the tree trunk. He'd barely lifted the camera. He never had a chance.

Ras stared up at the tree for several heartbeats. No matter how hard he peered, he saw nothing. And of course, he wouldn't. What was he expecting to find? A pulsing egg sac teeming with thousands of baby spiders...

Ras closed his eyes and massaged the bridge of his nose between his thumb and forefinger. He blew out a noisy breath. He didn't get spooked over a bad dream, or seeing a spider in the shower. Hell, he didn't have bad dreams, period. That he felt spooked bothered him, yet he wasn't sure why.

He opened his eyes and looked back up the tree. He'd seen two strange-looking spiders in two days. Spiders he felt quite sure didn't belong in the Adirondacks. He didn't know what to make of it at all. Somehow, he didn't think Aloysuis from the Nature Conservatory would offer any answers. Even if he knew them.

Of course, as much as he knew firsthand about spiders from photographing them over the years, he certainly didn't know everything. He remembered reading an article a few years back about a spider native to China and Korea—a Joro, if he remembered right, a kind of orb-weaver—popping up in Northeast Georgia about seven years ago. According to the article, researchers thought the spider had traveled to the U. S. in shipping containers, nestled in packing materials. They'd quickly spread, becoming an invasive species. Perhaps the same thing had happened here?

But two different species? The biggest cities closest to the Adirondacks—Syracuse and Utica—couldn't have much in the way of shipping traffic, except by tractor-trailer and by train. He supposed it was possible. Even so...

A couple of years ago a story from Upstate New York went viral. About how not one, but two baby alligators were caught in the Susquehanna River, near the small town of Lisle. Purchased as pets and abandoned, they'd grown and thrived on their own, until they'd gotten too big to avoid notice. They were eventually caught and safely relocated to a local animal conservatory. That couldn't have happened here, however. Could it? It didn't make much sense. Spiders from a similar climate surviving in shipping containers and then adapting to a new, but similar climate was one thing. Exotic spiders that didn't belong, surviving Adirondack winters, was another thing altogether.

Ras shook his head as he started back to the car. It was a shame he'd mouthed off to the kid at the conservatory center. Either he could shed some light on this, or he'd be equally interested. Which, of course, made Ras wonder if he indeed had seen a spider tattoo on the kid's wrist, and what it could mean if he had.

Ten minutes later he broke through the tree line and stepped onto Freivald Road. He was about to get into his car when his phone vibrated in his pocket. He pulled it out, swiped the screen, and saw notifications from his various social media platforms. Probably from the selfie he'd taken in front of the spa's gated drive.

He was correct. On Instagram, several hearts and one comment in all caps: YES! EXPLORE DO-EEET. On Twitter, about thirty likes and several re-tweets. On Facebook, about forty likes and ten comments, ranging from similar encouragements to good-natured laments of: "NOOO! WE'LL NEVER SEE YOU AGAIN!"

The last comment on Facebook caught his attention. He frowned and read it again. "Dude, who's the creeper in the background? Spooky." The comment had about twenty reactions to it, all using the shocked-face emoji.

"Creeper? Where?" Ras tapped the picture to enlarge, then zoomed in with several finger-swipes. His breath hitched slightly as he saw, in the background, about halfway up the drive to the abandoned spa, a figure standing in the middle of the drive. Looking at him.

Ras zoomed in more. The picture lost some of its resolution, but he could see the face more clearly. It sent cold ripples across his flesh, a sensation he wasn't used to. There, standing about ten feet away, was a man dressed in jeans and a red/black checkered flannel shirt. Sleeves rolled up to the elbows. At first, Ras thought the man's eyes were black, but when he squinted, he saw the man wearing sunglasses.

The man stood casually. Hands in pockets. The picture wasn't clear enough for Ras to see his expression, but he felt sure the man had been staring at him while he'd taken the selfie. How long had he been standing there? Why hadn't Ras seen him when he'd first pulled up? Was he still around?

Better yet...how had he gotten onto the drive to the spa? Climbed over the fence, as Ras had been considering? Or was there a break in the fencing, somewhere farther back in the woods?

Ras glanced up, crossed the road, and approached the gated drive. He looked as far as he could up it until it twisted away into the woods. He saw nothing. Of course, the man from the photo could be hiding around the curve (but why would he?) and Ras would never see him.

He stood there a few minutes, considering. Wondering if there was anything to worry about. It made sense to dismiss the man as another fellow hiker. Maybe, as he'd speculated, there was a break in the fencing behind the spa. Also, he'd noted himself how easy it would be to scale the fence. Why couldn't someone else do it? Especially someone local, who knew the area better than Ras did. If it was someone local, their interest in a stranger taking pictures made sense.

Even so, Ras still felt a chill creeping along his shoulders as he gazed at the man in the picture. He shook his head, put the phone away, and was about to brush the whole thing off when he noticed something on the metal warning sign he hadn't, before. A series of faint scratches. Done by a jackknife, perhaps.

He stepped closer. Squinted, reached out and touched the scratches with his fingertips and traced them.

It was a spider. He traced the rough approximation of a thorax and body. Each side had four legs. If he let himself imagine, the scratched spider appeared eerily similar to the tattoo on Sandy's wrist.

Ras swore the scratched spider hadn't been there when he'd first arrived. It must've been, though. He'd overlooked it, taking everything in for the first time. Also, when he'd first gotten here, he hadn't stood this close to the sign. Easy to see how he could've missed it.

Still. A part of him—a newly superstitious part he wasn't used to—insisted it hadn't been there when he'd first arrived. Someone (the man in the picture) had etched the spider onto the sign while he'd been taking pictures in the hollow across the road. But why? Was it...a warning?

Ridiculous.

He shoved those thoughts down and turned away from the sign and its scratched-on spider. It had obviously been there and he'd missed it. It wasn't a warning. Only the work of bored juvies with nothing else better to do.

Regardless, he couldn't help glancing in the rearview mirror several times as he drove away.

10.

Hyland's Place
1:00 PM

Despite his resolution to avoid eating at Hyland's Place so he wouldn't risk running into Sandy, Ras decided on the bar for lunch. It was the closest place to eat on his return from Freivald Hollow. Maybe Sandy wasn't a regular at all. Regardless, even if she did coincidentally show up, much of his reservations about her had faded. He wasn't nearly as worried about her, anymore.

As he finished a surprisingly robust fried Haddock sandwich, Ras decided to ask the bartender about the old spa. See if he could get some backstory. His interest in the place still lingered.

As the bartender—a tall, stout, bald man with a fixed scowl—came to collect his dishes, Ras leaped right in. "So. I'm from out of town. Was at Freivald Hollow taking some nature pictures, and I'm curious about the old spa. The one all fenced in? You know anything about it?"

The bartender's scowl deepened, but Ras thought it was more at the mention of the name "Freivald" than anything else. Wiping his hands on his apron, he turned down the bar and said, "Clive Hartley can tell you about that. He knows about everything goes on around here."

The bartender barked at a skinny man with a lined face sitting about four feet down the bar. "Hey, Clive! Why don't you tell this fellow about Omar Freivald's spa?"

The man—Clive—snorted and glanced up from the glass of beer he was nursing. "Omar Freivald. I ain't heard his name in a coon's age."

Ras turned on his stool to better appraise the man. Dressed in drab gray khaki pants, a matching gray khaki long-sleeve shirt with the sleeves rolled up, and a mesh CAT ball cap on his head, Clive Hartley sat on his bar stool as if he'd grown there, a permanent fixture. He sipped from his beer leisurely and said, "Why th' hell you wanna know about it?"

The grizzled man's question—and obvious disdain for the spa—only piqued Ras' interest more. "No reason, I guess. I'm a nature photographer, and I also like abandoned buildings. They intrigue me."

The man—Clive—snorted again. "Thinkin' of sneakin' inside an' takin' pictures? I wouldn't if I was you. Ain't a place for tourists to be pokin' around."

"Why? Because of the possible contamination sign? I'm not a rule breaker, but I gotta admit. It didn't appear official."

"Don' matter. Land's poisoned. Omar Freivald's spa had some bad shit goin' on there, an' the land ain't never been the same."

"How do you mean?" Ras pressed, though carefully, not wanting to repeat his mistake with Aloysuis from the conservatory. "If you don't mind me asking, I mean."

The bartender grunted and crossed his arms over a barrel chest. "He don't mind. If it's one thing Clive Hartley loves to do, it's talk."

Hartley cackled at this and gave the bartender a crooked middle finger. "Fuck you, Malfi," he said casually. To Ras, he said, "Sure, I don' mind tellin' you. Specially if it keeps you away from the damn place."

Hartley sipped his beer and began. "Omar Freivald's Daddy use to own half the businesses in Clifton Heights. They're an old family. Go back to the town's founding. Use'ta have lots of money to play with. Omar, his eldest, got fucked up in Vietnam." He sobered a bit, staring into his beer. "We all got fucked up in Vietnam."

He took a breath and continued. "But he was a tunnel rat. Saw some real fucked up shit. When he got back stateside, he wandered all over the country. Doin' drugs, drinkin' himself blind, messin' with the occult. At least, that's the way the stories go. Anythin' to make the memories stop, y'know? We all medicated in our own ways, I guess.

"Anyway, couple years later, he came home. Said he'd found his inner peace and wanted to share it with his hometown. Was gonna build a health spa for 'holistic healin' of the body an' spirit'," Hartley snorted. "Daddy was just happy his prodigal son had returned, so he backed the idea. Built his son a goddamn spa on the natural springs across from the hollow."

Ras nodded, guessing what happened next. "The whole thing flopped, right? Ruined his family's resources and reputation?"

Hartley waved. "Not right away. Actually did all right first four years or so. Omar's Daddy knew his contractin' an' his construction. Built a real nice place, with wood panelin' inside, and all sorts a finery. And it was the seventies, yeah? That shit was real trendy. But it didn' last, sure enough."

"Why?"

"Omar was fuckin' crazy. Lots of drugs done in there, by everyone. He put drugs in the pool water, in the springs, too. Aromatic shit in the saunas. Fucker was into bath salts years before anyone else." A sip from his beer. "Also, rumors of orgies an' animal sacrifice an' pagan shit started spreadin'. Place started puttin' out a real cult vibe."

"The police shut it down, then?"

"Nope. No one ever caught them doin' shit there. Old man Freivald was good at greasin' the wheels so's folks would look the other way. No, by the time police busted in there, place was abandoned, Omar an' his followers long gone for parts unknown. Never found 'em, neither."

Ras leaned forward, even more intrigued. "What happened?"

"Well, couple local boys decided they wanted to see them orgies up close for themselves."

Ras chuckled. "Of course they did."

"Well, they sneaked out of their houses one night to break into the place. Three days later, they ain't come home. Cops finally got it from the one kid's younger brother what they'd been plannin'. Then they raided the place."

"But they found it empty."

"Hell yes." Another sip of beer. "Empty for weeks. Mebbe months. Found them boys, too. Dead, an' all swollen up. An' covered with spiders. Spiders not from the Adirondacks, let me tell you."

A slight shiver ran down Ras' spine. "What do you mean?"

"Turns out Omar an' his followers had gone off the rails worse'n anyone figured. Goin' through his papers at the spa, cops learned Omar had been buyin' exotic an' poisonous spiders from all over the world, an' bringin' them to the spa. Probably used his military connections to skip customs."

Ras couldn't help but think of the spiders he'd seen. "But why?"

Hartley grinned, and it wasn't a pleasant sight. "'Parently, he an' his followers had taken to lettin' the spiders crawl all over them an' bite them. Cause the venom took 'em to an' 'altered state of consciousness.' Let them see 'the spider god' or some shit."

Ras shivered and experienced a brief flash of irritation at his mounting unease. He wasn't normally prone to falling for theatrics. That's what this was, pure and simple. An old coot with a natural flair for storytelling. "Wow. Quite a story. Is that why it's fenced off? All the drugs in the waters?"

Hartley nodded. "They was never able to find out exactly what drugs he used. Only that the spring waters was fouled, an' they stayed fouled. Lucky it ain't part of our water table, an' it's far away from Clifton Lake an' Black Creek, so it don't affect us none. But they could never get the place clean. Plus," he grinned at Ras again, "there's all them spiders, too."

The bartender snorted, his perma-scowl deepening. "Here it comes. This part's bullshit, so's you know."

Ras glanced between the two men. "What do you mean?"

"Well," Hartley said, "Animal Control came in for those spiders, but they never found 'em all. Not accordin' to Omar's records. So there's always been rumors some of those spiders survived an' started breedin'. They weren't normal spiders, neither. All those drugs changed 'em, somehow. Makin' 'em...different."

A quiet pause, until Ras licked his lips, swallowed down a tight, dry throat, and asked, "Different how?"

Hartley's grin spread. "Just ... different."

"Bullshit," the bartender scoffed.

"Again, Malfi. Fuck you," Hartley said demurely. He gave Ras a penetrating stare. "You're a nature photographer. You see any weird spiders round here so far?"

Ras forced his best poker face. "Not yet," he lied.

"Well then." Hartley turned back to his beer. "You stay clear of there. Place is bad news, whether you believe the stories or not." He glanced up at the bartender. "Even old Malfi'll tell you."

"Uh. Thanks."

"Don't mention it."

That was it. Hartley resumed sipping his beer quietly, apparently dismissing Ras.

Sensing it was time to go, he quietly turned to pay his bill. For all his scowling, even Malfi acted subdued, accepting Ras' payment silently. Ras got up and walked out.

11.

Chestnut Road
2:00 PM

Ras drove slowly back to The Motor Lodge, his mind spinning. A small part of him still felt irritated. How much of Hartley's story could he trust? Old coot could tell a story, sure enough. But the part about Freivald's spiders. Could they have survived the frigid Adirondack winters? Enough to propagate for several generations?

changed, makin' 'em...different.

As Chestnut Road turned into Chestnut Hill on the way back to The Motor Lodge, Ras thought about Sandy's spider tattoo and the one he'd thought he'd seen on Aloysius' wrist. He also thought of the young man's evasive behavior regarding the strange spider Ras photographed last night. And the man lurking behind him in the selfie he'd taken, whom he'd initially believed was a hiker. Hartley had used the phrase "his followers" several times to describe Freivald's spa patrons. Did he mean...

Was Omar Freivald still around?

He'd never been found, according to Hartley. But where had he been? Hiding in the Adirondack wilderness? At the very least, the man would now be in his seventies.

Ras was no spring chicken himself. But he still loved hiking and camping, and sleeping on the ground had never bothered him. Which wasn't the same as living in the wilderness for over forty years, hiding out from the authorities. Freivald would've needed help.

Of course, cults came in handy for those sorts of things. Hiding their leaders in the woods. Stocking them with provisions and supplies. But his "followers" would have to be the same age as he was. Unless he'd recruited more over the years.

Ras snorted and shook his head, amused and disgusted with himself all at once. If by some crazy chance, Omar Freivald still slummed in the woods around Clifton Heights, he was probably nothing more than a drug-addled old man incapable of supporting himself. Any of his "followers" were lost folks without purpose, willing to hang around anyone who gave them the illusion of meaning.

His thoughts faltered when he considered Sandy. If indeed she was part of some weird cult, she hadn't appeared lost or without purpose.

She'd acted confidently, aggressively, with an eerie kind of drive. Aloysuis, on the other hand, was just the type who might get taken in by a cult leader. Sandy, not so much. She was more like...

A leader.

Ras slowed as he neared The Motor Lodge, scoffing at this train of thought. Sandy was nothing more than a consenting adult who'd enjoyed last night and wanted to see him again. Suggesting she had some authority in a cult also suggested last night had been more than a good time. Ridiculous in the extreme.

Ras' thoughts trailed off as he saw a figure standing alongside the road past The Motor Lodge. A figure dressed in black pants; a red-black checkered flannel rolled up to the elbows, and wearing dark glasses. His gray and receding hair was pulled back into a ponytail, and his heavily-lined face was looking at him.

It was the man from the selfie Ras had taken at the hollow. He felt sure. The same man, staring at him...

Something soft tickled his forearm. He glanced down. In doing so, he lifted his foot from the brake. As his car coasted forward into the other lane, he watched hair-thin legs creep around his forearm, bringing a head and thorax into view. It appeared similar to a Huntsman spider, except it...wasn't. The wire-thin legs were the same, but the thorax was strangely bloated and lopsided, unlike any Huntsman spider he'd ever seen. Also, it was oddly colored. A strange mix of orange, yellow, turquoise, and red swathes over its grossly misshapen thorax.

A loud horn blasted. Ras jerked the wheel instinctively to his right, flailing his left hand at the same time, hoping to send the strange spider flying. His car veered out of the opposite lane as a big diesel pick-up truck roared by, horn blasting again. Ras cursed, pulled over onto the shoulder opposite The Motor Lodge, put the car into park, and examined the forearm where he'd seen the bizarre spider.

His forearm was bare. He checked all the way up his arm to his shoulder, going so far as to stick his hand under his shirt and pat around. Nothing there, nor did he feel anything scurrying around. He glanced quickly at the seat next to him, on the floor, already knowing what he was going to find.

The strange spider was long gone, as he somehow knew it would be. Even if he searched the entire car, Ras knew he wouldn't find it. Frantically, he wondered if he'd even seen it in the first place. He'd never been prone to hallucinating (at least, not sober), but after the day he'd had, he was starting to think nothing would surprise him.

Ras took a deep breath and collected himself. He looked up. As he'd also expected, the man he'd seen standing alongside the road was gone, too. He must've retreated into the brush and woods alongside the road. So far as Ras could tell, he hadn't gone up or down the road.

Where the hell was he?

Ras shook his head. "What the fuck," he muttered. "What the fuck is going on?"

Having no answer to this, he glanced both ways, put the car into gear, and pulled into The Motor Lodge's parking lot.

12.

Ras headed straight to the small refrigerator. Opened it, grabbed the bottle of vodka he'd put in there last night, snatched a glass off the counter, and walked into the den. He sat down on the futon, setting the bottle on the coffee table with a dull thunk. He opened it, poured himself a finger, and promptly tossed the whole thing back. He winced at the initial burn, then sighed as a boozy warmth trailed down his throat. He leaned back onto the futon, closed his eyes, and massaged the bridge of his nose.

What should he do? Pack up and leave? Head to Indian Lake early? Considering how weird things were getting, was he crazy to stick around?

Ras didn't consider himself timid. Quite honestly, he was a bit reckless. Even so, he felt a strange uncertainty when it came to Clifton Heights. On the surface, the place was the picture of in-nocent, American-small-town goodness. A Norman Rockwell and Thomas Kinkade painting rolled into one. A quaint little town, homey and welcoming. Yet for some reason, the thought of another encounter with Sandy left him unsettled. And this guy with the black glasses. Who the hell was he?

Of course, Ras had a curious quirk when it came to unsettling things. Instead of running from them, he ran *into* them. To confront them, demystify them, or because he didn't enjoy feeling unsettled. Usually, in his experience, running headlong into your anxieties proved those anxieties to be without substance.

But.

The guy wearing the black glasses was more than his anxiety.

Ras leaned forward and poured himself another finger. He picked it up, leaned back, and sipped it more thoughtfully. He'd pack up some of his things, and then go for a walk on one of the trails he'd scouted before coming here. Take his camera and simply shoot whatever nature offered.

Then, maybe he'd eat dinner at The Skylark and call it an early night. Get some much-needed sleep. He'd pack the rest of his things and head to Indian Lake. Maybe he was being overcautious in avoiding Sandy and getting out of town early. Maybe not. Either way, he wasn't a young sailor on shore leave anymore. He and the enigmatic Sandy had enjoyed a nice time. Better to leave it and move on. If he happened to see the guy in the glasses again? Ras certainly wasn't a brawler anymore, but he could take care of himself.

Ras finished the vodka. He set the glass down and got up to start organizing his camera supplies. Part of him whispered he was ignoring some things and sweeping them under the rug, but he'd worked in Naval Intelligence for over ten years. Sweeping things under the rug had become a way of life.

13.

Boden Hill Trail
Raedeker Park
5:00 PM

After some deliberation, Ras chose Boden Hill from the three trailheads near the entrance of Raedeker Park Zoo. It was the shortest, and it overlooked Owen Pond. He thought it might offer a nice view. Perhaps he'd get some striking sunset photos.

Boden Hill proved to be an easy walk. A smooth incline, it was well-worn and simple to navigate, relatively free of rocks, ruts, and deadfall. On his way, Ras didn't even bother to raise his camera. He merely walked at a leisurely pace, breathing deeply and enjoying the stillness. He felt much calmer, his thoughts more ordered. He had a good plan. Hike to the overlook, take some scenery pictures, eat dinner at The Skylark, hit the sack early, then check out and head to Indian Lake tomorrow morning. All sound and reasonable. His anxieties had fallen quiet, for now.

Twenty minutes later, Boden Hill Trail opened into a large clearing. Ras saw traces of old campfires. To his left, the brush and trees descended into a gentle slope that led down to a hollow. Ford Hollow, he assumed. Beyond the hollow, the blue-green waters of Owen Pond glimmered under the setting sun.

Ras approached the edge and gazed at Owen Pond. He made no move for his camera, content to enjoy the transcendence of the sunlight reflecting off Owen Pond. Coming up the trail in the evening had been the right choice.

Ras eventually pulled out his iPhone, turned, and snapped another selfie with the pond in the background. He cross-posted the picture to Hootsuite, writing: "Nature's Finest." He pocketed his phone, uncapped his Nikon (which was hanging from his neck), and started shooting.

He took several wide angles of the pond. Shots of the sun setting over the trees. Close-ups of the tree line past the far shore. Shots of a small promontory with a tall Adirondack pine jutting up from it. He'd snapped several shots of a small island in the middle of the pond and was aiming the camera at the near shore (about a hundred yards away) when he stopped and sucked in a breath.

At the bottom of the slope stood a man. Through the Nikon's high-powered lens, Ras saw the most detail yet. The same black pants and red/black checkered shirt with its sleeves rolled up to the elbow. A thin face lined by age and weathered by time and the elements. The man's gray hair was pulled back into a long ponytail and was receding at the temples. He wore the same tinted glasses as before. This time, Ras could see the man's facial expression clearly.

He was smiling. Content, satisfied, knowing. Almost serene. As Ras stared at the man through the camera's lens finder, the man tilted his head in greeting.

Before Ras could think or move, he heard a chittering behind him. A familiar sound, one he knew well. He turned. Sure enough, a large gray squirrel sat up at the edge of the clearing, on its hind legs. Head darting back and forth. Ras had no way of knowing for certain, but it appeared to be in distress.

It chittered again.

Dropped onto all fours. Stepped in one direction, sniffed, and hesitated. It turned the other way. Tail twitching, as if ready to flee…

A pile of leaves scattered. The longest insectile legs Ras had ever seen reached for the squirrel's hindquarters. As the squirrel squealed in animal terror, an impossibly large spider leaped out of the hole that had been concealed by the leaves. It pounced on the squirrel. The poor animal stiffened. Before Ras could even think, the gigantic spider dragged the squirrel back into the hole it'd sprung from, out of sight.

Ras stared, mind racing. The spider—*fucking huge spider bigger than my goddamn foot*—had behaved like a trap-door spider. It had dug a hole. Hid inside, then pulled leaves over itself, and waited for its prey. Its prey being a fucking squirrel. But trapdoor spiders didn't get that big. NO spider got that big. Not even the Goliath Birdeater from Australia, or the Giant Huntsman from Europe.

He stared at the spot for several heartbeats. Took a deep breath, and slowly approached the spot where the squirrel had disappeared. Feeling a cold unease, Ras peered down a hole much bigger than he'd originally thought.

He saw the tip of the squirrel's tail, about four inches deep. It twitched and spasmed. Despite his best efforts, Ras couldn't help but think of the spider's fangs, sunk deep into the squirrel, pumping it full of paralyzing venom, preparing to store it for feeding. It was what spiders do. It was natural. It shouldn't repulse him so deeply. But it did, because spiders shouldn't be this big. They shouldn't be snatching fucking squirrels. It was wrong. Out of balance with nature, instead of being part of it.

The doomed rodent's tail twitched once more. Then, it vanished into the darkness, as the spider dragged it deeper into the hole. From his informal studies, he knew trapdoor spiders dug surprisingly deep burrows. He couldn't imagine how deep this one had dug, given its size.

A heartbeat later, the spider scuttled back into view, startling Ras into a yelp. Part of his mind insisted this was normal behavior. It had stored the squirrel deep in its burrow, and now it would wait for him to leave so it could re-camouflage itself with leaves...

Wait for him.

For him.

Ras backed away from the hole. Backpedaled several feet then turned and walked stiffly for the trail leading back down to Raedeker Park. He didn't feel ashamed of his haste. He focused on putting as much distance between himself and the freakishly huge spider. He gave no thought to the man he'd seen on the shore of Owen Pond. The same man he'd seen twice already today. The man who'd nodded at him. Ras wouldn't even think about him until well on the way back to his cabin.

14.

The closer Ras got to The Motor Lodge, the more convinced he became his time in Clifton Heights had come to an end. He felt ready to move on to Indian Lake, and then eventually Lake George. He saw no reason to wait until tomorrow morning. Enough was enough. He'd seen that strange man (Omar Freivald? Was it even possible?) three fucking times in one day. Once, near his lodgings. He was being stalked.

It didn't frighten Ras. It alarmed him and angered him. Everything felt like a huge setup. From Sandy to Hartley's wild tale. Did Sandy and

Aloysuis have the same spider tattoo on their wrists? Who knew; who cared? He was being toyed with. He didn't enjoy it. At all.

He was leaving. He'd pack his things and wouldn't bother checking out. He'd call The Motor Lodge's office when he checked into a place in Indian Lake.

He told himself he wasn't scared. Wasn't scared of seeing Sandy again, or scared of running into the guy in black glasses. He was pissed off, and he didn't know how he'd act or what he'd do if he did run into either of them. He told himself this, and it felt true.

Mostly.

When he pulled into The Motor Lodge's parking lot, however, something fluttered in his gut, undercutting the hot anger inside, and cooling it considerably. Rising from the Adirondack chair on his cabin's front porch was Sandy. She smiled, free and easy, and descended from the front porch and approached him, as he shut his car off and got out.

15.

"Well, I gotta be honest," Sandy said with a genuine-sounding chagrin, "'What the fuck are you doing here?' was not the greeting I expected."

Ras winced slightly, embarrassed at what he'd blurted upon exiting his car. He unlocked the cabin door, and—though he wasn't sure it was a good idea—held it open for Sandy, gesturing her inside. She didn't enter, however. Only folded her arms, gave him an arch expression, and said with a mischievous smile, "Dunno. Don't exactly feel welcome, at the moment."

Ras knew he should tell her to fuck off and leave. If there was some sort of fucked-up spider cult in Clifton Heights, some remnants of Omar Freivald's freaky spa crew from the 70s, and if Freivald was—impossibly enough—still around pulling strings, Ras needed to leave town, now. He'd attracted their attention, which was bad. He was kicking himself for reacting so slowly. He'd seen it often enough in his military career. Sandy was the bait and switch. They wanted him on the hook, either as a new cult member or someone they could fleece for cash. Regardless, the safest thing was to tell her to piss off and slam the door in her face. Get packing, and get out, now.

Instead, he felt oddly ashamed of his knee-jerk reaction. With good reason, he supposed. He got as mad as anyone else, but usually, he didn't blow up at people. For some reason, he felt the need to make amends before leaving.

"It's been a weird day," he said, doing his best to keep his voice level, "I'm tired and out of sorts."

Her features softened. She nodded. "Fair enough." As she accepted his invitation and walked past him, into the cabin, her smile brightened as she eyed him speculatively. "Will I see you at Hyland's Place tonight?"

Despite a mounting urgency to get out of Clifton Heights, Ras experienced a momentary twinge of regret. He flickered a weak smile. "I'd love to, but I need to get on the road." He waved, feeling oddly meek, and hating every minute of it. "Think I'm gonna pack up and head over to Indian Lake for a few days."

Sandy wrinkled her nose as if she smelled something sour. "Indian Lake? Yuck. Nowheresville, USA. Nothing but a rundown town with closed stores. Can't imagine you'll find anything interesting to shoot over there. Don't even know if you'll find a place to stay."

Ras shrugged as he moved toward the bedroom. "I've read they have a robust population of black and yellow orb weavers," he said, which was true. "They're my favorite kind of spider, honestly. Also, pictures of those sell well on the website. Lots of people tend to attach memories of childhood summers to them."

All this was true, and the real reason why Indian Lake was his next stop. Even so, as he hauled his suitcase (which felt oddly heavy with a weirdly shifting weight) out of the small closet and onto the bed, he knew it was an excuse. He was engaging in small talk so he could pack and slip away without Sandy trying to stop him, though he couldn't imagine what she could do to stop him, even if she wanted.

"Even so," Sandy argued as she followed him into the bedroom, "Indian Lake is only an hour away. You could drive out there tomorrow, spend the day there, then come back here."

"I suppose," he admitted reluctantly as he unzipped his suitcase, knowing what she was doing, "but I prefer to use the area's natural lighting, which is easier to time when I don't have an hour drive there and back..."

He flipped open the suitcase.

And staggered back with a cry. His shaking hands up. His heart freezing and stomach clenching at the teeming mass of small, black, hairy spiders pulsing inside his suitcase. Wriggling, twitching, and scuttling over each other. A mass of hairy black legs, all moving as one, bristling...

Before he could turn, Sandy's hand clamped on the base of his neck from behind. On the other side of his neck, he felt a lightning-quick poke, a jabbing pinch. A needle's cold, metallic sting. An icy fire spread from the prick. Within seconds, Ras felt his muscles seize. His throat tightened. It didn't close entirely and he could still breathe, but he couldn't speak, or utter a sound, at all. He couldn't move, either. He stood there, joints locked, muscles twitching, his whole body throbbing with a dull ache.

He felt Sandy's warm breath as she pressed her lips to his right ear. "Sorry, sweetheart. You're not going anywhere."

She bit his earlobe playfully. Placed both hands on his shoulders, and slowly turned his frozen body around so he faced her. Bizarrely, Ras felt himself greatly aroused at the sight of her. To his horrified surprise, he felt himself stiffening into an unwanted—and yet incredibly painful—erection.

She snuggled up to him and teasingly, ran her hand over the jutting bulge at his crotch. Waves of confusing pleasure mixed with pain pulsed throughout his body. "Did you know," she said, lips curling into an almost sinister smile, "one of the side effects of a Brazilian Wandering Spider's venom is prolonged, sometimes painful erections in men? As you can imagine, that particular little fellow was in high demand back in the heyday of Freivald's spa."

She reached down and deftly plucked a spider from the teeming mass in his suitcase. She held it up before him, pinching its thorax between her fingers. Its legs flailed.

"Did you also know," she said softly, "that the dangerous venom of a black funnel spider isn't harmful if you eat it?"

In a flash, and to Ras' horror, the furry black spider disappeared into her mouth. She snapped her jaws shut, crunched three times, and swallowed. A satisfied smile spread. The expression of someone who'd eaten a favorite treat. "Even the most venomous spider isn't harmful if you can manage to eat it before it bites you. Your stomach acids neutralize the spider's toxins, rendering them harmless. The worst thing you might suffer is heartburn. Of course, the trick is getting it down before it can bite your tongue or the inside of your mouth."

She produced the hypodermic needle she'd pricked him with. "Thanks to our stomach acids, ingested spider venom has no effect. Spider venom harvested, distilled, and purified, however. Powerful stuff."

She brandished the needle. "Spider venom blocks nerve impulses to the muscles. Causing cramps and rigidity. Also, it overstimulates the production of the neurotransmitters acetylcholine and norepinephrine. This causes a temporary paralysis of your nervous system. It's how spiders paralyze their food."

Sandy produced a slim black pouch from her back pocket. Unzipped it, unscrewed the needle from the hypodermic syringe, stored them both in the pouch, zipped it up, and returned it to her pocket. She talked all the while.

"This is a heady cocktail. Consists of venom harvested from a black and red widow spider, a brown widow spider, a cobalt tarantula, funnel spiders, and—as your fantastic boner can attest to—a Brazilian Wandering Spider." She eyed him lasciviously. "And don't worry, we are not letting that go to waste."

The pouch stored away, Sandy brushed her hands and placed them on her hips, as if she were discussing the weather. "It took Freivald's bootleg chemists a while to get the mix right. Had to get rid of the toxins which cause tissue necrosis. Didn't want those. Only the paralysis, and, of course," she stepped close and squeezed his painfully engorged member through his jeans, "the aphrodisiacal results."

"Now," she said, slowly unbuttoning her blouse, "we get to have some fun. As I said, I want more. But it's not just fun. It's an invocation of the great Atlach-Nacha, the Old One who lives in the Void and spins our destinies. Last night was merely the preparation. Tonight, we call Him forth, and invite Him in."

Sandy's blouse dropped to the floor. She smoothly slipped out of her bra, setting her breasts free. Unzipped her pants, and with little ceremony pulled them and her panties down, until she kicked them to the side. A confusing wave of sensations buffeted Ras. Fear, and revulsion. However, there was also his insane (and painful) throbbing erection, only made more painful (and pleasurable) by the sight of Sandy's naked form. When she stepped close, she unzipped his pants, stuck her hands inside, and tugged his erection free. This only made him harder, as she grasped it and started stroking. Her skin felt silky smooth, and each stroke sent painful yet mind-numbingly wonderful pulses of electric heat throughout his whole body.

She pressed close, breasts and erect nipples pressing against his chest. Even through his shirt, the contact set him on fire. She gazed deep into his eyes as she slowly continued to stroke him and began speaking strange, guttural words. A chant, or a prayer, or a song, though the words didn't sound human, at all. He did catch one phrase repeated, over and over. Ia, Ia, Atlach-Nacha, fhatgn!

With each stroke the pain and pleasure intensified, fracturing his thoughts into incoherent splinters. With her free hand, she unbuttoned his flannel shirt and pulled it off. Pressed her free hand against his naked chest. Pushed him backward. Helpless and paralyzed, he couldn't resist, even if he wanted to...and he no longer did, as he fell with her, back onto the bed.

Onto the suitcase, still teeming with black funnel spiders.

He knew he should feel fear and revulsion at the sensation of hundreds, perhaps thousands of small spiders scuttling about under his body and around him, their legs and bodies brushing against his skin, but even as they swarmed up his neck and over his arms and started scuttling across his bare chest, he felt nothing but the glowing and painful lust burning in his core. All he could do was stare at Sandy's awesome beauty as she crawled onto the bed and mounted his unbelievably erect and throbbing member.

She started riding him. Slowly, at first. Hips rocking back and forth, sex latched onto him tighter than he'd ever felt before. Quickly enough, she began to pump harder and faster. Goading him closer to a climax Ras found himself silently begging for, but also fearing, because of the pain which wound its way through his mounting pleasure.

However, as she fucked him, the spiders crawled all over his arms and legs and began to crawl up her, as they fucked in a mass of teeming and bristling spiders, as Sandy kept screaming *Ia, Ia, Atlach-Nacha!* over and over, Ras realized he didn't care if the orgasm killed him. He needed release. If it ended with a stroke, a heart attack, or a seizure, so be it. So long as the release finally came.

She never slowed. Kept bucking and took him straight past the point of no return. When he finally came, his body bucked so powerfully—despite his venom-induced paralysis—he arched his back and lifted her off the bed with his hips. His cramping muscles screamed in agonizing pleasure. He kept thrusting upward and coming forever. She threw her head back and cried out, and the overwhelming pain and pleasure sent Ras hurtling into a black and all-consuming oblivion.

Before he lost consciousness, however, he saw something that filled him with cold fear and drove every ounce of pleasure from his body, though the venom kept his member rigid as Sandy bucked her sex up and down it. As Sandy bent forward and opened her mouth, mandibles spread, exposing dripping fangs. She had more than two eyes; she had six of them. Madly glittering, opening and shutting across a bristling, misshapen face.

Ras tried to scream. All he could manage was a dry croak. Mercifully, darkness fell as her horrible face descended upon him.

16.

He's at his grandparents' house. Standing at the base of the stairs leading to the attic. One of his favorite toys lives there. Yes, lives, because he believes his toys come alive. They have personalities. They have wills. They dream as he's dreaming now. After all the hours he's spent gleefully riding his Radio Flyer Rocking Horse, he's convinced himself it loves him as much as he loves it.

This moment is always fraught with anticipation. When he asks his grandparents' permission to play in the attic. They smile indulgently and say, "Of course." He stands at the foot of the stairs for a moment. Thinking of all the prairies he will ride. All the outlaws he'll chase down. He is only limited by his imagination, and his imagination knows no bounds.

However, something feels wrong this time. He doesn't remember asking his grandparents' permission. In fact, they're sitting at the kitchen table, his grandfather reading the newspaper, his grandmother sewing, both of them ignoring him.

Also, he's not filled with his usual breathless anticipation. Rather, his heart pounds to the beat of something far different. Something dark and cold. Fear. He fears what's waiting for him in the attic because something has changed. Something is wrong with his Radio Flyer Rocking Horse, and...

A heavy body slams against the closed attic door from the other side. Hard enough to send vibrations rippling down the stairs, and through the floor underneath his feet. It slams against the door again. And again. Now it presses against the door, and Ras' breath hitches and his stomach lurches as the door bends out of the doorframe, as if it were made of rubber, as wood creaks and groans.

He wants to run but can't. Wants to turn and shout to his grandparents for help, but his voice is stuck in his throat, which is closed tight. His neck feels frozen. Bladder twitching. It lets go. As urine runs down the inside of his legs, he hyperventilates and his heart pounds to the tune of the thing crashing against the attic door.

A soul-shuddering smash and the door slams open, the doorknob banging against the wall. Silence falls. All Ras hears is the thudding of his heart and his breath roaring in his ears. A swirling darkness fills the attic doorway, ink-black and impenetrable. There's nothing to see. For the briefest of moments, Ras wonders if he's somehow been spared the wrath of what waits for him in the dark...

He sees them.

Clustered together. Something about the image doesn't make sense. Doesn't fit. It's not natural. Deep inside, however, he knows what they are.

Eyes, gazing at him.

A shape protrudes from the darkness, probing the first step. An all-too-recognizable, bristling, fuzzy shape. A foreleg. A nerve-jangling hysteria fills Ras, but he still can't move. All he can do is stand and watch as more bristling black and fuzzy legs emerge from the darkness. Touching the first step. The walls, the ceiling, the railing. Legs, testing the air.

A low, sibilant hiss leaks from the darkness. The rest of the thing clambers into view as it scuttles out through the attic door.

Ras stares, his mind blank and stuttering because he can't make any sense of what he's seeing. It appears too big for the attic door, too big to fit in the cramped stairwell, and yet it does. It does and it sits and glares at him, its six eyes blinking.

It's his Radio Flyer Rocking Horse.

But it's not.

It doesn't have four legs frozen in an eternal prance, and four metal legs steadying it on the floor. It has eight massive, bristling, grossly misshapen tarantula's legs. Too big for the stairwell, but still it scuttles down the steps toward him, those abominable tarantula's legs scuffing the steps and walls and even the ceiling with a hairy rustling.

Its body—a hideous cross between spider and horse—pulses with some malevolent heartbeat as it descends. On its thick neck is a horse's head, but one drawn by a lunatic, or fashioned by a mad god. Its six eyes glitter madly. In place of a mouth, grossly oversized mandibles snap, tips glistening with venom.

It continues to scuttle jerkily down the steps, this spider-horse, a ludicrous description which somehow is still terrifying. As it looms closer,

Ras sees someone on its back. Riding it, as Ras himself has ridden his beloved Radio Flyer Rocking Horse for hours on end.

With a gigantic heave, the spider-horse leaps the rest of the way to the bottom of the stairs. It lands before Ras with a sickening squelch. With a shrieking hiss, the spider-horse rears back on its hind legs, its forelegs splayed wide. It hisses again, and then its forelegs slam down with a shuddering boom. The thing scuttles toward him and then halts, mandibles splayed, fangs poised.

The spider-horse's rider dismounts smoothly and stands next to the grotesquely mutated horse's head. The man is dressed in black pants and a red/black checkered flannel shirt rolled up to the elbows. His graying hair is pulled back into a ponytail. He wears black glasses, and his heavily lined face smiles at Ras.

"I first saw Atlach-Nacha in the Củ Chi tunnels in Vietnam," Omar Freivald says in a hoarse whisper. "I was a tunnel rat. My job was to clear the Viet Cong's tunnels. Flush the bastards out. But one time, as I was crawling through a tunnel, I was attacked by a swarm of tarantulas. It wasn't uncommon to come across a few. Part of the job. But this wasn't normal. This was...unnatural. Dozens upon dozens of tarantulas swarming out of nowhere. Crawling all over me. Biting me. Poisoning me."

Freivald shakes his head. "Later, the infirmary doctors couldn't believe it, surprised I survived. But years later, I understood why. Those weren't any ordinary tarantulas." Freivald smiles beatifically. "They were His children. The Spiders of Leng. And they were preparing me to see Him."

The monstrous spider-horse makes a ghastly chuffing sound. Freivald pats its blasphemous head and continues. "When I finally pushed through those spiders in panic and cleared the tunnel, I didn't see a

VC barracks. Instead, I saw a vast, black abyss. Cavern walls stretching downward into darkness. Walls teeming with spiders clambering over each other. And in that cavernous abyss, suspended in the middle of its infinite web, I saw Him. Sitting, watching, waiting. His bulk indefinable and grotesquely wonderful. His eight legs impossibly long,"

"As I teetered there, twitching from dozens of spider bites, I gazed upon Him. He lifted his head, and with a strangely human face, looked at me. He saw me. The Spinner in the Darkness. The Spider King. Atlach-Nacha. He saw me, and He knew me."

Freivald takes off his glasses and smiles. Cold horror flushes through Ras as he sees not two eyes, but six. Two rows of three eyes, glittering at him. "He sees you, Ras," Freivald whispers. "He sees you, and he knows you. Run, Ras. Run. Atlach-Natcha prefers to chase His kill."

Freivald reaches for him. Mouth spreading wide, as grotesque mandibles unfold and spread. Ras wants to scream, wants to run and hide, but he can't, he's frozen as Freivald's mandibles stretch and grow and grow, poised above him to strike...

17.

Ras jerked awake, covered in sweat, his chest pounding, breath roaring in his ears. He felt feverish and weak; but at the same time, adrenaline pulsed through him, making him jittery. He was lying on his back, not on his bed, or...

on a suitcase full of teeming black spiders

...but on a gritty, tile floor. He blinked several times, astonished to see the hazy light of morning. He covered his face with his hands. Breathed deeply and rubbed his temples with his fingertips. His head throbbed with a dull, distant ache. He felt awful. Of course, who knows what Sandy had really dosed him with before they'd...

fucked on a suitcase full of spiders

Shit.

Had that happened? Or was it a hallucination from the drugs, or spider venom, or whatever? And that fucking dream. Of his beloved Radio Flyer Rocking Horse turned into a fucking spider, and Omar Freivald riding it, telling some insane story about Atlach-Nacha and the Spiders of Leng...

wasn't a dream

it was a vision

Ras breathed once more. Probed his temples with his fingertips again, trying to massage away the ache. He uncovered his face, and pushed himself upright, into a sitting position. He tried to piece together his fragmented memory. The last thing he remembered clearly was Sandy jabbing him in the neck with a needle and injecting him with something. After was nothing but a mix of jumbled images, a strange mix of the terrifying and the erotic...

Still sitting, Ras glanced around. To his right, he saw a check-in desk. Behind him, a wide flight of stairs led to the next level. In front of him, were several doors with narrow, rectangle windows. It was the lobby of sorts, for...

A spa.

An abandoned spa.

"Son of a bitch," he whispered. Ras shakily stood, knees buckling slightly. Grit crunched under his shoes. He realized gratefully he was fully clothed. The spa lay in a deep silence, the only sound being his feet on the littered floor.

He took a deep breath and examined the lobby, which was only lit by the sunlight coming through the narrow rectangular windows in the front doors, and from the second floor, where there must be bigger windows. He cracked his neck, head still aching, though he felt clear and sober. He still felt a little unsteady, but he thought whatever Sandy had dosed him with last night had largely worn off. Despite the weakness in his knees, his headache, and a general ache all over, he should be able to walk out to Bassler Road, at least. If he could get out of here.

First, he should try and call someone. He checked his pocket for his phone and found it empty. With a sinking feeling, he checked all his pockets. He found them the same. No phone, no wallet, no car keys, and no cabin key. Pockets completely empty.

Anger kindled in his belly. "Fuck," he whispered. He'd been robbed. Pure and simple. All his ridiculous notions about a spider cult run by the mysterious Omar Freivald, and Sandy seducing him into it, were bullshit. She'd seduced him, all right. Then she—and whoever the hell the guy with glasses was—had robbed him, then dumped him here. Who knows, maybe Hartley was in on it. Maybe he set up rubes with those crazy stories about Freivald. He imagined Sandy, the guy in the sunglasses, and Hartley ransacking his cabin, and got even angrier.

Spurred on by his frustration and his anger, Ras stalked to the front doors. Hazy morning light filtered through the narrow windows. When he reached them, he tugged experimentally on the handles and found each door locked. He was trapped. Wasn't getting out this way.

An icy ball of dread formed in his guts. He knew nothing about Clifton Heights. The fencing around the old spa and the warning sign took on a new, disturbing meaning. Maybe this is where victims got left. Maybe every now and then, a small group of people—Sandy, the guy in the sunglasses, Hartley, a dirty cop—identified a new mark in town. Someone they'd lure in, drug, rob, and then leave in the gated abandoned spa outside town. If he searched the building, would he find the remains of others?

Ras tugged on the doorhandle one last time in vain while peering out the door's rectangle window. The glass was wire-reinforced. Even if he could break it, he'd never be able to crawl through.

Movement down the drive caught his gaze.

It was the man he'd seen all day yesterday. Standing in the middle of the drive. Wearing black pants. Red/black checkered flannel shirt, sleeves rolled up to the elbows, hands in his pockets. Dark glasses and graying hair pulled back into a ponytail. Staring placidly at the building.

For a moment, Ras' hallucination of the man having two rows of three eyes flashed in his head, but his blossoming anger pushed the image away. "Hey!" He pounded on the door with his fist, yanking on the unyielding handle with the other hand. "Hey, you motherfucker! Let me the fuck out of here, you crazy bastard!"

Ras couldn't tell if the man heard, but he thought maybe so. The man in the dark glasses (Omar Freivald? Who the fuck knew?) smiled slightly and nodded. He didn't speak. Merely nodded once more, then turned and walked slowly down the drive, away. In minutes, he disappeared around the bend.

Ras jerked on the door once more. "Motherfucker!" He turned away, anger blazing inside. He desperately fought for a sense of equilibrium, so he could assess the situation calmly, and get himself the fuck out of this mess. He was going to get out. When he did, he would track down Sandy, Hartley, or this guy in the dark glasses, and...

Even amid his rage, a cold terror had blossomed in his belly. Throughout his Naval career, he'd heard stories of similar things happening to American tourists in foreign countries, or lonely Seamen on shore leave. Folks who had wandered off on their own, and got waylaid by the locals, never heard from again. Alive, anyway.

It had never happened to anyone he knew, of course. The stories always came third-hand as cautionary tales from Chief Petty Officers before shore leave. Better not get blind drunk, or go off alone with a hooker. Don't know where you might wake. Or if you'd wake up at all.

"Fuck that," he whispered as he surveyed the lobby and the short flight of steps which led to the second floor. "I'm getting out of here, even if I have to jump through a fucking window or climb down a fucking tree."

Ras began a cursory examination of the lobby. Bypassing the stairs first, he checked the doors on either side of the stairs. Both were locked, also. Behind the front desk was a door, but it was locked, too. Which left the stairs to the second floor, which Ras hoped might prove more fruitful, based on the gray haze of light coming down the steps. He hoped it meant bigger windows he could break and crawl out of. Hopefully, the second floor wasn't too high off the ground, but still. Jump or climb, he was getting the fuck out of here.

With this resolve, Ras trotted up the stairs, a desperate energy pulsing through him. When he reached the top of the stairs and turned left, however, toward the source of the light, he skidded to a stop and gasped. His resolve faltered, replaced by a fear colder than anything he'd felt before.

The hallway ahead was indeed windowed, on its left side. However, the hallway was a phalanx of dense, interconnecting spider webs. One gigantic network of gossamer filaments, so dense it filtered the sunlight into the gray haze he'd seen spilling down the stairs. The webs almost glowed, iridescent in the sun's rays.

Ras had never seen anything like it. The webs were thick, layered, and interconnected. Also, filled with spiders of all kinds and shapes. Some content to hang motionless in the webbing. Others, crawling back and forth. Some at measured paces, others darting quickly. Some were impossibly large. Larger even than the one that had killed the squirrel last night. These either crawled along the floor or lay motionless on the windowsills.

Such a collection of spiders in one area wasn't just unlikely. It was impossible. Unnatural. Yet here he stood, staring at an entire hallway filled with nothing but spider webs and spiders. Which wasn't even the worst part. Far more terrible than the impossible spider web tunnel were the multitudes of dried husks suspended in the webs and wrapped in webs. Small to medium-sized masses. Some the size of birds, mice, squirrels...some, the size of a small dog or a raccoon or a fox, and even worse...

Human-sized shapes.

Human remains. At least ten, hanging throughout the webbed hallway. Transfixed by this gut-churning discovery, Ras slowly approached the edge of the webbing to get a closer look at the nearest human-sized mass. It wore fairly contemporary clothing, not much different from his. Though he had no way of knowing, he didn't think it had been here more than ten years.

Unlike the other human-sized masses, this one wasn't wrapped completely in webbing. Its head and face were visible through several thin layers of webs. Ras saw with muted horror the skin and muscle tissue had dried to the consistency of parchment paper against the skull. As if something had drained every drop of essential fluid from it. Several somethings, or one impossibly large something. As a spider would.

He sees you, too.

Ras refused to believe that. He couldn't. He had to believe this tunnel of webbing because it was tangible and visible. He thought it was clear what happened to this corpse, and all the others, considering they were in the hall with the wide windowpanes. Past victims of Sandy's scam, they'd also probably tried for the windows after they'd been drugged and locked in here. They'd thought as Ras had. Get out through the windows. However, they must've either not known anything about spiders or thought they could get through the webbing to the windows in time. They hadn't been able to, obviously. Whatever toxins these spiders carried...

drugs...makin' 'em different

...had obviously proved fatal. Here they were—ten, if Ras counted correctly—suspended in webbing. Given the unfathomable number of spiders here, they must've all fed on the bodies, as they would've fed on anything caught in its webs.

A question occurred to him, one which chilled him even further. These ten people had been desperate enough to try and escape through a hallway of webbing full of unknown species of spiders. What had made them so desperate? What could've possibly forced them down this hall?

Ras was about to turn away when a glint of silver in the webbing covering the corpse caught his attention. He dared a step closer, narrowing his eyes. The corpse's skeletal hands were clenched in tight fists as if they'd been gripped in a seizure at its death. The sliver glint came from the nearest hand, which poked out of the webbing. Peering closer, he saw what it was.

A lighter.

To ward off spiders? Burn a path through the webbing to the windows? Ras could see the merit but also imagined a mere lighter wouldn't have been enough. Even so, the idea of having fire at his disposal was an attractive one. Before he even knew what he was doing, Ras found himself reaching for the web-covered, desiccated hand. He grasped the lighter's exposed edge between two fingers, and gently tried to tug it free.

Vibrations tremored through the webbing, up the length of the corpse. Something fat and hairy, the size of Ras' hand, crawled lightning-quick out of the corpse's gaping mouth to perch menacingly on its chin. A reddish-gray spider, similar to a tarantula. Alerted by Ras trying to pull the lighter free, no doubt.

"Shit," Ras muttered, tugging on the lighter harder, which was proving surprisingly difficult to remove from the corpse's grip. "Shit, shit, shit."

He tugged harder. The lighter came halfway, then got stuck. The webbing shivered again. In a heartbeat, the spider scuttled down the shriveled corpse's web-sheathed shoulder toward Ras. Revulsion and adrenaline pulsed through him. "Fuck," he muttered and gave up trying to be gentle. He yanked the lighter with all his weight.

With a sickening crack, the lighter didn't come free...the hand holding it did. Ras stumbled backward, nearly falling, but somehow he managed to maintain his balance. He backpedaled away quickly, about ten feet.

The reddish-gray spider stopped at the corpse's wrist, where its hand used to be. Though Ras knew the vibrations had attracted the spider, he couldn't help attributing malicious intent to the arachnid. Couldn't help imagining it watching him flee. Waiting for his next move. He didn't think spiders could see far away. But nothing about the spiders he'd encountered in the last two days had been as they were supposed to be.

About fifteen feet away, Ras slowed and came to a stop. He took a deep breath and felt himself relaxing, especially with the thought of having a lighter at his disposal...when he felt them, crawling all over his hand.

He looked down. A jolt of fear pulsed through him. Dozens of the tiniest spiders he'd ever seen were swarming from the inside of the skeleton's hand out onto his, and spreading up his wrist. Bright red, and the size of fire ants, their itching touch was maddening. A manic frenzy consumed Ras as he unabashedly shrieked and cursed, frantically swiping the tiny red spiders off with his other hand. All the while, still clutching the skeletal hand, desperate not to lose the lighter.

Still, the tiny spiders kept coming. Finally, with an animal bellow, Ras threw the hand down and stomped on it. Brittle bone and dried flesh crunched into dust. He kicked the lighter—now free—to his left, away from the crushed remains, and the spiders which now spread in all directions. He strode away quickly, frantically swiping his hand and stomping his feet.

He felt himself unraveling. Deep inside, he felt the wall separating him from blind hysteria tremble slightly. Not much of a poetry reader, he did remember one line from a poem he'd read in junior college, years ago. "Things fall apart; the center cannot hold." Things weren't falling apart yet, but he wasn't sure how much longer his center was going to hold.

Several feet away from the remains of the corpse's hand, Ras finally stopped and took a deep breath. Turning his hand over and over, he didn't see any more red spiders, nor did he feel them. He bent over and brushed his pant legs and stomped both feet for good measure. Finally, when he was relatively sure nothing was crawling around under his clothes, he bent over and scooped up the hard-won lighter off the floor.

He stood. Took another breath, not daring to think the lighter wouldn't work, after all. "Here goes," he muttered. He flicked the top off and spun the lighter's wheel with his thumb.

He nearly shouted in joy when a vibrant orange lick of flame shot up and burned bright and pure. He snapped it shut right away because he had no idea how much fuel it had left. He needed to save it and use it carefully.

A gentle lapping sound caught his attention. To his right, Ras saw what had once been a giant observation window, now reduced to jagged shards poking out of a frame. He stepped carefully toward the opening and peered through it, down into a large, dark, cavernous space. He couldn't tell how large the space was. But he distinctly heard water rippling. Far across the dark expanse, he saw a rectangle of light. Through the rectangle, he glimpsed green undergrowth and a tree trunk.

An open door.

A way out.

But how to get down there?

Ras walked away from the webbed hallway past the observation window. On the wall, he could still read faded printing and arrows. An arrow pointed back toward the webbed hall, and next to it, he read:

"Yoga, Mediation, Acupuncture, Massage." Another arrow pointed in the direction he was heading, and next to it: "Pool, Spa, and Sauna."

Ras glanced ahead. About twenty feet away, the hall ended at a corner. Though it was darker there, he could still read on the wall, next to an arrow pointing down, around the corner: "Pool, Spa, and Sauna." Downstairs. Where the pool must be. The lapping water he'd heard. Across the pool area, an open door led outside.

Ras stood, momentarily paralyzed by his choices. A bizarre, webbed hallway filled with unnatural and venomous spiders, or stairs that descended into the unknown, where anything could be hiding.

Reluctantly, Ras pulled the lighter from his pocket. He'd only use it when he couldn't see. He cautiously approached the corner, leaving the phalanx of webbing and spiders behind him. Before the stairs, he saw a slightly open door right before it, marked MAINTE-NANCE, but decided not to explore it for now.

As Ras walked, he told himself the soft crunching he heard was from his footsteps on the gritty floor, and not the reddish-gray spider scuttling up from behind.

18.

The flight of steps led to a landing, turned right, and descended again. This time into an inky, dark murk. The landing sat in the early morning sunlight, which leaked through a dusty, narrow window high in the wall. Ras paused there and inspected his surroundings, telling himself he wasn't afraid of the steps descending into darkness. Not at all. He was only catching his breath.

Multi-colored graffiti covered the walls, but it wasn't the sloppy work of kids sneaking around. The designs painted on the stairwell walls were the products of talented artists. They'd painted nothing but spiders. Of varying size and shape. Some stick-figure caricatures, though artfully done. Others were startlingly realistic portraits. And even other images, rendered in an almost cartoonish grotesqueness, with bloated, hairy bodies, glittering eyes, and mandibles dripping venom. Ras tried not to think of the hideous hallucination he'd suffered, of his beloved Radio Flyer Rocking Horse turned into a mutated spider-horse, and failed.

On each wall, Ras saw four symbols in a line, which appeared occultic in nature, more than mere graffiti. Three of them were spiders. The fourth, three question marks spiraling around a dot. With the symbols, Ras saw strange phrases written in what might be Latin, though he couldn't be sure.

The symbols and strange words inspired a profound unease. They didn't speak of a group of murderous thieves or bored teens. They spoke of people who believed in something ancient, old, and powerful. A genuine, actual, for-real cult.

Bullshit, he told himself. *All this shit could've been Googled. It doesn't mean anything.*

This weak protest faded, however, when he glanced down and saw a painting on the landing so realistic, he nearly leaped back in shock. Under his feet, someone had painted a mural of a gigantic spider poised on a web over an incredibly detailed chasm. The artist had detailed the painting so finely, that the spider appeared as if it was truly hanging suspended in a web beneath his feet.

The spider was gazing up. At him. Its face had been given grotesquely twisted human features which stared with such cold contempt, that Ras' stomach lurched slightly.

in that cavernous abyss, suspended in the middle of its infinite web, I saw Him

The Spider King

Atlach-Nacha

He sees you, and He knows you

Threaded into the web above the abomination, the artist had painted: *Atlach-Nacha Spins in Darkness.*

Ras looked up, closed his eyes, and took a deep breath. He clenched his fists at his sides, pressing his fingernails into his palms. The dark stairwell ahead led to the pool and spa area he'd seen through the shattered observation window above. Where he'd seen the rectangle of daylight leading into the woods.

All he needed to do was brave his way down the dark stairs, using the lighter he'd wrested from the corpse in the webbed hallway. Make his way through the pool area if he could, and get the hell out of here.

Then, somehow, he'd get back to town. Best case scenario, the local police weren't inept or corrupt, and he could find some sort of justice, or at least recompense for his trials. Worst case scenario, he'd been robbed blind and his resources would take a hit getting new supplies and probably a new car. At least he'd be out of this place, and he could get away from this fucking crazy town, alive.

Ras opened his eyes. Took another deep breath. Flicked the lighter on. The faint light from its flame flickered partway down the steps before him. Marshaling what little resolve he had left, he descended.

19.

The second flight of steps proved to be short, as did the hall leading to the pool and sauna area. This gave energy to Ras' legs as he walked at an ever-quickening pace, lighter held high above him. From the corner of his eyes, he saw yet more spider graffiti on both walls, along with symbols and phrases in strange languages, but he didn't stop to inspect them. He pushed on, focusing only on the door waiting at the end of the hall. Faint white letters reading POOL AND SPA floated in the gloom.

When he reached the door, however, what he saw painted above POOL AND SPA gave him pause. In dripping red paint which had gone a reddish-brown, someone had written in scrawling letters: Ia, Ia, Atlach-Nacha fhatagn!

Swallowing down a sour taste in the back of his throat, Ras realized he'd heard the phrase before. If he hadn't hallucinated him and Sandy fucking on a suitcase full of spiders, it had been the garbled phrase she'd screamed over and over while she rode him. No arousal came with the memory, however. Only a gut-churning, ill feeling.

Below POOL AND SPA, in the same reddish-brown paint, someone had written: *The Court of the Spider King.*

Cold fear wound down Ras' spine and spread across his back. He tried to tell himself the words meant as little as all the other graffiti. If not products of bored teenagers, then of delusional minds with no grip on reality. It didn't mean anything. It couldn't mean anything. It wasn't possible.

Of course, neither was anything else he'd seen the past two days.

"Stop it," he whispered through clenched teeth. "Stop. It. This is your only way out. Suck it up and fucking deal with it."

His resolve slightly bolstered, he grasped the door's handle, praying to a god he'd never bothered with before. He nearly yelped in relief when it opened stiffly.

He yelped again as nearly a foot of water rushed out and splashed over his feet, putting him ankle-deep in foul-smelling water stinking of rot and decay. Ras cursed as he lifted his feet to no avail as the brackish water soaked through to his skin.

Though it meant getting even wetter, Ras cautiously waded toward the door. He held the lighter up and peered into the darkness beyond, which was faintly illuminated by the daylight streaming in from the door across the way. Water rippled, as far as Ras could see.

Flooded. The whole damn area was flooded. With the natural springs beneath the spa, all the years of rain and run-off, and no one around to maintain the place, it made sense. Which didn't make the truth any easier to swallow, however.

"Fuck. Fuck." Ras tried his best to shine the light around the room, but from his vantage, he saw nothing but gently rippling water. He had no way of knowing what debris lay underwater, especially in the pool itself. Regardless of his desperate situation, it would be foolish for him to try and navigate his way across the dark, flooded expanse. He had to find another way.

Much as he didn't want to, Ras considered the webbed hallway filled with all those spiders, and the shriveled corpses hanging in there. Especially the corpse he'd taken the lighter from. Whomever they'd been, they'd had the right idea. Except...

He needed an accelerant. He thought of the maintenance closet he'd seen before the stairwell. Maybe he'd find something in there. Cleaning fluid or something else flammable he could soak a mop in, and then light.

As he walked away, Ras took one last fleeting glance at the rectangle of daylight across the flooded pool area. A tantalizing glimpse of brush and trees. Muttering a dispirited curse under his breath, Ras turned away, eager at least to get his feet out of the cold, stinking water...

Something heavy splashed in the dark pool area, through the darkness, toward him. Something with many legs, treading water. Another splash, and a watery thwap. A heavy body heaving itself out of the pool, and onto the flooded floor around it.

Ras' knees locked, his thighs trembling. An invisible hand squeezed his heart. His breaths stuttered into painful rasps. He knew he should leap forward, slam the door shut, and run, but all he could do was stare into the darkness, as he saw something roughly the size of a cow...

or a horse

...or even a small fucking elephant clamber slowly toward the door.

Spiders don't live underwater, his mind gibbered, *they don't!*

Of course, he knew this wasn't true. A spider he'd always wanted to photograph was the diving bell spider, found in parts of Europe, Asia, and Australia. They lived their entire lives underwater breathing through the bottom of their abdomen, which stuck up through the water. It hunted everything from small fish to crustaceans.

The heavy thing splashed closer. Ras' mind spun; gears locked over two options. Rush forward and try to shut the door, or run away. The door had opened stiffly. He'd be shutting it against nearly a foot of water. A door ten feet away. Trying to close it would put him closer to...

Atlach-Nacha

The Spinner in the Darkness

If he ran, wouldn't it chase him down? And it wasn't a thing. It was a spider. A fucking gigantic monster spider. It would pounce on him and plunge those fangs into him...

Exoskeletons.

Biology was biology. Even grossly mutated. The bigger a spider, the heavier its exoskeleton. Would have to slow it down. Especially as massive as it was...

That doesn't matter! None of this shit matters because nothing here is the way it's supposed to be!

Four spiky forelegs longer than his whole body crept through the doorway. A head the size of a small dog poked out, and two rows of three eyes glimmered in the darkness.

Fuck.

Ras flicked the lighter shut. Turned and ran. As he scrambled through a foot of water toward the stairwell, he heard the spider hiss as it scuttled through the water after him.

20.

Somehow, Ras managed not to slip and fall face-first into the water. Somehow, he scaled the stairs without slipping and scrambled up the next set of stairs to the second floor. As he ran, his heart pounded in his chest. His breath roared in his ears, to the tune of a hissing which rose and fell behind him. A body thumped along the floor, and eight legs scuttled across the tile.

As he ran up the stairs, the garish spider graffiti on the walls filled his peripheral vision, distorted and amplified by his terror. As if spiders were materializing on the walls. Called into being by his own fear, and the thing—the Spider King! —clambering behind him. All he could think about were the dried corpses hanging in the webbed hallway. Even though his rational mind still tried to rally, he knew. He knew. The thing behind him had been the cause of their demise.

However, as Ras scrambled up the last step and onto the second floor, he realized the hissing sounds had faded slightly. As he darted around the corner and yanked open the maintenance closet door, he thought maybe he'd been right. A spider that big would have to be weighed down at least a little by its exoskeleton. Ras found some comfort in this. Small comfort, to be sure. But he'd take what he could get.

Abruptly, the sounds of the thing clambering up the stairs silenced. It had stopped. So far as Ras could hear, anyway.

He stood, knees and thighs barely responding. Taking a deep breath, he forced himself to back out of the closet and peek around the corner, and down the stairs.

"Fuck me," he whispered.

There it sat.

His initial impression had been accurate. Its abdomen was easily the size of a bull. Its head larger than an average-sized dog. Its legs were impossibly long, and it barely fit on the landing. Its legs bent at multiple, unnatural angles. It was wet-black and shiny, bristling not with hairs but tiny spines. Its six eyes blinked and stared, and its unbelievably large mandibles quivered in its mouth.

It sat there. Still.

Another scrap of memory occurred to Ras. Most spiders had poor eyesight. They tracked their prey through vibration, taste, and touch. Nothing was normal about these spiders, but he'd been right about the exoskeleton slowing it down. Maybe he was right about this, too.

He eased back into the closet. On a shelf, he saw a large can of aerosol cleaner. He gently grabbed it and eased it back out of the closet. He peeked around the corner. The thing still sat there, its front legs in the air, quivering.

Ras held the can aloft, hoping his aim was true. Whispering another prayer to a god he'd never believed in; he chucked the aerosol can down the stairs as hard as he could.

It flew above the spider, ricocheted off the wall above it, and flew down the other flight of steps, out of sight. Instantly, as if tugged by a leash, the thing lumbered around and clambered away, around the corner and down the other stairs.

Ras didn't waste time. He'd only been granted a temporary respite. He ducked inside the maintenance closet and began digging through old and dusty buckets and bottles, searching for anything that might burn.

He found an old mop with a long handle. Leaning against the back of the closet. The mop-head was big and scraggly, stiff and dry to the touch. He thought it would light quickly and burn well. He set it aside.

Next, he found what he'd been searching for, stacked against the back of the wall. Four huge, sealed buckets of chlorine, which made sense given the pool. Not flammable by itself, but it would certainly aid in making something else more flammable. Next to those buckets was a stack of eight buckets of what proved to be paint thinner. Acetone. Useful for all sorts of cleaning and de-greasing jobs, Ras knew.

Far away, still on the lower level, Ras heard a medley of thumps and a confused hissing. Feeling time racing away, Ras dug through the debris on the closet floor until he found a rag to tie around his nose and mouth and a screwdriver to pry open the cans of chlorine and acetone. He also found a length of metal pipe. He tied the rag around his lower face, covering his nose and mouth, set aside the pipe, and went to work on the buckets with the screwdriver. He worked quickly. By the time he heard another hiss and a heavy scuttling back up the stairs, he'd pried the lids off all the buckets of chlorine and had only two buckets of acetone remaining.

The thing scuttled up the first flight of stairs to the landing. Ras popped off the last two lids of acetone. Thankful for the rag shielding his nose from the worst of the fumes, Ras still held his breath as he grabbed the first bucket of chlorine and dragged it into the hallway. He did his best not to splash it onto himself, but by the time he'd gotten the bucket to the top of the stairs, his fingers and the back of his hands throbbed with a chemical burning.

The thing was rounding the corner, about to lumber up the stairs. Grunting, Ras tipped the heavy bucket over and dumped its contents—bitter, acrid, undiluted chlorine—down the stairs at the spider.

The result proved greater than Ras had hoped. Even before the chlorine hit the landing, the spider scuttled backward around the corner and down the stairs, hissing in distress. Ras heard another sound, also. Sizzling. He hoped it was the chemicals burning that unnatural abomination.

Ras dumped the other three buckets of chlorine down the stairs. Each time, he was rewarded with more hissing, which sounded even more distressed. Breathing sparingly through the rag wrapped around his mouth, Ras next emptied six buckets of acetone down the stairs. He set the other two next to the mop, and the pipe.

He tossed the empty buckets down the stairs. Ducking back into the closet for another rag, Ras moved too quickly and swooned, almost succumbing to the fumes despite the rag over his nose. He sagged against the inside of the closet, realizing a sober truth. Even with his improvised mask, his lungs and throat burned. He was probably scarring his lungs and throat with each breath. There was also nowhere for the smoke to go. Once the fire was lit, the smoke would roll back up at him.

He didn't have any choice.

He braced himself against the closet wall and straightened. Grabbed another rag, stiff with old age and dry rot, off the shelf. He pivoted out of the closet and stood at the top of the steps.

Below, the spider's forelegs were probing the landing. Peeking around the corner. Twitching and pulling away when it encountered pools of the noxious combination Ras had poured down the steps. Even so, it was attempting to overcome its aversion to the chemicals, as Ras knew it eventually would.

"Fuck you," Ras muttered. He held up the rag.

Flicked the lighter open and snapped it aflame. He lit the rag, which caught instantly. Dropped the rag on the top step and backed away.

21.

Ras wasn't sure what he expected. Certainly not the immediate wall of flame that Hollywood movies made so popular. However, he also knew acetone was highly combustible, and chlorine was extremely volatile when mixed with other accelerants.

So when a sheet of flame immediately whooshed upward in a curling fireball toward the ceiling, Ras stumbled back, crying out in surprise. The fire settled almost immediately, but it also raced down the steps toward the landing. The faux wood paneling along the stairwell began smoking almost immediately. The flames danced in weird blue and green waves. An acrid, chemical stench washed over him, forcing him to cover his mouth and nose with his forearm, even with the mask.

He saw no sign of the spider, but he heard it. Hissing angrily and scuttling away.

He grabbed the mop with his left hand and tucked the pipe under his arm. With his right hand, he grabbed both handles of the remaining buckets of acetone. Still feeling the seconds ticking away, he walked as quickly as he could toward the webbed hallway, awkwardly holding everything, gasping as an oily smoke followed him.

It seemed to take forever to reach the webbed hallway. Wheezing, his eyes burning and nose running, he glanced over his shoulder as he neared the webbing. The wood paneling in the hallway behind him was beginning to smoke now, too. Ras realized he'd done more than buy himself some time. Omar Freivald's abandoned spa—and the dumping place for Sandy and her playmate's victims—was going up in flames.

"Good," Ras muttered as he set the buckets down in front of the webbed hallway. "Fucking A."

He dunked the mop into one bucket of acetone. Kicked them both over, so the acetone ran down the floor of the webbed hallway. However, before he could do anything else, a coughing fit bent him double, as he hacked and gasped. He spit several times, convinced he was going to throw up. The ground wobbled and his legs felt weak and unsteady. The air grew hotter and the stench of burning chemicals grew more intense. For a moment, he teetered on the edge of passing out. Somehow, he forced himself to straighten.

He dug into his pocket and pulled out the lighter. Snapped it open and flicked it on. He lit the acetone-soaked broom head, and it caught instantly. Realizing he had nothing to save the lighter for, he tossed it onto the floor at the end of the webbed hallway, into the pool of spreading acetone.

This time, Ras was rewarded with an eruptive conflagration worthy of a Hollywood action blockbuster. Flames sprung up and raced down the hall along the spreading river of acetone. The dense webbing—no doubt clogged with decades worth of dust and debris—flashed into mini-explosions of fire, disintegrating almost immediately. Webbed carcasses fell to the ground and burst into flames. Most of the spiders had fled already, fearing the waves of heat rolling down the hallway. Stragglers caught fire and fell to the ground in light pattering thumps, curling into blackened, charred blobs.

Ras bent over and grabbed the metal pipe, coughing into the now sodden and sooty rag covering his mouth and nose. A path was quickly clearing to the window. He'd have to move fast because the heat would be almost unbearable, and as soon as he broke the window, the in-rushing air might explode, but fuck it all, anyway. If that's how he was going out, so be it. He started forward, shoulders hunched, eyes squinting against the heat.

An angry, loud, high-pitched hissing filled the air. A heavy, spiny object slammed into his back and knocked him sprawling forward. He hit the ground hard, landing on the edge of the still-smoldering tile. The pipe flew from his hands, into the flaming hallway, but somehow he kept his grip on his improvised torch as he gazed up at the hellish thing poised above him.

Man was never meant to see such a sight up close.

Man was never meant to see a spider's hungrily twitching mouth in such detail. But as the spider crawled fully over the ledge of the broken observation window overlooking the flooded pool area, Ras saw what man had never been meant to see. A bristling and wetly pink, V-shaped mouth pulsing, quivering, and drooling as two hideous fangs extended from thick, spiny mandibles. Ras could see into the thing's mouth. Could see its throbbing pink muscle and ridges. Its forelegs raised, it lurched forward, fangs dripping a bright green fluid.

It leaped after him. All Ras could do was scream and with both hands jam the burning mop at the oncoming behemoth.

The mop-head—almost charred to coal, but still hot—plunged straight into the thing's pink, wet mouth. A rancid-sweet burnt meat stench wafted over Ras. He screamed and jammed the smoldering mop deeper into its mouth, twisting and pumping it repeatedly.

The spider thrashed and its entire body spasmed. It jerked back, yanking the mop out of Ras' hands. Ras scrambled to his feet and leaped toward the windows. The webbing had mostly burned away, and he found a patch of floor in which the fire had burned out.

Behind him, the spider hissed again, though it had a broken quality to it. Ras glanced over his shoulder and saw it, free of the burning mop, staggering after him. Its mouth was a charred, blistered ruin. Swollen and torn, cracked and weeping strange-colored fluids, but it was coming after him, regardless.

Ras cast his glance downward, searching frantically for the metal pipe. He found it on the floor to his right, thankfully away from the flames. Without thinking, he bent and grabbed hold with both hands and screamed shrilly in pain as the red-hot metal seared the flesh on the palms of his hands, sending pulses of fire along his nerve endings. He felt his skin crack and melt, and yet, he didn't let go. He squeezed the pipe even tighter, screaming all the while. He raised it and turned to face the spider.

"C'mon, motherfucker! Come and get me!"

The spider roared and lunged for him. Instead of swinging the pipe at the spider, Ras turned and swung it away. At the windows.

If he hadn't swung with enough force, or the windows had the same security mesh as the windows on the front doors, he would've maybe cracked it, nothing more. He would've felt the spider's fangs plunge into his back before he could take another swing and would've died praying for the fire to take them both.

But the pipe smashed clean through the window.

Ras dove for the floor and threw the pipe away, screaming again as several layers of charred flesh stuck to the pipe and tore from his palms. He fell hard to the floor and cowered against the wall under the window, hands covering his head.

Incoming air washed over his head.

A concussive boom shook the whole building and rained shards of glass everywhere. The heat of the already blazing hallway nearly tripled. Ras dared to peek under his arms. Even though his hands screamed in agony and his throat and lungs burned, his heart leaped with glee.

The spider was on fire.

It feebly backed up to the broken observation window. Either desperately trying to return to the stagnant water of the pool or mindlessly lumbering backward. Regardless, it was dying. Flames raced over its already blackening and shriveling body, growing higher. Its legs twitched slower and slower.

Ras covered his head once more. When he was a kid, his cousin had once thrown a large wolf spider into a campfire. It had blackened, shriveled, and then...

A muffled, liquid-sounding whump shook the floor. Ras looked up and saw the split remains of the spider sagging into a wet pile. Green-black viscera dripped from the ceiling and pooled on the floor. He'd learned later in life that fire caused a spider's exoskeleton to heat up, and then...explode.

Which he felt like doing now.

He stood, but a wave of vertigo passed through him. Again, he fought against passing out. He'd killed the damn thing. Now he was getting out. Even if only long enough to taste the sweetness of outside air on his way down to the ground.

Coughing, battling faintness, he did his best to knock out the remaining jagged shards of glass with his elbow. He spared one last glance over his shoulder at the spider's corpse—now nothing more than an unrecognizable, charred lump—and then Ras toppled, more than jumped, out the window.

For a moment, he felt at peace.

Suspended in time.

Then he fell. He landed hard on his shoulder. Another electric jolt of pain flashed through him, then he fell further, into the dark.

22.

Wednesday Evening
Clifton Heights General Hospital

"Let's go over it once more, Mr. Saeger. This morning you went to Freivald Hollow because someone recommended it as a good place to take pictures for your website. Once there, you noticed the gate to the old Freivald Spa was open. And—even though it was clearly posted—you decided to go poke around. When you found the front doors open, you went inside to take pictures for your website. While inside, someone jumped you and knocked you out. You woke up smelling smoke and found the place on fire. A fire you think was set by the folks who jumped you. Somehow, you managed to break a second-story window, jump out, and then knock yourself unconscious yet again? Which was how Emergency Services found you." He paused with incredulity. "You're very lucky. By the time EMS got to you, the whole place was going up."

Ras shook his bandaged head slightly, trying not to move too much. He still felt horribly weak and was having trouble breathing. He'd probably received lung damage from inhaling chemical-laden smoke and had hoses up his nose providing supplemental oxygen. He was alive, though, and the spider was dead. He'd take it. "Yes," he rasped quietly, his burnt skin stretching painfully over his cheekbones. "I am."

Sheriff's Deputy Phelps consulted his notes. To Ras' relief, the young man had acted not only serious and sympathetic but also was thorough and capable. He'd taken Ras' fabricated story at face value, not questioning it at all. For his part, Ras didn't mention Sandy, Aloysuis, Hartley, or the man he'd seen stalking him. The one with the dark glasses. They'd gotten what they wanted, whatever it was. Better to not prod them with a stick by sending the police after them. Especially when Ras felt sure it would do nothing more than make him a target.

Deputy Phelps tapped the notepad he held with his pen. He looked up, and with a regretful expression said, "We've checked your room at The Motor Lodge. Unfortunately, it's as you suspected. Your room has been trashed. The expensive equipment you mentioned—laptop, camera equipment—gone. They left your wallet, but empty. Your rental car is gone, too."

Ras swallowed and tried to avoid clenching his tightly wrapped hands. He was only partly successful. Waves of pain radiated out from his devastated hands despite the pain medication he was on. He was alive. His stuff was gone. He was alive, but that didn't stop him from feeling angry.

The deputy jotted a few more notes down. Re-read them, grunted in approval, and stood. He nodded at Ras. "I'll do my best to find your rental car. Can't promise anything, but I do have a few trees I can shake. Smitty at The Motor Lodge says not to worry about the cost of the cabin. He's going to refund the whole week to you, in cash. Especially because your cards are missing.

"You're going to be here a while. Anyone you want me to call?"

Ras shook his head and rasped, "Not at the moment, no."

"All right. Doctors say you're not out of the woods completely, so you rest. I'll see what I can do." Deputy Phelps nodded again, then walked out.

Ras settled back and closed his eyes. He must've drifted off because when he opened them again, it was sufficiently darker outside the window. He hadn't even noticed the male nurse who was checking his vitals come in. "What time is it?" he asked, voice still raspy from smoke inhalation.

The nurse—a rather plain young man with thin brown hair—smiled down at him. "Almost ten-thirty. How are you feeling, Mr. Saeger?"

Ras managed a limp shrug. "I'm alive, I suppose."

The nurse's smile widened. "Well, that's good. After all."

He turned to face Ras, holding up a syringe filled with a bright green fluid. "Atlach-Natcha prefers to chase His kill."

Before Ras could make a noise or even think, the nurse bent over and jabbed the needle into the base of his neck, in the same place Sandy had the night before. The nurse plunged the contents into Ras' bloodstream with one vicious push. Ras opened his mouth, but nothing came out. A crippling numbness gripped his vocal cords tight and spread throughout his body.

The nurse sat on the edge of his bed, adjusting Ras' blankets. Ras' heart slammed against his ribcage as he saw the multi-colored spider tattoo on the man's wrist, under the sleeve of his scrubs. "That wasn't Atlach-Nacha at the spa, of course. It was a Spider of Leng. One of His children. Its venom was supposed to take you into the Court of the Spider King, not kill you outright. Because you see..."

The nurse bent close and whispered into Ras' ear. "The Spinner in Darkness spins his web in the Void between worlds. One cannot go there physically, so Atlach-Nacha doesn't consume your body. He consumes your mind. A Spider of Leng's venom takes you to a higher level of consciousness, and it is there you meet the Spider King. Luckily, over the years, we've harvested a plentiful supply of his children's venom. Which is what I just injected you with."

The nurse straightened. "Ia, Ia," he whispered reverently and comfortingly as he patted Ras' bandaged hand, "Ia fhatagn, Ia Atlach-Nacha."

The nurse stood and exited the room, whistling a jaunty tune. Ras heard none of this, however. Nor had he heard the nurse's exposition. He lay motionless, expressionless. Eyes stared at nothing as he screamed mindlessly inside. He felt the maddening weight of Atlach-Nacha's bulk and the maddening touch of its legs scurrying over the folds of his brain as it hunted Ras in the Void between worlds because Atlach-Nacha preferred to chase His kill.

TO SLIP THE SURLY BONDS OF EARTH

Oh! I have slipped the surly bonds of Earth
Put out my hand, and touched the face of God.

– "High Flight," by John W. Gillespie

1.

Riding the Steamin Demon
Great Escape, Six Flags
Lake George, New York
Saturday, August 9
7:30 PM

As he neared the peak of the Steamin Demon's first drop, Todd Houts adjusted his grip on the lap bar locked against his upper thighs. He flexed his knees against the armature, taking comfort in its resistance. It was something he did on every roller coaster—big or small—with the devotion of a minor league pitcher who always wore the same armband pushed up to his right elbow. It was a reflex. Something he never thought about. A quick flexing of the thighs to produce a satisfying thunk.

The Demon click-clacked as it crested. Todd saw the park spread out in miniature below. Other rides and concessions were tiny models on a scale model. This was his favorite moment. The brief space of tranquility, high above the world, before the first plunge.

The Demon cleared the first rise, but instead of rocketing downward, it coasted around a deceptively gentle right turn, a leisurely prelude to what came next.

"To slip the surly bonds of Earth," he whispered, "and touch the face of God."

With a suddenness that stole Todd's breath, the coaster plunged downward, descending sixty-five feet in a clacking roar. A delicious sense of weightlessness swelled in his belly. Before he could blink, the Demon rocketed out of its descent into a loop. For one lovely heart-pounding moment, the world turned upside-down.

Todd screamed with joy. The Demon whipped out of the loop into another deceptively calm turn. He had enough time to swallow before the cars whipped into a double-inversion corkscrew which spun the world around in dizzy circles.

This was when he was supposed to hear it.

The ghostly scream that haunted The Steamin Demon at Six Flags, Great Escape. Specifically, the double-inversion corkscrew. Cecy Leonard, who—because of a defective lap bar—fell to her death on the coaster's maiden voyage in 1984.

For a second, Todd thought he heard it.

The hysterical screech of a doomed ten-year-old girl.

But the wind whisked the sound away (if it had ever been there to begin with) and the Demon hurtled out of the corkscrew and around the last bend, toward the boarding platform. As the coaster slowed, the excitement faded, leaving Todd hollowed out with a jaded disappointment that became the epitome of his existence.

The Demon rolled to a clacking stop, jerking slightly as the brakes engaged. While the other riders clambered off, uttering breathless exclamations of wonder, Todd disembarked slowly, bereft of joy.

2.

Six Flags Great Escape Lodge
11:00 PM

At the desk in his hotel room, Todd opened his laptop and started Adobe Premier, the video program he used to produce his web series, Ghost Coaster. He loaded the template for "on the road" reports and checked to make sure his webcam and microphone were connected. He paused, took a deep breath, and then grinned for the camera. The expression still came easily, despite the increasing emptiness that filled him when producing the show. His excitement was a charade, but one he could still pull off. He clicked record and plunged ahead.

"Hey there, Ghost Coasters! As promised, here's my Road Report of The Steamin Demon at Six Flags Great Escape in Lake George, New York. First, the basic coaster deets. The Steamin Demon is one-thousand, five-hundred and sixty-five feet of steel that's every inch its name. The first hill is an eighty-five-foot climb, with a jarring sixty-five-foot drop slamming you through a five-story vertical loop, giving you about a nanosecond to recover before rocketing through a double-inversion corkscrew that'll leave your head spinning, even if you're an experienced coaster. It's a short ride, but what a ride it is. Definitely worth the price of admission."

Todd paused. What he'd said was true. From a coaster enthusiast's perspective, The Steamin Demon had proved a fun ride. He'd meant every word.

Next, however?

Next came the true performance.

He held up a dramatic finger. "Ah, yes, Ghost Coasters. I know your next question. What of its haunted history? What about the legend of Cecy Leonard, the ten-year-old girl who fell to her death at the inversion corkscrew because of a faulty lap bar on the Demon's debut ride, back in 1984? Does she scream in the corkscrew? Do you feel invisible hands grasping at you, replaying the instant before she fell from her mother's side?"

He leaned forward, playing his role to the hilt. He was good at it, and the tiniest spark of the old enthusiasm stirred inside. Not enough for him to believe, of course. Just enough to offer his audience a convincing charade.

"Let me say this. I'm not sure I heard anything, but I definitely felt something. Sitting in that same front car Cecy and her mother did. A strange disorientation unlike anything I've felt before, and believe me, I've been on plenty of inversion corkscrews in my time. This felt different somehow. Almost as if I was falling. As if my lap bar had disengaged.

"And what of the ghostly image that's supposed to show up on the Demon's Coaster Cam? The hazy outline of a little girl next to anyone who sits in the front car of the Demon?"

He paused several heartbeats, which gave him space to insert a scan of the over-priced Coaster Cam photo he'd purchased after the ride. The photo he'd edited digitally with a blur, carefully placed next to him.

"I'm not sure what you'd call that, folks. A camera malfunction? A smear on the lens? When I pestered the bored attendant shilling these photos," (which he hadn't), "the young squire—with a carefully wooden expression, I might add—claimed the corkscrew Coster Cam had been 'acting up lately.'" (which the attendant hadn't said).

He rubbed his hands, then shrugged. "What to believe? As always, that's up to you. All I know is the corkscrew section felt weird," (it hadn't), "there's a blurred spot next to me in the car Cecy fell from," (which he'd made in Photoshop), "and there are dozens of other pics circulating the web, with similar blurs on them." (This was true because it was where he'd gotten the idea). "Anyway, I can highly recommend The Steamin Demon at Six Flags Great Escape to anyone in the Adirondack area, for all of these reasons. Tune in for the main show this weekend, when I'll give an in-depth breakdown of the timeline leading up to Cecy Leonard's tragic accident and other detailed reports of her hauntings over the years. Saturday, live at 8 p.m. Eastern Standard Time."

He paused, acting as if he'd almost forgotten something. "Oh! Almost forgot. I've got some free space in my schedule this week before I move on to one of my favorite haunted and abandoned amusement parks, Chippewa Lake, in Ohio. Sound off in the comments about places to explore in the Adirondack area. Amusement parks with ghost stories, or even better, abandoned amusement parks, which you all know I love exploring! If I choose your destination...free Ghost Coaster merch for you!"

Yay, great. A crappy ceramic coffee mug, a cheap, ill-fitting T-shirt, or a keychain. Yay, cheap-ass Ghost Coaster merch.

"In any case, Ghost Coasters, I'm out. Have a good night. Choose my next destination below. Ride scary, my friends!"

Todd flashed another white-toothed smile. Gave the camera a jaunty salute. Tapped the mousepad on the laptop and stopped recording.

His face fell slack, his smile vanishing. He cut the camera's feed so he didn't have to see himself anymore, and began editing. The sooner he posted his report to YouTube, the sooner he could have a drink—or five—and watch some Kolchak reruns before bed. Or maybe an old horror movie. Something by Val Lewiston. Anything to relight the spark inside. A spark he feared was gone forever.

3.

12:30 AM

About an hour later, his report on The Steamin Demon had been edited, composed, and posted to YouTube. The process had become routine. Trim the footage, insert it into a template, and add graphic elements. Preview it, hit produce, grab a beer during the twenty minutes of composition time, review it once more, and then upload it to YouTube. He'd done it so often that he could edit in his sleep.

Of course, that's how life felt these days. As if he were going through the motions half-awake. What had once been a dream gig had turned into an odd kind of drudgery. It had lost its shine long ago. He felt as if he'd drifted on cruise control for years.

A part of him (not for the first time) wondered if maybe the "jig was up." Maybe it was time for Ghost Coaster's curtain call. Time to return to school. Get his master's degree in college administration and find a desk job working in Campus Health and Safety, or in some other kind of college administrative office, as he'd originally intended.

As he reclined on the hotel room bed and sipped his third (fourth?) Corona, watching Kolchak on the room's flat-screen TV ("The Energy Eater," the one about a haunted hospital), Todd wondered if returning to the "normal world" was even possible. The groove he'd dug over the past ten years hosting and producing Ghost Coaster ran deep and smooth. Though his passion had faded, his YouTube channel was monetized and produced consistently. The views still rolled in. Ghost Coaster's ratings on Roku had remained consistently good for the last five years. While it wasn't one of Fast Forward Media's highest-rated shows, it was one of their most reliable. They'd already renewed him for another season. His producers had even dropped tantalizing hints about deals with Netflix, Amazon Prime, and Vudu.

Of course, he still drew revenue editing shows for CoasterRadio.com, the first gig he'd landed while working Amusements and Rides at Disney World. He also wasn't hurting for freelance digital video work. His Ghost Coaster Patreon page, where he featured exclusive raw footage, outtakes, and behind-the-scenes interviews with amusement park owners and ride operators, also produced a steady stream of revenue.

Would he make more working a desk job at a university or community college, with the security of health benefits and a 401(k)? Sure. If he found his way into the right graduate program and pressed the right palms, he'd eventually land a comfortable job with benefits. Ditch his small apartment (which he rarely saw anymore, being on the road so much) and buy a house. He hadn't had a nice place since the one he'd shared with Bob, and...

He took a deep drink of his Corona.

Shut the door on the thought. Continued watching a Kolchak episode he'd seen so many times, that he knew the plot by heart. Could recite the lines, if he wanted. But he didn't. He watched the episode from afar, sinking into its reassuring familiarity.

Maybe that's why he felt so loathe to quit Ghost Coaster. Though his enthusiasm had faded, the show had become familiar, and therefore comfortable. A reassuring muscle memory. Maybe he didn't want to trudge back into domestic life because even though the thrill of Ghost Coaster had dulled, it was home. Familiar country. Reassuringly easy.

C'mon now.

You know that's not why you still chase ridiculous ghost stories all over the country. Why you chase ride after ride, searching in each drop, loop, and corkscrew for something you know you'll never find. You know why you can't quit.

You know.

Todd closed his eyes.

Breathed in deep.

Opened his eyes, and in one swift gulp, downed the rest of his Corona. With practiced ease, he also shut the door on this sly voice. To ensure the door stayed closed, he slipped off the bed and shuffled to the desk, where a half-full bottle of Tullamore Dew sat, waiting.

4.

The dream begins the same as always. He's on a coaster screaming around a hairpin turn. He's sitting in the last car with Bob because it's Todd's favorite car. He always wants to ride in the last car, because he enjoys seeing the rest of the cars, full of riders. Bob doesn't often ride roller coasters with Todd, but when he does, he always sits in the last car with him.

It's night. Below, a hazy amusement park glows with the lights of other rides and concession booths.

The coaster rockets out of the curve and plunges down a vertical dive which defies physics. The force lifts Todd off the seat, slamming his thighs against a lap bar which rattles. A wild exhilaration fills him. His heart pounds. Breath roaring in his ears. He feels more alive than he has since Bob left. Yet, beneath it all?

An icy fear pulses.

Because he can't look at Bob. He's not allowed.

Why?

After what feels like an eternity, the coaster's impossible descent swings into a series of gentle hills, each one higher than the last, each one less gentle, more abrupt. Todd's stomach rises, filled with a giddy lightness, an all-consuming delight...

Oh! I have slipped the surly bonds of Earth!

I've topped the wind-swept heights with easy grace.

The words of his favorite poem whisper in his ears as the coaster ascends the steepest hill yet, banks left and approaches a tight corkscrew that goes straight down. Nothing supports the tracks. The coaster spirals downward into a yawning, black nothingness, filled with the thickest darkness Todd has ever seen.

The coaster slows.

Comes to a hissing stop.

Bob stirs next to him, but despite how much he wants to, Todd still can't look at him.

He sits there, in the last car next to Bob, staring into the swirling darkness at the end of the coaster's track. A greasy cold fills his belly, replacing the glee he felt only moments before. His child-like wonder vanishes, smothered by a wave of terror.

Something is waiting for them down there.

Something has always been waiting for them. Waiting for him, in particular. It is waiting, hungry, and can't be denied.

He hears Bob fidget next to him. Does he groan fearfully? Todd still can't make himself look at him, because he knows, deep down...

He doesn't deserve to.

The coaster issues a pneumatic sigh. A low, sibilant, almost reptilian hiss. With a clanking lurch, it rolls forward, toward the corkscrew heading into nothingness.

Todd grasps the lap bar so hard his knuckles ache. His sweaty hands slip on cold metal. As the coaster goes faster, he slides his right hand down the lap bar for Bob's hand, but all he finds is cold metal. As the coaster speeds into darkness, the last bit of the poem comes to him, and he wonders with cold fear lodged in his throat if he's about to touch the face of God, and how God will reward such impudence...

5.

Six Flags Great Escape Lodge
Sunday, August 10
7:00 AM

Todd opened his eyes. He immediately wished he hadn't. Though the hotel room was still dim, a dull, insistent ache throbbed in his temples. Which, of course, only made sense. Considering he'd polished off the rest of the Tullamore Dew after the four or five (six?) Coronas he'd downed last night.

Fuck.

He closed his eyes and grunted. Covered his face with his hands and started kneading his forehead with his fingertips. "Getting old," he muttered. "Used to put away twice as much. Fucking lightweight."

At least he'd brought a bottle of Jack Daniels, too, because, despite his drinking last night, he'd still dreamed of riding that coaster with Bob at his side. Unable to look at Bob, or hold his hand, as they plunged into a bottomless darkness...

Todd fought to empty his mind. He'd gotten good at it over the past five years. Almost immediately, his thoughts about the dream vanished. His headache remained, however, so he lay there for several more minutes, rubbing his face, hoping the pain would eventually subside.

It didn't.

It remained, pulsing in an aching metronome.

"Fuuuuck."

He slowly sat up. Thankfully, the headache didn't worsen. He ran a trembling hand through sweat-damped hair. Swung his feet to the floor, pushed off the bed, and stood. When his headache didn't go away but also didn't get worse, and his stomach didn't protest too loudly, he shuffled to the bathroom. For Advil, then a hot shower.

6.

8:30 AM

An hour and a half later, after showering, dressing, hydrating, and eating a cautious breakfast at Johnny Rocket's Cafe, a refreshed Todd disembarked the elevator and approached his room. He'd revived adequately. The cafe hadn't been crowded. He'd sat in a booth far from other patrons. He'd taken his time, eating slowly as he scrolled through the comments for last night's YouTube update.

The update had received 350 views so far. Par for the course. His shorter videos didn't garner lots of views immediately. They tended to accumulate over time. He had received over 100 comments so far. Ranging from "Awesome!" or "Sick coaster!" to "Spooky story!" Of course, there was also the smattering of, "Ghost looks fake," which he couldn't take offense at, of course. It did look fake because it was.

To his disappointment, he saw no suggestions for abandoned amusement parks to explore. He hadn't visited one of those in quite some time. Not since the ruins of Joyland Amusement Park in Central Kansas, which closed in 2006 after a teen girl's death. She'd had a heart condition and suffered a heart attack on the appropriately named coaster, Nightmare. Which, incidentally, had been one of the nation's last surviving original wooden roller coasters at the time of Joyland's closing.

Apparently, he'd have some downtime. He'd stay busy, of course. Research on abandoned parks for the fall, after active parks in the Northeast shut down for the season. Line up freelance editing work to fill the gaps over the winter, as he'd travel less frequently.

However, just as he was making himself content with time off, his phone vibrated in his pocket as he turned the door handle to his room. He stopped, pulled his phone out, and saw he'd received a new YouTube notification. A comment. He tapped the notification. The new comment had been posted by someone with the username "HighFlight33."

Todd stared at the username for several seconds, feeling an odd chill. "High Flight" was a poem by World War II pilot John Gillespie. Todd loved the poem because it embodied his love of roller coasters. Was the YouTube user's name intentional? Or chance? Todd tried to remember if he'd ever talked about the poem's importance to him on the show, but he couldn't remember.

He swatted aside his unease. He must've talked about it. He'd never seen a comment by this user before, but maybe they were a loyal listener commenting for the first time. It was common enough. The majority of his viewers lurked, rarely commenting, at all.

Chuckling (though he still felt oddly uneasy), he read HighFlight33's comment: "Raedeker Park Amusements. Clifton Heights, New York."

He'd never heard of Raedeker Park Amusements or Clifton Heights, but that didn't mean anything. Over the years he'd visited many destinations he'd never heard of. Given his request for local destinations, he assumed Clifton Heights was somewhere in the Adirondacks.

On a whim, he tapped HighFlight33's name, which sent him to an empty channel. Only three videos were posted, in 'Uploads.' Short ones, too. He skipped those for a moment to examine the channel itself.

HighFlight33's channel was bereft of identifying information. The 'About' tab was empty. No external links were in the channel's blank profile. Of course, blank YouTube channels proved fairly common. Many folks only created YouTube accounts to follow their favorite content. Empty pages with no videos weren't so strange.

Even so, something about HighFlight33's channel bothered him. There was no avatar or header image. Again, not unusual. Regardless, Todd felt vaguely unsettled the longer he examined the channel.

On a whim, he tapped on the channel's first video. He enlarged it to full screen, and tapped 'play.' The video was of an amusement park fairway at night. Whoever was filming walked slowly. The hazy glow of a flashlight danced ahead of them, flitting over asphalt. As the camera progressed, it panned slowly back and forth. Todd caught glimpses of shadowed bulks he assumed were concessions, but the camera didn't focus on anything for long. It kept progressing down a weirdly long fairway. Almost never-ending.

Abruptly, the video cut out. Despite a chill running along his shoulders (which he couldn't explain) Todd clicked 'Next' to view the following video. This one began with a circular structure looming in the video's foreground, as the cameraperson walked past. A Ferris wheel, but with no carriages.

He'd seen Ferris wheels without carriages before, of course, at other abandoned amusement parks. They were usually stripped of them so urban explorers wouldn't be tempted to climb them for a better view. He'd never seen a denuded Ferris wheel appear so menacing, however. So bereft of meaning. Purpose.

The video continued silently, save the distant scraping of shoes on asphalt. Oddly sized and humped shapes lurked in the dark. Flat rides, Todd guessed. What remained of them.

As the camera neared a circular shape on the right, the cameraperson shined their flashlight on it, revealing horses forever frozen in leaps, their faces eternally screaming in agonized terror. A carousel. Todd had always found them slightly unnerving. Children riding the horses, kicking their heels against them and screaming in glee as their mounts suffered otherworldly torment. The cameraperson approached the carousel. Their flashlight played over dozens of horses forever captured mid-prance, poles rammed through their spines, invoking images of bugs impaled on pins. Their faces bore timeless expressions of stark terror. Lips pulled back from gnashing teeth. Eyes bulging madly.

Though the carousel horses appeared pale under the flashlight's beam, Todd could see how worn they were. Chipped and flaking paint. Cracks running along legs and necks. One black stallion even had a fist-sized chunk missing from its flank. Next to it, a palomino had somehow been uprooted. It lay on its side. Hoofs were missing, broken off at the ankles.

The video emitted a slight scuffing, then a thump. The video jerked slightly as the cameraperson boarded the decrepit carousel. The camera continued until it came to a boot-scuffing stop. Pointed down and focused on another horse that had been uprooted.

The view jerked to the right as if something startled the cameraperson. Todd inhaled sharply at a shadowed form staring at the cameraperson. Staring out of the video, at him. He instantly relaxed, however, as the cameraperson shined their flashlight onto the figure. It was simply their reflection in the carousel's mirrored center column.

The video panned away, ending as abruptly as the first.

Feeling a completely irrational certainty that his life would be better, by far, if he didn't click on the third video, Todd nevertheless tapped 'Next.' Competing with this odd foreboding was a healthy disdain. What the hell was he scared of? These were videos taken by an amateur explorer poking around an abandoned amusement park at night. That was all.

Still.

At first, there wasn't much to see. The camera was pointed at the ground ahead as the cameraperson walked. Occasionally, the toes of their white sneakers flashed into view. All Todd heard was the distant scrape of those sneakers, the muffled night breeze, and the cameraperson huffing in the background.

As if they'd been running.

Then, a sharp gasp.

The footsteps increased in tempo. The cameraperson's white shoes flashed quicker as they broke into a run. The video jerked up. In the moonlight, Todd saw the humped back of a brontosaurus, a dragon, or...

A roller coaster.

The camera's viewpoint tilted upward. The coaster dominated the night sky. Over the coaster loomed the tree line. The hulking image filled him with cold dread, inexplicably reminding him of the nightmare that plagued his sleep since Bob left.

The camera's perspective dropped. As the person neared the coaster, their flashlight flickered over wooden beams. The coaster was a woodie.

The camera's perspective shifted again. Now the cameraperson was running alongside the coaster. After what?

The video ended.

Todd stood in the empty hallway and watched the videos a second time. A third.

A fourth.

7.

10:00 AM

Todd sat back from his laptop at his hotel room's desk. Laced his fingers together and cracked his knuckles. After an hour's worth of researching Raedeker Park Amusements, he hadn't found much. He'd confirmed the existence of Clifton Heights. A modestly sized town west of Old Forge. He'd also confirmed the existence of Raedeker Park Zoo, and Raedeker Park Zoo and Amusements. Supposedly the zoo shut down their rides in May of 1979. The article—found on WebbHistory. com—proved vague. It only said after a rash of fatal accidents, the park's insurance became too expensive. To preserve the zoo, the amusements closed.

Todd couldn't find anything else. Nothing about rides, how big the park had been, or its maximum occupancy. The only picture with the article was a grainy black and white photo taken from atop the Ferris wheel, of a fairway dotted with vague blobs which could be buildings, concessions, or other rides. He couldn't find any other pictures, regardless of how he worded his Google searches.

Even more interesting was the lack of information about the park's ruins. He couldn't find any references to it on local sites for rural exploration. His go-to—AbandonedAmusementParks.com—archived articles on the smallest parks in the smallest towns. It had nothing on Raedeker Park Amusements or Clifton Heights. The other websites he used—CoasterChasers.net and CreepyCarnivals.org—didn't have anything, either. Further compounding his confusion was the dearth of information about the park on local history websites.

Todd sighed, wondering if this was worth his time. It might be wisest to book a flight home to clear his head. Get his thoughts in order. Besides, something still nagged him about HighFlight33's YouTube channel...

A sudden revelation struck him. He sat upright in his chair. "Holy shit," he whispered. "Are you...are you fucking afraid?"

He sat there for several seconds, mulling over his strange reticence to visit Clifton Heights. The whispered foreboding saying maybe it would be better if he passed on HighFlight33's suggestion. He'd thought it was his bullshit detector going off. When he analyzed his feelings more closely, however...

He felt fear.

Not a heart-pounding fear, certainly. More like worry. That he'd be walking into something dangerous, albeit in an ill-defined way. That maybe Highflight33's motivations might not be friendly, and might also be darker than a prank.

Oddly enough, this realization provoked a strange excitement. Wasn't fear the missing ingredient? Even when the show had been fresh, he hadn't ever expected to encounter anything threatening. Even at the abandoned amusement parks. It felt exciting, but not dangerous. He'd always known, deep down, that no harm would come to him. It was a fun show that gave himself and his viewers a delightful shudder, nothing more.

Ever since Bob left, however, the show's sparkle had worn off. Things had become routine. He'd "ride" a "haunted" coaster or explore a "haunted" abandoned amusement park. Put on a convincing show. Fake images in Photoshop, then afterward return to his hotel room and get shit-faced. Maybe he'd have the same dream he'd been having since Bob left; maybe not. Regardless, the next morning he'd either head to his next destination or return home and trudge through several days of work-for-hire projects before striking out on the road again. Drifting along, until...

Sudden inspiration pulsed through him. He was tired of it. He wasn't sure how much more he could take.

Maybe HighFlight33 wasn't legit. Maybe their suggestion to visit Raedeaker Park Amusements was a snipe hunt. So what? He didn't know it was. He had no idea what it was. That uncertainty alone felt refreshingly different.

If it proved dangerous? If HighFlight33 had ill intentions? It may be unwise, even plain stupid. He didn't care.

"Fuck this," Todd whispered. He began searching for places to stay in Clifton Heights.

8.

Hosting his own web series had never been Todd's vocational goal. Of course, he'd never had a clear vocational goal to begin with. He'd attended community college in Columbia for two years, pursuing a liberal arts education. Because he loved the strange, he'd toyed with the idea of writing fiction, but a few creative writing electives proved enough to convince Todd he simply didn't have the gift. He'd felt a little disappointed, but not terribly so.

He continued his education at the University of Missouri, majoring in the vague field of "Public Administration." Maybe someday he'd work for a community college or university. Or a law firm, or a marketing company. His goals, as always, hazy.

He'd been a good student who'd pursued his studies with detached diligence. In his final semester, he'd dutifully started examining his graduate school options when he stumbled into a life-changing opportunity.

He'd finished speaking with his advisor, weighing his graduate school options in a factual, passionless manner. His advisor had praised him for lining up several "sensible" choices. Todd hadn't felt anything about any of them. They were the same. He could tack them to the wall and make his choice by throwing a dart at them blindfolded.

Then he walked into the common area of the Student Union. A dozen or more booths had been set up for the Senior Internship Fair, which the University of Missouri held every spring. Todd had never once considered pursuing one. Even so, he glanced over the booths and their offerings. Law firms, marketing firms, companies of all kinds...

He stopped and stared when he saw it.

A vividly colored booth to his left. The banner read DISNEY WORLD. Flanking the booth were cardboard cutouts of Mickey and Minnie Mouse. It was the booth for summer internships at Disney World, in Orlando, Florida.

Something switched on inside Todd. A flame that burned clear and true. Ever since he could remember, he'd loved amusement parks. Riding roller coasters, in particular. Plunging down nearly vertical drops. Rushing around hairpin turns. Twisting upside-down in a corkscrew. He'd gotten this love from his father. Every family vacation involved amusement parks in some form. It was the only thing he and his father had bonded over. In fact, it had been his father who'd first quoted Gillespie's "High Flight" to him. Todd forevermore associated the poem with riding roller coasters.

All through high school and into college, Todd's love of roller coasters and amusement parks flourished. He visited them whenever he could. Also, during a time when most college students were pulling free from their families, Todd still traveled with his on their vacations to amusement parks. How Mom had put up with it all those years, Todd never knew. She did, however, with her trademarked gentle tolerance.

Though it might sound foolish, something spoke to Todd when he saw Disney World's booth. Drew him to it. When one of its attendants glanced up, he asked, "Do interns get to work with the rides?"

A young woman with brown hair and bright eyes—whose name tag read Erin—smiled. "They do! You might have to work in other departments first, but eventually, everyone gets a chance to work rides."

She held out a clipboard with an application packet. "Do you know about the Disney College Program? The details are here."

If anyone had suggested to Todd he'd end up working at Disney World in Orlando, Florida, he would've laughed them off. However, there he was, filling out an application for an internship at Disney World without bothering to read the packet fully.

Maybe the circumstances were perfect. Maybe he'd subconsciously felt dissatisfied with his graduate school plans. Maybe, if he hadn't seen the Disney booth right then, he never would've applied for their College

Program. Never would've spent the summer working at Disney World, and working the next six years there.

Whatever the reason, he applied for the Disney College Program, sending his life around a new and unpredictable curve with all the velocity of his beloved roller coasters.

9.

Todd worked at Disney for six years. After his summer internship ended, they offered him a fall internship. Considering the good pay and their company living arrangements, he accepted. Especially since they offered him a spot working rides.

His parents gave their blessing with little fanfare, which was their way. He still called home and visited from college. Still joined them on their family vacations to amusement parks, until Dad got too old. However, in many ways, Todd believed his parents didn't know what to do with their gay son. He didn't sense any condemnation. They treated him as kindly as ever.

Even so, it simply wasn't ever discussed. He longed to talk with them about it. Tell them they didn't have to treat him differently or give him special consideration. He was still Todd. Still the son who'd inherited his love of roller coasters from his father. Still the same teenager who'd grown up on a steady diet of Kolchak and Twilight Zone re-runs.

Sadly, that day hadn't arrived. Todd didn't foresee it coming any time soon. They treated his sexuality with the same aplomb they'd displayed when he initially came out: An unspoken sentiment of 'we love you and whatever you choose to do is your business and fine by us so long as we don't talk about it.' Their underwhelming reactions to his abrupt career change and coming out simply fit the standard for how they'd treated him his whole life.

Todd hadn't turned bitter. He didn't begrudge them for their distance. He also had the good sense to feel thankful, knowing others had experienced far worse when they'd come out to their friends and loved ones. Even so, he occasionally felt sad at the amiable gulf which had widened between them.

He spent six wonderful years working rides at Disney World. Most of the time, he worked coasters. Doing the morning checklist for Ride Ops. Checking tires, restraints, brakes. His favorite part was the ride through, which meant he got to ride the coaster before anyone else, alone. Nothing quite compared to plunging down stomach-lurching drops and hurtling through dizzying corkscrews in the crisp morning air. By himself, screaming as loudly as he wanted.

As a hobby, Todd had always been handy with digital video and audio production, so when a friend inquired if he'd be interested in volunteering as a production assistant on a podcast called CoasterR adio.com, he jumped at the chance. Born in the early podcast boom, by the time Todd joined the team, Coaster Radio had become the premier coaster-centric podcast in the country.

Todd mostly remained behind the scenes, doing production work. Occasionally, he filled in when one of the hosts was unavailable. He'd been working on Coaster Radio for a year when, on their Halloween Haunting Special, he was invited onto the show to share his experiences at Disney. He enjoyed it far more than he'd expected. Not only did he share his experiences, but they also discussed stories about haunted roller coasters and abandoned amusement parks.

Afterward, Todd thought nothing of it. He returned to production, content. Three months later, the executive producers of Fast Forward Media (they managed Coaster Radio), contacted him. The Halloween Special had gathered three times as many downloads as the rest of Coaster Radio's shows. The producers floated the idea of his own show. A podcast about haunted roller coasters and abandoned amusement parks.

Todd accepted in a heartbeat.

The show wasn't an overnight success. It began life as a weekly podcast covering the lore of both haunted roller coasters and abandoned amusement parks. He didn't travel in the beginning. He worked at Disney World, worked on Coaster Radio, and produced Ghost Coaster on the side.

Gradually, however, the show gathered momentum. The idea of a YouTube channel was his. After getting clearance from Fast Forward, Todd started traveling on weekends to amusement parks within a day's drive from Orlando. Parks with reported instances of "hauntings." He recorded everything. Trips to and from destinations. His thoughts at the hotel. His experiences at the amusement parks. On several occasions, he interviewed park employees, getting their stories of the supernatural.

His YouTube channel exploded. On a whim, he bought advertising on Coaster Radio. His YouTube channel and podcast began cross-promoting. A year later (still working days at Disney World), he purchased a reliable web-hosting package and launched Ghost Coaster's official internet presence. The full-blown version of the web series was still a few years away (which happened shortly after he and Bob moved in together), but it had started taking its first steps.

None of this escaped Fast Forward's notice. About five years in (a year after he first met Bob), executives from Fast Forward approached Todd with an attractive proposal. Let them host Ghost Coaster on a much larger, more professional web platform. They'd pay him to travel to parks throughout Florida. If the show continued to succeed, they'd greenlight out-of-state trips, also. They would, in turn, develop Ghost Coaster as a Roku channel, with an eye toward other streaming platforms if the show continued to succeed.

He signed on the dotted line. Ghost Coaster got a sleeker, more professional appearance. He no longer had to produce it by himself, though he continued to manage the YouTube channel. When the Roku app debuted a year later, he launched his Patreon page, offering unfiltered behind-the-scenes footage. Five years later, his Patreon boasted several hundred patrons at various tier payments. The ratings for the Ghost Coaster Roku channel remained consistently positive.

He worked in rides at Disney for one more year, until the Roku channel officially launched. Shortly after, he resigned. He and Bob moved into their first place. A nice, tidy townhouse not far from Disney World. They began their life together. A life that had a far shorter lease than either of them could've foreseen.

10.

Clifton Heights, New York
The Motor Lodge
1:30 PM

The Motor Lodge had been the only place to stay in Clifton Heights. Todd booked their last available space, Cabin 14. Worried it'd be an overpriced hunter's shack when he pulled into the front office's parking lot, he saw (with great relief) modestly sized and well-maintained cabins on neatly trimmed plots. Each cabin had a tidy parking space before its front steps. The main office appeared well-maintained, also.

The main office lobby was neatly furnished. The clerk at the front desk didn't say much as Todd checked in, dutifully reciting house rules as Todd filled out paperwork, also rattling off all the best places to eat in town. Todd signed his name at the bottom of the registration form. Laid down his credit card and slid it across the counter. "So, I was wondering if you could tell me a little about some of the town's attractions. You guys have a zoo, right?"

The clerk nodded absently while he examined Todd's paperwork. "Yep. Raedeker Park Zoo," he said in a disinterested voice. "Second oldest zoo in New York, after Ross Park Zoo in Binghamton."

"Didn't it used to have an amusement park, too? With rides, a coaster, the whole bit?" Todd crossed his arms as the clerk continued entering his information into an old, dingy-white PC, whose keys clacked dully with each finger stroke. "I heard its coaster was the second oldest wooden roller coaster in New York."

The clerk—still staring dully into the old PC's screen—shrugged. "Yeah. Got torn down in the seventies, I think."

"Any ruins left? I run a web series specializing in this sort of thing. Someone on YouTube recommended it."

The clerk hit 'enter' and met Todd's gaze with watery, distant eyes. "Don't know. Grew up in Booneville. Still live there. About thirty minutes west. This is only a part-time gig. I don't spend much time in Clifton Heights. Not if I can help it, anyway."

The apathetic clerk handed Todd's card back, along with a key attached to a yellowed tile with a faded black 14 on it. "Anyway, if there's anything you need, let me know. Enjoy your stay."

Todd looked into the clerk's pale eyes for another heartbeat. The clerk stared dully back, not unlike a cow sunning itself in a pasture. Another heartbeat passed. Feeling an increasing discomfort he couldn't explain, Todd jingled the key and offered a spare nod. "Thanks."

The clerk nodded, turned in his chair, and started typing on his keyboard, apparently done speaking. The young man's dismissal didn't offend Todd in the least. In fact, he felt relieved, for some reason, to be freed from the clerk's empty gaze. He had to force himself not to rush out of the office.

11.

Raedeker Park
2:30 PM

An hour later, Todd parked his car in front of Raedeker Park's main office building, which sat on a hill. The zoo itself lay nestled in a valley below. He hadn't unpacked yet. Would do so later. After a cursory examination of his cabin, he'd stowed his belongings in the bedroom and called the park's director, Patrick McDonough, to set up an appointment.

The cabin had proved to be nicer than Todd anticipated. The furniture was all rustic -hewn wood, with a polished hardwood floor. The small den felt comfortable. There wasn't a desk, so he'd set up his laptop and its webcam on the coffee table. The kitchen—which had all the necessities—was spotless. The bedroom, cozy. The bathroom, off the bedroom, was a tight fit, but spotless also. There was a fifty-two-inch flat-screen television in the den. A small sign on the wall had the guest password for Apple TV.

At Raedeker Park, Todd turned off his car, slid out, and closed the door behind him. He'd left his video camera at home, thinking if there were any ruins, his iPhone's camera would work fine. Unfortunately, his skepticism had grown since his encounter with the lackluster clerk at The Motor Lodge. Even if the young man had grown up elsewhere, if there were ruins of the old amusement park to explore, he should've heard about it. Also, on the phone, Patrick McDonough had sounded as if he'd forgotten Raedeker Park once had rides, which didn't bode well.

In the office building's lobby, a blond woman informed Todd that Mr. McDonough would be along shortly. She directed him to a waiting area that lacked the personality of the picturesque Adirondack town he'd briefly glanced at on the ride over. It also struck him (uncomfortably) how similar the receptionist's behavior was to the clerk at The Motor Lodge.

He tried to push away his unease. They were two bored young people trudging through boring jobs. He'd probably feel and act the same in their shoes. A plausible explanation, one he mostly believed.

What the receptionist lacked in personality, however, Patrick Mc-Donough made up for in spades. A large, gregarious man who smiled easily, Patrick McDonough opened his office door not ten minutes after Todd sat down. He approached Todd, grinning, eyes bright.

"Mr. Houts! Patrick McDonough." He extended a huge hand Todd feared would crush his own. "Sorry to keep you waiting. Was chatting with the elementary school principal about their annual zoo field trip."

McDonough pumped his hand once and released it. Todd smiled. McDonough's infectious goodwill made it hard not to. "No problem. Thanks for making the time to see me."

"My pleasure. Your call certainly intrigued me." He gestured into his office. "Come in. Make yourself comfortable."

Todd rose and followed McDonough into his office. The park director allowed Todd by, then closed the door. He gestured to a chair before a battered oak desk cluttered with papers. Todd sat as McDonough rounded his desk and took his desk seat.

"So," he began, "you're a podcaster covering abandoned amusement parks. Someone recommended us, because of old Raedeker Park Amusements?"

"Yes. A listener suggested I visit what was left of it."

McDonough's smile faded slightly. He sat back in a black leather chair and steepled his fingers before him. "That's what intrigues me. I didn't address it over the phone, because I wanted to make sure what you were asking, in person. There aren't any ruins. No old rides, concessions, roller coasters, or anything. All torn down not long after the amusement park closed."

Todd sighed, his worst fears about this being a prank seemingly confirmed. He pulled his phone out of his pocket. "There were some videos of someone exploring the park at night..."

He could hear the shrug in McDonough's voice as he pulled up his phone's browser and the bookmarked YouTube channel. "Videos of someone exploring an amusement park at night, maybe. Not Raedeker Park. There's nothing to explore."

Of course, McDonough could be right. He'd seen nothing in the videos which had identified what park they'd been taken in. They could've been taken anywhere, then posted on the YouTube channel as a prank, as he'd feared.

Why or to what end, Todd didn't know. As the host of a niche paranormal investigation web series, he did have his share of trolls who (ironically) accused him of altering photos. Maybe High-Flight33 was a sock-puppet created to send him on a snipe hunt, nothing more.

That didn't feel right, however. Todd didn't know why. Maybe the videos felt too ominous to be a prank. He would've expected over-enthusiastic narration in an attempt to bait him. Unless this was the work of an incredibly insightful prankster.

He glanced down at HighFlight33's YouTube channel. No videos. Sometime between this morning and now, HighFlight33 had deleted them. Which, Todd knew, was easy to do. It took two clicks. That's all.

He glanced at McDonough, struggling to keep the dismay from his face. Seeing the park director's sympathetic face, it was obvious he'd failed. "They're gone," he said. "Whoever posted those videos must've deleted them."

"Huh." McDonough crossed his arms, looking even more sympathetic, which only made Todd feel worse. "This the first time a listener had recommended a fake place to visit?"

"This has never happened before, trust me. I've got my share of internet trolls, but no one's ever tried to bait me on a snipe hunt."

"Wow. Crazy." McDonough shrugged. "Look, I feel bad. You came all this way for nothing. Why don't I take you down there? Nothing left except the zoo entrance and the Shelby Road entrance, which is blocked by debris. Gated, too. All grown over where the rides used to be, and while it's probably not what you want, it's still a bit spooky. And, I will say this." He smiled. "Some of our more domesticated animals need to stretch their legs. Keeps them happier and healthier. Even though the field would be the perfect place for it, my employees won't take them there. Also, townies hardly ever sneak in there. So maybe the place does have kind of a vibe."

Todd thought it over. A quick spot touring the park's empty grounds could serve as a good space-filler. Especially if he could dredge up some more actual information about why the park closed. At the local library, more likely than not.

Even so. Perhaps it would be good to call things even. He'd been suckered by a troll. Led to a destination that didn't exist. First time in his career, which wasn't bad odds. If he walked away now, maybe it would be for the best.

Of course, walking away meant going home to an empty apartment. He'd have to confront the same things he always did. Memories of Bob. His smile. Bright blue eyes. The way he laughed. How his curls lay wet on his brow after he got out of the shower, and he smiled...

Todd shrugged. "Sure. Why not?"

12.

3:00 PM

Concrete steps descended from the park's office building to its entrance, bypassing the front drive, which meandered through the trees. Neither of them spoke, but as they reached the entrance, Mc-Donough remarked, "You need a camera?"

Todd held up his iPhone. "This has Dolby Vision, HD recording."

McDonough nodded and said nothing further. As they passed the ticket booth at the entrance, he nodded at the attendant, and they entered the zoo.

While they walked past a road branching sharply uphill to the left, Todd felt conflicting things about the Zoo. On one hand, it boasted an impressive array of diverse animal exhibits in such a narrow valley. Todd saw exhibits for everything from an alpine goat to black howler monkeys and two-toed sloths.

However, while some of the exhibits were extremely well-done, a curious air of benign neglect hung over others. Some were empty and appeared long unused, with no signs of recent occupation. He couldn't form a concrete opinion of the place. Whoever oversaw the day-to-day operations didn't appear to have a coherent vision for the zoo.

After about twenty minutes, Todd noticed the last few exhibits they'd passed had been empty. The asphalt path felt more uneven, with shoots of grass pushing up through cracks. As if sensing Todd's thoughts, McDonough said, "My predecessors stopped using this stretch twenty years ago. For some reason, the animals here never fared well. Many of them died, for no reasons veterinarians could ever tell."

He gestured vaguely. "This stretch leads to the entrance of the old amusement park. The previous directors never came out and said this end of the zoo was haunted. They just stopped using it."

Todd nodded, thinking he'd get some footage of the empty cages and the cracked walk on his way back.

The director withdrew a large keyring from his pocket. Sorted through them, until he found one. He gestured ahead. "There it is. The old entrance to Raedeker Park Amusements, and the only remaining ride."

Todd had to force himself not to stumble. A cold sensation pulsed through him. His thighs felt slightly weak. McDonough had gestured at an old stone archway that stood about fifteen feet high and twenty feet across. On the arch, he could make out RAEDEKER PARK AMUSE-MENTS chiseled in ornate script. It appeared incredibly old. Almost antiquarian, but the archway itself hadn't provoked his reaction.

It was the carousel that sat past the arch. The same carousel he'd seen in one of Highflight33's now-deleted YouTube videos. He felt sure of it.

A strange sensation curdled in his belly. His mouth and throat felt oddly dry. He swallowed and said, "I thought there wasn't anything left."

McDonough stopped at the chain-link fence barring the way. He shrugged as he unlocked the gate's padlock. "Yeah, it's weird. I forget it's here, most of the time."

He snapped the padlock open and unlatched the gate. Pushed it in-ward. "After you."

For the briefest of moments, Todd felt another burst of hesitancy. A warning that he stood on the brink of a threshold. A ridiculous notion, one he shook off as he walked through the gate. McDonough followed, closing the gate behind them.

The padlock snapped shut.

Todd glanced over his shoulder. McDonough turned away from the now-locked gate and shrugged again. "Don't want any visitors wandering back here. Lots of debris under the tall grass. Last thing we need are a bunch of insurance claims."

The explanation rang hollow, for some reason. There wasn't much Todd could say in return, however. He nodded and continued forward.

As he approached the old carousel, which sat crooked on its axis, Todd's guts clenched. It was the same carousel from the video. Had to be. The eternally screaming horses were chipped and worn in all the same places. He saw a bucking black stallion missing a chunk from its flank, like in the video.

Of course, that could be a coincidence. Any carousel left to the elements would show considerable damage. With the video now deleted, he'd no way of comparing them. As he rounded the carousel, however, he couldn't help but come to a stop when he saw the same uprooted palomino lying on its side.

"There it is," McDonough said, "what's left of Raedeker Park Amusements."

Todd followed McDonough's gaze across an empty plot of land about three or four football fields long and wide. He saw nothing but knee-high weeds and clumps of small, low-lying brush, interrupted occasionally by heaving patches of sun-bleached asphalt. It was on the smallish side as amusement parks went, but Todd had visited smaller.

"It's odd," McDonough said, "you'd think the zoo would've explored the idea of paving this and expanding our exhibits here. Could've easily doubled or tripled our capacity. A few folks—myself included—have brought the idea to the board of directors numerous times. It's always shot down. You'd think we'd try to develop this land. I don't believe we ever will, though. Don't know why, but I've learned the hard way that discussing it is a losing battle."

As Todd examined the overgrown expanse, his misgivings faded. A plan formed. Maybe this wouldn't be such a waste of time after all. He had no explanation for the videos posted to and then deleted from High-Flight33's YouTube channel. It seemed more and more likely (though it didn't feel that way) the whole thing had been a prank. Ironically, however, he realized he could spin the supposed prank into an intriguing mystery. Were the videos a prank? Or were they ghostly in nature?

He glanced over his shoulder at McDonough. "I don't suppose you have any employees with strange experiences they'd be willing to share on the record?"

McDonough nodded; his expression neutral. "Sure. How long will you be in town? I can put the word out. See if anyone bites."

"Maybe two more days? Three, if there's a strong response from your employees. Also," he gave McDonough what he hoped was a reassuring smile, "I promise I'll paint Raedeker Park in a positive light. Always a priority for me."

McDonough's face relaxed as if this indeed did relieve him. He extended a beefy hand, which Todd accepted in a quick handshake. "Sounds good. Hey," he nodded back to the zoo proper. "I've got some paperwork back at the office. Mind if I split? Feel free to wander and take all the footage you need. Just be careful. As I said. Lots of debris lying around."

"Thanks."

"All right then. I'm off." McDonough turned back toward the zoo. As he left, he said over his shoulder, "If you don't mind, I'm going to lock the gate after I've left. When you're done, call the ticket booth. Someone will let you back in."

He smiled again. "Insurance reasons, of course."

Todd nodded. "Sure. No worries."

However, as Todd looked away from McDonough to the weed-filled space before him, he couldn't deny a cold shiver. Part of him scoffed. He was getting himself worked up over nothing.

Part of him relished the sensation, however. It filled him with a watchful energy he hadn't experienced since the show's early years. He walked into the empty field so he could explore the sparse remains of Raedeker Park Amusements before the feeling faded, as it always inevitably did.

13.

Todd picked his way carefully through the underbrush. McDonough hadn't exaggerated. Chunks of asphalt and metal hid under the weeds, as well as the crumbling foundations of concession booths and rides. Also, the asphalt was heaved and cracked. He'd already stumbled several times.

Of course, as Todd had expected, his sense of foreboding had already faded. The demolition of the old amusement park had been total. Apart from the rubble, little remained. Certainly, nothing worth filming.

Also, he didn't recognize the layout from the videos. He saw nothing but knee-high weeds. If it wasn't for the weird similarities between the carousel here and the one in the video...

bullshit, they're the same one

He stopped in the middle of the field and panned his phone in a slow circle, recording nothing but weeds. He remained silent, not offering any commentary. Quite frankly, there wasn't anything to comment on. If he wanted, he could always add a voice-over later.

As he completed his slow pan of the area, his stomach felt heavy with the dull weight of routine. Nothing of interest remained here. Still, as planned, he'd spin HighFlight33's now-blank YouTube channel and its deleted videos into something weird and spooky. Interviews with zoo employees recounting "strange" experiences would spice things up. Sure, they'd be products of over-active imaginations from folks eager to perform. As always, he could knit them all together in an entertaining way. He'd done it before.

He'd visit the local library. Poke through old newspapers for anything odd. At the very least, maybe he'd find more details about the accidents that led to the park's closing. His viewers would eat that up. He'd name the episode "The Vanishing Carnival." The usual trolls would cry foul, of course, and (rightly so) accuse him of making it all up. Most everyone else, however, would shut them down. This episode certainly wouldn't gain as many views and ratings as the others, but over time it would perform well enough.

Todd panned the far tree line, about three hundred yards away, when movement in the corner of his phone's camera caught his eye. He glanced up in time to see something white flash into the trees at the field's edge. Branches shook in its wake.

Todd found himself rooted to the spot. Unable to move, he stared at the tree line where something had plunged through the brush, into the woods. Though he couldn't be certain, he didn't think it had been an animal. Something in his gut also whispered it wasn't gone. It remained, hidden past the tree line, waiting.

Watching.

"Okay," he said in a slightly breathless voice, "I know we've all seen this bit in every paranormal investigation show over the past twenty years, when someone whips their camera around wildly at nothing, saying, 'What was that?!' BUT. But."

He paused, swallowed, took a deep breath, and forced himself to speak slower. "You know what? Fuck it. What the hell was that?"

He took slow, measured steps toward the tree line. His heart had sped up. It took considerable effort not to pant. Nervous energy again pulsed through his thighs, down into his calves, making them twitch. "I definitely saw something dart into the woods at the far tree line. Maybe three hundred or so yards away. It wasn't an animal. Whatever it was, it wore light-colored clothes."

As he walked, Todd's heart slowly eased. His well-oiled habit took hold. In a much calmer voice, he continued. "I need to do more research here in Clifton Heights. Maybe at the library, because online information on Raedeker Park Amusements and the accidents which closed it proved scant. It shut down in 1979 after a rash of fatal accidents. Which would be uncommon for bigger parks with riskier rides. For such a small park, it must've been downright bizarre. Frightening, even. Which makes it odd that there's not more stories about it on the Internet."

A hump of indeterminate rubble—asphalt, dirt, rock, rusted metal—rose from the weeds, blocking his path. He slowed and changed course, picking his way around the pile, wary of tripping. When he cleared the debris, he refocused on the tree line, resuming his narrative.

"The deaths interest me, of course. I know what you're thinking. Morbid much? Even so. I know it's terribly cliché, but I believe deaths leave a stain. I'm sure of it."

And that, he was sure of.

In the worst, most personal way possible. He pushed those thoughts away, however, as they scrabbled against the door he'd constructed in his mind to contain them. Later tonight he'd again numb them with booze. Try to put them back asleep. For now, he'd ignore them, because he had a job to do, and for the first time in a long time, it felt real.

14.

Thirty yards from the tree line, Todd's foot thunked against something metal running through the waist-high weeds. He angled the phone down and parted the weeds with his free hand, revealing a set of rusted rails. They ran parallel to the tree line.

Were these the remains of Raedeker Park's coaster? Or its miniature train? He studied the rails for several minutes. Based on their thickness, Todd thought coaster. A chill shivered through him, prickling his skin. In one of the now-deleted videos, someone had been running next to a roller coaster. Trees had loomed above it. The coaster in the video had run along a tree line. As this one had.

Abruptly, "The Vanishing Carnival" didn't sound so contrived after all.

"So," he said, after clearing his throat, "I think these are remains of the park's roller coaster. It runs along the tree line at the field's edge, like the roller coaster in those videos HighFlight33 posted on YouTube. I don't know what that means."

Todd fell silent.

Panned the phone up and down the rusted coaster rails once more. Pointed it forward, stepped carefully over the rails, and continued on his way.

15.

He stood at the tree line, staring at the rusted, leaning archway. Its faded wooden banner read: *Wonderland!* Traces of a path crept through it. In the woods beyond, Todd saw small buildings and other odd structures. Also, weirdly shaped people. Standing still.

Next to the archway stood the remnants of what might've been a white hut with a yellow roof and blue trim. Now it was old and decayed. Wooden siding weathered and peeling. It slumped sideways as if sinking into the ground at an angle. Todd thought if he pushed it, the wreck would fall over. Scattered on the ground around the old building, Todd saw rusted mini-golf putters.

A miniature golf course. Wonderland had been a miniature golf course. McDonough hadn't said anything about this, either.

Odd.

Todd resumed his narration as he approached the entrance, getting shots of the old building and the archway. "Looks like what's left of an old mini-golf course. Strange McDonough failed to mention it."

As Todd neared the archway, he saw the remains of a wooden gate stretching into the woods on either side of the archway. He felt a little nervous walking under the arch, but he figured since it probably stood for this long, it would probably stand a few minutes longer. Also, the brush on either side of the arch had twisted itself around the remains of the fence. He didn't want to fight his way through it.

He took a deep breath. Steadied himself and walked quickly under the banner. Having cleared that hurdle, he released a breath he didn't realize he'd been holding.

He took stock of what lay before him and sucked in a sharp breath.

He'd encountered many strange things over the years exploring abandoned amusement parks. This ranked up there with the weirdest. Here, inexplicably intact, lay a miniature golf course in the woods. He didn't know anything about forest growth or how quickly trees grew, but based on the size of the surrounding tree trunks, Todd guessed it originally had been built here in the woods, albeit with less overgrowth.

The course was of average size. About the length and width of three or four basketball courts, though its boundaries meandered in gentle curves. As Todd panned the phone back and forth, he could barely make out putting greens and holes under layers of underbrush. What could be seen, however, was the attraction at every hole.

Todd eased forward. Most of the course features had little in common. An old windmill to his left. To his right, was a crumbling Gothic castle. Farther ahead, a temple or a church, though its shape was weirdly pagan in a way Todd couldn't identify. Despite leaving behind his Methodist upbringing years ago when he'd embraced his sexuality, he couldn't repress a shiver. Somehow he thought the rites in such a church would be strange. Profane, even.

Figures stood among the buildings. Some of them were wooden cutouts. Others were plaster statues that had somehow withstood the ravages of time. They were mostly intact, though riddled with cracks here and there, wire armatures peeking through crumbling plaster. As Todd drew nearer, phone panning back and forth, he slowly realized their connection. A bizarre mix of fairy tale, fictional, and folklore characters.

A hulking, broad-shouldered lumberjack to his left was most likely Paul Bunyan. A crudely shaped ax rested on his shoulder. His hand rested on his jutting hip in a haughty air. Though he knew it was his imagination, Todd thought he glimpsed a cruel bravado in Bunyan's sculptured features.

Past Bunyan stood a wooden cut-out of a little girl in a blue jumper with blond pigtails. Her expression was empty and vapid. Obviously, because it had been painted by inexperienced hands, not because she was empty and vapid. Regardless, the deadness he saw in the caricature's expressionless eyes bothered him, though he didn't know why.

The blond girl's identity became clear when Todd saw the shorter cutout standing next to her. A white rabbit dressed in a black tuxedo, wearing a matching top hat, and a monocle, and holding something Todd thought was a stopwatch. The perpetually late rabbit from Alice in Wonderland. This, of course, made the little girl Alice.

Todd pivoted to his left. He saw a cutout of two generously rounded men connected at the hip, with an arm around each other's shoulders. They wore faded green overalls and were jabbing fingers at each other. One wore a foolish, screwball expression. Crossed eyes over a gap-toothed smile. The other scowled meanly. Cruelly, even. Tweedle-dum and Tweedledee?

Todd grunted. "More like Tweedle-Dumb and Tweedle-Fuck-You."

Past the squabbling brothers stood another sculptured figure. This one was not from Wonderland but from the far off country of Oz. Another ax-wielder in a crude rendition of the Tin Woodsman. Its silver paint had long since dulled to an ashen pewter. The ax it brandished was missing its head. Its face was oddly blank, painted expression washed away by the years.

As he slowly continued, Todd encountered another resident of Oz. The Wicked Witch of the West. She stood ramrod straight, holding her broomstick to one side. Strangely enough, this sculpture had fared much better against the elements. Her pointed hat and cloak were still a deep black which glimmered in the sunlight. Her face a dark, disturbing shade of green. Her eyes were far more detailed than the others. They glared with a cruel malevolence. Though he felt loathe to admit it, Todd turned away from her quicker than the others.

He jerked reflexively.

Something flickered in the corner of his vision. A silvery movement. In minutes he realized what it was. A poor reflection of him in dull tin. A reflection marred by a creature painted on the tin. A crude rendition of something dragon-like. The Jabberwocky, lurking on the other side of the Looking Glass.

Todd completed his circle, returning to the statue of Paul Bunyan, ax brandished in both hands. He started to offer commentary but remained silent. Something snagged his thoughts. Something different about Paul Bunyan...

He looked at it through the camera's viewfinder, peering closely. Blinked, then raised his eyes and looked directly at the statue. It took a few seconds before the thought clicked into place. The position of

Bunyan's ax had changed. He felt sure of it. Initially, the ax had rested on the statue's shoulder.

Hadn't it?

On a whim, Todd panned the phone back to the Tin Man. A chill rippled across his flesh. The statue's ax was now raised above its head as if it was about to deliver a killing blow. Before, the ax-head was missing. Now, it was on the handle.

Leave, an inner voice whispered, now.

"No way," he said through clenched teeth. "No. Way. Okay, folks. Something weird is definitely going on. Those statues moved. I'm sure of it."

As he panned his phone, Todd felt a creeping unease bordering on fear. Even so, he forced the feeling down. This is what he'd wanted. Something he didn't have to exaggerate or make up. Something real. A cold rush of frightening yet thrilling adrenaline flushed through him, rippling icy prickles across his skin. A sensation he hadn't felt in years...

Something rustled in the brush.

To his right.

Todd spun, muttering "Shit!" He stared at Alice, his mind again trying to decipher why the cutout looked wrong. After a couple more minutes, he realized that the white rabbit in the tuxedo had vanished. Before he could fully adjust to this impossibility, he heard another rustle. To his left, near the Tweedle brothers.

The first difference he noticed was their expressions. Mouths howling in silent pain, eyes wide and staring at...

Todd could only gape. The White Rabbit had transformed into a ravening beast. Its wide mouth—riddled with needle-sharp teeth—was sunk into Tweedle Fuck You's leg.

Beyond them, he saw another absolute impossibility. The reflective tin had transformed into a real mirror, which was shattered. Through it, a nightmarish creature with shiny black hide was frozen in the act of crawling through. It wasn't a wooden cutout. It wasn't a plaster statue. Todd didn't know what it was, and he didn't want to find out.

As Todd backpedaled away, he saw something that threatened to send him into screaming hysterics. The Tin Man had advanced upon the Wicked Witch. She bent double over the Tin Man's ax, the head of which was buried in her guts. The Tin Man held the ax handle as if frozen in the delivery of his death blow.

Todd gave up. He turned and ran, mind a frightened blur.

At the archway, he skidded to a stop. He closed his eyes. Pressed his free hand to his forehead and drew several deep breaths. He felt strange, his sudden dread gone.

He took another breath. Opened his eyes, turned, and forced himself to look at Wonderland. It had returned to normal. Paul Bunyan's ax had returned to his shoulder. The Tin Man's rested in his hands, missing its head. The Tweedle Brothers were as snide and as petulant as before. The White Rabbit was once more a cartoonish thing at Alice's side. The Wicked Witch of the West stood, holding her broomstick, belly unmarred. The Looking Glass was once more dully reflective tin, its "Jabberwocky" painting comical.

Other figures loomed beyond those. The Mad Hatter. Queen of Hearts. A dull green castle Todd took for Emerald City.

What had happened? Had his over-active imagination gotten the best of him? It had felt so vivid. So real.

Todd stared at the mini-golf course a heartbeat longer, then pivoted and walked away. He tried his best not to conjure up strange eyes watching his departure.

16.

McDonough frowned. "Come again? Not sure I follow."

"Wonderland. The old mini golf course in the woods. Why didn't you mention it?"

When the park director had re-admitted Todd into his office, he'd exuded a slight air of annoyance, acting as if he'd spent enough time on Todd's situation for one day. However, his demeanor quickly shifted to confusion when Todd asked about Wonderland.

"The mini-golf course. Was wondering why you didn't mention it."

McDonough sat back and crossed thick arms over a barrel chest. "Because there's nothing left. Wonderland is older than the amusement section, I think."

Todd frowned also, a slippery sensation winding in his guts. "But I saw them. Paul Bunyan, the Tin Man, the Wicked Witch, Alice and the White Rabbit..."

McDonough nodded. "Those are the ones. At least according to pictures from sixty years ago. Last time I was down there, the statues had crumbled into nothing, and the wooden cutouts fallen over and rotting."

Todd fumbled his phone out of his pocket. "But I saw them. I have video." He tapped the camera app and started the video he'd taken in Wonderland. He pressed 'Play' and handed the phone to McDonough, who accepted the phone with an oddly hesitant hand. He watched it for several minutes.

His expression relaxed. He grunted and handed the phone back. "As I said. Barely anything there."

Todd accepted his phone back numbly, seeing nothing in the video but piles of debris and shapeless mounds.

It was wrong.

All wrong.

"I saw them," Todd whispered.

"Listen." McDonough's chair creaked as he stood. Todd met the man's sympathetic gaze. "I know you were hoping for something more. But the carousel's still there. And as it turns out, I've got more than a few employees who swear they've experienced weird things there. I'm sure they'd be happy to chat."

McDonough's attitude had shifted completely. He acted eager for Todd to come away with something. And? Todd thought the park director appeared relieved. It was written on McDonough's face. Relieved about what, Todd wasn't sure.

Todd tried to project an air of gratitude. "Sure," he said, his voice surprisingly even. "I'll be at The Motor Lodge for another day or so."

He was about to say more...but what could he say? That the video on his phone was wrong, somehow? He simply mumbled, "Have a good day," turned, and left McDonough's office.

17.

5:00 PM

Todd sat in his car as it idled in the parking lot, staring blankly forward. The first thing he'd done was review the footage. Hoping this time he'd see Wonderland as he remembered it.

Instead, he saw the same thing he had in McDonough's office. Nothing but indeterminate ruins. He re-watched the footage multiple times. Afterward, he closed the camera app, tossed the phone on the passenger seat, and stared out the front window.

Confusion roared in his mind. He'd seen Wonderland differently. He knew it.

A twinge in his stomach reminded him he hadn't eaten anything since breakfast. He'd passed a deli on Main Street. Dooley's Ice Cream and Subs. He'd grab something to eat. Maybe time and some food would clear his head.

He paused as he rested his hand on the gearshift. Met his reflected gaze in the rear-view mirror. He didn't like how haunted he looked. He snorted and said, "Well, you were the one who wanted something real. Happy?"

Unsurprisingly, his reflection didn't respond. Only stared back with its slightly haunted gaze, unbowed by his snark. Todd shook his head and glanced away. He put the car into drive and pulled out of the parking lot, heading toward Dooley's for a quick dinner.

18.

The roast beef sub proved serviceable. Not the best he'd eaten; certainly not the worst. Of course, it could've been the greatest sub in the world and Todd wouldn't have noticed. Right now, eating was a mechanical function, so focused was he on his objective.

The town library. Bassler Memorial Library, according to Google Maps. Hopefully, he'd find more information there about Raedeker Park Amusements. Maybe the library had old newspapers on microfiche. At least physical copies of old newspapers. Regardless, he needed to dig into the park's background. He always researched locations, but in the past, his research had been manipulative. To not only "wow" his viewers, but oftentimes, to trick himself into feeling something. The more well-developed the story, the more he could half-believe it, if only for the camera.

This was different, however. Something was actually happening. This was the real thing. A true haunting. He felt it, in his bones. Believed in a way he hadn't for years. He was (mostly) relishing the sensation.

A small part of him was recoiling from it, however. Whispering he should leave Clifton Heights immediately. Get back on the road and resume "business as usual." He wasn't in any danger of losing Ghost Coaster. The ratings were steady and consistent. The Roku channel was doing well. His producers at Fast Forward Media had supported all his programming choices.

Up until now, his existence had been safe. Predictable. Maybe things had turned a little stale. Maybe he was getting burned out. Tired of the dog and pony show. But he understood it. Could plan for it.

He didn't understand what was happening now. On some primal level, he didn't like it. If he kept pursuing this, would he encounter more than he could ever unsee? Things that would damage his view of the world forever? Wouldn't it be safer to flee?

His frustration and burnout were proving louder than his fears, however. Yes, his life had become safe, comfortably routine, and predictable. But he didn't feel whole. Something was missing. If he was honest with himself, it had been missing since Bob left.

He stopped before Bassler Memorial Library's front door. Closed his eyes and breathed in deeply. He wasn't going to think about Bob leaving him. Couldn't take the time. Wouldn't take the time. He had a job to do, and for the first time in a long time, it felt real. He had no time to spend wallowing in self-pity.

He grabbed the door's handle and pulled it open.

19.

At the front desk, a bland but agreeable man named Earl informed Todd that while the library didn't have microfiche and all physical copies of newspapers from before 1985 were archived at the town hall, the library did have a searchable intranet database of scanned newspaper articles dating back to the mid-1950s. He absently directed Todd to a table in the back of the library, on which sat four old PCs. Todd thanked him. Earl nodded perfunctorily and informed Todd he'd be at the front desk if further assistance was needed. Todd nodded. Earl left him without a glance.

Todd sat, pulled out his phone, and opened the voice recorder app. He tapped record. "Today is Sunday, August 4. I'm at Bassler Memorial

Library in Clifton Heights, New York, to search through the library's intranet for scanned news articles pertaining to the closing of Raedeker Park Amusements in the late 1970s. It's about six PM."

He paused, and then added, "Here's my first note: It's odd this information is stored in an intranet system not accessible online. In my experience, these documents are usually accessible through the library's website. Having these scanned articles on a separate system not accessible online feels oddly secretive."

He tapped *pause*, and clicked the old PC's mouse, bringing up a menu. It proved simple enough. Before long, he found the first newspaper headline about Raedeker Park Amusements. He read it silently, grunted in dissatisfaction, and tapped record.

"Unfortunately, the first article I've found doesn't say much. Only that the park was closing its rides because of climbing insurance rates and lawsuit threats stemming from this still-vague 'string of unfortunate accidents.' Oh...wait a minute."

He tapped pause, collected himself, tapped record, and said in a more formal tone, "The ending of this article—from the 1978 edition of *The Clifton Heights Tribune*—offers the first specific details about these accidents. Four total. Occurring in 1974, 76, 77, and the last in 78. Also...and this is unexpected, but here it is...in October 1973, the year before the first accident, a Brianna Ward was found dead on the carousel. No cause was ever determined; no one ever charged with her death."

Todd hit pause again. Stared at the scanned article, his mind spinning. Several minutes passed before he tapped record and continued.

"Why keep this from me? McDonough would have to know I'd conduct my own research. I mean, I get how this is probably something the whole town wants to forget, but letting me find out on my own makes me think they're hiding something."

He hit *pause* and clicked links to previous scans, searching for the accidents themselves, and anything more about the mysterious death of Brianna Ward. After about ten minutes, he'd found and read articles about each. He collected himself, hit record, and began.

"I don't think I've ever heard of so many serious accidents so close together. Especially given the park's modest size. Also, while two of them are probable, the others are unlikely. At the least, strange.

"The first accident occurred in 1974 when ten-year-old Sophie Jenks fell to her death from the top of the Ferris wheel. While it was stopped with her and her parents at the top, Sophie somehow worked out of her harness while her parents were arguing. Authorities speculated she was leaning out of the car when she toppled over the edge. This story is tragic but plausible, given the poor quality of restraints back then, and her distracted parents. The next accident, however,..."

He took a breath and continued. "This one is a little weird. A year later, Gladys Brown, single and thirty-two years old from nearby Booneville, died on the carousel. Apparently slumped over dead on the horse she was riding. No one discovered her until the ride ended. Doctors later testified to a weak heart due to a birth defect. A condition her personal physician confirmed. Witnesses reported her face was frozen in an expression of terror.

"In 1976, sixteen-year-old Clifton Heights sophomore Scott Belman was fooling around on the roller coaster—the Sky Diver, the second oldest wooden roller coaster in New York at the time—when he fell to his death. Drunk and trying to impress his girlfriend, fifteen-year-old Sheili Gotlinsky, he managed to get free from his harness and stood up on the coaster's first descent. He made it but fell over the side when the coaster made its first sharp turn. He died instantly when he hit the ground head-first and broke his neck. Again, a sad story, but not so strange, especially given Belman's intoxication.

"The next is fairly mundane, too. In 1977, eight-year-old Timmy Rogers—after ride jockeys allowed him on the Tilt-a-Whirl by himself, despite being far too small—suffered severe head trauma when he lost his grip on the lap bar and slammed temple-first into the metal interior of his car. He died several hours later at Clifton Heights General. Again, an awful death, but not so strange, especially considering how jerky those old Tilt-a-Whirls were. Honestly, I hate the damn things.

"The final accident, in 1978, is another odd one. Downright bizarre, really. And the one that drove the final nail in Raedeker Park Amusements' coffin. On the Teeny Train, of all things. On the morning of August 8, 1978, the train operator, Elmer Devlin, showed up drunk. Somehow no one noticed. Regardless, on the last ride of his shift, Devlin's attention drifted enough for him to not see the child who'd stepped onto the tracks. Despite people screaming for his attention, Devlin didn't come around until far too late. The train plowed into the boy and dragged him for about twenty feet, mangling him beneath its wheels.

"The strange part is this: witnesses say the boy—Johnny Novak—stepped onto the tracks purposefully. He turned, stared at the oncoming train, and didn't move as it bore down upon him."

Todd hit *pause* again. Sat back and rubbed his mouth, thinking. Now he understood the scarcity of information online. Conversely, he felt even more surprised he hadn't found any mention of these on the local folklore websites. In his experience, these unfortunate incidents always spawned urban legends about hauntings.

Of course, the park was torn down immediately after it closed. He supposed that explained the lack of legends. If there was nothing to explore, there wasn't anything to 'haunt.' This history also occurred decades before the internet, so he could understand how these accidents had been shuffled into relative obscurity.

Which, of course, didn't explain how HighFlight33 posted videos of someone exploring the ruins of Raedeker Park Amusements at night. Ruins which hadn't existed in over forty years.

Todd shook his head and hit record. "The first death—which remains unresolved—occurred in 1973. On Saturday morning, November 1, workers discovered Brianna Ward's lifeless body on the carousel. Curled up on one of the benches, appearing to be asleep. Police found no prints at the scene, or on her. No one was ever charged."

Todd paused, mouth open, at first hesitant to say exactly what he thought. Realizing he could edit it later, he continued. "This whole thing is shaping up strangely. A mysterious death of a town girl, followed by four fatal accidents, led to the park's closing. It's odd, but honestly, this whole town is odd. I've only been here a few hours, but all the folks I've encountered have acted distant. Not forthcoming at all. McDonough 'forgot' about the carousel still being up. He clearly left out the bit about a dead girl being found on it a year before the accidents started. And I still can't get over the town's secretiveness. These meticulously scanned newspaper articles are available only on a library intranet, with hardly any information online. The brevity of the press coverage of Brianna Ward was ridiculous. How little effort was expended in solving her death. Or, at least, that's how the article reads. At best, it seems no one tried to find out how she died. At the worst..."

He trailed off, thinking. After several minutes he tapped pause, wondering how he should proceed. Or if he should proceed. He didn't like where this was heading. Investigating his first real paranormal event was one thing. Getting tangled up in a decades-old unsolved death was something else entirely.

Was he putting himself in danger?

He couldn't see how. Clifton Heights certainly was odd, maybe even secretive, but surely town thugs wouldn't come knocking on his cabin door later tonight and "encourage" him to leave town. Surely (if Brianna Ward had been murdered) her killer wasn't still in town. Lurking in the shadows, ready to strike again.

Even so, he could easily stir up unneeded complications digging indiscriminately into sensitive town history. His producers at Fast Forward Media certainly wouldn't enjoy dealing with that kind of fallout.

"You're not Kolchak," he whispered. "Not here to uncover a crime or expose a murderer. You're here for a good and entertaining story, and that's it. This is backstory. For once, backstory you didn't have to make up."

He logged off the PC's intranet, pocketed his phone, stood, and headed for the door.

20.

On a whim, Todd stopped at the library's front desk before leaving. Earl, who had been diligently typing something on a PC that was as obsolete as all the others, looked up and asked in a pleasantly bland voice, "Find what you needed?"

"Enough for my purposes, yes. I do have a question, though. Out of curiosity, more than anything else. Why are all your archived newspapers on a closed intranet, instead of available through the library's website?"

Earl shrugged, expression placid. "I couldn't say. The system was developed before my time. Making it accessible online has simply never come up."

Earl smiled wider, his eyes flat and empty. "Was there anything else I could help you with?"

Todd offered a fake smile. "Nope. Thanks."

Earl nodded again, then resumed typing on the computer, as if Todd no longer existed. He stood there for a heartbeat longer. Shook his head, turned, and walked away, out the library's front doors.

21.

As Todd approached his car, he felt adrift in a sea of contradictory emotions. He didn't quite know what to do. McDonough was hiding something. Todd felt sure of it. Also, there was something sinister about Brianna Ward's death and the fatal accidents that closed Raedeker Park

Amusements. How it was sinister, he wasn't sure. It was a feeling. A sensation in his gut, nothing more.

Even so.

Todd passed a hand over his face and rubbed the bridge of his nose between his thumb and forefinger. He was trying to connect dots that kept moving. The only thing he knew? Something strange was happening to him, and he didn't know how far he wanted to pursue it.

Todd snorted. Did his viewers want something real? Or did they want to "play pretend?" As much as he wanted (hell no, needed) an actual supernatural experience, did his viewers want it? Would they even believe it?

"Ironic," Todd muttered, shaking his head, "fucking ironic."

He wasn't going to reach a solution to his dilemma standing on the sidewalk in front of the library. He'd booked two more nights at The Motor Lodge. Might as well head back to his cabin, transfer his phone's footage and audio files to his laptop, and record tonight's brief YouTube check-in, which his subscribers would be expecting.

He'd stick to the routine. Make his update overly general, dropping a few vague teases. He'd leave out HighFlight33's strange YouTube channel and its disappearing videos for now. He'd also skip over his apparent hallucination in the ruins of Wonderland...

it had been real

...as well as leave out the mysterious death of Brianna Ward. For now, he'd keep it simple. Stick to the basics. Give his viewers what they expected. He'd figure out the rest later.

22.

The Motor Lodge
8:00 PM

"There you have it, Ghost Coasters. I've taken a brief survey of what's left of Raedeker Park Amusements, and I can definitely say, without a shadow of a doubt, there's interesting things going on here, and an equally interesting story, too.

"Over the next few days, I'll explore some more. Maybe even interview a few park staff. Whatever happens, I can say with absolute confidence this is perhaps the most unique case I've ever worked on. You'll get the full scoop, as always, live Saturday night, 8 p.m., Eastern Standard Time. Until then, fellow Ghost Coasters...*ride scary.*"

Todd offered his customary two-fingered salute, then ended the live YouTube feed. The instant it cut, his face fell slack, smile disappearing. He sat back, covered his face with both hands, and breathed out, kneading his forehead with his fingertips.

He'd decided against a full-blown story about the accidents and Brianna Ward's unsolved death. He'd keep the footage of Wonderland for atmosphere. He'd cut narration about the statues moving because he'd obviously imagined...

he hadn't

it happened

Best to use clips and with a voice-over saying he'd "felt something strange" in the mini-golf course. At the least, it would be the first time in a long time he'd meant it.

Tomorrow, maybe he could interview a few park employees. If he was lucky, they'd share spooky or weird experiences. Testimonials always went over well.

Would he try to explore the field at night? He didn't think so. Even though night exploration videos performed well, he doubted McDonough would allow him night-time access. Those pesky "insurance claims" again.

Though it annoyed him, Todd had decided not to mention High-flight33's channel. Something about it bothered him. The name, for one. Taken from the title of his favorite poem, which he didn't remember quoting on the show. Also, he refused to believe those deleted videos had been a prank. Somehow, they'd been taken at Raedeker Park Amusements.

Impossible, he knew.

Even so.

The carousel he'd seen this morning was the same as the one in the video. The rails he'd stumbled over belonged to the coaster. They ran along the tree line, as in the video. Those videos were impossible, were deleted, and only he'd seen them. But he had seen them. For some reason, he thought it unwise to mention them on the show.

Todd shook his head, realizing he was going in circles, wondering if he should produce this episode or not. Of course, he'd just posted an update about it. In all the years of his show, he'd never failed to follow through. He wasn't about to start now.

He closed the video editor on his laptop. Got up and headed to the fridge for a few beers.

On a whim, he grabbed the bottle of Jack Daniels and a tumbler glass along with the beer and returned to the futon. He'd get a little lubricated. Watch some Kolchak, then head to bed. He'd sort things out tomorrow.

Or so he told himself as he poured himself his first whiskey.

23.

Todd was halfway through his fourth Kolchak episode in a row when his phone dinged. He picked it up off the futon next to him and glanced at it, expecting another comment on his live update. He'd received fifty so far, mostly generic remarks from viewers looking forward to Saturday night's show. He figured this was one more.

His guts twitched, however, when he read the notification. *High-Flight33 is now live.*

He straightened, his previously relaxed mind snapping into an icy clarity.

HighFlight33 is now live.

He didn't remember subscribing to HighFlight33's channel. He'd meant to, of course. But the day had gotten away from him, and he'd forgotten. Here was a notification from Highflight33's channel, all the same.

His thumb hovered over it. Darrin McGavin's voice as Kolchak faded into a vague background mutter. Again, Todd felt the dreamy certainty that if he chose not to watch the video, things would go as he'd planned. He'd shoot some interviews with zoo staff tomorrow. Collect some creepy shots of the carousel and empty field. Catch a flight home, and produce a show that would receive its usual amount of consistent acclaim. Then he'd move on to the next show. No fuss, no muss.

Also, he believed if he didn't click on the live notification, it would eventually disappear. He wouldn't hear from HighFlight33 again. Wouldn't be able to find the channel, even.

Maybe that would be for the best.

"But I want to see," he muttered, "dammit, I want to see."

He tapped the notification. YouTube opened. He enlarged the video to full screen. Stared at it, ice forming in his belly, spreading fiery cold throughout his body.

Like the other videos, this showed the camera's perspective of someone walking down a country road. As the perspective approached a road sign, the view shifted up, framing it. White letters blazed in the darkness.

Shelby Road.

Todd's breath caught. He swallowed down a dry throat, thoughts smashing into each other, making no sense. With great effort, he shoved aside his mental turmoil as he gazed at the video of someone walking down Shelby Road. Here in Clifton Heights. His hands started to shake. He fumbled his beer in his other hand as he set it down on the coffee table, almost spilling it.

The camera moved slowly. The white lines running down the strip of asphalt glimmered in the night. Todd heard nothing in the video save the muffled rustling of the wind and the measured scuffing of footfalls on asphalt.

The camera panned left. A stone archway loomed into view. The camera approached it, panning upward, until the arch's banner came into view. He read Raedeker Park Amusements in faded letters.

The camera panned down. The Shelby Road entrance appeared clear. The camera advanced under the stone arch. Shadowed buildings huddled on either side of a fairway. The outline of the Ferris wheel loomed above. In the distance, along the tree line, he saw the faintest outline of the roller coaster.

The live video snapped off so abruptly that Todd cried out and stood. His shin banged the coffee table. His beer fell, landing with a dull thunk on the floor. It gurgled out its contents, but Todd's thoughts were far away. All he could think about was the live video he'd watched. Of someone walking through the Shelby Road entrance into Raedeker Park Amusements.

"Fuck it," he muttered. He stumbled around the cabin, grabbing his coat, his hand-held DV camera, and his car keys.

24.

Shelby Road
Midnight

Though Google Maps claimed Shelby Road was only ten minutes away, the drive took forever as he followed a needlessly convoluted route through town. Not knowing his way around, and driving at night, Todd didn't dare try to find it himself, so he followed Google's directions, regardless. Even so, he couldn't help thinking something was toying with him. Making it harder for him to reach Shelby Road. A ridiculous notion, but it persisted as the drive went on.

He passed no one. The streets and sidewalks were empty. He didn't see any police. The picturesque, bucolic small town felt strangely ominous under the cover of night. Streets lit only by dim orange streetlamps and the moon. A profound sense of emptiness crawled over him. He felt as if he were driving through an abandoned town past condemned buildings whose only occupants were rodents, dust, and time. A powerful illusion, he knew. Even so. At night, Clifton Heights shed its pleasing exterior for something more menacing. A beautiful flower that was carnivorous in nature.

Finally, Google instructed him to take a right onto Shelby Road. Five minutes later, he braked his car at Raedeker Park Amusements' old entrance. For several long minutes, he sat and stared, a slippery sense of unreality slewing around him.

The entrance was clear and ungated. It shouldn't be. Not according to McDonough. A well-worn path lay under the stone arch. He saw the buildings, never-ending fairway, Ferris wheel, and along the tree line, he saw one of the roller coaster's hills.

Todd blew out a shaky breath. He turned the car off, fumbled for his DV camera with numb hands, opened the car door, got out, and walked on weak legs toward the archway. At it, he stopped, closed his eyes, took several deep breaths of cool night air, counted to ten, and opened his eyes.

It was still there.

"This is fucking insane," Todd whispered.

C'mon, Kolchak, a voice whispered in his head, a voice which sounded, bizarrely enough, like Darrin McGavin. *This is your chance. Your shot. If you don't check this out...you're going to regret it for the rest of your life.*

Todd felt the truth in that statement. He felt another truth, however. A darker one. This was an offering. An invitation. From what, he didn't know. He wouldn't be offered this chance again.

C'mon, sport, Darrin McGavin whispered, *don't turn back now.*

Todd took a deep breath. Raised the DV camera, took the lens cap off, and thumbed record. He walked through the archway, and into the ghostly ruins of Raedeker Park Amusements.

25.

Todd stepped carefully over the train tracks skirting the park's exterior. Tracks for Teeny Train. They arced in an easy-to-see curve. More than likely, he was standing where Johnny Novak inexplicably stepped in front of Teeny Train, before a drunk Elmer Delvin ran him down.

The final nail in Raedeker Park Amusements' coffin.

The tracks should be overgrown. Ties heaved out of the ground and rotten with disuse. Rails should be corroded with rust. They weren't, however. They sparkled under his flashlight's beam.

He approached the fairway, which stretched much further away than seemed possible. Indeed, the fairway and the park itself looked twice the size of the empty field he'd explored during the day. Maybe three times bigger. He tried to rationalize this disparity. Things appeared different at night. Loomed larger, more foreboding. He couldn't convince himself, however. There wasn't a rational explanation for any of this.

As he walked down the fairway, panning his camera back and forth, a strange sense of familiarity dawned on him. He recognized something about this. What, he couldn't tell. It just felt familiar. As if he'd been here before. Done this before.

The feeling of déjà vu persisted as he continued. Flashlight beam dancing on the ground ahead. The night felt still. No sounds, save the occasional sigh of the breeze and his shoes scuffing an asphalt fairway which should be cracked and shot through with weeds.

Between the concession stands he glimpsed shadowed hulks. Flat rides, he figured. Some he could barely make out in the gloom. He wondered if he was near the Tilt-a-Whirl, where Jimmy Rogers had his head bashed in.

Around the middle of the fairway, he stopped beneath the Ferris wheel. It loomed impossibly high above. For some reason, it looked abnormally large. Grotesquely bloated, warped, and misshapen. It was too large to be real, though he didn't know what that meant.

He stared at the Ferris wheel for several minutes. Thinking of poor little Sophie Jenks, who'd somehow gotten loose from her restraints while her parents argued about something probably stupid and trivial, then plunged to her death.

He thought of being in one of those carriages, trapped at the top. He'd never enjoyed Ferris wheels. Especially when they stopped so high in the air. He'd take the most nausea-inducing roller coaster any day over being suspended helplessly in the air. Just thinking about dangling up there churned his guts, so he lowered his camera and walked on.

As he continued, it got harder to make out the flat rides beyond the concession booths. He thought about leaving the fairway to explore, but the idea made him profoundly uneasy. He thought (crazily enough) that if he left the fairway he'd never find his way back.

Abruptly, he found himself at the park's far end. The fairway curved to the right, toward the far tree line where the roller coaster sprawled. He shivered involuntarily at the thought of exploring Wonderland in the dark.

it was a hallucination

no, it wasn't

He frowned and gazed over his shoulder at Shelby Road. It didn't make sense how quickly he'd come so far. It should've taken much longer to walk. Yet here he was.

He faced forward. His flashlight's beam fell on the old carousel. He approached it slowly, then carefully mounted it. His footfalls thumped onto the platform, sounding familiar. It took several seconds to place it. The footfalls of the mysterious cameraperson in HighFlight33's videos, when they had mounted the carousel.

Todd slowly navigated his way past leaping and screaming horses. It didn't take long to find the over-turned white horse, exactly like the one he'd seen this morning, and in HighFlight33's video.

Todd pulled his phone out and was about to snap a picture when he heard it. On the asphalt fairway, rounding the bend toward the roller coaster.

Footsteps.

Todd glanced up, quickly stuffing his phone back into his pocket. He aimed the flashlight back into the park and caught the barest glimpse of something white flashing around the curve of the fairway and out of sight. Indeed heading toward the roller coaster.

A strange urgency swelled inside. As Todd picked his way through crooked carousel horses, part of him knew he should flee, not pursue.

Even so, his instinct wasn't to head back to his car. He wanted to catch the figure. Wanted to know who…

or what

…it was. More than wanted. Needed.

He hopped off the tilted carousel and onto level ground. Caught his balance and broke into a swift jog. Panting, he rounded the fairway's corner. It reached out into the darkness before him, running parallel to the roller coaster looming to his left.

Part of him recoiled at the strangely terrifying prospect of him reenacting one of those mysterious videos. Running alongside a coaster at night, flashlight stabbing the dark. He didn't remember if the faceless cameraperson had been chasing anyone or not, but in some ways, it didn't matter. Here he was, like in the video. Running alongside a wooden roller coaster in the dark.

The white figure darted left. Todd ran faster, a compulsion urging him onward. If he didn't reach the figure before it climbed to the boarding platform at the top, if he didn't stop them before they boarded a car…

As the figure fled up the steps, Todd shouted, "Wait! Stop! Please!"

The figure was halfway up the steps. Todd reached the stairway, but before he mounted the first step, he bellowed, "Stop!"

The figure jerked to a halt and stood there, frozen. Even from such a distance, Todd could see the figure quivering.

"Who are you? Why…why are you here?" Then, at the behest of a crazy leap of intuition, "You're Highflight33. Aren't you? You suggested I come here. You posted those videos, then deleted them."

Silence.

The figure didn't move. Todd cried out again. "What is this? Why am I here?"

The figure shivered once, then fell still. For a heartbeat, and then another, they both stood locked in their positions. Him, at the bottom of the steps, somehow unable to climb them. The distant figure, wearing a white T-shirt and jeans, frozen halfway up the stairs, its back to him...

The figure glanced over its shoulder. Todd could see its face somehow clearly, despite the distance between them. At first, he couldn't comprehend what he saw. It didn't make sense. It couldn't be. He was hallucinating. Had to be.

It was impossible.

The figure stood a heartbeat longer. Eyes wide and oddly empty. Face expressionless and weirdly plastic. Todd opened his mouth to speak, to call out, to scream "Why?" Nothing came out but a dry rasp.

The figure turned away and continued its ascent. Todd stood there and watched it disappear. Even after the figure vanished, Todd stood there, paralyzed and helpless, belly full of ice-cold fear.

Bob.

It was Bob.

26.

The week things ended between them, Todd was on Ghost Coaster's first cross-country tour, in California. First, he'd visited Six Flags Magic Mountain in Valencia. Then, Knott's Berry Farm in Buena Park. Nothing supernatural happened, but he had a great time.

That's how he'd missed the signs, of course. He'd been having so much goddamned fun. In the weeks leading up to the California trip, they hadn't fought outright about Ghost Coaster, though there'd been several sharp-tongued close calls. However, Bob's questions about their future had grown more frequent, though he hadn't given Todd an ultimatum.

Yet.

Bob's growing distance when he was on the road hadn't troubled Todd much. When he returned home, Bob was happy to see him; Todd was happy to be home, and Bob's questions about their future would subside for a time. Until, of course, Todd's next trip approached. Though something about this cycle nagged Todd, he continued on his merry way, assuming life would sort itself out.

Fate, of course, proved him dreadfully wrong.

When Todd opened the door to their shared duplex upon his return from California, several odors assaulted him at once. A musty smell. As if the house hadn't been opened all week. Beneath it lingered a potent mix of bloated, gaseous odors, and a sickly sweet, rotten smell. The kind associated with food left in the fridge too long.

Especially meat.

The smells pulsed ice through Todd's veins. His knees felt so weak with fear, he didn't think he could take another step. He didn't have to, of course. Bob was sitting in the den. In his favorite recliner. Next to the beat-up but wonderful couch they often made love on after several drinks.

Bob sat, slumped over in his recliner. Numerous liquor bottles sat at his feet, empty or half-empty. Also littered around Bob's feet were empty pill bottles. Some were generic. Others, prescription. Which ones Todd couldn't tell, and he wasn't about to check.

He wanted to look away. Sink to his knees and bury his face in the floor. Turn and run out of the duplex, jump into his car, and speed blindly away.

He couldn't do any of these things. Instead, his gaze continued to travel numbly over Bob. His lap was covered with crusted-over piles of vomit. One hand still clutched an empty bottle of Tullamore Dew. A terrible image flitted through Todd's mind. Bob, in his final hours, methodically washing down pills with deep swigs from the Tullamore Dew. Throwing up in his lap, not moving. Sitting there, drinking. Vomiting in his lap. Drinking more booze and swallowing more pills, until the end finally came.

He'd avoided Bob's face. Which had been fairly easy, with Bob's head bowed, dead eyes staring into the congealed puke in his lap. But now, against Todd's will, his gaze traveled to Bob's downturned face. He couldn't see much of Bob's glazed, yet pained expression, wide eyes forever fixed in panic and terror. All Todd saw was a swathe of forehead (where he'd always playfully kissed Bob on his return home), and bloated, mottled cheeks. That was all he saw, but it was enough.

Todd's legs finally gave out. He sank to his knees, threw his head back, and screamed.

27.

Todd blinked and came to with a start. He felt confused, disoriented, mind fuzzy. His recollection of the last twenty minutes was disjointed. He had to sit still and stare straight forward for several minutes to try and piece his thoughts together.

He sat behind the wheel of his rental car, hand on the shift. The engine idled smoothly. He must've unbuckled himself—or driven without a seatbelt—because he wasn't wearing it.

His vision focused. Through the windshield, he saw Cabin 14, cast in the eerie glow of his car's headlights. He'd driven back to The Motor Lodge. He could barely remember. Snatches of Clifton Heights' night-shrouded side streets flitted in and out of his memory, along with ghostly images of an amusement park that shouldn't be there. Also, images of...

Bob.

Climbing the steps of a roller coaster, disappearing at the top.

Todd closed his eyes, covered his face with his hands, and rubbed his temples with his fingertips. After several minutes, he opened his eyes, shut off the car, got out, closed the door, and stumbled toward his cabin on legs that felt far away.

He let himself inside, gently closed the door behind him, and flicked the light on. He made his way to the futon, sat, and poured himself a glass of Jack Daniels from the bottle still sitting on the coffee table. Methodically, he began to drink.

28.

Todd jerked upright off the futon. He immediately wished he hadn't. His stomach sloshed dangerously, hot gorge rising in the back of his throat at the sudden movement. A powerful headache throbbed in his temples, to the pounding tune of his heartbeat.

Todd covered his face with his hands and sat still. He took measured breaths. In, out. In, out. He didn't move until his unsteady guts calmed somewhat, and the pounding in his temples eased.

When he felt a bit more certain he wasn't about to puke, Todd uncovered his face and straightened slowly. He ran a shaking hand through his hair and gazed blearily at the empty bottle of Jack Daniels sitting on the coffee table before him, surrounded by several empty bottles of beer. *Shit. Did I drink all that?*

He caught the faintest whiff of whiskey and beer. His guts lurched slightly. He covered his mouth and belched. Though his stomach lurched, he only belched again, nothing more.

Slowly, he dug his phone out of his front pants pocket. Thumbed it on. Saw the time. 3 a.m. The Witching Hour. From some book he'd read or movie he'd seen. He couldn't remember which.

It didn't matter. He needed to sleep. He was going to feel awful in the morning. Spending the rest of the night on the futon was only going to make him feel worse. The trick, of course, was getting to bed without heaving his guts.

Todd breathed deep, then slowly pushed himself off the futon to a wobbly, sitting position. His thighs quivered. The floor tilted slightly under his feet. A dizzying numbness spread through him. Still drunk.

Feeling as if he were miles away from his body, or as if he were floating above it, Todd slowly inched his way to the kitchen. He grabbed a bottle of Gatorade off the counter. Turned, and shuffled back across the den toward the bedroom.

He didn't bother with the lights or getting undressed. He set the Gatorade on the nightstand next to the bed. Sat on the bed, gently fumbled each shoe off, and then slowly laid down and worked himself under the covers, praying the room wouldn't spin.

It didn't.

He dropped off almost instantly into a deep slumber.

He didn't dream.

29.

Bob hadn't left a note, a video, or anything indicating his reasons for killing himself. At first, Todd had felt a shameful kind of gratitude. It was hard enough grappling with the impossibility of Bob taking his life. During the first several days after, Todd wasn't sure he could've handled knowing why. The mystery of it was better, at first. Kinder, even.

As the weeks passed, however, bleeding over into months, this mystery grew teeth and claws and latched into Todd's heart. Todd began to agonize over what kind of creeping darkness had been growing in Bob's mind, and for how long it had been growing while he'd been out gallivanting around the country hunting ghosts that didn't exist.

After the funeral, Todd found himself alone. Worse, he felt guilty. As if he'd fed Bob the pills and poured the booze down Bob's throat. He knew it was irrational, but the signs were so clear in hindsight. How could he have ignored them?

Bob hadn't killed himself.

Todd had killed him. With his negligence, his inattentive selfishness, and his pride. As surely as he'd pulled the trigger or tied the noose around Bob's neck, Todd had killed him. And instead of haunting him, Bob had done the opposite. He'd never shown up at all. Even worse; he'd taken all the ghosts with him, so there'd never be anything to discover. The final punishment for a would-be-ghost hunter.

30.

Monday, August 11
11:00 AM

Todd woke slowly. Layers of unconsciousness peeled away, revealing the morning world. A deep ache blossomed in his temples. He licked dry lips. Tasted whiskey in his mouth and on his tongue. Apparently, he hadn't managed to drink any of the Gatorade he'd brought with him.

He didn't open his eyes right away. Instead, he covered his face with his hands. Rubbed his eye sockets with his palms. Tried to pull together shredded strings of memory and weave them into a coherent tapestry.

God. How much did I drink?

He vaguely remembered waking up on the futon after passing out. Somehow standing and making his way to the bedroom without throwing up. Miraculously he hadn't, but he instinctively sensed he wasn't out of the woods yet. He needed to move carefully.

For at least fifteen or twenty minutes he lay on the bed. Many years stood between him and his drunken college exploits, but he remembered the drill. Move slowly. Hydrate carefully. Talk softly...

An image flashed in his mind.

Of Bob, standing at the top of the coaster steps. Staring down at him. Of Bob, sitting in the recliner at home. Head bowed. Surrounded by empty beer and whiskey bottles. Lap full of empty pill bottles and clumps of dried vomit.

Todd's guts surged.

Bile flooded the back of his throat.

He scrambled out of bed, caution thrown to the wind. Head pounding, stomach clenching, and throat suddenly full of bile. Somehow, he made it to the bathroom in time. Luckily, the seat was already up. Vomit gushed from his mouth even as he collapsed to his knees before the toilet. His head pounded, pain squeezing his eyes shut, as his stomach heaved and he puked again, hands grasping and sliding over the toilet's slippery porcelain.

His intestinal heaves tapered off. After a few minutes, Todd's stomach settled into an uneasy stillness. He licked his lips. Spat several times, trying to rid his mouth of its acidic bitterness.

He sniffed. Blindly grabbed a towel off the rack next to the shower and passed it over his face, wiping his eyes first, then his nose and mouth. When he felt reasonably sure his stomach had settled, he shut the toilet lid and flushed the mess away. As the toilet emptied, he bent his head and rested his temples on the toilet's cool plastic lid. He closed his eyes and quietly began to sob, the image of Bob standing at the top of the coaster in the night fixed in his mind's eye.

31.

1:00 PM

Though Todd hated puking (who didn't?), in his moderate drinking experience, he always felt better afterward. This time proved no exception. Even so, he'd moved slowly around the cabin. A hot shower had helped. After he finally started (with great care) sipping from the Gatorade he'd gotten last night.

By noon, after slowly clearing up last night's fallen soldiers, he was sitting on the futon, finishing the Gatorade, carefully chewing his second piece of unbuttered toast. His stomach finally felt settled. Thanks to slow hydration and a liberal dose of Advil, his headache had abated. He still felt exhausted, however. Exhausted, and emotionally wrung out.

He had no idea what to do next.

What happened last night, what he'd seen...in a field which had been vacant during the day...

It had been real.

He knew it. He also knew if he drove out to Shelby Road right now, he'd find the entrance gated and blocked by rubble, with nothing but an overgrown field beyond. Last night, however, the entrance had been clear of debris and open, almost as if it was welcoming him...

Home.

With great difficulty, he pushed the troubling thought aside and tried to focus. He'd reviewed the footage on his camera after dressing, half-expecting it to be altered. To his shock, it had recorded the buildings, rides, the carousel, and the figure that he'd chased alongside the coaster. When they stopped on the coaster's steps and looked back?

Not Bob's face.

It was blurred by a fuzzy distortion.

He'd paused the video and stared at the blurry face for several minutes, confused. Maybe the figure had never been Bob. Maybe he'd imagined it. Even worse?

Maybe he'd just wanted it to be Bob. Even so.

He had it.

Proof of the supernatural. But he would never use it.

So why was he still here? To interview zoo staff members? This was an excuse, Todd knew. He simply wanted—no, needed—to know if anyone else had experienced strange things in Raedeker Park.

Todd sat forward and grabbed his phone off the coffee table. He swipe-unlocked it and dialed McDonough's office. After two rings, the park director answered with a brisk, "*McDonough.*"

"Mr. McDonough, this is Todd Houts. Was wondering if any zoo employees had stories to share, as we discussed yesterday."

McDonough grunted, sounding as if he'd hoped Todd would've forgotten. "*Actually, yes. A few folks. Why don't you come by around three.*" A pause, and then, in a slightly gruff tone, "*I trust you'll honor your promise to cast Raedeker Park in a good light?*"

"No worries. If I do my job right—though I make no promises—you might see an increase in business after the show. It's happened before."

Another grunt. "*Okay then. Give me a call when you're on the way. I'll make sure they're available.*"

"Thanks, Mr. McDonough. See you then."

"*Sure.*"

The zoo director hung up. Todd did also and rose slowly from the futon. He headed for the kitchen, where a bottle of Advil waited. For now, the mild pressure in his temples diverted his thoughts, but he knew it was only a matter of time before they seeped back in and took over.

32.
Raedeker Park Zoo
Carousel
3:00 PM

Even though he was sober, his stomach settled, and his headache faded, Todd's drive to Raedeker Park Zoo drifted through a hazy fog. He didn't feel connected to anything. He felt adrift as if he was numbly watching himself sleepwalk. In McDonough's office, he smiled and chatted about meaningless things with the zoo director; things which he instantly forgot as soon as the words passed his lips.

The brief peace he'd felt after talking to McDonough on the phone had vanished. All he could think about were the strange things he'd experienced. His hold on reality felt slippery. As if the world had become a greased snake he could barely hold onto. Even as McDonough asked questions about how the episode was shaping up, Todd numbly offered placating half-truths while his under-mind spun with what had happened in the last two days.

They left the office to walk down to the old carousel. They'd agreed he'd film his interviews there. The only remnant of the amusement park in the background would make for excellent cinematography.

"So. Where do I start?"

Todd swallowed and blinked furiously, abruptly dizzy and slightly nauseous, with a dull headache throbbing in his temples. He no longer felt hazy and distant, but disturbingly and vividly there. He coughed, rubbed his mouth, and focused on a young woman with shoulder-length brown hair and bright green eyes, whom he'd managed to frame perfectly in the camera's viewfinder, with the derelict carousel in the background. "Tell us the first time you felt something strange in the park," he somehow managed to say. "Your general impressions, and why you think it was supernatural. Oh, and start with your name and how long you've worked here."

The young woman flashed a smile, obviously excited to share her experiences. Todd wouldn't use the whole video, of course. He'd edit it, take the best parts, and use some of its audio as voice-overs for close-ups of the old carousel, the panoramic shots of the empty field, and the closed entry on Shelby Road.

"My name is Emily Brown-Bauer. I'm a second-year student at Webb Community College, studying Creative Writing and English. I've been working at Raedeker Park for five years since I was fourteen. First few years as a summer intern, then as an official employee in the zoo. I run concessions, work in the ticket booth, and help manage the petting zoo."

Something flickered in the camera's viewfinder, over Emily's shoulder, on the carousel. Todd frowned but dismissed it, assuming it was a variation of light, nothing more. "Great. So, when would you say was the first time you experienced something strange here at the zoo? Something you might call...supernatural?"

Emily beamed, clearly excited to share her story. "Well, it was about two years ago. The summer after my senior year at Clifton Heights High.

I'd heard lots of rumors about people hearing voices around the park and seeing things, but I'd never experienced anything myself. Anyway, it was a Friday night. July, I think. I was doing rounds, checking the animals, closing. I was down here, not far from the old entrance to the amusement park, when..."

Todd squinted.

Something flickered in the viewfinder again, beyond Emily. He glanced over her shoulder at the old carousel but saw nothing. As the young woman continued with her story (which Todd listened to with only half an ear) he looked back into the viewfinder as Emily rattled on.

"...I swore I heard someone whispering 'come with me' down in the shadows by the old entrance. I knew I probably should ignore it. How many times in horror stories has the dumb chick died checking out weird things they shouldn't have? But I followed the voice anyway, and..."

It happened with such swiftness, that Todd could only stare, eyes wide. When the body fell from the rafters of the old carousel; he twitched slightly when it jerked, its fall arrested by the noose around its neck. He shivered at the sharp cracking sound it made as its neck broke with its fall. Otherwise, he managed to remain mostly silent as Emily chattered away.

The body slowly swung around to face him.

"...I was overcome with this powerful feeling of, I don't know," Emily gestured excitedly with her hands, expression animated, as the corpse's face slowly swung into view, "sadness, maybe? Loneliness?"

The young woman's voice faded into a light background murmur as the corpse's face came into view. Todd gasped slightly (ironically Emily smiled even wider, assuming he was reacting to her story), because the corpse's face was ruined. Eyes wide and bulging. Face a mottled red-purple. Tongue poking out between obscenely swollen lips. Head at an angle on its broken neck, nearly parallel to its shoulder. It barely looked human, yet Todd knew who the face belonged to.

Bob.

"...you know about the deaths in the amusements during the seventies, right? And Brianna Ward, how they never figured out how she died? Well, I've heard places get scarred by death. Makes the barriers between past and present thin, lets violent emotions bleed through..."

Todd flicked his gaze from the viewfinder to the carousel. Nothing. No body hanging from the carousel's rafters. No bloated-face corpse with its tongue poking out between swollen lips. Heart pounding, Todd looked back into the camera's viewfinder.

The body, still hanging from the carousel's rafters, was now kicking at the end of its noose. Fingers grasping at the rope around its neck. Eyes bulging, face twisted into a grimacing mask of pain and fear. Mouth stretched wide, tongue lashing, drool and bloody froth slicking its mouth and chin.

Bob hadn't hung himself. He'd taken pills and drank himself to death. But there he was, in the camera's viewfinder behind Emily Brown-Bauer, hanging from the carousel. Flailing and dying at the end of a rope.

places get scarred by death

makes the barriers between past and present thin

lets violent emotions bleed through

The body hanging from the carousel jerked. A flesh-ripping sound filled Todd's ears as a red stain spread across Bob's white T-shirt. As if his abdomen had been slit open by an unseen hand...

his hand

he'd killed him

Bob's entrails spilled out from under his shirt in a viscera-coated mess and landed with wet, meaty slaps on the carousel's deck. The blood splattered, Bob twitched, and Emily Brown-Bauer prattled on, somehow oblivious to the dawning horror that must be spreading across his face.

The body jerked once.

Twice.

The rope snapped. Bob fell to his hands and knees in the pulped remains of his insides. He didn't collapse, however. He shakily lurched upright. Gore dripping from his hands and knees and still falling from under his shirt and pattering onto the carousel's deck, sounding as if someone was emptying a bucket of skinned tomatoes into a sink.

"...and anyway, it makes me think this spirit or whatever wants to connect, y'know? It doesn't want to hurt anyone or scare them, it wants to feel connected again..."

Bob stumbled off the carousel and onto the pavement. Somehow kept his feet and started lurching toward him. Feet dragging, neck still bent, head practically laying on his shoulder. Face swollen and bruised, engorged tongue flopping out of a swollen mouth, moist eyes wide and bulging, face screaming in agony. Even though Todd could only see through the camera's viewfinder, he could hear crooked feet dragging against the asphalt. Could hear fluids pattering as Bob lurched toward him.

Todd's mind slammed into a wall. Without a word to Emily Brown-Bauer, who at this point was trailing off, finally noticing his horrified expression, Todd spun awkwardly on one heel and stumbled away.

He didn't bother taking the camera with him. Fuck the camera. Fuck this place and his show. He didn't hear Emily Brown-Bauer calling out and asking what was wrong, her voice drowned out by the sound of crooked feet dragging against asphalt, which pursued him all the way to his car.

33.

5:00 PM

Todd moved around the cabin bedroom, hastily and clumsily packing his clothes, his hands numb. He felt separated from himself. Disembodied and watching from a great distance as invisible strings worked his limbs, as he moved at the behest of some great, unseen cosmic puppeteer.

A part of his mind knew he was in shock. A result of yet another hallucination...

no, real

...at Raedeker Park. Another part of him, however, insisted it hadn't been a hallucination at all. None of the things he'd seen had been hallucinations. He'd seen them. These things had been there, they'd been real. Not hallucinations, or mental manifestations of the guilt he felt over Bob's suicide. They were real.

Todd threw one last handful of clothes into his messy suitcase. He carelessly mashed the clothes, flipped the suitcase closed, and zipped it up, pressing down on the lid as he did. After, he closed his eyes and covered his face with his hands, trying to still his thoughts and force them into some recognizable order.

He had to get the hell away from here. He couldn't explain what was happening to him. Didn't even want to try. He wouldn't produce an episode about this place. Hell, he wasn't sure if he'd ever produce another episode ever again.

Part of him argued he just needed distance from this awful place. Needed to return home (a bland single-bedroom apartment which wasn't haunted by Bob's memory), and sort himself out. He could easily run a Top Ten episode this weekend to give himself breathing room before he needed to produce another one. Once he escaped this place and got on the road, he'd drive south as long as he could. Find a hotel, check in, and drink himself blind drunk. Wash away all the dread fancies capering in his mind...

His phone buzzed in his pocket. He stood there for several minutes. Eyes closed behind his hands, trying to ignore the phone's buzzing. Trying to wait it out. A call, a message, a notification. If he waited long enough, the buzzing would stop, and he could finish packing up his stuff and get the hell out of here.

But the phone kept buzzing.

As he stood there, frozen in Cabin 14's bedroom, hands covering his face, he thought it might go on forever.

"Fuck it."

He uncovered his face, opened his eyes, and dug his phone out of his front pocket. Swipe-unlocked it. With his thumb, he pulled down the notifications list.

Highflight33 had posted another video.

His thumb hovered over the notification. The video wouldn't make anything better. Whatever he saw would only push him closer to hysteria. He should ignore it. Put the phone away. Finish packing, and get the hell out of this fucking town. When he felt more stable, he'd unsubscribe to HighFlight33's channel, and block them, so their videos couldn't torment him anymore.

It made perfect sense.

Perfect, logical, common sense. Even so, his finger hovered over High-Flight33's notification because, quite simply, he had to know. Had to see, because he sensed this would be HighFlight33's last video. His thumb hovered over the notification for a heartbeat longer, until (quite without realizing it) he tapped it.

The YouTube app opened on his phone, loading the video. He tapped 'play,' and watched it unfold. It started where the last video had left off. With the cameraperson (who he somehow knew was him, now) chasing Bob up the steps to the coaster's loading platform. Bob was about ten feet away. He made no sound. Neither did the cameraperson, save their footfalls on wooden steps and slight gasping. The climb went on forever, with no end in sight. The moon hung high overhead, casting the steps in an ethereal, pale, unearthly glow.

Without warning, Bob ducked left and disappeared from view, apparently having reached the loading platform. The cameraperson continued ascending. Within minutes, the cameraperson (him) reached the top of the steps and turned left, onto the roller coaster's loading platform.

There Bob sat, in the last car of the coaster's train. Todd's favorite seat. Bob knew that, of course. Even though he hated the back car—and coasters, and amusement parks in general—he always rode in the back seat, for Todd. All for Todd, even though in the end, amusement parks and Ghost Coaster had come between them. Even though Bob knew he could never compete with Todd's obsession.

The cameraperson focused on Bob, sitting in the last car. As Todd watched, he felt overwhelmed with guilt, shame, and grief. His stomach clenched with self-loathing, eyes welling up with tears he didn't dare shed, for fear of never stopping.

"Go," Todd whispered to the camera person. "Go to him. Before it's too late."

The cameraperson didn't. They stood there; unseen feet rooted to the loading platform. Even as the coaster's launching mechanism creaked. Even as the coaster began inching forward, wheels clacking. He stood there, camera focused on Bob, who sat rigidly in the last car, white hands clutching the lap bar, back ramrod-straight, tendons standing out of his neck as the coaster gathered speed and clacked away, out of frame.

The cameraperson didn't chase after.

They panned the camera left, as the coaster rocketed away.

The video flickered, then ended.

"Damn you," Todd whispered as he blinked through the tears he could no longer hold back. "Why didn't you go to him? Why?"

A nearly overwhelming urge surged through Todd to throw his phone against the wall as hard as he could, smashing it to pieces. He repressed it, barely, and instead tossed it weakly on the bed. His knees buckled, thighs weak and quivering, and he sank to his knees. Slumped over the bed, buried his face into the blankets, and screamed muffled cries of shame and heart-rending grief, as a loss greater than he'd ever known filled him, and swallowed him whole.

34.

Shelby Road
7:00 PM

A numb kind of awareness seeped into Todd. He slowly woke, sitting in his rental car, parked on the shoulder of Shelby Road, before the old entrance to Raedeker Park Amusements. He had no idea how long he'd been sitting there. He'd little recollection of stumbling from the cabin to his car and driving through Clifton Heights.

Regardless, here he was. Parked in front of the old entrance to Raedeker Park Amusements, as twilight fell. As it had been during the day, the old entrance was blocked by debris and rubble. It was also gated. The rubble and the fence looked strange under the growing dark, however. As if they were slowly growing thinner. More insubstantial.

He raised a bottle of Dewar's to his lips, tipped it back, and swallowed. The scotch burned down his throat to settle into his already warm and glowing belly.

Todd hated scotch. Certainly hadn't brought a bottle with him to Clifton Heights. He must've bought it at Cutting's Spirits, the small liquor store on Main Street, though he didn't remember stopping there. He also didn't remember drinking half the bottle, but as he belched up fire and smelled the scotch on his breath, and slowly blinked heavy eyelids, he figured he must have.

He stared at the old Raedeker Park Amusements entrance, his mind a sludge-filled morass of despair. He tried to think, but couldn't. He tried convincing himself he had no idea what he was doing here, but he knew that was a lie. He knew, deep in his heart, what he was doing here, and why.

But he didn't want to admit it. Couldn't. So he tried to piece together the tattered fragments of his scotch-sodden memories, retracing his steps from The Motor Lodge to here.

He'd remained on his knees, screaming into the bed for a long time. How long, he didn't know. Eventually, he stumbled to his feet. Walked away from his luggage, exited his cabin, got into the car, and drove across town to here. He didn't remember making any stops, though the half-empty Dewar's bottle he clutched spoke otherwise.

And here he was, sitting in his car, parked on the side of Shelby Road. Outside the old entrance to Raedeker Park Amusements, as the sky darkened into twilight, and the debris and chain-link fences blocking the old entrance grew thinner and more insubstantial, as the booze in his belly warmed his insides, and slowly turned the world into a soft, fuzzy place.

A great drowsiness settled over him. A warm, heavy blanket. He leaned his head back against the seat's headrest, sighed, and closed his eyes.

A warm shudder passed through him. Something was coming. Coming for him. He surrendered himself to it, willingly.

35.

Todd blinks, feeling lost. He's plagued by the sensation of being somewhere else, doing something else, but he can't remember what. He's sitting in a car. With Bob. They're fighting (as they have been a lot lately) over something stupid. Bob's saying something, and he's desperately trying to listen.

But he can't understand Bob's words. They're jumbled, slurred, and Todd feels blurry. Has he been drinking? He thinks so, but he's not sure...

Bob's voice, finally understandable, breaks into his thoughts. "Why, Todd? Why the hell do you love roller coasters so much? You're obsessed with them. Don't fucking deny it. Hell, you love coasters more than you love me. I don't get it."

Todd opens his mouth to answer, but his head is a vast wasteland of buzzing white noise. He closes his mouth and shakes his head, trying to gather his thoughts, but the words are slippery. When his mind tries to grab hold of them, they squirt out of its grasp.

Todd senses Bob facing him, but even though he glimpses his partner from the corner of his eye, he can't see him distinctly. Bob's face is nothing but an indistinct oval with the barest suggestion of features. Todd stares straight ahead out the front window, unable to turn and meet Bob's gaze, because he knows, deep in his heart, he can't stand to see the pain in Bob's eyes.

A voice whispers, however: *this isn't Bob*. But if it isn't Bob...who is it?

What is it?

Suddenly, he can understand Bob again.

"Why, Todd? Can you tell me why? Why do you love roller coasters so much? Why do you love them...more than you love me?"

"'Oh, I have slipped the surly bonds of Earth,'" Todd whispers, "'put out my hand, and touched the face of God.'"

Bob doesn't answer.

"That's from one of Dad's favorite poems." He takes a healthy swing from the Dewar's bottle. "He used to say it before every coaster ride. He quoted it before he took me on my first coaster ride. No idea how he got me past the height requirement. Couldn't have been tall enough. Somehow he did, though. And you know what? I screamed the whole way through. Screamed with joy, at every bank, plunge, and corkscrew. It felt like I was flying. Slipping the surly bonds of earth and touching the face of God. I never wanted it to end. Ever."

Bob doesn't speak. He stares at Todd with a hungry glare Todd can feel. Todd wishes Bob would say something, but he doesn't. He sits and stares, until...

The car shakes as the door slams shut.

Bob's ghostly figure flickers through the rental car's headlights, across the road. Todd sits there, paralyzed by conflicting feelings of anger, betrayal, shame, regret, and soul-crushing sadness...

"No," he whispers through gritted teeth. "No. Go to him. Fucking go to him."

Manic resolve pulses through him, flashing his system with adrenaline. He tosses the empty Dewar's bottle aside (how did he fucking finish the whole thing?) and scrambles out of the rental and into the road. He almost falls, but grasps the car's open door and leans against it. Closes his eyes and takes a deep, steadying breath. Opens them, straightens, steps forward, and closes the door behind him. He turns and looks at the Shelby Road entrance to Raedeker Park Amusements.

It's completely clear of debris, now. No chain-link fence blocks the way.

This isn't right.

In the end, it doesn't matter. Todd crosses the road, passes under the arch, and enters Raedeker Park Amusements.

36.

Bob flickers ahead of Todd, too far, too fast. He follows, trying in vain to catch up with the figure. As he walks along the fairway, the concessions and vendor booths flicker in the corner of his eyes. They're empty, of course, because the park is closed...

or is it abandoned?

...but even so, he thinks he sees and senses shapes and figures in the concession booths, lurking, swelling, thrashing about silently. Something tells him he shouldn't look at them, can't look at them, so he doesn't. He walks forward. Gaze straight ahead. Down the fairway at the too-rapidly fleeing form of Bob.

not Bob

Abruptly, Bob cuts right, leaves the fairway, and darts between two concession booths. His heart pounding, Todd breaks into a run. Now he can feel the booze sloshing in his belly as the ground beneath his feet tilts, feeling untrustworthy and strangely springy. His run is a shambling lurch, yet he pushes himself forward, consumed by the fearful certainty that if Bob leaves him behind, he'll be lost to Todd forever. That's unbearable, so despite the haze clouding his mind and the alcoholic lethargy numbing his limbs, Todd pushes himself even harder.

After an eternity, Todd reaches the place where Bob left the fairway, and he ducks between an old shooting gallery and a boarded-up food vendor. As Todd passes the gallery, he catches the barest glimpse of things hanging on the gallery's back wall. Not stuffed animals. dolls, or toys, but gelid and reptilian things that squirm and thrash against their cruel impalement. Their limbs are ropy, fleshy, and thick. They glisten wetly in the moonlight as they twitch and flail. He refuses to look at them directly as he passes, but he can't ignore their fishy, rotting stench. Against his will, he wonders what decayed remains could be found in the shuttered food concession, and his gut lurches at the thought.

As he clears the shooting gallery and its abominable "prizes," Todd finds himself on a narrower strip of asphalt which leads to a looming building. Above the building's entrance, a faded banner reads: SPOOK HOUSE. Bob's form drifts up the Spook House's front steps and through its front door.

Dread bubbles up inside as Todd stumbles to a halt. A numb indecision spreads through him. He doesn't want to go in there. He senses—he knows—things much worse than plaster statues of monsters, vampires, and werewolves, and wire-operated ghosts await him. He doesn't want to see. He can't.

What choice does he have? Go back to his car? Drive back to The Motor Lodge? Or simply drive straight out of town, along dark night roads, cruising aimlessly, until he falls asleep and wraps his car around a tree?

Bob is in there. And even if it isn't Bob...can he possibly turn away?

He knows the answer, even as he asks. Squeezing his hands into tight fists, his fingernails digging into his palms, Todd walks slowly toward the SPOOK HOUSE, to follow Bob one last time.

37.

Spook Houses, Fun Houses, Mirror Mazes...these have always been Todd's least favorite amusement park attractions. They're the antithesis of everything glorious about roller coasters. Instead of flying you through wide open air, free and unbounded, the wind rushing through your hair, Spook Houses dragged you through crowded, dimly-lit claustrophobic passageways that smelled musty with dust, time, age, old sweat, and rot.

These thoughts swirl in Todd's mind as he stands in the Spook House's foyer, horrified confusion gripping him. Much as he hates Spook Houses, he'd much prefer them to this. This isn't a Spook House.

It's his house.

His and Bob's.

Impossibly, he's standing in the foyer of the house he shared with Bob. The house he fled several months after Bob killed himself, unable to withstand the memories that lingered there. And yet, it is and it isn't their house. The foyer appears the same. To his right, stairs ascend to the second story, as they should. Immediately ahead is the front den, with the same furniture. A couch and coffee table, and the same recliners sitting at either end of the couch.

However, the furniture is dusty, pockmarked with holes of rot, slashed with tears, and they appear as if they've sat here moldering in the darkness for decades. Past the recliner on the far end of the couch, against the wall, stands a bookcase where there should be one. It's leaning crookedly, however. Shelves warped and askew, spilling books swollen with damp to the floor. And not paperback suspense, romance, science fiction, and crime fiction novels. These are bound in strange, old leather.

The pictures on the wall—one above the couch, the other two on either side of the bookcase—are different, also. They're not Van Gogh's Starry Night or bland but acceptable landscapes of vague, abstract countryside. These portray images of hell; the kind Gustav Dore or Bosch would've favored. Depraved and lost souls flayed alive by capering, animal-faced beings in craggy grottoes filled with brimstone, fire, and bubbling pools of blood.

None of this is as horrifying as the thing sprawling on the couch. Todd has sensed it there, but he's refused to look at it directly, sliding his gaze over and past it, but part of him knows the time has come. He has no other choice. His insides twisting and clenching, he finally looks and beholds a sight born of his worst nightmares.

It's Bob.

One arm draped over his chest, the other dangling off the couch's edge. Legs splayed as if they'd kicked and jerked in his death throes. On the floor lay a .38. The back of Bob's head is blown out. Todd can see the ragged, gaping exit wound. The wall above the couch is painted with dried splatters of blood and brains. Bob's glassy eyes peer at something in the far middle distance.

Todd stares.

Guts heaving, bile rising in the back of his throat. He can't do this. He won't. He won't endure this depraved mockery of what was once his and Bob's home. A shiver pulses down his spine. He jerks around and staggers toward the Spook House's front door, which closed behind him. He reaches for the doorknob to yank the door open...

Something growls beyond the door.

A low, bestial, and hungry rumble. It slams against the door, rocking it in its frame. The doorknob twists wildly, jerking and rattling. Todd's heart skips a beat. For a dreadful moment, fear clenches his guts so tightly, he's close to vomiting. He swallows and somehow manages not to. Lurches around, and stumbles away from the door and the thing snarling past it. He stumbles past the horrid thing lying on the couch, down the hall of this mockery of a home, a hall which stretches out much longer than it should.

He stumbles against the wall and fights to keep upright, as the floor tilts beneath his feet. His stomach once again spasms and waves of nausea buffet him. All at once, he feels every ounce of scotch he gulped down in the car. He presses himself against the wall (which feels strangely sticky, and fleshy, and expands and contracts slightly, almost as if it's breathing, as if it's alive) and inches forward, desperate to remain upright. Somehow he knows if he falls and blacks out in this place, he'll never leave.

Doorways in this too-long hallway open into rooms which, as he stumbles past, are re-creations of the den, offering different yet equally hellish and grotesque scenes. The first several he pushes past. Eyes sliding over the same furniture and bookcase, and the different renditions of misery. Inevitably, however, Todd's gaze is drawn against his will to behold the rooms' offerings as he numbly stumbles forward.

In one room, Bob lies sprawled on the floor, not the couch. His hand clutches a rifle. Nothing remains of his face but shredded and glistening viscera. In the next, a too-familiar scene. Bob sitting in the recliner, feet surrounded by empty booze bottles, head down, lap filled with fresh vomit.

In the next, Bob's in the recliner again, but this time sprawled at an angle, body frozen in one last spasm. Hands clutching at his guts, face staring at the ceiling, expression fixed in a soul-shattering expression of mindless pain and terror. A strange blue foam bubbles and oozes from his mouth, coating his chin, flowing down his neck, and soaking his shirt. Lying on the floor is an economy-sized bottle of Drano.

Todd hears it several steps before the next room. The slow, rhythmic creaking of something heavy swinging at the end of a rope. He gibbers, close to hysteria. He can't. He won't look, goddammit, he won't...!

But he does.

As he inches past yet another door, back pressed against the strangely fleshy and pulsing wall, thighs quivering, knees watery. He gazes upon Bob's rigid body, swaying gently back and forth at the end of a rope tied to the ceiling fan. His feet jut out in different directions at the end of still legs, face frozen in a gasping rictus of fear, hands dangling loosely at his sides...

Bob opens his eyes.

They bulge. Staring at Todd, glittering with malignant hate. Inhuman anger ripples across Bob's bloated and bruised features, as he opens his mouth wide, far wider than a mouth should open, especially with a noose around the neck.

He bucks at the end of the rope. Body heaving, shoulders lurching forward as if he's coughing and gagging something up.

Blind panic flashes through Todd, shooting manic vitality through him. He pushes off the wall and scrambles away, but not before he hears a great intestinal heaving. A loud, ripping hurrrrk, and something gushing outward. No matter how hard he runs he hears it splashing onto the ground as the body keeps vomiting...

He closes his eyes and runs blindly, not caring if he slams face-first into a wall or if he trips over something because it doesn't matter anymore if his eyes are closed he still sees those rooms, somehow, as he sprints down a hall which never ends, past doors showing him terrible things, even though his eyes are closed...

Bob sitting in a recliner, methodically drawing a razor up the inside of his forearm, the blood welling and pulsing out of the slit and down over his arm. Bob reclining on the couch, rubber tube tied above his elbow, hypodermic needle ready to overdose him with something, even though Bob never used drugs, ever.

Bob shooting himself in the temple. Through the mouth. Under the chin. With a handgun. A rifle he triggered with his toes. Washing down bottles of pills with beer, wine, whiskey, laundry detergent. Bob on the couch vigorously fucking another man or even a woman or sometimes both, anything and anyone to fill the empty spaces Todd had carved out of him.

An endless stream of images and sounds assaulting his mind and soul through his clenched eyes as he scrambles and lurches forward, sobbing aloud at the phantasmagoric collage of Bob after Todd abandoned him, after Todd left him alone and hungry.

Todd's outstretched and flailing hands touch the door before he slams into it face-first. He manages to absorb the blow from his momentum with his shoulder. Eyes still closed, tears streaming down his face, his hands scrabble for the doorknob. He shouts in hysterical release as his flesh finally finds cool metal. He turns the knob, throws open the Spook House door, and tumbles out into the night, falling to his knees on the fairway's rough asphalt beyond.

38.

Todd lies face-down, sobbing. He wants nothing more than to roll over onto his side, curl into a fetal ball, and cry until he no longer has the will to move. However, Todd somehow knows if he gives up now, if he stays lying face-down in the night, he will never leave. He'll lie here, face-down in the dark, sobbing forever.

With a force of will, Todd sits up and stumbles to his feet. He sways for a moment, seeing double and even triple, through eyes blurred by tears. But he closes his eyes, squeezes his fists tightly, and somehow regains his equilibrium.

Not real.

It wasn't real.

But it doesn't matter. Bob's still dead. Dead, because of me.

At the last, a strange lassitude settles over him. An odd mix of apathy, resignation, and acceptance. Bob is dead. Dead because Todd left him alone too much, took him for granted. Nothing can change that. Not his guilt, shame, or remorse, or the nightmarish images he's witnessed. Bob is dead, and he is responsible.

Something cold grows inside Todd. A numb sense of detachment. Is this acceptance, or surrender?

Does it matter?

Todd breathes the chill night air and opens his eyes. He glances over his shoulder, strangely feeling no fear. Of course, all he sees is the faded exit door of the old Spook House, nothing more. He knows with certainty that now there's nothing inside but dust and decayed remnants of a long-abandoned amusement park attraction.

He faces forward. Though it makes no spatial sense, his trip through the Spook House has taken him to the other side of the amusement park. He stands before the humped, dinosaur-shaped wooden roller coaster. Right before the steps to the loading platform, where Bob is waiting for him. He knows this, deep down.

Not Bob.

Something else.

At this point, it doesn't matter. Nothing has mattered since the moment he left his car and followed Bob into Raedeker Park Amusements. If he turns back now, he'll be stranded here forever. There's only one way out, now.

Embracing the distance growing inside, Todd grasps the railing and begins to climb.

39.

Todd's climb up the coaster's wooden steps to the loading platform takes forever, yet it also happens in the blink of an eye. Even so, he moves calmly, with none of the manic fear he felt before. As he climbs, his mind is paradoxically empty yet filled with a slideshow of his life with Bob.

The day they first met at Disney, working in the gift shop. The first rush of recognition, of affection, then quickly, attraction. Their first date, at an unremarkable restaurant and an equally bland movie. The first time they made love, several months later. Walks in the park. Camping in the woods. Vacations to the beach, before Ghost Coaster took over his time and left Bob adrift. Bob's unabashed smile when Todd goaded him into grinning over something stupid and silly. All these images, snapshots of minutes frozen in time, fill his mind, even as a great roaring nothing also fills his mind.

He notices nothing else along his ascent. It takes forever; it ends in an instant. Time has no more meaning as he steps onto the loading platform and approaches the last car in the lone coaster waiting to depart. In the back, someone sits, wearing a white T-shirt, his head down on his arms, folded on the backseat of the car in front of him. Todd walks to the car. Stops, and whispers, "I'm here. I came.

"I'm ready."

The figure shifts and sighs. Then slowly raises its head and meets Todd's gaze. His instinct is right. It's not Bob, at all. It hasn't been, this whole time.

It's him.

As Todd stares into his own face—which is cast in a wooden expression—dismay pierces him. The loading platform sways under his feet. Confusion roars in his mind, devouring the slideshow of his life with Bob.

He opens his mouth. Closes it. Swallows down a dry, tight throat, and tries again. "I don't understand."

His reflection, his double, his twin, his ghost speaks slowly. "It's never been Bob. It's always been me. You. I'm the one you've been searching for this whole time."

"Who are you? What are you?"

Todd's ghost shrugs. "The part of you that loved wonder. Amazement. Joy. Mystery. Which slowly died, after Bob."

A pressure builds behind Todd. Something creeping up the steps to the loading platform. It's the same thing he felt in Wonderland, the same as the things hiding in the darkness between the concession booths, what lived up the stairs in the Spook House, what had chased him through the Spook House. It's here, creeping closer. If he stands here much longer, it will take him, and he'll never leave this place. Will be stuck here forever.

"A part of me died. After Bob."

Todd's ghost shakes his head. "I didn't die on my own."

An icy horror blooms in Todd's gut, spreading through him as he understands. Even as the darkness creeps up behind him, he understands, at last.

"I killed you," he whispers. "Didn't I?"

"Yes."

An all-consuming guilt washes over him, drowning him in its stinking waves. His thighs quiver in shame, his knees feel loose with self-loathing, and his stomach sick with self-hate. It takes all he has left not to collapse to his knees and let the gathering darkness consume him.

He forces himself to speak. His thin voice quivers with fear. "What happens now?"

His ghost shrugs. "It depends. If you don't come with me right now, you'll never leave. You'll stay here forever." He pauses. "With the others."

"Others?"

"You haven't seen them yet. Only sensed them. In Wonderland. In the shadows between booths and rides. In the Spook House. Damned to spend eternity here."

Todd swallows. "That's what I feel behind me. Isn't it?"

A sad, regretful nod. "Yes."

"If I go with you, where will we go?"

His ghost shakes his head. "I don't know. It may be better. It may be worse. But it won't be here."

"Will I see Bob?"

Another shrug. "I don't know that, either."

Todd stands there, grieving. As the darkness gathers behind him, a deep paralysis grips him, and he finds it difficult to move, to think, to choose.

His ghost extends a hand. "Please."

Todd takes it. Climbs into the car next to his ghost. Instantly, the dark pressure behind him fades. Over the clacking of the roller coaster, he hears a distant scream of frustration and anger, keening, and then fading with the darkness.

He meets his ghost's eyes. Sees nothing but a peaceful emptiness there, and then looks ahead as the roller coaster builds speed and rushes ahead into an unknown darkness. He wonders if, at long last, he'll finally touch the face of God, and if so, how he'll be rewarded for his impudence.

Clifton Lake

Wednesday

10:00 PM

Sitting at the kitchen table in my cabin at Clifton Lake, I turned over The Motor Lodge's last page. I felt a strange, disquieting, surreal disconnect. Especially after the manuscript's dry, matter-of-fact tone. It read with all the meticulous attention to detail of a stenographer's court records.

I grunted and pushed away from the kitchen table. Stood and got a cold bottle of Pepsi from the fridge (years ago, it would've been a bottle of Jack Daniels). Twisted the cap off, tossed it into the sink, and pushed through the screen door onto the front porch. With a sigh, I sat down on my Adirondack chair, kicked my feet up on the railing, and looked out over the moonlit waters of Clifton Lake.

I sipped my Pepsi. Thought about places like The Motor Lodge. Hotels. Motels, boarding houses, bed and breakfasts. I'd certainly stayed at my share of hotels early in my career when I'd traveled more. Never liked them much. Not sure why. I'd stayed in all sorts of places. Expensive presidential suite rooms to cracker-box single-bed efficiencies. They'd all left me cold. Still do.

I sometimes wonder if all those hotel rooms worsened my drinking problem. As if I'd had to drink more while in them, so their featureless, bland, identical nature didn't drive me over the edge.

They were transitional spaces, of course. In-between places, liminal, both literally and figuratively. Most of the time, the literal wasn't the problem. They were stop B on the way from A to C. A practical necessity on long trips that most folks don't think twice about.

For many others, however—like those Old Man Kretzmer had written about, and countless more—transitional places ran together like colors on a kid's messy watercolor painting, each place bleeding into the next, until life was nothing more than a blurred transitional space. An endless in-between with no meaning or purpose, or even worse: No end. Just one more stop along the way.

Old Man Kretzmer's stories weren't dated, except for vague references to smartphones and other minor things which placed them sometime in the last six to eight years. I thought of asking a clerk at The Motor Lodge about the people Kretzmer had written about, but I figured I'd just be told that was private information. I could get Sheriff Baker to lean on

The Motor Lodge...but to what end? Knowing this town as I do, the only thing they'd be able to tell me was that each person either quietly checked out in the dead of night or they mysteriously skipped out on their bill. End of story.

I could ask Sheriff Baker about Deputy Phelps' meeting with Ras Seager, but most likely, Tony Phelps probably wouldn't remember much about the encounter. And I felt sure Ras' death certificate read: "Death due to fire-related complications."

I usually liked to research details from these stories, but for some reason, this time I didn't. Some of the things I knew. Jesse from Rich's Auto did die several years ago. I knew because he'd always worked on my car. We did have a Nature Conservatory. So far as I knew, it was underfunded, understaffed, and no one went there.

I'd heard rumors about Zoo Town over the years, but I'd never had the courage to explore the gated access road above Raedeker Park. Same thing with the old Freivald Health Spa, which did indeed mysteriously burn down about four years ago. Folks suspected teens screwing around.

Ras Seager does have a website. It hadn't been updated in over six years. Likewise, the Roku channel GhostCoaster was finally canceled three years ago, after falling dormant. I do know the story about Raedeker Park Amusements, but I'd never driven down Shelby Road at night, and I had no plans of doing so anytime soon.

Of course, I knew the man who sat in his chair outside his little yellow clapboard house on Chester Road, the man who talked in a gibberish code to everyone. I'd always wanted to write a story about him but hadn't yet, nor had I ever discussed it with the shopkeeper at Handy's. I also hadn't received a strange phone call from a David Roth about it, either.

At least, not yet.

Through my re-readings of The Motor Lodge, I considered Googling names and local Irish immigrant history but didn't.

Why?

I decided it didn't matter.

So I sat there. Drinking my Pepsi and staring at the moon-glittering waters of Clifton Lake. Barry Spellman said there were more stories Kretzmer had written. Stories I could have if I wanted. I wondered if I dared. I wondered if I could say no, even if I wanted to.

I decided not to think about it further. I sat, drank my Pepsi, silent in my own transitional space on my cabin's porch, more aware than ever that I had no idea where I was headed, or how many more stops there would be along the way.

Gavin Patchett

July 28, 2021

Clifton Heights, New York

BONUS EXCERPT
From October Nights

We are delighted to bring you this bonus excerpt from
October Nights by Kevin Lucia.

CAMEO

When it's time
Say goodbye to warm
blood,
Shut the window,
And lean into the shadow.
See what happens
just after Midnight.
– Jessica McHugh

"Notice where we are?"

"A bridge?"

"Not just *any* bridge."

"Ah. The bridge over Cocytus."

"Where the veils are thin, and once we

cross, we leave the mortal realm."

"And into the world of enchantment, where we

see things as they really are."

"Where dreams are true."

"*Stories*, too."

– Boys in the Trees, 2016

October.

Red-orange sunsets bleed into purple-bruised skies shot through with yellow streaks. Crisp air nips at noses and earlobes. Trees wave red, orange, yellow and burnt umber tapestries, and withered leaves crackle across sidewalks. Jack-o'-lanterns grin joyful fire from porches. In front lawns skeletons, witches, ghosts, zombies, and other monsters sway and gibber. Everywhere, anticipation awaits the dark, magical birth of mystery on the last night of the month.

October.

My favorite time of year.

And, as it happened this October, I was in-between projects. I'd just completed the final edits for my novella *The Night Road* and sent them to my publisher. Two other manuscripts were with beta readers, so I had some free time. Seeing as how my best friends Chris Baker (the town Sheriff) and Father Ward (Headmaster of All Saints School) were out of town, this meant lounging on a late October Saturday morning at Bassler Memorial Library. Skimming books on folklore and mythology, as well as town history, looking for a spark to light the flame of a new story.

In many ways, I enjoy this process as much as the writing itself. So early on in a project, *ideas* were all that mattered. Gut instinct. Atmosphere. Sitting at a table tucked in a quiet corner of the library, books spread before me, notepad and pen to the side, I didn't worry about character motivations and whether they made sense. Plausibility was of no concern. I wasn't getting a headache from rooting out overwrought metaphors. I didn't care if plots seemed too convenient.

At this moment, nothing mattered but the sparks. As I browsed legends and sifted through our town's history, I reveled in a very Bradbury-esque "tingling of the ganglion and detonation of the dendrites." If a folktale caught my fancy, I jotted down the free-association ideas it generated. When odd historical occurrences gave me pause, I scribbled existential questions about their probable (and maybe supernatural) catalysts.

I'd spend an hour or so (three, if my synapses were really humming) filling up a composition notebook with ideas, questions, quick descriptions and plot sketches, and sometimes even badly rendered pictures which looked like they were drawn by a two-year-old. Of course, several days later, after the glow of my mania faded, I'd flip through the notebook with a cooler eye, looking for concepts "with legs", as they say. But at that moment, only *ideas* mattered.

I'd decided to write something Halloween-themed, possibly for release next year. I'd gathered several books about autumn myths and legends from different cultures. I skimmed the town history books specifically for strange events occurring around October. By fortune's gracious whims, I'd also found a slim volume of poetry which included a long poem called *Halloween, A Romaunt with Lays Meditative and Devotional,* by Arthur Cleveland Coxe. Several stanzas were thought-provoking, so I jotted them down into my notebook.

I hadn't yet formed an outline for the collection, but I was well on my way. My "ganglion tingling and my dendrites detonating." So absorbing was the work, I didn't notice anyone standing next to me until I heard a gentle cough.

I looked up and saw a smiling Kevin Ellison standing at my elbow. Kevin owned Clifton Height's only used bookstore, Arcane Delights. The same store his father owned before he passed away from Alzheimer-related complications six years ago. Like his father, Kevin had retired from teaching English to run the store.

He nodded at the pile of books before me. "Must be engrossing."

I smiled sheepishly. "Sorry about that. How long have you been standing there?"

Kevin chuckled softly. "Not long. No worries. I know how you get. Any good ideas?"

I gestured at my notebook, which was already filled with several pages of notations. "I do. The hard work will come later, when I have to figure out what's really good and what's not."

"Ah, yes. 'Kill your darlings.' The hardest part about writing. Well, I'm only here to complicate matters, I'm afraid."

I affected a stone-face and lifted an eyebrow, doing a very poor imitation of Mr. Spock. "Fascinating," I smiled. "Whaddya got? You know me. I'll take ideas from anywhere. Beg, borrow, even steal."

Oddly enough, Kevin didn't smile at my self-deprecation. "Remember when I re-opened Arcane Delights? When someone left us that box of... odd donations?"

I leaned back, interested. "Of course. That journal you found, containing stories someone wrote about Clifton Heights. They inspired *Through a Mirror, Darkly*." I offered him a wry smile. "I still think you should've let me credit you as co-author."

He shook his head, smiling... but an odd uneasiness lingered in his eyes. "Thanks, but no. *Through a Mirror* is all yours. Anyway."

He paused, smile fading. For a moment he looked deeply conflicted, as if he wasn't sure what to say next.

"Kevin. What?"

"We got another donation this morning. A box of books someone left outside the front door, before we opened."

I looked at him for several seconds, my ganglion tingling and my dendrites fairly exploding. "What are you saying?"

For the first time, I saw the black leatherbound book he carried under his arm. I recognized it, of course. I had one just like it in my office. The one Kevin found in a box of donations when he first opened Arcane Delights. The one containing stories which helped me write *Through a Mirror, Darkly.*

I gestured at the book. "Is... that what I think it is?"

He nodded, almost regretfully.

"I dunno, Kevin. Maybe you should use it this time. Write your own collection and take full credit."

Kevin shook his head. Shifted the black leatherbound book into his hand and held it out to me. "Nah. These aren't... my kind of stories. They're your kind. Plus, they're the kind you could probably use, right now."

My mouth fell open. I probably gaped like a fish for several minutes before I summoned the wherewithal to stammer, "They're Halloween stories? From Clifton Heights?"

He didn't say anything. Just shrugged, and held the book out to me. Barely restraining my eagerness, I took it—but didn't open it right away. I set it down on the table and glanced back at Kevin, feeling slightly shocked at the glimmer in his eyes. I saw what I took to be guilty regret. Even a little sadness.

I grinned. "It's fine, Kevin. Really. It's just a book, right?" I patted it with a forced nonchalance. "What's the worst that could happen?"

He offered me a small smile, turned and left. He didn't say anything, of course, because he knew better.

So did I.

Which of course didn't stop me from opening the book and reading.

THE RAGE OF ACHILLES

'Tis the night — the night
Of the grave's delight,
And the warlocks are at their
play!
Ye think that without,
The wild winds shout,
But no, it is they — it is *they*!

Halloween, A Romaunt with
Lays Meditative and Devotional,
by Arthur Cleveland Coxe

1.

Halloween
8 PM
All Saints' Church

The confessional door creaked shut and someone sat on the bench. Father Ward straightened from a state of quiet meditation and listened.

Only silence.

Father Ward wasn't expecting visitors. Normally All Saints was closed on Halloween but, as a new priest freshly home, he wanted to serve his community as best as was possible. He loved hearing confession and offering what comfort he could—and for some reason he couldn't put his finger on, tonight of all nights, he felt called to the confessional booth. Whether or not anyone actually came was secondary. He was here, ready to listen to whatever troubles anyone needed to share.

Hoping to set his visitor at ease, he bent close to the grate. "Welcome to All Saints," he said. "How can I help you?"

A cough. Then, "I... I need to talk to someone."

"How long since your last confession?"

The man coughed again. "I honestly can't remember."

"What matters is you're here now. What's on your heart?"

A deep sigh. "I've been away, but I've come back. I need to do something, but I don't... don't know if I can...."

I got back in town a few hours ago, Father. First thing I did was walk around. It was quiet, but of course things usually are, here. Clifton Heights is a rarity. Our worst offenses—at least, when I lived here—usually amounted to petty larceny and low-grade vandalism. At any moment, I knew a patrol car would roll by.

Yellow lights glowed from living room windows. On each porch were jack-o'-lanterns of all kinds. Here a round Jack, carved with the classic triangle nose and eyes and a buck-toothed grin. There a taller pumpkin, eyes more rounded, with a serpentine smile. Over there, one whose grin threatened to eat the world. All of them lit by blazing candles, throwing orange flickers on front walks.

I walked on, smelling the dust of autumn leaves and the faint scent of cooking pumpkin. It reminded me, too well, of one kind of Jack-o'-lantern in particular.

The kind Evan loved making.

The kind he'd never make again.

2.

All Saints' Church

"I'm sorry for your loss."

A rasping sigh. "Thank you. Evan was gentle and mostly soft-spoken, unless in the midst of an... episode."

"What kind? If you don't mind my asking."

"Evan had difficulty controlling his emotions, and he was large for his age. He suffered from poor coordination. Often bumped into kids without meaning to. But he never intentionally hurt others. When he got angry, he just wasn't rational."

"He loved Halloween, I take it?"

Father Ward heard the man's smile. "Yes. He adored it. Over the years he dressed up as superheroes, cowboys, knights, astronauts. He loved dressing up."

"And he loved carving jack-o'-lanterns?"

"Yes. He preferred friendly jacks, though. Cross-eyed with gap-toothed grins. He wanted a funny face on our doorstep, inviting all the kids to our house. That was the interesting thing about Evan, Father. He didn't want to go trick-or-treating. He wanted kids to visit our house, so he could give them candy. But every year he was disappointed. No kids showed up. I don't know why, exactly, though I can guess. No one in school ever bullied Evan directly, Father... but you remember how kids are. They dislike what they don't understand.

"He didn't have many friends. Didn't participate in any school functions, except the year he was a bat boy for the varsity baseball team. That ended in disaster, when one of their best players shoved Evan to the ground because he got in the way at the plate. He wouldn't go back after that.

"His outbursts in school earned him a reputation. Kids and even their parents were always looking at him oddly. As if expecting him to do something strange, at any moment. That didn't stop Evan from believing trick or treaters would come, though. Every Halloween, he'd sit in a chair next to the door, a bowl of candy in his lap, dressed in his chosen costume, rocking back and forth, waiting.

"No one ever came."

Emotion tightened Father Ward's throat. "Must've been hard."

"He always hid his disappointment well. Always smiled and nodded, with only a small glimmer in his eye as he said, 'It's okay. They'll come next year. I know it.' But they never came. And now... none ever will."

"Again, my condolences. Outliving your child is a horrible burden."

"It's worse. I blame myself for allowing Evan to...." A sniff. "If I had never...."

A gasp, which dissolved into quiet sobs. Father Ward waited, his heart twisted by the pain he felt radiating through the grate. Finally, the man swallowed and continued.

"Linda felt the same way. That it was my fault. Why shouldn't she? I made a decision without her input. Anyway. Several weeks after, she packed her things and left. Three days later I got a call from a divorce lawyer in Utica."

Night was falling, the sky darkening. I was walking, not sure where I was headed, but I felt pulled somewhere regardless. Though I imagined the houses on both sides were filled with laughter and giggles of excitement over the night ahead, silence surged around me, the only sound my shoes scraping asphalt, crisp autumn leaves skittering along the sidewalk, and the breeze ruffling the trees.

When I reached Main Street, I saw it was lit in yellow and orange. Storefront and restaurant windows were strung with harvest-colored lights. On doorframes, orange and black streamers fluttered. The windows of several shops were populated by cardboard cutouts of ghosts, goblins, vampires, werewolves and Frankenstein monsters. They passed by in a blur, until I found myself standing before Handy's Pawn and Thrift, on Acer Street.

Don't know if you've been there, but Evan and I visited Handy's regularly. After a bad day of school one September, when Evan was eight, I picked him up early and was driving around town while he sobbed *'It's not fair!'* over and over. He said a boy had stolen his box of crayons during Art class. He'd responded the way he always did when angry. He slammed the table with both fists as hard as he could and screeched at the top of his lungs. The boy called him a retard. Evan threw himself on the floor, kicking and screaming.

I believed Evan's story. I figured his teachers did too. As usual, however, *Evan* was the one sent home. I didn't fight it. You get used to it, after a while.

Anyway, I'd turned onto Acer Street and was heading toward the Salvation Army when Evan shouted "There!"

I stopped the car and found myself before Handy's. I'd heard of the store but had never driven by it before, much less gone inside. From what I saw, couldn't figure why I'd want to. The front windows on either side of the door offered nothing but old shoes, stacks of dusty board games, and piles of rusted tools.

I'm not sure what caught Evan's eye. It didn't matter, however. Evan had switched from sobbing to bouncing with excitement, so I didn't care what he saw in Handy's.

"What's up, bud? Want to check it out?"

As an eight-year-old, Evan acted younger. It's part of his condition. A developmental delay, they called it. I remember him pressing his face against the rear passenger window, breath fogging the glass. "Yeah."

"Okay. We'll stay ten minutes. Then we leave. Deal?" Linda and I had learned early on Evan needed specific timeframes to help him transition from one activity to another.

"Deal." A pause, and then, "If I see something I like, can we get it, Daddy? Please?"

I didn't answer right away. Whatever I bought would become Evan's obsession for the next few weeks. He would carry it everywhere. Home, on the bus, at school, in the car, to church. He'd sleep with it. Bathe with it, bring it to dinner. It would consume him, and drive us insane.

But.

I couldn't deny Evan this small comfort. Especially after the day he'd suffered. It would drive us crazy and I'd catch hell from Linda, but even so.

"Sure, Evan. If it's small. Okay?"

I glanced in the rearview mirror, and Evan's delighted grin nearly broke my heart.

"Okay!"

3.

All Saints' Church

"How long have you been gone from Clifton Heights?"

"A year. A week or so after Linda's divorce lawyer called, I left town. Went to stay with some friends down in Cortland. Stupid to skip out, but I just couldn't stay around anymore."

"Why have you come back?"

A pause.

Feet shuffling.

A deep breath, and then, "To make things right."

Handy's was the junk shop I'd taken it for. Tins full of screws and marbles, old tools, cameras, and jumbled piles of toys. I figured it wouldn't be long until Evan grew bored.

Surprisingly, he made a bee-line to some ceramic figurines cluttering a nearby shelf. He didn't hesitate and picked up a bird. A grayish-blue one with black wing tips. "This one, Daddy." Evan held it up, beaming. "I want this one."

I was impressed. Initially the figurines had appeared chipped and yellowed with age. In Evan's hands, however, the ceramic bird looked painstakingly crafted and life-like. Honestly, I could almost imagine it taking flight.

"Nice. What is it... a barn swallow?"

"It's a mockingbird. I take it you're not a birdwatcher."

I turned to see the shopkeeper standing behind us. He was tall, with a neatly-trimmed white beard and hair. His face was almost stern, but warm green eyes glimmered. He smiled gently.

"Not a birdwatcher, no," I admitted. "Not like my dad, anyway. He knew every bird around here by sight. Had most of the trees memorized, too. Me, I know a birch tree when I see one, can pick out a maple leaf...."

The shopkeeper nodded. "We all have our callings." He regarded Evan, who still cradled the ceramic mockingbird. "You've got something more special to mind."

Most folks looked at me with pity. In the shopkeeper's eyes I saw only admiration.

"He's not like the rest of us, is he?"

Something in his tone struck me. "No. He's not. He's different."

"Not different." The shopkeeper folded his arms and regarded Evan warmly as the boy continued to examine the mockingbird from every angle. "He's better. Better than us, anyway. And the mockingbird suits him." He paused, then said, "Mockingbirds don't do one thing but make music for us to enjoy... they don't harm anyone, but sing their hearts out for us. That's why it's a sin to kill a mockingbird."

I swallowed, my throat suddenly tight. I knew the quote, of course. We read *To Kill a Mockingbird* in high school. But as much as the shopkeeper's quote moved me, it hurt, too. "I appreciate the sentiment. At times, maybe you're right. Maybe he is like a mockingbird, and his uniqueness is music."

I gazed at Evan holding the mockingbird, and thought of his irrational rages over a picture he'd drawn wrong or a toy not working the way he wanted. I thought about how the slightest change in routine could send him into earthshaking meltdowns. "Too often, though, the sounds Evan makes are not musical."

"'O sing gods, the rage of Achilles,'" the shopkeeper whispered.

I sighed. "Not so romantic. He's not Achilles, or the gods, I'm afraid."

The shopkeeper nodded, instantly apologetic. "It is, of course, none of my business. I can't imagine the daily toll."

His curious spell over me faded. I glanced at my watch. "Wow. Almost four. Linda's going to think we disappeared."

The shopkeeper nodded. "By all means. The mockingbird is twenty-five cents. Feel free to bring Evan back. I have many more figurines in stock. Don't expect to have a demand for them anytime soon."

I nodded. "Sure. Evan, would you like to come in next week?"

Evan had wandered down the aisle as he'd examined the ceramic mockingbird. He glanced up, blinking slowly, looking more peaceful than I'd ever seen him. "Sure, Dad. Sounds great."

I shrugged. "Looks like we've got a deal."

The shopkeeper waved toward the sales counter. "A pleasure to serve you. If you'll follow me?"

Oddly enough, Evan didn't obsess over the figurines he would go on to collect like I'd feared he would. He did love them, however. We often came across Evan in his room, gazing at them on the narrow wooden shelf I mounted the day after purchasing the mockingbird. He sat on the edge of the bed, hands folded in his lap, rocking gently, humming to himself.

Evan's collection grew. He added more birds, along with owls, hawks, eagles, foxes, raccoons, and deer. In the five years Evan collected them, never once did the shopkeeper indicate they were in danger of running out. Up until the last day, the shelves stretched around his bedroom.

After it happened, I sat on his bed, staring at the figurines. They glared at me, their eyes accusing me for my failure to protect him. I sat there for hours, taking their judgment.

Two weeks later, Linda left while I sat there. I didn't hear her leave. Didn't hear if she said goodbye.

I never spoke to her again.

To continue reading, please visit Amazon to purchase *October Nights* by Kevin Lucia.

Continue reading
October Nights now.

Scan here to see all of Kevin's books

About the Author

Kevin Lucia has contributed short fiction to many venues, most notably with Neil Gaiman, Clive Barker, David Morell, Peter Straub, Bentley Little, and Robert McCammon. His first novel, *The Horror at Pleasant Brook*, was released from Crystal Lake Publishing in October 2023.

THE END?

**Not if you want to dive into more of Crystal Lake Publishing's
Tales from the Darkest Depths!**

Check out our amazing website and online store or download our latest
catalog here.
https://geni.us/CLPCatalog

We always have great new projects and content on the website to dive into, as well as a newsletter, behind the scenes options, social media platforms, our own dark fiction shared-world series and our very own webstore. Our webstore even has categories specifically for KU books, non-fiction, anthologies, and of course more novels and novellas.

Readers...

Thank you for reading *We All Go Into the Dark*. We hope you enjoyed this novel. If you have a moment, please review *We All Go Into the Dark* at the store where you bought it.

Help other readers by telling them why you enjoyed this book. No need to write an in-depth discussion. Even a single sentence will be greatly appreciated. Reviews go a long way to helping a book sell, and is great for an author's career. It'll also help us to continue publishing quality books.

Thank you again for taking the time to journey with Crystal Lake Publishing.

You will find links to all our social media platforms on our Linktree page. https://linktr.ee/CrystalLakePublishing

Follow us on Amazon:

MISSION STATEMENT

Since its founding in August 2012, Crystal Lake has quickly become one of the world's leading publishers of Dark Fiction and Horror books. In 2023, Crystal Lake officially transitioned into an entertainment company, joining several other divisions, genres, and imprints, including Torrid Waters, Crystal Lake Comics, Crystal Lake Games, Crystal Lake Kids, and many more.

While we strive to present only the highest quality fiction and entertainment, we also endeavour to support authors along their writing journey. We offer our time and experience in non-fiction projects, as well as author mentoring and services, at competitive prices.

With several Bram Stoker Award wins and many other wins and nominations (including the HWA's Specialty Press Award), Crystal Lake Publishing puts integrity, honor, and respect at the forefront of our publishing operations.

We strive for each book and outreach program we spearhead to not only entertain and touch or comment on issues that affect our readers, but also to strengthen and support the Dark Fiction field and its authors.

Not only do we find and publish authors we believe are destined for greatness, but we strive to work with men and women who endeavour to be decent human beings who care more for others than themselves, while still being hard working, driven, and passionate artists and storytellers.

Crystal Lake Publishing is and will always be a beacon of what passion and dedication, combined with overwhelming teamwork and respect, can accomplish. We endeavour to know each and every one of our readers, while building personal relationships with our authors, reviewers, bloggers, podcasters, bookstores, and libraries.

We will be as trustworthy, forthright, and transparent as any business can be, while also keeping most of the headaches away from our authors, since it's our job to solve the problems so they can stay in a creative mind. Which of course also means paying our authors.

We do not just publish books, we present to you worlds within your world, doors within your mind, from talented authors who sacrifice so much for a moment of your time.

There are some amazing small presses out there, and through collaboration and open forums we will continue to support other presses in the goal of helping authors and showing the world what quality small presses are capable of accomplishing. No one wins when a small press goes down, so we will always be there to support hardworking, legitimate presses and their authors. We don't see Crystal Lake as the best press out there, but we will always strive to be the best, strive to be the most interactive and grateful, and even blessed press around. No matter what happens over time, we will also take our mission very seriously while appreciating where we are and enjoying the journey.

What do we offer our authors that they can't do for themselves through self-publishing?

We are big supporters of self-publishing (especially hybrid publishing), if done with care, patience, and planning. However, not every author has the time or inclination to do market research, advertise, and set up book launch strategies. Although a lot of authors are successful in doing it all, strong small presses will always be there for the authors who just want to do what they do best: write.

What we offer is experience, industry knowledge, contacts and trust built up over years. And due to our strong brand and trusting fanbase, every Crystal Lake Publishing book comes with weight of respect. In time our fans begin to trust our judgment and will try a new author purely based on our support of said author.

With each launch we strive to fine-tune our approach, learn from our mistakes, and increase our reach. We continue to assure our authors that we're here for them and that we'll carry the weight of the launch and dealing with third parties while they focus on their strengths—be it writing, interviews, blogs, signings, etc.

We also offer several mentoring packages to authors that include knowledge and skills they can use in both traditional and self-publishing endeavours.

We look forward to launching many new careers.

This is what we believe in. What we stand for. This will be our legacy.

Welcome to Crystal Lake Publishing—Tales from the Darkest Depths.

9 781964 398327